SPLENDOR

Janet Nissenson

Copyright © 2014 by Janet Nissenson

All rights reserved. No part of this publication may be reproduced, distributed or transmitted in any form or by any means, without prior written permission.

Janet Nissenson
www.janetnissenson.com

Publisher's Note: This is a work of fiction. Names, characters, places, and incidents are a product of the author's imagination. Locales and public names are sometimes used for atmospheric purposes. Any resemblance to actual people, living or dead, or to businesses, companies, events, institutions, or locales is completely coincidental.

Book Layout © 2016 BookDesignTemplates.com

Splendor/ Janet Nissenson. -- 1st ed.
ISBN 978-1514383964

Dedication

Thanks to my family for tolerating all the hours I spent on this book. I promise to get to all of the projects I've neglected for months any day now.

Thanks to the fans, reviewers, bloggers, etc. who so graciously welcomed Serendipity. Your words of praise and encouragement make all of this worthwhile.

And a huge thanks to the entire world of indie publishing, for helping to make a thirty year old dream finally come true. It's no longer just the lucky few who can hope to share their literary creations with the rest of the world.

CONTENTS

Chapter One	1
Chapter Two	15
Chapter Three	35
Chapter Four	49
Chapter Five	63
Chapter Six	79
Chapter Seven	109
Chapter Eight	125
Chapter Nine	143
Chapter Ten	159
Chapter Eleven	173
Chapter Twelve	195
Chapter Thirteen	211
Chapter Fourteen	235
Chapter Fifteen	261
Chapter Sixteen	281
Chapter Seventeen	307
Chapter Eighteen	327
Chapter Nineteen	351
Chapter Twenty	381
Chapter Twenty-One	405
Chapter Twenty-Two	437
Chapter Twenty Three	453
Chapter Twenty Four	483
Epilogue	511

Chapter One

September

There were very few things that could rattle Ian Gregson, or threaten the iron control he typically wielded over his emotions. If he were to attempt to explain this state of affairs, he would likely point to the years spent in strict, rule-abiding English boarding schools. As a young, often rowdy boy of ten he might not have appreciated the discipline imposed on him by his teachers, but as a grown man of thirty-seven he was able to fully appreciate the guidelines that had been instilled in him so long ago.

In the high-profile position he held within his family's company, Ian made crucial decisions, dealt with multiple levels of managers within his region, and met with patrons and potential new customers of his hotels on a daily basis. It was during these times that he was most grateful for what the years in boarding school had instilled in him – supreme self-control and the ability to mask his emotions when needed. He seldom if ever lost his temper, but it typically only took a slightly raised eyebrow or the merest hint of a frown to signal his displeasure, and those barely imperceptible gestures were often all it took to get his message across loud and clear.

But no amount of schooling or years of experience dealing with argumentative employees or difficult customers had prepared him for the very unexpected – and very compelling – reaction he had to the young woman who stood framed in the doorway of his office.

Ian's very capable and almost frighteningly efficient PA – Andrew Doherty – was ushering the girl inside, but he paid scant attention to what his assistant was saying. Instead, his gaze was fixated on the arresting face and figure of the stunningly beautiful blonde who was approaching his desk hesitantly, hanging back behind Andrew uncertainly.

"Mr. Gregson, may I introduce you to the newest member of our Management Support Team?" asked Andrew briskly. "This is Tessa Lockwood, sir. She's just transferred here from the Tucson resort two weeks ago."

Ian had just returned to the office this very morning after a nearly three week business trip visiting several of the hotels under his direction. That would explain why he hadn't met the lusciously tempting Tessa until now. He knew instinctively that he would never have forgotten seeing *that* face before today.

He rose to his feet smoothly, extending his hand across the desk. The smile he pasted on his face was, he hoped fervently, one of polite welcome and nothing more blatant.

"It's a pleasure to meet you, Tessa," he told her gently. "I trust you're settling in here without any difficulty?"

Tessa placed her slim, smooth hand in his rather tentatively and returned his smile sweetly. "Yes, sir. Everything has been just fine, thank you. I'm – it's an honor to be working here for you."

Her voice was breathy, a little high, and astonishingly the sound made him instantly and uncomfortably aroused.

Ian was shocked at his uncharacteristic reaction to this girl, and he drew his hand away almost brusquely. "Well, I'm pleased to hear that. And I'm certain you'll be a fine addition to our team here."

"Thank you, Mr. Gregson. I'll do my very best, I promise," she told him in that sweet voice that went right to his groin.

There was a somewhat awkward silence for a few moments, until Tessa glanced down at the carpet uncertainly, and Andrew began to steer her out of the office. As his PA was about to leave, Ian called out to him.

"Andrew. A moment, please."

His usually unflappable assistant looked a bit on the uncomfortable side but merely nodded. "Of course, sir. Just let me get Tessa some data she needs for a spreadsheet and I'll be right back."

While Ian awaited the return of his PA – who would definitely have some things to answer for – the image of young Tessa Lockwood refused to erase itself from his mind. For a man who could easily have his pick of beautiful, desirable women around the globe, it was rare that he was rendered virtually speechless by the mere sight of one. And rarer still that he was instantly and almost uncontrollably aroused by one. Ian was as controlled and in command of his sexual needs as he was of every other aspect of his life, so it was more than a little unsettling for him to have this sort of reaction to a woman.

And Tessa Lockwood was barely a woman. 'Christ,' he thought in near-disgust. 'She looks like a damned teenager.' But the fact that he was likely almost twice her age did absolutely nothing to diminish the attraction he felt for the breathtakingly beautiful girl who, by some rather unfortunate set of circumstances, was now working for him.

Ian's Management Support Team was a group of six administrative assistants who worked both for Ian and roughly a dozen of his highest level managers. Each manager had their own PA to perform more complex and confidential duties, but relied on the support team to handle jobs such as word processing, making travel arrangements, setting up A/V equipment and ordering refreshments for meetings, compiling reports, and a long list of other tasks. In past decades, before political correctness had prevailed, the team would have been called a secretarial pool. Ian's father Edward and his uncle Richard, now both semi-retired, would most certainly still refer to the team by that rather antiquated term.

He recalled now that just prior to his departure on this most recent business trip one of the team – Sarah – had requested an immediate transfer out of the regional headquarters, and a position at the hotel here in San Francisco had been found for her. Ian grimaced as he remembered the reason behind Sarah's eagerness to be transferred – namely, the overly amorous attentions she'd received from one of his managers.

Unfortunately, it hadn't been the first time that a female employee had caught the attention of Jason Baldwin, or the first time that upper management had been forced to smooth over the resulting fallout. With nearly any other employee – manager or not – such actions would have resulted in immediate termination. However, Jason had the extreme good fortune to be married to Ian's cousin Charlotte, the only child of his Uncle Richard. Jason and Charlotte were parents to three very young children, and it was for this reason and this reason only that he hadn't been canned some time ago. He was a decent enough employee but definitely expendable.

And Jason would most certainly be *very* attracted to the gorgeous, tempting girl who had just walked out of Ian's office moments earlier. Ian somewhat vaguely recalled Sarah, Tessa's predecessor, as a cute little brunette who tended to wear her skirts a bit too short and her blouses a bit too low to be appropriate for the type of office environment he insisted on maintaining. All in all, Sarah had been nothing remarkable and most assuredly had never caught his attention even for a moment. But if Jason had pursued her to the point where she'd felt the need to transfer immediately, Ian shuddered to imagine how his cousin's reprehensible husband was going to react when he saw Tessa Lockwood for the first time.

The red sheath dress she'd worn had skimmed over a tall, curvy figure. A thin black patent leather belt encircled her slim waist, setting off the fuller curves of her breasts and hips. Ian knew without having to glance at the label that the dress was inexpensive, as were the plain black patent leather pumps on her feet. Ian had grown up among fashionable, well-dressed women – his mother, grandmothers, aunts, cousins – not to mention the countless number of women he'd met over the years in his business and social circles, all of whom dressed in expensive designer apparel. But it didn't really matter that Tessa's simple dress had likely been bought at a discount store or off a sale rack, for she had the sort of figure that would look stunning in anything she wore.

As if the lush curves of her body weren't attraction enough, she also had a heartbreakingly beautiful face – high, sculpted cheekbones; big blue eyes framed by long, curly lashes; a full, kissable mouth; and the sort of flawless, porcelain complexion that only the very young or the very rich could boast of. And the cherry on top of the most delicious sundae he'd ever seen was the thick, lustrous fall of golden blonde hair that spilled over her shoulders and halfway down her back.

Tessa was stunning – young, ripe and sexy – and yet she somehow seemed to be unaware of how tempting she was. She had been shy and uncertain, and more than a little nervous when being introduced to him just a short time ago, behavior that was not in the least bit typical for a female who was supremely confident of her looks and sex appeal. It made him wonder anew just how young she was.

'Too damned young for you, mate' he told himself almost angrily. 'You're as bad as that bastard Jason, except at least you're not a married father of three.'

Ian was pacing distractedly back and forth in front of his desk when Andrew returned, and the PA could only blink and stare in disbelief at his boss. Mr. Gregson was always cool and controlled, was never agitated or even the least bit anxious. The only person Andrew had ever known to be in better control of their emotions was his own self. So it was with some amazement that he observed his normally formal, restrained employer so clearly displaying agitation.

Ian glanced up, his mouth tightening as he brusquely motioned Andrew inside. "Close the door. And then you can explain why a teenager is working for me."

Andrew suppressed the rather undignified urge to roll his eyes at his boss' uncharacteristic sarcasm. "Of course, sir. And if you're speaking of Tessa – which I assume you are – she is certainly young but not *that* young. She's twenty-two, Mr. Gregson. More importantly, she's been working for the company for three years already."

Ian frowned. "Straight out of high school?"

"Not quite." Andrew pulled some papers out of a dark blue folder, the sort used for employee files. "Apparently she was hired as a part-time employee after completing a year at community college. She transitioned to full-time a year later after earning an office technology certificate from said college."

Ian was only mildly appeased to learn the girl wasn't quite a teenager, and had already been employed by the Gregson Group for a few years. "She still seems a trifle young – and inexperienced – to work at this level, Andrew. I realize I left the matter of Sarah's replacement in your capable hands, but I have to question your decision on this issue."

Andrew adjusted his glasses and cleared his throat. "I can understand your concern, Mr. Gregson. But I assure you there were several very good reasons for placing Tessa in this position. If I may?"

Ian gave a terse nod before sitting down in his imposing leather desk chair. "By all means. Convince me why that child is qualified to work on the executive floor."

"Of course. First, the timing with Sarah's very abrupt transfer happened to coincide almost exactly with Tessa's arrival in San Francisco. Placing her in Sarah's position was quick and seamless. We avoided the need to interview and do security clearance for a new employee, or worry about having to replace an in-house transfer."

Ian waved a hand somewhat irritably. "Convenient, yes, but hardly a valid reason for giving her such a high profile job."

"She's got advanced training in Excel, sir. Certificates from continuing education classes, things like that. She's an expert at the program, able to perform functions that none of the others on the team could even begin to guess at. Even I'm not proficient at some of the more advanced functions she is," admitted Andrew somewhat reluctantly.

That revelation mollified Ian a bit. He relied heavily on the use of spreadsheets to keep track of all the aspects of the dozens of hotels he oversaw – expenses, profitability, occupancy rates, employee statistics, property maintenance, etc. It had always been a source of some annoyance that none of the support team seemed to be especially proficient in a program that was such a vital necessity to his business. Knowing that Tessa would possibly be able to produce the complex reports he needed might be reason enough to keep her on the team.

And, as if that wasn't sufficient cause, Andrew had another weapon in his arsenal. "Also, Tessa comes very highly recommended by her previous manager – a Mrs. Francine

Carrington."

That name got Ian's attention and he stared at Andrew in mild shock. Andrew realized he'd seen his normally unflappable boss show more emotion in the past ten minutes than in the entire three years they had worked together.

A slow smile crossed Ian's features. "It's hard to imagine Mrs. C. recommending anyone, much less highly so. Let me see that letter, please."

After scanning the sheet of paper, his smile broadened. "Well, I suppose that settles it, then. If Tessa made this sort of impression on Mrs. C. – the toughest boss *I* ever had – then she must be qualified. There's just one more thing, then."

Andrew raised a brow expectantly, wondering what else his boss could possibly object to. "What's that, sir?"

Ian grimaced. "Keeping her as far away from that bastard Jason Baldwin as possible. He'll think Christmas and his birthday have arrived wrapped up in one big shiny package when he sees Tessa for the first time. We are *not* going to have a repeat of the Sarah incident with Tessa. Not to mention the previous two sexual harassment incidents my uncle swept under the rug."

"Three, sir. There were actually three incidents on his record prior to this most recent one with Sarah," pointed out Andrew. "But in regards to Tessa, I doubt that Mr. Baldwin will bother her under the circumstances."

Ian frowned. "What circumstances would those be?"

"Tessa is married, sir. Hopefully that knowledge will keep all the males in this office at bay – whether they happen to be married themselves or not."

Ian thought he'd received all the shocks a person could handle in one day, but the knowledge that the beautiful, golden girl - who had caught his attention like no other woman ever had before - belonged to another man was almost enough to knock him on his arse. "Married?" he repeated hoarsely. "How is that possible? I mean – she's too damned young to be married."

"I happen to agree, sir, but the fact of the matter is that she's a married woman. Married to a Peter Lockwood. He's evidently a journalist."

"Children?"

Andrew glanced up from Tessa's personnel file in surprise at the almost desperate tone of his boss' voice. "No, sir. At least none that she listed as covered dependents for her medical insurance. And I've spent a good deal of time showing her the ropes these past two weeks so the topic of any children would certainly have come up. An unplanned pregnancy is most likely not the reason she got married so young."

'No,' thought Ian with a sense of near-despair. 'Her husband is probably as young and attractive as she is, and the boy wisely snatched her up before someone else could. Lucky little bastard.'

Andrew left his office moments later, leaving Ian to mull over everything they had just discussed. Almost without being aware of his actions, he pulled up the employee directory for the Tucson resort on his computer and dialed in directly to the woman who'd once put the fear of God into his nineteen-year-old heart.

"I was wondering when I might hear from you, young Ian," greeted the austere, no-nonsense voice of Francine Carrington. "I assume from this long overdue call to your former manager that you've met Tessa."

Ian couldn't help chuckling, recalling as though it were yesterday the first time he'd met the very intimidating and extremely daunting Mrs. Carrington. She had been in charge of the entire administrative staff at the company's worldwide headquarters in London, and Ian had been assigned to work under her direction during his summer break from Oxford. He and his brothers had been required since the time they entered their teens to learn the family business from the ground up. That meant spending school breaks working at one of the hundreds of worldwide properties owned by the Gregson Group, and most assuredly not at a cushy, executive level position. Ian and his siblings – Hugh and Colin – had all worked a wide variety of jobs – bellhop, front desk clerk, gardener, housekeeping, janitor, hotel laundry, and busboy. As they grew older and graduated from university, they had moved on to desk jobs and began the long, gradual climb up the managerial and executive ladders until each had achieved the position of Managing Director. Hugh, as the eldest, oversaw all of their European properties; Ian was in charge of the North and South American hotels and resorts; Colin, the youngest, worked out of their Hong Kong offices and was responsible for the Asian and South Pacific divisions.

Ian had learned a great deal from his formative years working in a variety of entry level and clerical jobs, but never as much as he had the one summer he'd spent under Mrs. C's stern eye. She cared not a whit that he was the company founder's grandson, and gave him zero leeway or tolerance. Like all of the employees under her direction, he'd been terrified of her and had done his utmost to abide by her strict rules of conduct and live up to her lofty expectations. But her Draconian-like rules had had the desired affect his father and uncle had hoped for – Ian and his siblings had emerged from their summers under Mrs. C's direction as capable, steadfast employees, ready to take on any task.

He'd kept in touch with Mrs. C. over the years, exchanging emails and popping in for a quick visit whenever he was in London. He recalled now that she had requested a transfer to the Tucson resort several years ago since her husband suffered from some type of pulmonary disease and would benefit from the drier climate of Arizona.

"Yes, I've met your dear Tessa," agreed Ian. "For a few moments I found it hard to believe that the Mrs. C. I knew could ever write such a glowing recommendation for anyone. So initially I had to assume that either the letter was forged or that you'd gone soft."

"Pah!" exclaimed Francine in mild disgust. "You know me better than that, boy. If anything I've become crankier and even harder to please in my old age. As for forging a letter, Tessa is the very last person who would think of doing something so unethical. The girl is the most timid little thing I've ever met, afraid of her own shadow half the time."

Ian drummed his long fingers on his desk. "So everything you detailed in your letter is true, then?"

"Every word. She's a good girl, Tessa is. Hardest worker I've ever seen, never slacks off, doesn't gossip – which you know I detest – no excuses, never late. She dragged herself in once sick as a dog and wouldn't leave until she'd finished some reports."

Francine's voice quieted as she added, "You know how difficult it is to earn my respect, Ian, and Tessa has it in spades. She'll make an excellent addition to your staff. You're lucky to have her. Meanwhile, I'm left to deal with the nitwit who was hired to replace her. Useless, annoying girl – I give her two months tops before I have to fire her or she runs out of here crying."

Ian couldn't suppress a chuckle. "Go easy on her, Mrs. C. It sounds like your Tessa is going to be a hard act to follow."

"She's *your* Tessa now, my boy. And you'd better treat her well. She's - " Francine hesitated. "Well, let's just say she's had a rough time of it in her young life. I admire her all the more for how she's overcome her misfortune."

"What sort of misfortune?"

"I can't discuss that with you, Ian, as I'm certain you know," admonished Francine. "Not to mention I'm not sure that even I know all of it. Tessa is a very private person, not one to broadcast her life's story around the office. Another admirable trait that I value. Just – go easy on the girl, Ian. Trust me, it won't take you long at all to realize her value. Not to mention," she added slyly, "she's quite easy on the eye, isn't she?"

Ian chose his next words carefully before replying. "She's a lovely girl, yes. But is it really true that she's already married at such a young age?"

Francine sighed. "Yes, it's true. It's – complicated, Ian. That's all I can say on the matter. Tessa rarely discusses her husband but he definitely exists. Nice enough boy and she dotes on him, but there's something a bit odd there."

He decided not to question her further about Tessa's marital status, not wanting to betray even the slightest indication to the extremely perceptive Mrs. C. that he was attracted to the girl.

"I am a bit worried about how Jason is going to act around her," confessed Ian. He knew that Francine had met his smarmy cousin-in-law on more than one occasion, and that she had an extremely low opinion of him. "Tessa's predecessor requested a transfer because of some difficulty with him."

Francine's voice was as biting as a whip crack. "Ian, promise me right now that you'll keep that randy bastard Jason away from

Tessa. If I learn that he's so much as blinked at her the wrong way, I swear I'll pack Oliver into the car along with my brand new shotgun and drive up there to deal with the little weasel myself. And I'm quite a good shot these days. They like their guns in Arizona."

Ian smiled in spite of himself at the ferocity of Francine's words. "You're quite the protective mama bear about this girl, aren't you?"

"She needs looking out for, Ian. More so than anyone I've ever met. So, please, do me the greatest favor and keep an eye on her, would you? Discreetly, of course, she can be quite stubborn when it comes to asking for help."

"I promise," he assured his former mentor gently. "And – thank you for sending her my way. If she managed to make this sort of impression on you, then I know she must be an excellent employee."

They exchanged pleasantries for a few more minutes before bidding each other good-bye. Ian replaced his phone receiver then shut his eyes, massaging the beginnings of a headache he felt welling up near his temples.

'Good Lord, what a disaster,' he muttered under his breath. 'How in the world are you going to cope with this one, mate?'

Against his will, the tempting image of Tessa invaded his thoughts once again. He longed to spread all of that glorious golden hair out against his pillow; to gently remove that discreetly sexy red dress and bare her lush, curvy body to his eager gaze; to wrap those long, shapely legs around his waist. Ian grew hard instantly as he imagined having her – nothing as crude as a quick, hard fuck - for Tessa was worth so much more than that. Instead, he would linger over her for hours, kissing, caressing, arousing, and making love to her over and over until he was finally sated. For a while, anyway, for he feared that Tessa was the sort of woman he could never truly have his fill of.

It would have been oh, so easy without the unexpected and inconvenient complication of her marital status. Had she been a single woman, the first thing he'd do would be to find her a job of equal pay and rank at another luxury hotel in San Francisco. The Gregson Group had a very strict policy forbidding managers and executives from dating an employee who could be deemed their subordinate, and frowned on employees in general dating each other. Ian in particular held himself to extremely high standards when it came to this rule. He'd fended off too many eager advances from female employees over the years, and each had received the message loud and clear. Except, of course, for the obnoxiously persistent Morgan Cottrell, his current Business Development Manager. When he'd transferred to San Francisco three years ago, the blonde had made it very clear on numerous occasions that she found him extremely attractive and would be open to any sort of after-hours relationship he liked. After several firm but polite brush-offs, he'd finally had to take the gloves off and let Ms. Cottrell know in no uncertain terms – and in a very icy tone – that if she wished to keep her elevated position in the company – or any position at all – that she'd keep her distance from now on. Morgan had been the model of professional decorum from that moment on.

After ensuring that Tessa was safely employed elsewhere, he would have pulled out all the stops to make her his own. Ian had rarely courted or seduced a woman before, for he'd never really had to make the effort. From the time he'd reached his teens, women had flocked to his side, attracted not only by his looks but by his money, his well-bred British family who could trace their roots back several centuries, and by his high-powered position in arguably the top luxury hotel chain in the world. He could at any given time have his pick of gorgeous women – executives, socialites, celebrities, models.

But Ian was picky and somewhat fastidious about his taste in women, unlike his brothers. Hugh had married his longtime sweetheart, a girl he'd met at university, and they'd been happily wed for years, parents to four children. Colin had been quite the notorious playboy for years, much to their mother's dismay, until he, too, had finally settled down just two years ago. He was married to a strikingly beautiful Eurasian woman from Hong Kong and they were expecting their first child in a few months.

That left Ian as the only bachelor among his siblings, and he didn't envision that status changing anytime soon. Since his one failed engagement a few years ago, he'd kept busy with work and hadn't really let himself think about settling down.

That is, until a ridiculously young, breathtakingly beautiful, and delightfully sweet girl had tentatively walked into his office a short time ago. He'd known – just *known* somehow – that she had been made for him. It had been the biggest shock of his life to realize that she'd already been claimed by another man.

And now, he was going to have to man up and find some way to keep his wayward emotions under control in her presence. Transferring her out of the team would raise too many red flags, especially given her level of competency and the shockingly glowing recommendation from Mrs. C. Ian knew he'd have to call on every ounce of self-control he possessed to treat young Tessa in a professional but impersonal manner, to keep her and his rampaging desire for her at arm's length at all times, and to remind himself constantly that she was strictly forbidden to him for more reasons than he wanted to count.

'Damn it,' he cursed beneath his breath. 'What in hell was Mrs. C. thinking of sending her my way? If I didn't know better, I'd swear that old witch was still trying to let me know who's really in charge around here.'

Chapter Two

September, two years later

Tessa Lockwood did not like Wednesdays. She was well aware that most people didn't share her feelings, that the majority of the world thought of this day as "hump day", when their busy work weeks were half over and they could begin winding down for the weekend ahead. But for Tessa, it seemed that nearly every bad thing that had happened in her life so far had occurred on a Wednesday.

Bad things didn't happen every Wednesday, of course, but when they did she usually had some sort of uneasy premonition. Like the butterflies kicking around in her stomach as she brushed her hair and got ready for work this morning. Or the chill that shimmered up her spine as she hurriedly ate a piece of toast with jam and drank a cup of tea before dashing out the door of her apartment.

The unsettled feeling continued during the crowded bus ride to work, and she tried desperately to quell her nerves. She wondered if her sense of unease had anything to do with the fact that Peter was supposed to be flying home today. After almost two years, one would think she'd stop worrying when he had to take a long flight home from a job assignment in Asia. Even though he frequently flew in and out of some less than stable socio-political countries, he'd never had any problems, at least none that he'd ever told her about. So she knew that her unsettled emotions this morning weren't due to unnecessary worry about her husband's incoming flight from Cambodia. But there was definitely *something*, some niggling little fear that something bad was going to happen. And her spidey-sense had yet to be wrong.

Tessa had to stand on the bus, as usual, and she assumed her normal position of never really making eye contact with anyone else on board. Most of the people riding the bus at this time of the morning were either going to work like her, or to school, but there were definitely a fair number of weirdoes along, too. San

Francisco was a very diverse city, after all, with people of varying ethnicities, sexual orientations, and socio-economic classes, and Tessa was pretty sure she'd seen a really good sampling of them all in the two years she'd been living here and riding the city buses.

The bus left her off a block away from her office building, and she exited the stuffy, crowded vehicle with relief. It had taken her a long time to get used to relying on public transportation when she and Peter had moved here from Tucson. Because both of their cars had been old and in dire need of repairs, they'd unloaded them before moving to San Francisco. Now they relied on buses, rapid transit, and walking to get around, which made good economic sense because the cost of maintaining even one car in this very expensive city would not have fit into their extremely tight budget.

And money was always tight, the budget always stretched thin. Tessa made a good salary but Peter only got paid when one of his news stories actually sold. Not to mention the fact that the cost of living in San Francisco was exorbitant, the rent on their tiny, cramped apartment more than twice what they'd been paying for a much larger place in Tucson.

As Tessa entered the building that housed the corporate offices for the Gregson Hotel Group's American headquarters, she hoped that Peter would arrive home with good news about his job. When they had moved to San Francisco two years ago, it had been for Peter's new job as a freelance reporter for an international news agency based in the city. His assigned territory was Asia, requiring him to make frequent and lengthy trips to such places as Vietnam, Malaysia, China, and Thailand. He was hoping to find a better position that didn't require nearly as much travel in addition to offering a regular salary, and had recently begun sending out resumes and doing some networking among the contacts he'd developed.

The past couple of years had been hard on Tessa, left alone and lonely for such frequent periods of time. Peter was all she had – he wasn't just her husband but her best friend, her family, her everything. And when he was away for weeks at a time she struggled constantly with her fears, her loneliness, her sadness. The fear that she would descend into darkness like her mother had done for so many years plagued her often, and she was determined that she wouldn't suffer the same fate. But it was hard to be alone, and she had to wage a constant battle with her emotions to keep positive and happy, to stay busy and not dwell on her sadness.

Tessa liked her job, finding the work both challenging and rewarding, though of course she would have preferred being a PA for one of the executives. Not only was the salary considerably higher but the position carried more prestige and responsibility, with some of the PA's even traveling with their managers on occasion. But she also knew she would need a college degree before she could even think of applying for a job like that, and going back to school at this time just wasn't in the cards. Her super-tight budget would never allow for college tuition and books. And, ironically, even though she and Peter lived in a cramped apartment in a questionable neighborhood; couldn't afford to own a car; and ate a lot of cereal, ramen noodles, and peanut butter sandwiches to stretch their dollars, they made too much money for her to qualify for most grants or scholarships. It was a cruel sort of Catch-22.

As Tessa put away her jacket and purse and booted up her computer, she thought it was likely all for the best that she couldn't afford to go to college. She'd admittedly never been a brain or the best student, getting by with mostly B's and C's during high school. Of course, there had been some real extenuating circumstances behind that – a mentally ill mother, moving around and changing schools multiple times, always teetering on the edge of poverty.

At least she'd done very well with the computer and business classes she had taken at community college back in Tucson. The certificate she'd earned from their Office Technology program had enabled her to get a job at the Gregson Resort in Tucson, and the eventual transfer to the American headquarters here two years ago.

But this would likely be as far as she could reasonably expect to advance in the company without that college degree, so Tessa had made up her mind some time ago to simply do the very best job she possibly could. She took a lot of pride in her work, and worked very hard to be an exemplary employee. She was never late, never left early, never took more than her allotted time for lunch. She'd dragged herself into the office on more than one occasion with a cold or the flu, doggedly refusing to call in sick. And unlike most of her co-workers, she didn't waste time during the work day gossiping, checking her personal email, sending texts or making phone calls. She was well aware that everyone who worked on the Management Support Team were watched like a hawk by Andrew Doherty, the Managing Director's sharp-tongued, eagle-eyed PA.

In the time she'd worked here, Tessa couldn't recall even one occasion when Andrew had so much as cracked a smile. He was all business all the time, and he didn't miss even a single detail. Tessa had seen him chastise her co-workers for all manner of minor errors or oversights, everything from a misspelled word on a contract to ordering the wrong sandwich for a lunch meeting to an executive's dissatisfaction with the flight that had been booked for a recent business trip. Andrew never raised his voice or used bad language or issued threats, but it was more than obvious by his icy, formal demeanor when he was displeased. So Tessa worked very, very hard to make certain she wasn't on the receiving end of one of his famously scathing dressing-downs.

The Iceman – as one of Tessa's co-workers had irreverently dubbed Andrew – arrived at the office about five minutes after she did. She knew he'd likely been at the office until early evening on the previous day, and probably had to deal with phone calls and emails after hours as well.

She offered him up a warm but businesslike smile as he passed by on the way to his office. "Good morning, Andrew."

He gave her a brief nod. "Hello, Tessa. First one in again, I see."

Her cheeks pinkened and she gave a small shrug. "I got the early bus. It's a bit less crowded than the next one."

"Mr. Gregson is going to need some spreadsheets done today," he told her briskly. "I'll be sending the information your way shortly."

It was a great source of pride for Tessa to know that her expertise with producing complex spreadsheets was highly valued by the Managing Director. Mr. Gregson used them on a regular basis for his reports and presentations, and the vast majority of them were delegated to her for processing.

"Of course, Andrew. Send them along at your convenience and I'll get right to them," she assured him. "I don't have anything else pressing on my schedule for today."

"Good to know. I'll email you the supporting data within the hour."

Tessa always paid extra attention to her work when she knew the project was for Mr. Gregson. It wasn't just the fact that he was the Managing Director – in charge of all the hotels in North and South America plus all of the employees here at the regional office. She couldn't – or perhaps more truthfully – *wouldn't* define her feelings for the incredibly handsome, dynamic man but she knew that they were not appropriate emotions for a married woman to be having for a man who wasn't her husband.

She felt guilty every single time she saw Ian Gregson, or even thought about him, and recognized the little thrill that shimmered through her body as attraction. Tessa always dismissed her reactions to her charismatic, compelling boss as nothing more than a silly little schoolgirl crush, the same sort of harmless infatuation one might harbor for a movie star. God knew she would never, ever consider acting on her awareness of him. Besides the very obvious fact that she was completely devoted to Peter and would never consider being unfaithful to him, there was the matter of Ian Gregson being her employer. And he was so far above her in every way – intellectually, socially, economically – that it was laughable to think he would ever notice a lowly employee like herself. He dated socialites, businesswomen, and occasionally celebrities. Tessa's co-workers were constantly tracking their boss in the society and gossip columns online, and chatting about the current woman in his life. And whether Tessa cared to hear about Ian Gregson's personal life or not, she typically wasn't given a choice in the matter. Just like she was rarely given a choice of the other mind numbing topics they chattered about incessantly – clothes, makeup, celebrities, a variety of TV shows, what club they had hit last weekend, the latest argument they'd had with their boyfriend. The list went on but none of the topics of conversation were of particular interest to Tessa, and certainly none of them could be called intellectually stimulating.

But she was far too shy and retiring, and too intimidated by her co-workers, to speak up. It had been that way for her ever since childhood. Moving and changing schools so often had made it difficult for her to make friends easily. She had always felt like the new girl, the outsider, and just when she'd finally started to fit in and make a friend or two, her flighty, emotionally unstable mother would uproot them and move on to the next town where Tessa would have to start all over again. And old habits died hard it seemed, for Tessa still felt like the outsider at the office, even though she'd worked here for two years. She had never really bonded with any of her co-workers, didn't feel as though she could honestly call them her friends, and, sadly, didn't trust any of them.

She had been at her desk for more than half an hour before the rest of the team began to filter in. As usual, Marisol was the first one in and she gave Tessa a weary smile as she put her things away. At twenty-eight, Marisol was a pretty, petite Filipina woman, married with two small children under the age of four. Even though she and her husband got a lot of support from their families, working full time and caring for two young kids wore her out. She yawned constantly during the day, drank endless cups of coffee, and seemed to operate in slow motion most of the time. Still, Marisol was sweet and quiet, was always kind to Tessa, and generally didn't join in most of the incessant gossiping and chatter as the others did.

Next to arrive was Shelby, a giggly, easily distracted strawberry blonde who reminded Tessa of a bird. Of medium height, Shelby was stick thin, her arms and legs spindly. She had a small face with a pointy nose and chin and deep-set, almost beady eyes. Her high-pitched voice and annoying little laugh at times sounded just like a chirping bird.

Andrew seemed to pick on Shelby more than any of the others, to the point that she was now terrified of him and would start quaking whenever he was close by. Privately, Tessa thought Andrew's methods could be a little less intimidating but nonetheless could understand his constant irritation with the silly, not especially bright Shelby. Tessa wondered how she'd ever been hired to work in this very high profile unit given her overall lack of ability.

The next two to arrive were BFF's Gina and Alicia. Since they were roommates, they arrived and departed the office together every day, and at times it seemed like they were joined at the hip. They gossiped all the time, were merciless in their critique of other employees' wardrobes and grooming, and Tessa neither liked nor trusted them. They were always nice to her – almost sickeningly so – but she knew for a fact that they talked about her behind her back, made fun of her inexpensive clothes, and cattily speculated why she always seemed to get the best assignments from Andrew.

Both women were obsessed with clothes, shoes, hair, makeup and manicures, read fashion magazines and online blogs on a daily basis, and were always smartly dressed. Gina was the more exotic, flamboyant of the two with her olive skin, big dark eyes, and masses of dark brown hair. Alicia was classier, more refined, with a chin-length bob of wheat blonde hair, ivory skin and a designer wardrobe she was able to afford via her monthly trust fund stipends.

With their sly, almost predatory mannerisms, Gina and Alicia made Tessa think of the conniving Siamese cats from *Lady and the Tramp*. She was extremely careful not to give them any fodder for gossip, rarely if ever discussing her personal life, and generally not contributing to their almost nonstop commentary about the goings-on in the office.

Gina gave her an overly-friendly smile, while Alicia greeted her with a saccharin sweet "Good morning." Tessa tried to ignore how both of them none too discreetly checked out the dress and shoes she'd worn today.

"That's such a cute little dress, Tessa," Gina told her in a phony voice. "Every time you wear it I think what a good color it is for you."

Tessa merely smiled politely in response to Gina's not-so-subtle dig. Tessa never tried to pretend that she had much beyond her rather limited wardrobe, or that she could afford to shop anywhere besides the big discount chains like Marshalls, Forever 21 and H&M. She could never dream of buying anything at the places she knew Gina, Alicia and Shelby preferred – big-name stores like Barneys, Nordstrom or Neiman Marcus. Not only wasn't it even remotely in her budget, but Tessa didn't let things like a label or price tag bother her. She knew all too well what it was like to have absolutely nothing, so she was always grateful for the little she did have.

The last of the team to arrive – almost fifteen minutes late – was Kevin, the lone male of their group. Though, as Shelby, Gina and Alicia loved to tease, Kevin was arguably the most effeminate of them all. He was flamboyantly gay – his clothing, haircut, mannerisms, speech – and he talked freely about his lifestyle to anyone who would listen. Tessa had learned far too much about Kevin's numerous boyfriends and hook-ups, including his sexual preferences and escapades. Even though she was married, she'd been more than a little naïve sexually, but two years of working with Kevin had opened her eyes – and not in a good way.

Kevin made his rounds to each of the girl's cubicles, air-kissing them in turn. He cooed over Gina's new shoes, admired Alicia's manicure, made a whispered comment to Shelby that caused her to make one of those chirpy little bird laughs, and told Marisol he'd had dinner at the restaurant she'd recommended to him last night. He came to Tessa last since they sat next to each other.

He pressed his cheek to hers lightly, and she had to force herself not to recoil at the heavy scent of his cologne.

"Morning, sweet pea," he grinned. "How's my girl today?"

Tessa couldn't help but return his smile. Kevin might be a promiscuous airhead with atrocious taste in clothes and cologne, but he was almost always cheerful and could usually put her in a good mood.

"I'm good, thanks. Peter's due home later today," she told him.

Kevin's eyes twinkled mischievously. "Oooh, bet someone's good and horny by now. You'll be walking funny tomorrow morning after he's through with you."

Tessa felt her cheeks grow warm at his very straightforward innuendo. No matter how many ribald stories Kevin shared with them, she wasn't sure she'd ever really get used to his very frank way of talking about sex. And, rather sadly, it was quite unlikely that Peter would be the least bit horny, despite the fact that they hadn't seen each other in weeks. Or had sex for even longer. Things were – complicated.

With everyone settled in at their cubicles, the noise level in this section of the office began to rise dramatically. The sounds of telephones ringing, keyboards clacking, and voices speaking all co-mingled and seemed to get a bit louder with each passing minute. Tessa sighed, wishing for perhaps the thousandth time that she had a more private space – a secluded cubicle or desk in front of one of the private executive offices. Fortunately, she'd honed her powers of concentration very well over the past two years, so she could block out nearly all of the distractions around her. Except, of course, when her very favorite topic of conversation was brought up, as it was nearly every day. Then she was all ears, even though she was painstakingly careful not to betray even the slightest interest in what was being said. All it would take would be the tiniest hint she was interested, and her gossipy co-workers would be spreading the news of her infatuation all over the office. And Tessa would be mortified – absolutely mortified - if anyone ever guessed that she had a crush on Ian Gregson.

"Any sign of His Hotness yet this morning?" asked Gina in the sly, sultry tone that for some reason really grated on Tessa's nerves. She also hated the rather undignified nickname that Gina, Alicia and Kevin had bestowed upon their boss. Oh, there was no question that the man was hot but he was also the epitome of suave sophistication and class, and Tessa privately thought such a nickname didn't do him full justice or pay him the proper respect.

"Not yet," offered Marisol. "He's addressing a group at the

Convention and Visitors Bureau this morning."

One of Marisol's jobs was to keep track of all the executives schedules, so that one could tell at a glance where a particular employee was on a given day and time.

"Mmm, guess we'll have to wait a while longer to see what he's wearing this morning," lamented Gina. "He hasn't worn the Dolce and Gabbana suit for a few weeks so maybe today will be the day."

Tessa had zero idea how Gina and Alicia were able to identify which designer suit Mr. Gregson wore from one day to the next – and wondered why on earth they cared. She didn't know an Armani from a Dior and it didn't really matter, anyway – their gorgeous boss looked mouthwateringly handsome in whatever suit he wore, no matter the color, style or fabric.

"He was also out pretty late last night," offered Alicia. "My mother texted me this morning that she saw him at a benefit dinner for the symphony last night."

"Oooh, and what very lucky lady was he escorting last night?" asked Kevin, his pale blue eyes sparkling with interest. "Was it the bank president, the news anchor or the ballerina?"

Alicia gave a shrug that was meant to seem careless. Tessa knew that despite her co-workers feigned indifference, Alicia was actually very interested in who Mr. Gregson dated. And that it bothered her to no end that the man had such a rigid policy of never dating employees. Alicia had reportedly been one of many in a long line of hopefuls who had found that hard truth out. And while she never outright flirted with Mr. Gregson, she always went out of her way to greet him with a very interested smile, making it quite plain that if he were to ever change his mind she was ready, willing and available.

"I couldn't say," replied Alicia a little huffily. "My mother didn't mention it and I didn't care to ask. But he's rarely seen with the same woman twice so whoever he escorted it can't be too serious."

"So that means there's still hope for you, Ali," teased Kevin, using the nickname he knew she despised. "Have you considered finding another job so that he might actually ask you out? I mean, that way he wouldn't have to worry about his hands off the employees rule."

Gina smirked. "She talks about doing that all the time. The fact that she hasn't actually quit must mean she doesn't think he'd ask her out regardless."

Alicia threw a wadded-up piece of paper at her roommate. "Hah, hah. I haven't noticed you turning in your resignation, either."

Gina shrugged. "I've got my hands full with Alex at the moment. He's not as hunky as His Hotness, and of course nobody's even half as rich, but he'll do for now."

Kevin heaved a dramatic sigh. "Well, whoever the lucky lady he escorted last night was she's probably wobbling around this morning. If that man isn't built like a bull, I'd be shocked speechless. And for me, you know, that's saying something. No pun intended."

Shelby emitted one of her annoyingly chirpy little giggles. "What's that saying about a man's shoe size? I'll bet he wears at least a size thirteen."

Kevin cackled with glee, and for the next twenty minutes the conversation turned downright bawdy as he, Shelby, Gina and Alicia continued to speculate on Mr. Gregson's sexual prowess. Tessa kept her attention focused on the report she was working on, trying desperately to conceal the embarrassment she felt and the flush that stained her cheeks. It certainly wasn't anything she hadn't heard before – or much worse after sitting next to Kevin for two years. But she was more embarrassed for Mr. Gregson than herself, finding this talk about the size of his "equipment", or how many women he'd nailed, or what sexual position he would probably prefer, to be completely disrespectful to a man who wasn't just their boss and part of the family who owned this company, but a kind, dignified and almost regal man. If Mrs. Carrington could overhear even a snippet of their crude commentary she would fire every one of them on the spot.

Tessa missed the cantankerous office manager who had been her boss, her mentor, her friend, and at times her surrogate mother. Mrs. C. – as she preferred to be called – had taught Tessa everything about office etiquette and had instilled a strict work ethic in her. The very fearsome office manager had put the fear of God in her about gossiping, being late, eating at her desk, not proofreading everything she typed at least three times, or wearing her skirts too short. The rules of conduct the older woman followed were, by her own admission, very strict and more than a little old-fashioned. But Mrs. C. had insisted that if Tessa followed them to the letter that she would be successful and go far in the company.

Considering the behavior of all five of her co-workers, Tessa doubted any of them would last a day with Mrs. C. And the stern office manager would certainly be outraged to hear the gossip being spread about Mr. Gregson. Tessa was aware that her former and current bosses knew each other but had never been told what the exact connection was. The only thing Mrs. C. had told her was that Ian was hardworking and demanding but a fair employer who prized diligence and loyalty above all else. Tessa had strived to be the hardest working and most loyal employee he'd ever had from her first day in the office.

She only wished she had the nerve to stand up and tell her co-workers to shut up, that they were being horrible, rude people to discuss such a dignified gentleman like Mr. Gregson like he was some sleazy gigolo. Like that nasty, creepy Jason Baldwin, for example.

Tessa shuddered as she thought of the way Mr. Baldwin leered at her every single time he saw her. She knew the other girls thought him attractive – Gina insisted he could be David Beckham's twin – but he gave Tessa the willies. She knew he was married to Mr. Gregson's cousin and that they had three young children. Mrs. Baldwin and her brood visited the office occasionally, and from all appearances she was a very pretty, sweet woman who certainly deserved better than her lecherous, cheating husband. Tessa had heard all the rumors and gossip about what women Jason had hit on and slept with, and she wondered how on earth he could live with himself for constantly cheating on his poor wife.

But even if Jason Baldwin had been single, Tessa still wouldn't have found him attractive. Oh, he was handsome enough, with his expertly cut dirty blond hair, evenly tanned features, and leanly muscled body. No, it was the predatory look in his eyes and his leering smirks that gave her the creeps. She had made it very, very clear to him – albeit in a polite, respectful manner considering that he was her superior and an extended member of the Gregson family – that she was most definitely not interested in him and was a happily married woman. But Jason persisted in flirting with her, trying to find ways to be alone with her or touch her in some manner, and making all sorts of suggestive comments.

Fortunately for Tessa, Andrew seemed to be very well aware of Jason's interest in her and did as much as he could to keep her away from him. He never assigned her any projects where she would have to work with Jason, even though Tessa knew Mr. Baldwin had specifically requested her on multiple occasions. And somehow, as though he had radar, Andrew always seemed to appear whenever Jason was being especially obnoxious. Jason would mutter something like "here's your guard dog again" before slinking off. Tessa didn't know why Andrew had quietly appointed himself her protector, but she was exceedingly grateful to him. She had heard all the stories about Jason's past troubles with female employees – including the one with Sarah, her own predecessor – and surmised that Andrew perhaps had been given strict orders to make sure no more unpleasant incidences occurred.

It was close to ten a.m. when Mr. Gregson arrived at the office after his morning appointment. Tessa could hear him greeting other employees before he reached her cubicle, his crisp British accent giving her a little thrill as usual. His voice was deep and cultured, and it never failed to enthrall her.

"Ah, His Hotness is finally here," said Kevin in a stage whisper. "It's show time, ladies."

Six heads popped up simultaneously as Ian Gregson walked past their cubicles with his long-legged, supremely confident stride. He gave the team an almost perfunctory nod, greeting them with a "Good morning, ladies. And Kevin."

There followed a rousing chorus of "Good morning, Mr. Gregson", including Tessa's own softly murmured reply. And then he continued on his way to his office, leaving half a dozen admiring gazes trailing in his wake.

Gina sighed. "God, he just gets hotter with every passing year. Most men get fat and gray as they age but not him."

"He's wearing the Savile Row suit today," volunteered Alicia. "And wearing it very well, I might add."

Kevin sniffed. "We'd all look good if we wore custom sewn five thousand dollar suits. Unfortunately, most of us are doomed to shop at Banana Republic for the rest of our lives."

Tessa thought privately that even a moderately priced store like Banana Republic was way out of her budget. And the thought of spending so much money on just one suit was so far beyond her scope that she failed to comprehend the idea. Her entire wardrobe – including underwear and shoes – wasn't worth the total of that sum. It was yet one more fact that widened the cultural gap between her and someone as splendid as Ian Gregson.

The rest of the morning went by quickly. Tessa had received the data she needed from Andrew, and was busily constructing the intricate spreadsheets. Though she didn't consider herself to be especially brainy and wasn't exactly a math whiz, she did enjoy working with the Excel program and the more detailed the worksheet the better.

But as she was reviewing the completed sheets before sending them on to Andrew, she frowned, for one of the pie charts didn't look quite right. Remembering Mrs. Carrington's teachings to proofread everything at least three times, Tessa checked and re-checked the data Andrew had sent her and was flummoxed over where the chart discrepancy was originating from. She hated to bother Andrew with anything, fearful that he would see her as incompetent. But she wasn't about to send an incorrect file to Mr. Gregson, either, so she printed out the offending sheet along with the back-up data, knowing that Andrew would prefer looking at the physical sheets rather than a computer monitor. It was already past the noon hour, and half the team was at lunch. Marisol was off making photocopies, which left just Shelby and Tessa to mind the fort.

"I need to ask Andrew about one of these reports," Tessa told her co-worker. "Are you okay here by yourself for a few minutes?"

Shelby visibly trembled at the mere mention of her tormentor. "God, poor you, having to deal with the Ice Man. Maybe you should put a sweater on so he doesn't give you frostbite."

Tessa merely smiled and headed towards Andrew's office. The PA had his own private space just outside of Mr. Gregson's commanding office suite, and the space was as tidy and organized as it always was. Except that Andrew himself was nowhere in sight. Tessa knew that he took his lunch break at precisely one p.m. every day, so she guessed he was off doing some task for Mr. Gregson.

She bit her bottom lip uncertainly, not wanting to just hang around as though she had nothing better to do. She was in the middle of jotting a detailed note to leave for Andrew with the reports when a voice from just behind startled her.

"Tessa. This is a surprise to see you here. Was there something you needed?"

She dropped the pen she'd picked up from Andrew's desk abruptly, and looked up as Ian Gregson appeared by her side. Tessa felt like all of the air had been sucked out of her lungs, and she suddenly forgot how to breathe. He had this effect on her every single time she was within a few feet of him, and she felt her cheeks flush.

"Um, I was just leaving a note for Andrew, sir," she murmured. "There's a bit of a discrepancy with one of the spreadsheets he asked me to do for you."

"Ah, well, we can't have that, can we?" he replied in a gentle voice. "Why don't you show me the problem and let's see if we can figure it out, hmm?"

"All-all right." Tessa struggled to maintain her composure, for she was hyper-aware of the man standing right next to her. With her sensible heels on, she stood at five ten, but he still towered over her by a good six inches. He had removed the aforementioned custom tailored dark blue suit jacket and hovered next to her in his shirt sleeves. She stole a quick glance sideways and had to stifle a gulp when she noticed how the fine linen fabric stretched across his broad shoulders and the wide expanse of his chest.

And she thought faintly that no one had ever smelled as good as Ian Gregson did. It was an irresistible combination of soap, aftershave, and pure male, and it made Tessa long to burrow her face against that strong, muscular chest and take a long, luxurious sniff. Even without making any sort of physical contact, she could feel the heat pouring off his big body, and her nipples hardened automatically in response against the thin fabric of her dress. Hoping fervently that he didn't notice, she self-consciously smoothed down the pleated skirt of her pale peach polka-dot dress.

She pointed to the pie chart in question. "This isn't accurate, Mr. Gregson. But I've checked the input data four times and it's all correct."

Ian studied the two sheets of paper for a long moment before pointing to the one with the background information. "Except that you were given the wrong report. This is the previous quarter's report, even though someone put the current quarter's date on it. Who prepared this report anyway?"

Tessa feigned ignorance, even though she knew that Shelby was usually the one who was in charge of the report in question. Andrew would figure that out soon enough on his own and give Shelby yet another icy admonishment.

"I'm not certain, sir. But it should be a simple matter to fix this. And now that you've identified the discrepancy, I can go ahead and adjust the spreadsheet. It will only take a couple of minutes."

The smile he bestowed on her made her knees go weak and her panties grow damp. "I don't know what I'd do without you here, Tessa," he told her earnestly. "You're the only one I trust to get all of these done correctly. Thank you for all of your diligence."

She couldn't resist smiling at him in return and hoped faintly that her cheeks weren't too red. "It's – I'm happy to help, sir. I'll – um, just take these back to my desk and fix the problem. I'm sorry to have bothered you, sir."

"It was no bother at all, Tessa," he assured her kindly. "I appreciate your conscientiousness in catching the error."

Trying in vain to conceal her flustered state, Tessa quickly picked up the papers from Andrew's desk and spun around to make a hasty exit. Except that Mr. Gregson hadn't moved an inch and she bumped smack into him. He placed a hand on her arm to steady her, and her cheeks grew even hotter to realize that her breast was crushed up against his iron-hewed arm.

He released his grip on her arm immediately and took two steps back. He didn't say another word but his hazel eyes had darkened noticeably, and the smile on his face had faded as he gazed at her somberly.

With a hastily mumbled "thank you", Tessa almost bolted out of the office back towards her own desk. 'Oh, God,' she pleaded silently. 'Please do not let him have noticed my nipples were hard.'

She was both mortified at what had just happened, but also incredulously, ridiculously aroused. It upset her to realize that her own husband failed to arouse those same types of feelings in her, and that she was so unsuitably attracted to her gorgeous, debonair boss.

She made it back to her desk on shaky legs and sunk down gratefully into her chair. She closed her eyes, and the image of Ian Gregson's ruggedly handsome face filled her thoughts despite her best efforts to dispel it. He was more striking than classically good looking but his strong, masculine features were irresistible – the intelligent, all-knowing hazel eyes; broad cheekbones and square chin; the firm, full mouth that rarely smiled but when it did his whole face softened and became even more compelling. His face was framed by his expertly cut dark hair, the back and sides cut short and close to the head while the top was left longer.

It was the return of Kevin and the others from lunch – all giggling and gossiping together – that jolted Tessa out of her almost trancelike state. She swiftly located the correct report she needed from their file sharing system, and made the required changes to the spreadsheet before emailing it to Andrew.

But as busy as she strived to keep for the rest of the workday, she couldn't completely forget about the brief but disturbing encounter with her boss earlier in the day. And each time she did her cheeks would flush anew and she'd curse herself for having such a strong and unsuitable reaction to him. She had no reason at all to believe that Mr. Gregson found her attractive, or even gave her a second thought. She was simply one of his many employees, and not a very important one at that.

The unwanted sexual attraction she felt for him was only because of the frustration she was currently experiencing due to Peter's long and frequent absences, she told herself fiercely. She was young and healthy and craved affection and physical contact, a perfectly normal state for a woman her age. Especially a woman who was alone as much as she was, and whose sexual relationship with her husband was as messed up as hers. It was only natural, Tessa assured herself with a confidence she didn't really feel, that her body would react to a man as virile and physically appealing as Ian Gregson. From what she'd heard from gossip and such, most every woman he came in contact with had the same sort of reaction to his charm and extreme good looks, so she was far from the only one.

'So it doesn't mean a thing, silly,' she told herself with a sense of relief. 'It doesn't mean that you don't love Peter or that you'd ever think of cheating on him. Especially since Mr. Gregson certainly doesn't think of *you* that way. I'm sure he hasn't given you a single thought the entire day.'

Chapter Three

Ian cursed softly as he tried for perhaps the fifth time to concentrate on the report in front of him. He'd had a ridiculous amount of work that needed to get done today, starting with the speaking engagement first thing this morning, and due to wind up with a business dinner this evening. In between, he'd had reports like this one to review, phone calls to return, employees to meet with, and plans to make for an upcoming trip to visit several of the properties in his region.

But it was as if all of his brain function had become stuck in quicksand ever since the all-too-brief encounter with the constant object of his desire – Tessa.

He shut his eyes, rubbing at a tense spot at the back of his neck. Christ, what a muddled-up mess this entire situation was with the woman he'd become positively obsessed with over the past two years. Ian thought rather sourly at times that he ought to have followed his instincts the first time he'd seen her, and arranged for a swift transfer to another department where he wouldn't have to see her every day. It might not have completely stopped his infatuation with her, but he would have had an easier time of it day to day.

But he'd been too weak – or too kind, not wanting to hurt the girl's feelings – and as a result had condemned himself to the hell of having to see his golden girl every day and know she was not his to claim.

He'd tried to fight his attraction to her, of course, using a variety of methods – none of which had worked. Ian had dated a string of beautiful, desirable women until he'd realized that none of them interested him in the least. He kept his distance from Tessa as much as possible, relying on Andrew to delegate assignments to her. And he had made it quite clear to Andrew that he did not want Tessa filling in as his PA whenever Andrew was out of the office. Passing by her cubicle en route to and from his office was one thing – it would be beyond the limits of even his ironclad control to have her sitting directly outside his office for hours and days at a time.

Ian was quite sure that his very perceptive PA knew of – or at least strongly suspected – his attraction to Tessa. He knew that he'd given Andrew more than adequate cause for such suspicions and really only had himself to blame. In addition to his refusal to have Tessa work as his fill-in PA, Ian had also given Andrew very strict instructions to do whatever was necessary to keep that bastard Jason away from her. Fortunately, Andrew took his duties very seriously and he'd done an admirable job at subtly looking out for Tessa. However, Andrew would also be well aware that his boss had never asked him to keep a watch over any of the other female employees on this floor before, and Ian would be shocked if the sharp as a tack PA wasn't supremely confident that his boss lusted after the beautiful Tessa something fierce. But Andrew was also wise enough to not so much as hint at the idea. The two men did not discuss personal issues, and Ian knew very little about what Andrew did after hours. Ian did know that Andrew had a longtime girlfriend, disputing the rumors floating around the office that he was gay, and that he originated from Seattle. Beyond that, much of Andrew's life was a mystery.

Ian was usually able to keep his attraction towards Tessa well under wraps, never betraying even a hint of it to anyone. But today he'd come perilously close to letting her know just how much he desired her, to dragging her into his arms and kissing her senseless. For starters.

She was wearing one of his favorite dresses today – the pale peach one with tiny white polka dots, belted at the waist, and a pleated skirt that fell to just above the knee. The silky fabric clung lovingly to her ripe breasts, the belt nipping in at her small waist, and the skirt draping softly over her gently curving hips. The color flattered her creamy skin and golden hair, and she looked as delicious as a sweet, juicy peach.

He was quite familiar, in fact, with nearly all of her outfits, especially since her wardrobe was anything but extensive. He'd overheard those two little cats – Gina and Alicia – make fun of Tessa's inexpensive, limited array of clothing behind her back, and he'd longed to sternly admonish the nasty little gossips.

He also longed to shower Tessa with all of the things she had to do without – dress her in beautiful, expensive clothes and shoes; buy her fabulous jewelry; make sure she was as pampered and indulged as a princess; protect and spoil her to her heart's content. He wanted her with him constantly – living in his home, sleeping in his bed, traveling with him wherever and whenever he had to go. But, instead, he continued to experience the frustration of not being able to betray his feelings for her – not while she was still a married woman.

Ian had been more than a little surprised when he'd met Peter Lockwood for the first – and only – time at last year's office Christmas party. Given that Tessa was such a knockout, he'd fully expected her husband to be a tall, well-built and equally good-looking young man. Instead, Peter had been a bit shorter than his wife, boyishly slim, and no more than average looking. It had been very obvious that he was uncomfortable at such a formal event, and certainly not used to dressing up. As Ian recalled, Peter had worn ill-fitting, mismatched trousers and jacket, a wrinkled shirt and skinny tie. His light brown hair had been on the longish side, secured back in a short ponytail, and one of his ears had been pierced.

Tessa's husband had been so completely unlike what Ian had imagined him to look like that it had been a struggle to contain his shock when she had briefly introduced them. Still, Tessa had seemed entirely devoted to him, sticking to his side like glue, and listening intently to his every word.

Ian had been almost overwhelmed with jealousy that night, and he'd had more to drink than was usual for him. But no amount of alcohol had dimmed the empty ache in his heart as he'd watched Tessa hold hands or link arms with Peter. He'd been consumed with envy over a pale, skinny boy who had somehow managed to claim the most beautiful girl Ian had ever seen.

That was the only time he'd ever seen Tessa's husband, and he had learned from Andrew that Peter was out of the country a great deal for his job. Ian thought passionately that if Tessa was his there was no way in hell he'd leave her alone for even two or three days, much less weeks.

His traitorous thoughts refused to let go of the memory of how it had felt – albeit very briefly – to have her lush body pressed up against his earlier today. His arm still burned from where one round, firm breast had been crushed against it. If he closed his eyes he could still feel the warm, silky skin of her arm where his hand had wrapped around it to steady her. He could smell the delicate, barely perceptible scent of her perfume or soap, a light, fleeting fragrance and not some overpoweringly strong odor. He'd been close enough to notice the charming blush on her cheeks, the wide roundness of her china blue eyes, and the way that decadently full mouth had trembled slightly. He didn't know if she was physically attracted to him, or simply terrified, but she had definitely been aware. The knowledge of her reaction to him had given him a least a small measure of satisfaction.

'What an ass you are, mate,' he chastised himself. 'So pathetically grateful for any imagined little reaction from her. You're ten times worse than a schoolgirl with a mad crush on her favorite movie star. And just as hopeless.'

***

The feeling that something bad was going to happen had gradually subsided as the day went on, and by the time Tessa got off the bus two blocks from her apartment, she was very nearly convinced that her premonitions had been all wrong. This was in spite of the fact that she hadn't received any sort of text or phone message from Peter confirming that he'd arrived home safely. She had reasoned that oddity away by assuring herself that he was undoubtedly exhausted after such a long flight, and had probably fallen asleep as soon as he'd walked in the door.

And then any worries she might have still been harboring flew away the moment she walked through the door of their apartment. The sound of one of Peter's favorite songs – *Hemorrhage* by Fuel – greeted her as she dropped her purse and slipped out of her shoes, leaving them by the tiny entryway table as was her norm.

"Hey, Tess."

Tessa smiled broadly and rushed to give her husband an eager hug. "Hey, yourself. I was starting to worry when I didn't hear from you. What time did you get in?"

Peter gave her a quick hug in return and pressed a kiss against her forehead. "I actually arrived in early this morning. We probably just missed each other."

Her smile faded rapidly as he gently disengaged her arms from about his neck. "What? I had no idea you were getting in so early. Why didn't you let me know?"

He shrugged, the shaggy, uneven ends of his light brown hair now long enough to reach his shoulders. "I was flying standby and literally didn't get on the flight until the last minute, so no time to text you before I left. And then when I got here I was pretty wiped out, I guess, plus I had some stuff to take care of. Sorry."

"No, it's okay," she assured him. "It's just – I've been a little unsettled today. I woke up with one of those weird premonitions – you know, it is a Wednesday after all. And I always worry when you have a long flight home from some of those places you travel to."

Peter gave her hand a squeeze. "Well, I'm okay, as you can see. Come on, I ordered pizza and it just arrived. Let's eat while it's hot."

Tessa frowned as she removed her jacket and hung it on a wall peg in the entryway. "I had already defrosted some chicken – thought I'd make that tortilla casserole you like. Are you sure getting pizza was a good idea? Things are a little tight for a few more days until I get paid."

He was already taking plates from one of their very few kitchen cabinets. "It's fine, Tess. Three of my stories from the last trip all sold and I deposited the check today. The chicken will keep. Sit down and take it easy."

Reassured, she sat across from him at their tiny table for two and eagerly reached for a slice of the mushroom and olive pizza that was her favorite. "Thanks, it looks delicious. It was really nice of you to order it."

Peter chucked her gently on the chin. "You deserve it. I know how hard you work, Tess, and how seldom you treat yourself to anything. And it's just a pizza, for God's sake."

She took a bite, savoring the warm melted cheese and thin crispy crust. "Mmm, it's awesome. Much better than chicken."

"Yeah, I admit I've been craving it myself. Too many weeks of one form or another of noodles and vegetables. But that's what comes from traveling through Asia as often as I do."

He told her about his most recent trip while they ate, and she listed as always with rapt attention. Peter was a master storyteller, whether in written or oral context, and she loved to hear his numerous tales. If she couldn't travel to these far-off, exotic places herself, then hearing his stories and reading his reports almost made her feel as though she was there herself.

Peter cleaned up the kitchen while Tessa took a quick shower. Normally she showered at the office after her daily workout at the employee gym, but she'd been in a rush to get home to Peter and had skipped working out today.

She'd been so happy to see him, had rushed inside the apartment so quickly, that she hadn't noticed his still unpacked bags until she reentered the living room after her shower. Tessa frowned as she towel dried her hair, especially when she realized there were a good half dozen bags piled together. Peter never took more than two bags with him on a trip, and he was usually always meticulous about unpacking not long after arriving home.

"Why haven't you unpacked?" she asked, an uneasy feeling starting to overtake her once again. The premonitions she'd felt upon waking this morning were returning in full force and then some.

Peter shoved his hands into the pockets of his baggy cargo pants, a sure sign he was feeling agitated. "Because I've got to leave again. Soon."

Tessa stared at him in dismay. "What? I don't understand. Why would the agency fly you all the way home from Cambodia just to send you back out again so soon? Especially with the tight budget they always have you on."

The international news agency that Peter worked for as a freelance reporter was notoriously cheap. The flights they scheduled for him always involved multiple stops and connections, and the accommodations they booked for him were anything but first class. The salary was barely adequate, and he often had to argue with them about getting paid on a timely basis. It was a fairly steep price to pay for doing the sort of work he loved, and had always dreamed of doing, but Tessa had done her best to support him these past couple of years. Even if it meant living on a shoestring budget and hardly ever seeing her husband.

Peter's thin mouth tightened into an even narrower line. "Tess, let's sit down, okay? We have some stuff to talk about."

Her legs suddenly felt wobbly, and the pizza she'd so eagerly devoured was beginning to burn a hole in her stomach. "Peter, you're starting to freak me out," she told him in a pleading little voice. "What's going on?"

"Sit down and I'll tell you." His voice was gentle but firm.

She sank down onto the futon that had originally been their bed, until they'd finally been able to afford a real one. She was starting to tremble and wrapped her arms around her torso in an effort to quell the tremors.

"Peter, please. I've got a really bad feeling about this now. What's wrong?"

He sat down next to her, taking her hands in his, his expression solemn. "I've got a new job, Tess. A hell of a lot better than this lousy gig. Better pay and actual benefits, a regular salary, living allowance. I've got to fly to New York to go through a two-week orientation before I actually start work."

Tessa almost laughed with relief. She had been convinced he was going to tell her something awful, but instead it was really, really good news. "But that's fantastic, Peter! I'm so happy for you!"

She flung her arms around his neck, hugging him close. Tessa pressed a kiss on his cheek, hoping, wishing, that tonight he might actually return her affections, might be able to make love to her for the first time in months.

But her hopes were dashed when he once again gently disengaged himself from her embrace and moved a short distance away from her. He kept her hands firmly clasped in his. "Thanks, Tess. It's a great opportunity, exactly what I've wanted for a really long time. I'm glad to know you're happy for me. Though

I'm guessing you won't be when you hear all the details."

Tessa regarded her husband warily. "What sort of details?"

Peter sighed, and ran a hand through his unruly hair. "The job is based in the Middle East," he told her quietly. "That's going to be my new territory. No more Asian trips."

She gave a small shrug. "Is that a bad thing? I mean, how much longer are the flights to and from the Middle East than they were to Asia?"

He paused, as though choosing his words very carefully. "You don't get it, Tess. *I'm* going to be based in the Middle East. Bahrain, to be exact. I'll be relocating there, living there full time."

Tessa felt like she'd taken a blow to the solar plexus, and struggled suddenly to breathe. "So – so we're moving? Leaving San Francisco and moving to Bahrain?"

He shook his head. "Not we – me. I can't take you with me, Tess. That's not part of the job offer. I'll be sharing a residence with three other journalists and photographers. And even if that wasn't the set-up there's no way I'd leave you alone for weeks on end over there. It's a very different world for a female in the Middle East. You wouldn't be able to get a decent job or go out and about anytime you wanted. Bahrain is a more modern country in that part of the world, but you still wouldn't have the sort of freedom you have here and would have to be very careful all the time. I'd worry about you constantly every time I was away."

The tears were beginning to well up hotly behind her eyes. "I'd be okay," she whispered. "I'll do whatever is necessary, just as long as I can go with you, so we can be together."

"No, Tess. It wouldn't be any kind of life for you. You'd be almost like a prisoner every time I was away," he explained. "And I'm expecting to be away for even longer stretches than I am now – maybe a month or two at a time – places like Syria and Egypt and Iraq."

The tears starting tracking slowly down her cheeks. "So – so how often will you be able to come home to see me?" she asked, her voice breaking.

Peter closed his eyes and took a deep breath. "I get two weeks off each quarter."

"That's it?" she cried. "I'll only get to see you eight weeks a year?"

"No. Let me finish. I'm not coming back to San Francisco. When I leave – that's it. We need to end this, Tess. It's way past time and we both know it."

She was weeping openly now, hiding her face in her hands as her body shook with sobs. "Please don't do this," she begged. "Don't leave me, Peter. I don't care if I can only see you a few weeks a year. Just don't leave me alone forever."

He took her into his arms gently, easing her head onto his shoulder. "Shh. Take it easy, okay? You know we have to do this, Tessa. We should have ended things a long time ago. This – what we have here – it isn't a marriage and it never has been, not really. You know it as well as I do. And it's never been fair to you for even one day."

"That's not true," she protested weakly. "We have a good marriage. We love each other. You've been so good to me, Peter, taken care of me for so long. I – I can't do this by myself."

"You're wrong, Tess. You've been taking care of yourself for almost two years now, every time I go away. And you've been doing great. I know you're going to do just fine on your own," he reassured her confidently.

She shook her head, clinging to his hand desperately. "That's different. I always knew you were coming home soon. And we Skyped and texted and emailed almost every day. Are we – can we still – "

"No. At least not as often. You need to start over, Tess, to break the ties and finally have a real life, a real relationship. Not all the crap you've had to put up with for so long with me."

"We do – I do -" she began to protest.

Peter stared at her in disbelief. "No, we don't, Tess, and we never have. I've never been able to give you what you need – what you deserve – and I doubt I ever will. You deserve so much more than what little I can give you."

"I don't care," she told him fervently. "I'm perfectly happy with the way things are."

"Bullshit. Come on, you're a beautiful, healthy, normal twenty-four year old woman. Every time we're out together I see the way guys look at us. They're all wondering how a pathetic geek like me landed someone as hot as you, wonder what the hell you see in me."

"Who cares what anyone else thinks?" asked Tessa passionately. "Our feelings are the only ones that matter."

"Exactly. And I've always felt like an asshole for not being able to give you what you really need." He squeezed her hand. "You know how fucked up I am, Tess. Everything that happened to me – it's not something I can forget or get over that easily. I'm not sure I'll ever really be normal or have a normal relationship. And I'm not going to make you suffer because of that any longer."

"I don't care about any of that," she insisted. "All I care about is being with you."

"Well, *I* care," Peter stated firmly. "How do you think it makes me feel knowing that I'm not giving you what you need – that I can't ever be the man you deserve? I feel like a total shit and certainly not like any sort of real man. So this has to happen, Tessa. For my sake as well as yours."

She slumped against the back of the futon, her limbs limp and lifeless. "How am I going to cope without you, Peter?" she whispered brokenly. "I'm so afraid of being alone. You're all I have."

He twined a lock of her damp hair around his fingers, a habit he'd picked up years ago. "You're going to be fine, Tessa. You're so much stronger than you think, you just don't see it now. And one day you'll meet a guy who truly deserves you – one who can finally give you everything you need – a real marriage, a baby."

"I don't want anyone else," she protested. "You're all I've ever needed."

"You've been the best wife any man could ever hope for – sweet, loyal, patient. You've never complained once about how crappy everything has been, how little we've had and how hard we've had to work. And you'll always be my best friend.

Forever." He kissed her softly on the temple. "But it's time for you to finally live, Tessa – *really* live, and not this shitty half-life we've been pretending to have for so long."

Tessa choked on another sob and dashed away a fresh onslaught of tears with the back of her hand. "So what – what happens now?"

"I visited an old college friend this morning – you remember Kyle?" At Tessa's nod, he continued. "He's finishing up law school here in San Francisco and working part-time at some big firm. He offered to draw up papers for us, do all the busy work, and then get one of the attorneys to sign off on them."

"Papers?" she asked in confusion.

"Divorce papers," he confirmed gently. "Kyle will have them sent here for you to sign, and then you just return them to him. He'll take care of forwarding them to me."

"Oh, my God." Tessa pulled her knees up to her chin, wrapping her arms around her shins. "God, are we really getting a divorce? It sounds so final."

"Our marriage will be over, Tess, but not our friendship," he reassured her. "We'll always be family, okay? And I'll help with money as much as I can. The lease on this place isn't up until April, you know, and you won't be able to afford the rent on your own. I'll put some money in your account each month until the lease is up and you can move to a cheaper place."

She hid her face against her bent knees, unable to think about practical things like paying bills or eventually having to move. "How long?"

"The divorce will take a few months to be final."

"No, that's not what I meant," she corrected. "How long until – you leave?"

"I fly to New York tomorrow morning. I'll be going through a two week orientation program, finalizing my work visa and stuff like that. I leave for Bahrain after that."

Tessa heaved a weary sigh. "So this is it, huh? Our last night together. Can't we have a few more days, Peter? So I can get used to the idea a little."

"It's better this way, Tess," he insisted. "I know you won't agree, but if I stay any longer you'll just try to convince me to forget about everything. And I've been putting a move like this off for far too long already. It's time, Tessa. Time for both of us to start over."

Her bottom lip trembled. "I know I've held you back. I know the only reason you stayed with me so long was because I was too helpless to take care of myself."

"That's bullshit, Tess. We've gone over this too many times to count. You are not helpless or incompetent or dumb. Or any of the other unflattering terms you always insult yourself with. You're smart and capable and you amaze me every day with how much you've grown."

She raised huge eyes to him. "I'm scared, Peter," she confessed in a trembly voice. "Scared of being alone. And terrified that I'm going to be like her."

"You aren't. You won't. You're nothing like your mother, Tessa, nothing," Peter assured her fiercely. "You're so much stronger than you're even aware of. And I know how hard this is but you're going to be okay. If I didn't believe that I wouldn't be leaving."

"Will you hold me?"

He took her into his arms, rocking her gently as though she were a small child. "Of course I will."

"I knew something bad was going to happen today. I felt it the minute I woke up. God, I hate Wednesdays," she said bitterly.

"Shh. It's just a silly coincidence, nothing more. Now, we should both get some rest. My flight leaves pretty early in the morning."

Tessa wasn't certain she could sleep, given how upset she was, but as she snuggled close against Peter she did manage to fall into a somewhat restless slumber, hoping against hope that she would wake to find all of this was just a bad dream.

But when her alarm went off the next morning, she was once again alone in the bed, as she was so often these days. And this time, Peter wouldn't be back.

Chapter Four

October

"How are you, Tessa? It's been a while since I've seen you here."

Tessa had been tidying up the refreshment table in the large conference room but glanced up at the soft, melodious voice of Julia McKinnon. Though smiles didn't come easily to Tessa these days, she couldn't help but return the interior designer's friendly greeting.

"I'm well, thank you. I'd ask how you're doing but I think that's fairly obvious," Tessa replied in a lightly teasing tone.

Julia's smile deepened into a grin. "And here I thought Nathan and I were being discreet. I guess I just can't help the way I look at him."

"You're in love. I don't blame you for being happy. And Mr. Atwood is obviously just as crazy about you," Tessa told her warmly.

Nathan Atwood was the co-owner of the architectural design firm that was currently creating the newest Gregson resort – this one in the Napa Valley wine country. Julia was the interior designer assigned to the project, and it had been rather obvious to Tessa the first time she'd met the gorgeous Julia that Mr. Atwood was extremely taken with her. They had been a couple for a few months now, and both of them positively glowed with happiness. And though they were discreet and professional, Tessa couldn't help but notice all the ways they found to touch each other – fleeting little touches, affectionately given, almost imperceptible. Tessa had found herself envying them the easy, natural affection they shared, something she and Peter had never come close to having.

Julia seemed inordinately pleased at Tessa's comment. "Well, it took him long enough to admit it, but now that he has it's awesome. It's – well, you know how it is – you're a married woman, after all."

Tessa knew her facial expression must have been a dead giveaway, because Julia instantly clutched her arm in concern.

"Are you all right?" she asked worriedly. "My God, you look like you're going to faint, Tessa."

Tessa closed her eyes, taking a deep breath before shaking her head. "I'm – okay, yes. Thanks for asking. I'd, um – better finish cleaning up here, though. I need to get back to my desk soon."

But Julia wasn't so easily dissuaded. "I'm so sorry if I said anything to upset you. Look, do you want to talk about it? Why don't we have lunch together? What time do you normally take your break?"

"Um, at one o'clock. But I – that is, I always bring my lunch every day. I don't think –" stammered Tessa. It would be too humiliating to confess that she couldn't afford to eat lunch out. Now that she was completely on her own, money was tighter than ever.

Julia seemed to sense her dilemma and laid a small, gentle hand on Tessa's forearm. "My treat. There's a cute little café about a block from here that I love. Nathan thinks it's too fussy and never wants to eat there with me. But they have really yummy desserts so you'd be doing me a huge favor if you'd go with me."

Tessa hesitated, not at all convinced that Julia wasn't just feeling sorry for her. It had to be quite obvious to the always beautifully dressed designer – with her chic sheath dresses, sexy high heels and perfectly coordinated accessories – that Tessa wasn't exactly in the same sort of financial circumstances. Her own clothes were very plain and inexpensive, and someone who had an eye for fashion like Julia did would have been sure to pick up on that fact. The navy pencil skirt and simple navy pumps were both items she wore often, though the pretty yellow blouse with the ruffle down the front was new. It had been an impulse buy a couple of weeks ago – a futile attempt to cheer herself up. Fortunately, the blouse had cost less than ten dollars on a clearance rack at Forever 21.

"I don't know," she demurred, looking down at her shoes. "I do have a lot of work to do."

"Do you want me to clear it with Andrew?" offered Julia. "He doesn't scare me in the least, you know, even though everyone else around here seems to be terrified of him."

Tessa gave a little laugh, probably the first time she'd done so in a month. "Andrew's not so bad. He just has high expectations. The first manager I had when I joined the company was much worse than he was. And – no, I don't need to check with him. I'd like to have lunch with you, thanks. Where should I meet you?"

Julia beamed and gave her the name and address of the little bakery café, arranging to meet just after one o'clock. She wrinkled her nose in distaste a moment later, though, as she glanced across the conference room.

"God, that guy gives me the creeps," she confided in a hushed tone. "At last month's meeting he actually came up to me afterwards and put his arm around my waist. I thought Nathan was going to break a couple of his fingers."

Tessa followed Julia's gaze and frowned. "Ah, Mr. Baldwin. Yes, he has something of a reputation around here. You're lucky you have your boyfriend to watch out for you."

"Does he harass you, too?" asked Julia in concern.

Tessa shrugged. "He tries, but I do my best to avoid him. I think Andrew's been told to keep him away from all the women on this floor."

"Hmm, I can see why. It doesn't seem to concern him in the least if a woman is married or otherwise spoken for, does it? And he must think he's God's gift to women, but he isn't *that* good looking," sniffed Julia. "My Nathan is ten times more attractive. And I can't understand why any woman in this office would look twice at a creep like Jason Baldwin when they have a hunk like Ian to stare at instead."

Tessa cursed her fair skin as she felt a warm flush stain her cheeks. Aware that Julia must expect some sort of response, she stammered awkwardly, "Um, yes. I – uh, agree."

To mask the sudden discomfort she felt at the mention of her boss' name, Tessa turned her attention back to cleaning up the refreshment table. Julia thankfully took the hint and left, reminding her about their lunch engagement at one o'clock.

But a few minutes later, after everyone else had left the room,

Tessa pondered the wisdom of going to lunch with the very perceptive Julia. It wasn't that she didn't like the bubbly, beautiful designer. On the contrary, Julia had been exceedingly kind to her from the very first time they had met back in February. And her boyfriend – Nathan – had always treated Tessa like a gentleman, never trying to flirt with her or ogle her the way so many others did. The entire design team for the Napa hotel had monthly meetings here at the office with management, and Tessa was nearly always assigned the job of setting up the room, taking meeting notes, and then cleaning up afterwards. Julia always sought her out, taking a few minutes to chat and thanking her for helping. Tessa was flattered by the attention, for she didn't really have any friends of her own, especially no one as pretty and outgoing as Julia. Tessa just knew somehow that Julia had been one of the popular girls in high school, while Tessa had always been a loner, an outsider.

She thankfully wasn't as socially awkward as she'd been back then – years of working so closely with others had helped improve her social skills a lot – but she was still extremely shy and not especially clever at conversation. Tessa just hoped she wouldn't be too boring for the vivacious Julia. She knew from past conversations as well as snippets of gossip she'd overheard that the designer had attended an Ivy League college, spoke fluent French, and was a talented artist. Not to mention having a wardrobe that Gina, Alicia and Shelby were all green with envy over.

Plus, Tessa was more than a little concerned that Julia suspected something was bothering her. She'd done her very best to conceal how devastated she was about the breakup with Peter, and hadn't said a word about it to any of her co-workers. She rarely discussed anything about her personal life anyway, and her separation and impending divorce were still too new, too raw for her to be able to discuss them with anyone. She very much feared, however, that Julia McKinnon had already surmised something was wrong, given the way Tessa had reacted to the comment about being married.

She had just finished tidying up the conference room, and was about to return to her desk, when Ian Gregson strode briskly into the room. He stopped short at seeing her, his expression as reserved and impassionate as always.

"Tessa. I didn't realize you'd still be here."

She simply couldn't help the little thrill that shimmered up her spine at the sound of his deep, cultured voice. Or the way her heart rate picked up at the sight of his tall, broad-shouldered body clothed in his elegant charcoal gray suit, impeccable white dress shirt, and expertly knotted tie.

She blushed yet again as she realized he was gazing at her somewhat impatiently, evidently expecting some sort of reply. "I, um, was just leaving, sir. Can I – is there something you needed?"

He frowned slightly, already looking around the head of the table where he always sat. "I seem to have misplaced my pen. Did you happen to find it when you were tidying up?"

Tessa shook her head. "No, I didn't, sir. But I'll be happy to help you look for it."

Ian waved a hand in dismissal. "It's no bother. I'm certain it will turn up somewhere."

From the corner of her eye she spotted an object on the thick carpet beneath the table that could be a pen. Dropping to her hands and knees, Tessa crawled the short distance, her hand closing around the pen at the exact same moment Ian squatted down beside her.

"Here it is."

"I've got it."

They spoke simultaneously, his hand brushing over hers as they both reached for the pen at the same time. Flustered by the feel of his warm hand on hers – however fleetingly – she glanced downwards only to have her mortification increase by leaps and bounds. For not only had her slim fitting skirt ridden up her thighs several inches, but the neckline of her pretty yellow blouse gapped open enough to reveal the lace of her bra. She could only hope that Mr. Gregson hadn't noticed, but those hopes were quickly dashed when she realized his gaze was fixed firmly on her cleavage.

She knew her face must be red as a beet as she somewhat

awkwardly got to her feet, smoothing her skirt down as she did so. Ian, too, stood up abruptly, then uttered a hasty "thank you" before striding out of the room in his usual authoritative manner.

Tessa was still cursing herself for her gauche, awkward behavior when she left to meet Julia for lunch. She had lost count of the times she'd made a fool of herself in Mr. Gregson's presence – always stammering or blushing or acting like she didn't have an ounce of sense. It was small wonder that Andrew had never once assigned her to fill in for him when he was on vacation or away on business. Marisol or Gina typically filled in, though Kevin and Alicia had also helped out before. There was no possible way Andrew would ever trust Shelby to work as Mr. Gregson's temporary PA but evidently Tessa hadn't been deemed worthy, either. She had always assumed it was because she lacked the college degree that nearly all of the others had. Marisol was the only one besides Tessa who didn't have a degree, but she did have seniority over everyone else and had obviously earned Andrew's trust because of her length of service.

But now Tessa wondered if perhaps Mr. Gregson simply didn't think she was bright enough or capable of handling the responsibility of being his temporary PA. God knew she'd done absolutely nothing to change his impression of her, given how tongue tied she always was when he was nearby. She hoped fervently that he only thought she was a silly, not especially bright girl rather than suspect the truth – that she had a massive crush on him. The former was embarrassing – the latter would be utterly devastating if he ever knew.

And for some reason, her crush seemed to have magnified tenfold ever since Peter had left last month. Perhaps it was the subliminal knowledge that she was now truly alone that was the cause of several erotic dreams she'd had in recent weeks about her very compelling boss. The most recent one had occurred just two nights ago, and recalling the specifics of it made her cheeks grow hot and her panties grow damp.

She'd been nude, laid out on the huge conference room table, her arms and legs spread wide. It was as though invisible bonds had been tied around her limbs, holding her in place. Ian had still been fully clothed, except for his jacket and tie, his crisp white shirt partially unbuttoned to reveal a ribbon of dark hair bisecting his muscular chest. His hands and mouth had been everywhere, it seemed – kissing her lips, cupping her breasts, sliding between her eagerly parted legs. He'd kissed his way down her body, licking her nipples until she'd squirmed with arousal, and then his head had ventured between her thighs.

Her dream had ended rather abruptly at that point, and she'd woken to find herself wet, her nipples taut, her full breasts even heavier and swollen. She had tentatively touched herself – one hand on her breast, tweaking a nipple, and the other between her legs, stimulating her clit. She had been startled at the swiftness and strength of her orgasm, how easily it had happened.

She'd groaned then, burying her face in her pillow, and trying not to feel ashamed. During their infrequent sexual encounters, Peter had never once been able to bring her to climax and had never wanted to give or receive oral sex. That she should dream about Ian Gregson going down on her was probably telling in some way, but Tessa didn't have a clue as to why. Sex was something she continued to be rather naïve about and definitely inexperienced, despite the fact that she and Peter had been together for a long time.

Tessa found the quaint little bakery/café easily and saw right away why Julia's boyfriend might not care for it. The outside awning was pink and the ruffled curtains at every window a floral print. Julia was just arriving, too, and Tessa marveled at how fluidly she could walk in her towering pale pink stilettos. She looked amazing in a form fitting sheath dress of gray lace, and drew admiring stares from every man she passed.

Julia's smile lit up her gorgeous face when she spied Tessa, and she gave her hand a little squeeze. "I'm so glad you were able to come. I've been wanting to have lunch with you for ages but work has been so crazy all summer. Let's go inside, shall we?"

The café was cozy and charming, with small tables draped in pink floral cloths, each with a vase of pastel flowers as a centerpiece, and attractively set with white dishes and gleaming flatware. It wasn't in the least bit stuffy or pretentious, and Tessa felt a sense of relief. She seldom went out to lunch with her co-workers except on special occasions like someone's birthday, and the others all seemed to favor trendy, upscale restaurants where the atmosphere wasn't nearly as relaxed and comfortable as this place.

Tessa continued to glance around the small interior as they were seated before smiling at Julia gratefully. "This is so lovely. It feels like someone's home instead of a restaurant."

Julie nodded enthusiastically. "It does, right? I thought the same thing the first time I ate here. But Nathan thinks it's too girly, reminds him of his grandmother's house."

Tessa laughed softly. "I must say I can't see him being comfortable here with so much pink and lace. Even the menu is printed in fancy pink script."

She didn't add that she had no real idea of what a grandmother's house might look like, since she'd never known either of her grandmothers. Or her father, for that matter. It had always been just Tessa and her mother, until there had only been Tessa.

Forcing herself to stop thinking about sad things and enjoy this rare opportunity to actually get out and do something fun, she studied the menu carefully. Fortunately, the café specialized in comfort food, nothing too fancy or exotic.

"Everything is delicious here," Julia offered helpfully. "Sandwiches, quiche, crepes. You can't go wrong no matter what you order."

Tessa grinned at the enthusiasm in her companion's voice. "Sounds like you eat here a lot."

"Quite a bit. My boss Travis loves it, too, and especially his partner Anton. *They* don't mind all the girly touches."

Tessa ordered the chicken salad croissant and Julia the smoked salmon quiche, along with a tall glass of sparkling French lemonade for both of them. They ate hungrily, and Tessa reflected on how many meals she'd been skipping lately. Her sadness and depression over Peter had contributed to most of that, but she'd also had to trim her already lean budget even further. She'd lost a few pounds as a result.

"I'm sorry if I said something to upset you earlier today," Julia told her quietly as they waited for their dessert to be served. "Maybe it was my imagination but you looked like you were going to collapse when I made that comment about being married. Is – is everything all right?"

Tessa nervously twisted the pale pink linen napkin between her fingers. "Um, it's – not something I -"

Julia placed a hand on her forearm. "God, I'm sorry. I don't mean to butt in. I was just worried about you, that's all."

Tears welled up in Tessa's eyes, touched at Julia's kindness. "No, it's okay. It's just – hard for me to talk about, you know? I haven't told anyone else – there really isn't anyone else to talk to." She bit her bottom lip to keep it from trembling. "My husband – we're getting a divorce. We, um – broke up about a month ago."

Julia gasped. "Oh, Tessa. I'm so sorry, honey. What an idiot I am, putting my foot in my mouth that way. Are you okay?"

Tessa shook her head, unable to stop the tears spilling down her cheeks. "No, not really. It's been so hard, Julia. I miss him a lot. He's – well, he was all I had. I don't have any family at all, haven't for years, so I'm all by myself now."

"You were close then – you and your husband?"

"Yes, very," replied Tessa tearfully. "Peter was my best friend as well as my husband. My only friend, really. I hardly even know anyone else here in San Francisco."

Julia looked aghast. "That's awful, honey. I had no idea, no idea at all. God, I can't even imagine not having my family or friends. Don't you have friends back in – was it Tucson or Phoenix you were from?"

"Tucson. And no, I really didn't have any close friends back there, either. For so long it was always just Peter and me."

"How long were you married?" asked Julia curiously.

Tessa hesitated before replying, knowing the answer would be startling. "Seven years."

Julia stared at her in disbelief. "Seven? How old are you anyway? I always thought you were a little younger than I was."

The subject of her marriage was always an awkward one for Tessa to discuss, and now was no exception. "I'm, um, twenty-four. I was seventeen when Peter married me."

"Seventeen!" Julia was visibly shocked. "God, you were just a child. Is that why – Jesus, never mind. I can't believe I'm asking you stuff like this."

"It's okay. And no, it wasn't because I got pregnant. It's – complicated."

"And none of my business," declared Julia. "I really don't mean to pry, Tessa. I'm just concerned is all. And it sounds like you could really use a friend right now, so please know that I'm here for you whenever you need me, okay?"

Tessa forced a teary smile. "You're so nice, Julia. I can see why Mr. Atwood fell in love with you."

Julia gave her a wink. "Well, it was definitely mutual – love at first sight and all that mushy stuff. Ah, here's our dessert. Nothing like a big old sugar rush to make you feel better."

The desserts came in huge portions so they had agreed to split the towering slice of black forest torte. Julia dug into the cake with gusto while Tessa merely picked at it, her appetite having waned abruptly after the discussion about her impeding divorce.

"Come on, don't make me be a pig and eat all of this myself," urged Julia. "Nathan already teases me about my ass getting bigger."

Tessa gave her a small smile and obediently ate a forkful. "It's really good. Thanks for this. Not just lunch but, - well, for being so kind to me."

"It's easy to be nice to nice people," assured Julia. "And you've always been so sweet to me every time I'm over for a meeting. Not like those bitches you work with. I'm not sure which one I dislike more – Gina or Alicia."

Tessa sipped her tea. "They're practically joined at the hip so take your pick. And they're roommates to boot."

"Figures. Though if I had to pick the nastier one it would be that sneaky little witch Gina. She tries to flirt with Nathan every time we're in the office, even though it's very obvious he's with me now. At least Alicia keeps her distance."

"That's because she's got her sights fixed on Mr. Gregson instead," Tessa blurted out. "But he never dates employees so she's out of luck."

Julia smiled mysteriously. "Hmm, bet I know of one employee he'd be willing to bend that rule for. Does Ian know you're getting a divorce?"

Tessa shook her head, frowning. "No, of course not. I haven't told anyone in the office yet. My co-workers tend to gossip a lot so I try not to discuss my personal life with them."

"Wise move. I wouldn't trust those two evil bitches for twenty seconds. And I know how fast office gossip can spread. My boss is a huge blabbermouth, I can't tell him anything really confidential or it would be all over the place within five minutes."

Tessa paused before asking her next question. "What did you mean about Mr. Gregson? The part about him making an exception to his rule."

"You really have no idea?" Julia regarded her curiously. "Well, our Mr. Gregson would deny it, of course, being that he's so prim and proper and always plays by the rules. But I've caught him more than a few times looking your way when you didn't notice and – well, let's just say I think he'd be *very* interested to know you're going to be a single lady soon."

Tessa stared at Julia in shock, her mouth hanging open in surprise. Slowly, she shook her head. "You've got to be mistaken. Badly. Mr. Gregson barely even speaks to me. And he is definitely not attracted to me."

Julia took a sip of her coffee and grinned wickedly. "If you say so. But I'd be willing to bet he'd speak to you a whole lot more if he got wind of your impending divorce."

"Please don't tell him," pleaded Tessa. "Not just him but anyone in the office. I'll tell them when the time is right but – well, it's just hard for me to confide in people. And even harder to talk about something as painful as this."

"I get it. And I won't say anything, even to Nathan. I swear, sometimes I think men are even worse gossips than women."

Tessa offered to split the check but Julia was adamant that this was her treat, plunking down a credit card casually.

"Thank you, Julia. Not just for lunch but for letting me cry on your shoulder. Not literally, of course," added Tessa with a little smile.

"But pretty close, huh? It was my pleasure. Look, I want to give you my cell number, okay? And I really do want you to call me if you ever need to talk or want to hang out. We can go have coffee or get a drink or just take a long walk. Do you like yoga?"

Tessa took the business card Julia handed her, the cell number written on the back. "I love yoga. I can't really afford it, though, so I mostly look for places that offer free or demo classes. What about you?"

"Yeah, it's kind of my obsession. I go to class almost every day. You should come to my studio with me some weekend soon. My weekend teacher Sasha is awesome. She kicks my ass every single time I take her class. I can get you a complimentary pass if you'd like."

"I'd love that," beamed Tessa. "I, um, don't really have any girlfriends so I appreciate your offer to – you know, hang out."

"Well, I don't have very many myself," confessed Julia. "So I'd really, really like to call you my friend. Okay?"

Tessa felt just a little bit less lonely as she smiled at her new friend. "Okay."

Chapter Five

November

Despite the fact that her abs were already quivering in protest, Tessa forced herself to do another set of crunches on top of the hundred she'd already completed. She was using the slant board today, which was always tougher for her than the fitness ball, and thus had to push herself hard to finish the grueling workout. Besides the core work, she'd done an hour of cardio, split between the stationary bike and the elliptical machine, then lifted weights, focusing today on her biceps and shoulders.

She'd always liked to exercise in some form or another, even though her mother had never been able to afford the various fees and equipment involved in playing organized sports like soccer or softball. Not to mention the fact that she couldn't be counted on to remember to actually pick Tessa up from practices or take her to games. From the time she had been a small girl, Tessa had more or less been responsible for getting herself to and from school, in addition to all of the other daily tasks she'd had to perform for herself.

At least she'd had the good fortune to attend some highly rated public schools over the years, all of which had offered excellent physical education classes and facilities. P.E. had always been one of her favorite classes, perhaps because it was one that she excelled at, and didn't feel far behind all the other students in class. Whether it was swimming, tennis, basketball, modern dance, or running, Tessa had looked forward to that class every day.

She'd been thrilled to discover the small but well equipped employee fitness room here at the San Francisco offices. Back at the Gregson resort in Tucson, employees had been allowed use of the expansive fitness facilities, so long as it was during off-peak hours when the hotel guests weren't availing themselves. Tessa was very disciplined about her workouts, rarely missing a day. Five days a week she exercised here at the office, always doing some sort of cardio – bike, elliptical, treadmill or stair climber – plus weight training and core work. She couldn't afford to belong to an outside gym, so she was extremely thankful to have use of this room. On weekends, she scoured the Internet to find the free or demo yoga classes she'd told Julia about, and also took long walks and hikes around the city. Peter had often accompanied her on these excursions when he'd been in town, and Tessa figured they had explored nearly every trail or pathway in San Francisco.

The thought of her soon-to-be ex-husband made her sad, as it always did these days. It had been over two months now since he'd left, and she was still miserable and lonely. She had to force herself not to contact him too often, to limit her emails to no more than twice a week. At first, Peter had always answered her promptly, telling her in detail about what he'd been doing, how he was settling in, and asking how she was adjusting. Lately, though, it was taking him just a bit longer each time to respond, and his replies were getting shorter and shorter. Tessa knew that this was Peter's way of gradually cutting her loose, and nudging her to look after herself.

She finished her crunches, now too wiped out to consider doing even one more, and reached for a towel to wipe the sweat off her face and neck. As she drank from her water bottle, Tessa fought off the guilt she always experienced when thinking of how much Peter had sacrificed for her sake over the years. If he hadn't felt obligated to take care of her and make sure she was financially and emotionally stable, he would have likely traveled more than halfway around the globe by now. Instead, he had stayed in Arizona with her to finish his college degree and make sure she had the job training and experience she would need to one day support herself. By then they had just grown used to being together, and Tessa had been prepared to follow Peter anywhere he wanted to go in return for his protection. All the while, she'd known that what he really wanted was to travel freely wherever his whims might take him, following one story after another, and she had felt responsible for holding him back.

She was happy for him – that he was finally getting to live his dream – and she was really trying hard not to resent him for it. She couldn't be Peter's responsibility any longer, the weight that dragged him down, and was determined to finally grow strong enough to stand on her own two feet and not depend on anyone else to take care of her. It was hard, the toughest thing she'd ever had to do in a life that had been filled with hardships, but she was getting through it a day at a time.

The loneliness was the worst – the nights when she was all alone in her tiny apartment with no one to talk to or hang out with. Julia had been wonderful, calling several times a week to chat, and they'd met for coffee a few times already. But at present Julia was still recovering from a near-tragic assault she'd suffered at the hands of Nathan's ex-fiancée. Tessa had wanted to drop by her new friend's flat for a visit but hadn't wanted to intrude, especially when Julia's parents had arrived for a visit.

And now Thanksgiving was only about ten days away, and she knew Julia was flying to Michigan to spend the holiday with Nathan's family. Tessa hadn't even begun to think about what she might do herself, since she'd always spent holidays with Peter. Last year they had gone to dinner at the home of one of his former co-workers at the news agency, but this year everything was different. She would most likely be alone on Thanksgiving, just as she was every other day now.

The punishing workouts she'd been putting herself through these past weeks had helped some – at the very least filling those empty hours after work so that she didn't have to sit around her apartment longer than necessary. And all the exercise had helped make her legs even more toned, her abs tighter and more defined, her muscles leaner. Not that she cared very much about how she looked these days. After all, it wasn't as though she had a man in her life, or any real desire to find one.

Before meeting Peter, there had been a couple of boys in high school that she'd flirted with, and even made out with a little, though it had never gone any further. And then when things had gone to hell with her mother and her entire life changed overnight, there hadn't been time for boys or any of the other pleasures girls her age normally enjoyed. Life quickly became about day to day survival and nothing more.

Tessa knew she was considered pretty and had a good body, but she'd never been vain about her looks. Still, she was fairly certain she wouldn't have a problem in meeting men and going on dates if she were so inclined. But her almost crippling shyness stood firmly in the way, and she wouldn't have a clue on how or where to begin. She'd only been to a club, for example, once or twice when she and Peter had rather reluctantly been persuaded to go out with her co-workers. Gina, Alicia and Kevin had spent the better part of the evening getting completely plastered, and Peter had made her promise to never go out with them again, calling them a bad influence. Plus, from what she'd observed of the scene inside the clubs, Tessa highly doubted she'd ever want to try and meet men in a place like that.

As usual, she'd had the fitness room pretty much to herself. One of the women from Accounting had been here when she'd arrived, walking on the treadmill, and then two geeky IT guys had stopped in to use the weight machines for a few minutes. The room had been empty for the last forty-five minutes, the only audible noise coming through the earbuds of her tiny iPod shuffle. Peter had bought the device for her in Japan for her last birthday, and had loaded a bunch of songs he knew she liked. It was one of her most cherished possessions, despite the fact it was really only worth about fifty dollars. Even now as she was cooling down before heading off to take a shower, she was tempted to sing and dance along with the throbbing beat of Bruno Mars' *Locked Out of Heaven.*

She had the volume of the iPod cranked up so loud that she didn't hear the door to the fitness room open. It was only when she turned away from the water cooler that she realized someone else was in the room, and gulped in alarm when she saw who it was.

Jason Baldwin was smiling at her in what he likely thought was a seductive manner, but to Tessa it more closely resembled a leer. Reluctantly, she turned off her iPod and removed the earbuds, all too aware of how close he was standing. A shiver of alarm traveled rapidly up her spine, and she instinctively took a step or two backward.

But Jason wasn't easily deterred and merely moved even closer, enough that she could smell the lingering scent of alcohol that clung to him. Tessa belatedly remembered that there had been some sort of cocktail reception on the schedule today, with most of the management team in attendance. In addition to the fitness room and showers, this floor held the employee lunch room, a few smaller conference rooms, and a large reception room complete with its own kitchen and bar that was used for entertaining clients.

"Well, if I had known the most beautiful woman in the office was in here working out alone, I would have left that god-awful party a long time ago and joined you," Jason told her in a deliberately seductive voice.

Jason was also British, as were quite a few of the upper management team, but his accent had no effect on Tessa whatsoever – not in the least like Mr. Gregson's smooth, cultured tones. The only effect it had was to give her the creeps, and make her very anxious to get out of this room as quickly as possible.

Tessa tried to brush past him without being too obvious. "I've actually just finished, Mr. Baldwin. If you'll excuse me, please."

He wrapped a restraining hand around her bare upper arm. "What's the rush, honey? You're always running away from me. Or else that damned guard dog Andrew is hovering somewhere in the background like he's your nanny or something."

She attempted to pull her arm free but Jason's grasp was unrelenting. "Please let me go, Mr. Baldwin. I – um, need to change clothes and then get home. My – husband will be expecting me."

But he refused to release his grip and instead raked her up and down with his heated gaze. She tried not to quiver in fear at the very obvious lust she saw in his eyes, and wished fervently that she hadn't worn such skimpy workout attire – tiny gray terry gym shorts and a bright pink racerback tank that clung a little too closely to her breasts.

"You don't have to change on my account, Tessa," he told her in a husky voice. "In fact, I'm very much enjoying the view. Mmm, someone's been working out hard, haven't they?"

This time she couldn't help the quiver of alarm that rippled through her entire body as Jason traced the beads of sweat that had gathered in the base of her throat down between her breasts. She gasped in outrage when his finger dipped into her cleavage before his thumb brushed over her nipple.

"I'd like to get you even sweatier." He bent forward to murmur in her ear. "I've wanted to fuck this gorgeous body of yours since the first time I saw you. Why don't I join you in the shower and we can have ourselves a real good time?"

Now Tessa was beginning to panic a little, and struggling to control her fear as she once again tried to break free. "Mr. Baldwin, this isn't appropriate. Both of us are married and -"

Jason interrupted her with a hoot of laughter. "I don't give a damn about that, honey. All I care about is finally seeing this hot body of yours. Especially these nice big tits."

She cried out in alarm as his hand closed over her breast, squeezing it painfully. And then she gasped in shock as a larger, stronger hand clamped forcefully over Jason's wrist.

"Let go of her immediately, you fucking little bastard."

Tessa didn't know whether to be greatly relieved or completely mortified at the sight and sound of an enraged Ian Gregson. He practically dwarfed the shorter and slighter Jason, and there was no question as to which man was more powerful – or more fearsome.

She had never seen or heard him this angry before. His hazel eyes were flashing, his cheeks flushed red, and his sinfully full mouth a tight, narrow line. Tessa could see he was almost shaking with rage as he forcibly yanked Jason's hand away from her breast.

Jason's fear was obvious but he foolishly still tried to make light of the situation. "Aw, come on, Ian old chap. I was just having a bit of fun with the girl. No harm done, just a little innocent flirting. Isn't that right, Tessa?"

Tessa was shaking so badly that she had to lean against a wall to steady herself. She felt the sheen of tears in her eyes and bit down on her bottom lip to keep it from quivering. Speech was not something she felt capable of, so she merely shook her head vehemently in protest.

Ian's hand tightened around Jason's wrist until he yelped in protest. Even then Ian refused to release him, his voice icy cold and filled with barely restrained anger as he bit out, "Shut your foul mouth, Jason. I want to see you in my office at once. Get your sorry arse up there right away and wait for me."

"But – but Charlotte is expecting me," protested Jason weakly. "We have an event to attend."

"Then you'd best call and let her know you've been unavoidably detained," retorted Ian sharply. "And our conversation won't take long. Now get out of here."

Jason rubbed his abused wrist as he exited, wisely not looking back on his way out.

Ian turned to Tessa, his voice and facial expression taking a complete 360° turn as he did so.

"Are you all right, Tessa?" he asked in the gentlest, most compassionate manner she'd ever known him to exhibit.

She was instantly enthralled by the tenderness in his gaze, the obvious concern in his voice, and nodded. "Yes, sir. He didn't hurt me. I was just scared."

Ian grimaced. "Is this the first time he's harassed you? And be honest, Tessa. That bastard doesn't deserve to be defended."

Tessa hesitated for a few brief seconds before replying. "It's – the first time he's ever – well, put his hands on me that way, sir. But, no, it certainly isn't the first time he's said – um, inappropriate things."

"I surmised that." The stormy look was back on his face but she knew it wasn't directed at her. "Why didn't you file a complaint about him with Human Resources?"

She was startled at his question. "I never considered it, Mr. Gregson. I mean, he's a manager. And part of your family. And I – well, I need my job, sir. I would never do anything to risk being dismissed."

He stared at her in mingled surprise and alarm. "Good Lord, why on earth would you think you'd be fired for something like that? Especially when it's common knowledge that this isn't the first time that weasel has done something like this." Ian's expression softened, and she was taken aback by the almost tender look on his face. "You're my most valued employee other than Andrew, Tessa. I would never allow you to be dismissed just for speaking up for yourself. And I certainly won't allow Jason Baldwin to put his stinking hands on you ever again, or utter one more inappropriate word. He'll be taken care of swiftly, I assure you."

She found herself speechless at the fervor in Ian's voice and the ferocity of his features. She had no idea what to say in response save for a hastily stammered, "Um, thank you, sir."

An awkward silence hung between them for several seconds, until Ian's gaze flickered over her miniscule gym shorts and clingy workout top, and she cursed beneath her breath as she felt her nipples begin to peak. Whereas Jason's amorous regard had made her skin crawl, her body evidently had no such problem with Ian Gregson looking at her in much the same way. Tessa just hoped he wouldn't notice her rather obvious reaction to his proximity.

He gave her what looked like a knowing little smile before holding the door open. "You ought to go shower and change now, Tessa. You don't want to catch a chill, after all."

Her face flaming, she hurried past him out the door, ready to sprint for the shower room two doors down. But the almost imperceptible touch of his hand on her bare arm stopped her, and she gazed up at him quizzically. The utter kindness on his beautiful face caused something deep inside of her to ache unbearably.

"I'll never let anyone in this office hurt you, Tessa," he told her with complete seriousness. "I want you to come directly to me in future if anyone dares say anything to upset you. Do you understand?"

All she could summon up in bewildered surprise was a nod, but it was enough for him to release her before striding briskly in the opposite direction.

Her legs felt like they were going to give out from under her, a condition that had nothing whatsoever to do with the grueling workout she'd just completed.

And, as she stood under a hot shower a few minutes later, it belatedly occurred to her what day this was – a Wednesday, of course.

***

Ian rarely engaged in outward displays of temper, but he could almost feel the steam escaping from his ears as he exited the elevator and headed for his office. He couldn't recall a single time in his life when he'd felt so much rage, such an uncontrollable urge to slam his fist through the wall, or curse vividly and loudly. That prick Jason had gone too far this time, had dared – *dared* – to touch his golden girl, his beloved, precious Tessa, and the randy bastard was going to pay dearly for that very unwise act.

He felt like a caged beast as his long legs covered the distance between the elevator and his office in record time. Rage shimmered through every muscle in his body, and he clenched his fists in a futile attempt to stem his anger. Every time he pictured Jason's filthy hand touching Tessa, or recalled the look of panic on her sweet, lovely face, he wanted to roar like a lion in the jungle. There was no punishment too severe for what that horny little bastard had done.

His anger was not diffused even a bit as he found Jason loitering around Andrew's desk. His cousin-in-law was in the middle of tapping out a text, and didn't look to be in the least concerned about the severe tongue-lashing he was about to receive.

Jason glanced up as he heard Ian approach, and actually had the balls to offer up a cheeky grin. "Ah, there you are, mate. I was starting to wonder where you were. Now, I managed to persuade Charlotte to be patient for a little while, but I don't have much time. What -"

"Get the fuck into my office and keep your bloody mouth shut," Ian spit out, longing to put his fist very capably into Jason's smug face.

Jason almost jumped at the icy anger in Ian's tone but obediently didn't say a word as he followed him inside the office.

"Close the door and sit your sorry arse down. This won't take long."

Jason was beginning to feel more than a little uneasy. He'd known Ian for a good ten years now and had never seen him this pissed off, the rage pouring off of him in waves.

"Take it easy there, old chap," soothed Jason. "No need to get your knickers in a twist. I was just having a bit of harmless fun with the girl. Hot little thing like her must hear that kind of stuff all the time. That husband of hers is a lucky bloke, isn't he? Can you imagine having someone like that to tap whenever you get the urge?"

Jason did jump this time, as Ian slammed the office door shut almost violently. And then Jason was the one being slammed, as Ian grabbed hold of his shirt and shoved him up against the nearest wall.

"I told you to keep your fucking mouth shut." Ian ground out every word with ill-concealed malice. "Did you think I was joking, Jason?"

Jason could only shake his head, his fear rendering him suddenly mute.

"Good. Now listen and listen carefully because I'm not a man who likes to repeat himself." Ian gave him a shake as though he were a repulsive gutter rat. "I'm sick to death of your manwhore behavior in this office. I've already had to transfer one employee off of my team in order to prevent her from filing a sexual harassment lawsuit. I'm not prepared to take that risk any longer, or lose another member of my team."

Jason was wide-eyed and listening very carefully to every word as Ian continued.

"Consider this your last day in this office. Tomorrow you are to report to your new assignment – as the manager of our hotel in the Silicon Valley. Fortunately we've just had an opening so you won't have to move the family elsewhere in the country."

"Silicon Valley!" burst out Jason. "But – but that's in bloody Scotts Valley! Do you have any idea how long it will take me to commute there and back from San Francisco every day?"

Ian smiled, but it was not a pleasant look. "I don't give a holy fuck how long it takes you. If you don't like it, Jason, then the other three options you have are Atlanta, Palm Springs, or – oh, yes - looking for employment somewhere else besides this company."

"But you can't do that!" protested Jason. "My father-in-law will never allow it. All it would take is a phone call to him."

Jason squealed as Ian shoved him even harder against the wall, his grip on the front of Jason's shirt tighter.

"I can do whatever I goddamn please." He enunciated each word with careful precision. "My uncle can't – and won't – do a bloody thing about it. And do you know why that is, Jason?"

Jason had to look away from the ferocity in Ian's eyes for fear he might piss his pants. "Nnnoo. I – I don't."

"Uncle Richard is well aware of the fact that you can't keep your dick in your pants, but for reasons of his own he chooses to turn a blind eye to your little escapades. However, brief, meaningless flings are one thing but a permanent girlfriend is quite another. I doubt Richard would be especially understanding of the arrangement you have set up over on Pierce Street."

The shocked expression on Jason's face would have been priceless had Ian not been so enraged with him.

"I see you don't even begin to deny it." Ian shook his head in revulsion. "And it's only for the sake of your three very small children that Charlotte isn't being made aware of – is it Greta or Gretchen, I don't recall exactly."

"Greta," replied Jason in a barely audible voice.

"Ah, that's right. A very pretty little blonde if I recall from the photo I saw. Swedish, is she?" asked Ian mockingly.

"How did you-" began Jason.

Ian regarded him in disbelief. "Do you really need to ask me that, Jason? I know everything. Or at least the things I need to know. And for obvious reasons I've kept very close tabs on you over the last few years."

Jason's expression was sullen as Ian finally released him. He straightened his rumpled shirt and tie, and ran a hand through his sun-streaked hair. "So what am I supposed to tell Charlotte about the reason for this sudden transfer?'

Ian shrugged. "Tell her whatever the hell you want. I'm certain it won't be the truth. But then you must have become quite the expert at lying to her after all this time."

Jason glared. "What I can't quite figure out is exactly what provoked these extreme measures. With the others, they were the ones who got transferred. Why can't you move Tessa somewhere else? She's just a fucking secretary while I'm part of the family."

The expression on Ian's face was scathing. "You're sure as hell not *my* family. At least not that I'd acknowledge. And frankly, that girl is a far more valuable member of my management team than you could ever be. So she stays – you go. Now, I've got a dinner to attend so you can leave now. I'll have your personal belongings packed up and delivered to you at your new office. Best get a good night's rest, Jason – don't forget you'll have a bit of a drive tomorrow."

But Jason wasn't quite through and a mischievous smirk turned his mouth up at the corners. "I get it now. The real reason you're sticking up for Tessa is because you fancy her for yourself. You're pushing me out because I dared to put my hands on her when you want to do the exact same thing. Is that it, mate? You're getting the competition out of the way so you can shag the hot little bitch to your heart's content?"

The grin on his face was abruptly replaced with a grimace of pain as Ian twisted his arm behind his back and held it pinned in an iron grip. Ian brought his face so close that Jason could count his eyelashes if he was so inclined.

"First of all," began Ian in a not so pleasant voice, "you would never be competition for me in any way, and especially not with a woman. Second, you are beyond offensive, beyond reprehensible. Tessa is a married woman, and unlike most of the others in this office – like your little fuck buddy Morgan – she's also a lady. Lastly, if I ever see you speak to her or – God forbid – touch her again, or even hear that you've done so, I'll break your jaw, all ten fingers, and kick you so hard in the balls you won't be able to fuck anything for a year. And if you think I'm not capable of all of those things, don't forget I was the heavyweight champion at Oxford for three years in a row. Now get out of my sight, you miserable piece of shit."

As Jason made a swift exit, Ian paced furiously around his office, finally stopping in front of the wet bar in one corner. He poured himself three fingers of a very rare single malt Scotch and bolted it down in two gulps.

He was on his third drink – which he was now sipping – before he felt the rage begin to subside. He had never come close to displaying this sort of anger before, to losing control of his ironclad emotions. But then he'd never felt this way about a woman before, and every protective instinct in his body had risen up automatically when Jason had tried to accost Tessa.

'I should have broken the slimy bastard's wrist,' Ian thought furiously. 'For starters.'

There had been no question in his mind – and zero delay in making it happen – that Jason simply had to go. Ian knew his uncle wouldn't be pleased but it was just tough shit. The family had stuck Ian with the horny little prick when he'd been appointed to this post, so it ought to be completely his decision on how to manage him. If it meant Jason now had an hour's commute each way to his job, then in Ian's opinion it was nothing less than he deserved. When Ian thought of how frightened Tessa had looked when he'd been fortunate enough to walk by the fitness room at the right time, he wanted to drag Jason back into this office and use him like a punching bag.

Christ, she had looked delectable – and very, very fuckable – in those tiny little shorts that had bared the long, streamlined length of her shapely legs. And that top she was wearing – more like a longer length exercise bra – had been molded to her lush breasts like a second skin. He hadn't missed the way her nipples had peaked and pressed against the Lycra fabric, either.

'Damn it!' He cursed softly to realize he was hard and throbbing, no better than that rutting rake Jason. But unlike his amorous cousin-in-law, Ian would never, ever harass Tessa or even give her the slightest hint that he was attracted to her.

He cursed again, for attracted was far too mild a term to describe what he felt for the beautiful girl who could never be his. Obsession was more like it, and he wondered in near desperation how much longer he could keep his hands off of her.

Chapter Six

December

"There, all done. Let me take a look, make sure I don't need to touch anything up."

Tessa continued to sit patiently at Julia's dining table while her friend carefully inspected Tessa's makeup. With brush in hand, Julia swiped another bit of powdered blush on each cheekbone, then finally smiled in satisfaction.

"Perfect. Wow, you look stunning, Tessa, just – wow. Every head in the place will be turning when they see you tonight."

'Tonight' was the annual office Christmas party that Tessa had somehow allowed herself to get talked into attending. Not only had all of her co-workers done their best to convince her, but once Julia had heard about the event, she too had gently but firmly urged Tessa to go.

"It will be good for you to get out a little," she'd prodded. "You're too young and too hot to sit at home every night. It's way past time for you to start having fun."

And when Tessa had still resisted, Julia had asked rather bluntly, "Don't you think it's what Peter would want you to do?"

That had finally convinced her, because Julia was absolutely right – going to the party was exactly the sort of thing Peter would have encouraged her to do. So she'd allowed Julia to drag her on a mini-shopping spree to find a new dress and shoes, mindful of Tessa's very limited budget. Julia had a knack, however, for finding beautiful clothes even at a discount store, and the strapless blue cocktail dress Tessa wore tonight was every bit as glamorous as one from a high end store.

Julia had actually offered to ask her aunt – who was the head buyer at some fancy New York department store – to send a dress and shoes for Tessa, but Tessa had gently but firmly refused.

"I just think it would look a little odd for me to show up in a really expensive dress," she'd explained. "Gina and Alicia in particular would be sure to recognize a designer gown, and then ask all sorts of questions about where I got it. And – well, you know I hate discussing anything personal with them."

"You mean Anastasia and Drizella?" At Tessa's puzzled look, Julia had laughed and clarified her question. "Those were the names of Cinderella's evil stepsisters."

"Oh." Tessa couldn't help giggling along with her friend. "Actually, I've always thought of them as the nasty Siamese cats from *Lady and the Tramp.*"

Julia had thought that hilarious, and they'd shared a good laugh. Then she had assured Tessa she understood her concerns about the dress, and instead offered to go shopping together.

"Not everything I wear is expensive or from my aunt, you know," she'd confided as they scoured the racks at several different discount stores. "In fact, Aunt Madelyn is the one who taught me how to look for the best dress in places like this one, and how to mix high and low end pieces. Oh, my God, Tessa. Look at this one – it's absolutely perfect."

Tessa had fallen in love with the chiffon dress with its strapless bandeau bodice and the way the fabric fell from the gathered bust to a few inches above the knee. Julia had declared that silver shoes and accessories would go best with the deep blue color, and they'd found a pair of strappy silver heels on the clearance rack at DSW. The rest of Tessa's ensemble this evening consisted of items loaned to her by Julia – a sparkling round brooch pinned to the gather at the bust; a wide cuff bracelet; a pair of dangly earrings. Julia had assured her that all the pieces were costume jewelry and not very expensive at all, so that Tessa wouldn't have to freak out about wearing actual diamonds or worry about losing them.

Julia was also loaning her a sparkly silver clutch, into which she was placing the tube of shiny rose lip gloss that she'd just painted onto Tessa's mouth. She had spent over an hour doing Tessa's makeup and hair, and now it was time for the "big reveal" as Julia teasingly called it.

"Come on, you can see for yourself how awesome you look," cajoled Julia as she propelled Tessa into her bedroom and inside the walk-in closet.

Tessa had been dumbfounded the first time she'd seen Julia's closet, never having imagined that one person could own so many dresses or shoes or bags. She only owned about three pair of shoes that were suitable for the office, and one oversized purse that she used for everything. Julia had been horrified at the thought of Tessa taking the rather beat-up bag to tonight's formal affair, and had set her foot down that she use the clutch instead.

"Okay, tell me what you think," prodded Julia as they stopped in front of the full length mirror hanging on the back of the closet door.

Tessa gasped and could only stare back at her reflection in disbelief. She had never, ever, looked like this before – or felt so beautiful – almost like Cinderella herself.

The dress fit her perfectly, the strapless top baring her shoulders and upper chest but stopping just short of revealing too much cleavage. Tessa offered up a silent thanks that she'd devoted extra time these last few weeks to toning her upper body, for her bare arms and shoulders looked lean and shapely. The sapphire blue shade was very close to her eye color, and flattered her ivory skin and golden blonde hair. The strappy silver shoes had a higher heel than she normally wore, and made her legs look even longer. She was glad Julia had suggested breaking the high heels in and walking around her apartment in them a few times so that she felt steady with the added height.

Julia had done a fabulous job on her makeup – making her eyes look twice as big with the silvery gray shadow, subtle application of liner and three coats of mascara. Her complexion glowed rosily with the light touch of foundation and blush, while her mouth appeared fuller and plumper with the shiny rose gloss.

Her thick golden hair had been curled into soft, loose waves, held back on one side with a rhinestone clip. It smelled like peaches or apricots, courtesy of the decadently rich shampoo and conditioner Julia had used on her, so much nicer than the cheap brands she bought at the drugstore.

Julia brushed a stray hair off of Tessa's cheek. "You look perfect. Gorgeous, sexy, sophisticated." Then she groaned. "I just wish I'd been able to arrange a better coat for you. No offense, but that raincoat of yours just doesn't do it for me."

The five-year-old beige belted raincoat was the only actual coat she owned, and was just going to have to do. It was cold outside tonight, the gusty winds making it feel even chillier, and any of her other jackets or sweaters wouldn't do a thing to keep her warm. Julia would have gladly loaned her a coat, but the five inch difference in their heights took that option off the table.

"It's fine," assured Tessa. "No one will even see me in the coat – I'll be checking it as soon as I walk into the hotel."

Julia shook her head. "If you'd given me even a week's notice, I could have had Aunt Maddy ship out something for you. Or I would have been happy to loan you the money."

"No. Thank you, but no. I've stretched my budget way too thin as it is buying the dress and shoes. But I just needed – you know – to -"

"To feel pretty," finished Julia. "I get it, honey. From what I can tell you hardly ever treat yourself to anything. You should make Ian give you a nice Christmas bonus. Or a raise."

Tessa was glad Julia had whisked an extra bit of blusher on her cheeks, because it masked the real flush that heated her skin. Just the mention of the handsome, enigmatic Brit was enough to set all her nerve endings on edge. Ever since the incident last month in the fitness room, she'd been even more aware of him than usual, forcing herself not to react whenever he walked by. Fortunately, he'd been traveling on business quite a bit these past few weeks and hadn't been around much.

She'd been shocked to discover that Jason Baldwin had been transferred out of the regional headquarters to manage the hotel down in Silicon Valley. And doubly shocked at the swiftness of Ian's promised actions, for Jason had been gone the very next day after the incident. Speculation as to why he'd been transferred had run rampant around the office for several days, but Tessa had kept her mouth tightly shut about the real reason. There was no way she would discuss that with anyone, even Julia. She had merely continued to echo what everyone else in the office surmised – that there must have been a complaint filed against Jason and that management had wisely decided to remove him.

"We should head downstairs. Our cab will be arriving within

the next five minutes," reminded Julia.

Tessa nodded, forcing thoughts of Ian Gregson from her mind. It was going to be hard enough seeing him at the party tonight with another woman, especially when she'd be there without an escort of her own. Julia had tentatively offered to set her up with a friend of Nathan's but Tessa had gently but adamantly refused.

"I appreciate the thought, but I'm just not ready to start dating yet," she'd admitted.

Julia had nodded. "I get it. When Nathan was still with his ex, I knew I should force myself to get out there and meet other guys, but I just didn't have the heart. Besides," she had added with a wink, "the few remaining single friends Nathan has are just about the biggest guy sluts I've ever met. And, my God, can those guys drink! You'd probably never speak to me again if I set you up with one of them."

The two women were sharing a cab downtown, dropping Tessa off first at the posh Gregson Hotel where the Christmas party was being held. Julia was continuing on a little further to meet Nathan and a group of his friends for dinner.

"It's his water polo teammates from college," she'd explained to Tessa. "They have this tradition of meeting over at Berkeley and playing in some sort of alumni game. Then they go get drunk at one of their old hangouts before hopping on public transit – thank God for that – and meeting their wives and girlfriends for dinner."

Tessa had frowned. "It doesn't bother you – him getting drunk, I mean?"

Julia had smiled impishly. "Nathan knows his limits, unlike some of his idiot friends. And when he gets a little tipsy he's really, really fun in bed."

The subject of alcohol and getting drunk had always been a touchy one for Tessa. Her own mother had overindulged in both booze and drugs at various times, though never to the point where it had become an addiction. Peter's mother, on the other hand, had been a raging alcoholic and, as a result, he'd sworn off liquor and refused to keep any in the apartment. Tessa hadn't minded, having been completely sympathetic to the hell Peter's life had been, and she seldom touched alcohol herself.

During the cab ride, Tessa gave Julia's hand an impulsive little squeeze. At her friend's inquiring gaze, Tessa told her, "Thank you. For all of this. Helping me get ready, encouraging me to go, sharing the cab."

"It's nothing," assured Julia. "I had fun getting you all girly. I hardly ever get to do stuff like that to my other friends. You've met Angela – the last thing on her mind these days is making herself look pretty. And my sister – let's just say it takes a lot of arm twisting to convince her to dress up. I don't really have any other close girlfriends – just the people I work with and now the wives and girlfriends of Nathan's buddies. And you, of course."

Tessa felt immensely pleased that Julia included her on the surprisingly short list of her friends. Julia was so beautiful, smart and accomplished that Tessa was more than a little in awe of her – and almost pathetically grateful for her friendship.

When the cab pulled up to the grand porte-cochere of the hotel, Tessa tried to hand Julia some cash for her share of the fare only to have it firmly refused.

"No. I told you this was my treat. God, when you mentioned you were going to take the bus or the metro here tonight I thought I'd faint." Julia shook her head. "And you'd better take a taxi home, too. Are you okay for that?"

Tessa understood that Julia was really asking if she had enough money, and nodded, trying to conceal her embarrassment. "Yes, thanks. Especially since you won't let me pay half of this fare."

Julia smirked. "I have a rich boss. Who also happens to be my rich boyfriend. I can afford a twenty dollar cab fare. Besides, it's something like the third – or is it the fourth – night of Hanukkah, so consider this a little gift."

Tessa laughed. "But neither of us is Jewish."

"Doesn't matter. Now, you go have yourself a fabulous time, all right? I wish I was going with you instead of to this overgrown frat boy party of Nathan's."

As Tessa walked inside the hotel, she wished Julia was accompanying her, too. She felt awkward and uneasy attending this fancy party alone, especially when all of her co-workers were bringing a date or their spouse. There would be very few people in attendance tonight who were here by themselves, and she fought off the feeling of being a pathetic wallflower.

'It's not like it's a high school dance, silly,' she chastised herself. 'Nobody's going to be gossiping about what a loser you are during first period English class on Monday.'

But as she checked her well-worn raincoat at the coat check just outside of the enormous ballroom, Tessa couldn't help feeling once again like the new girl in school – the outsider who had no friends, who was too shy to speak to anyone, who was always alone and lonely. Some things, she thought sadly, never seemed to change.

Fortunately, some of her unease began to fade as she spotted Kevin and Shelby nearby with their respective companions. Kevin was living with his current boyfriend – an older, wealthy attorney named Terence. It was very obvious from all of the disparaging, almost insulting comments that Kevin frequently made about his lover that he was merely using him for his money. But for tonight at least Kevin preened over the older man, touching his arm and laughing at whatever he said.

Shelby, who was wearing a skintight pink bandage dress that clashed oddly with her strawberry blonde hair, was already making the chirpy bird sound laugh when Tessa reached her side. Tessa had met Shelby's date – a slightly overweight, prematurely balding young man named Grant – when he'd taken Shelby out to lunch a couple of weeks ago. Tessa chose to ignore how Grant's close-set eyes lingered a little too long on her boobs.

"Sweetie pie, you look a-maz-ing!" exclaimed Kevin. "Wow! If there was any woman in the world who might have a shot at turning me straight, it would definitely be you!"

Tessa couldn't help laughing in delight at his praise, and let him envelop her in a hug, not even caring that his new cologne was even more pungent than his old one.

"Thanks," she answered demurely. "Um, a friend of mine helped me get ready."

She intentionally didn't mention Julia's name, fairly certain that no one at the office would mind her friendship with the interior designer, but thought it prudent not to advertise the news, either.

"Well, she did a fabulous job on you, sugar, just fabulous," gushed Kevin. "Now, aren't you glad we all talked you into coming tonight? Much better than sitting home all by your lonesome."

She had finally confessed to her co-workers that she and Peter had split. The news had sort of slipped out a few days before Thanksgiving, when she hadn't been able to stem the flow of tears that had started after Peter still hadn't responded to her email of five days earlier.

All five of her co-workers had been sympathetic, and even Gina and Alicia had seemed genuinely kind and concerned. When Kevin had learned that Tessa was going to be alone on Thanksgiving, he'd insisted she join him and Terence for dinner at their home. She had felt a little out of place among the two dozen or so people at their "little gathering", but it had definitely been preferable to spending the holiday by herself.

The group had next ganged up on her until she'd reluctantly agreed to attend the office Christmas party. And even though the round tables were really only set for ten, they were squeezing in an extra chair so that Tessa could sit with everyone else.

It had touched Tessa to have the support of her team, who had acted like real friends to her, helping to lift her spirits and give her encouragement. And, so far as she knew, they had kept the news of her impending divorce to themselves as she'd requested. At least, no one else in the office had said a word to her about it.

Within a few minutes. Marisol and her husband Raul, Gina and her boyfriend Alex, and Alicia and her date Ross had all arrived, the girls gushing over Tessa's dress and hair and makeup. Of course, Gina and Alicia were dressed to kill in obviously expensive designer gowns, their own hair and makeup flawless. Tessa tried not to worry about how cheap her own dress and shoes – the same ones Julia had assured her looked awesome – must appear next to not just Gina's and Alicia's but to every other woman's here tonight.

She accepted a flute of champagne from a passing waiter, but was careful to sip it very slowly. While Peter had never outright asked her not to drink, she had always tried to be supportive of him and had usually refrained. She'd never had more than a glass or two of wine at one time, and most definitely didn't want to experiment with more at the office Christmas party, where every member of the management team was in attendance.

She was aware of Ian's presence well before she actually saw him. He had that sort of magnetism, the kind that drew everyone's attention no matter who else might be in the room. Tessa merely had to glance in the same direction as everyone else around her to find him, and her heart did a rapid little flutter when she saw him for the first time this evening.

He'd been traveling these past two weeks to several of the hotels in Mexico and South America, and his ruggedly handsome features were deeply tanned. His hair had been cut very recently, and was as expertly styled as always. Ian wore a beautifully tailored black tuxedo, paired with a snowy white shirt and classic black bowtie. He was suave and sophisticated, classy elegance and overwhelming masculinity all rolled into one mouthwatering package.

To Tessa, he was far more attractive and compelling than any movie star. He could easily be some sort of diplomat or head of state, or even the prince of some small European nation.

She didn't realize how long she'd evidently been staring at him until Gina's voice murmured slyly in her ear. "His Hotness looks even hotter than usual tonight, don't you think?"

Tessa swiftly glanced away from her undeniably hot boss, but was afraid she'd already betrayed her attraction to him to the very perceptive Gina. Trying desperately to seem nonchalant, she gave a small shrug and smiled. "Most men always look extra special in a tuxedo."

Gina grinned. "You're right. Especially when it's a Brioni tux that probably set the boss man back eight or nine thousand."

Tessa gasped. "For one suit? And how do you always know this stuff – I mean, what designer and how much it costs?"

"Guess I'm a bit of a frustrated fashion designer," confessed Gina. "I really wanted to attend a fashion school, and get into either design or merchandising. But my parents were insistent I get a college degree and a quote unquote real job. So now I just settle for looking through as many fashion blogs and magazines as I can and keeping up to date on stuff. Just in case, you know."

Tessa shook her head. "I don't know the first thing about fashion, and can't tell one designer from the next."

"You don't really have to," admitted Gina almost wistfully. "You're lucky enough to be one of those very few people who looks good in anything, not to mention being gorgeous. I'm more than a little jealous of you, Tessa. Most of us have to work really hard to look good but not you."

Tessa was both startled and flattered by Gina's compliment and offered her a grateful smile. "That's nice of you to say, even if it really isn't true."

"Ah, but it is. You just don't see it. Oh, I see His Hotness has the banker lady with him tonight. Alicia and I were wondering who the lucky lady was going to be. I hope when I get to be forty I look as good as she does."

Tessa reluctantly followed Gina's gaze back towards Ian, who now stood with his hand resting lightly on the arm of a strikingly beautiful woman. The tall, gracefully slender beauty had raven hair cut into a sleek, perfect chin-length bob, her face expertly made up with dark eyes and carmine lips. She wore a stunning gown of deep burgundy, with long, fitted sleeves. It was gathered at the bodice and the long skirt was slit to just above her knee. Tessa just assumed the rubies and diamonds that sparkled at the woman's ears and throat were real.

"She's beautiful. They make a good pair, don't they?" asked Tessa in a small voice.

She wasn't sure why seeing Ian with a date was unsettling her. She would have just assumed he'd be here with someone tonight, just as he'd brought a date to the last two Christmas parties she'd attended. And if the gossip around the office was to be believed, Ian dated a lot of different women – all of them beautiful, sophisticated, and accomplished. And so very, very different from herself – a young, gauche and not very bright admin assistant who would likely never rise above her current situation.

Gina shrugged in response. "If you say so. She seems a little cold for him, actually. Her name is Rebecca Mellor, and she's the

President of Golden Gate Bank. I think she and His Hotness are just friends from what I've read."

Tessa didn't really want to think about the striking Rebecca's relationship with Ian. Instead, she gave Gina a teasing smile and asked, "Yes, but more importantly, who designed her gown?"

Gina laughed, then replied without hesitation. "Elie Saab. I saw that dress at Barneys last week. Do I have the gift or what?"

The cocktail hour passed by quickly, and Tessa was careful to make her one flute of champagne last. Meanwhile, Kevin and Alicia had both put away several drinks before dinner, and were well on their way to getting sloppy drunk. Gina seemed to be holding her liquor a lot better than her roommate, while Shelby and Marisol kept the drinking to a minimum.

From her peripheral vision, Tessa kept sneaking discreet little glances at Ian as he and Rebecca circulated the room. She knew from having helped compile the list of RSVPs that his parents were here this evening, over for a brief visit from England. It had been easy to pick the elder Gregsons out, for Ian greatly resembled his father. Edward was a bit shorter than his middle son, and his dark hair was liberally shot through with gray. Joanna Gregson was surprisingly petite, her delicate form beautifully gowned in glittering emerald green, her frosted blonde hair cut in short, feathery layers about her almost elfin face.

Ian's parents were every bit as regal and sophisticated as he was, and they would certainly expect him to eventually marry a woman with the same sort of elegance and class. Most definitely not a naïve, ordinary girl like Tessa, with her clearance rack shoes and rumpled raincoat and borrowed costume jewelry. It was a very good thing, she thought firmly, that she recognized her ever growing attraction to Ian as nothing more than a harmless fantasy.

But then she happened to glance his way only to find his own intense gaze upon her. Her heart slammed erratically against her rib cage as she stared back, mesmerized. Ian was unsmiling, his expression almost brooding, but his eyes remained locked with hers, silently refusing to let her look away. Tessa couldn't breathe, couldn't move, as she just stood there shell-shocked, too dazed to even begin to wonder what this all meant.

And then, the stare down that seemed to have lasted forever but had in actuality only been for long seconds, ended abruptly as the beautiful Rebecca touched Ian's arm and called his attention back to her.

Completely flustered, Tessa turned away and offered up a silent prayer of thanks that the call was being made to sit down for dinner. She was practically the first one to arrive at their table, and was relieved to realize her assigned place would not put her in any sort of direct view of Ian's table.

Even though Andrew was officially in charge of organizing tonight's party, he had delegated as much of the work as possible to the team. Gina and Alicia had jumped on the opportunity for they loved to handle all the social and travel related functions, as opposed to more mundane work such as word processing or filing. They had been working on invitations, seating charts, place cards and little else it seemed for the past few weeks, so Tessa had been afforded ample opportunity to take at glance at where everyone would be sitting.

It had been something of a nasty shock to learn that Jason Baldwin would be attending this evening. But Alicia had explained that quite a few of the hotel managers in California would be at the party, and since Jason actually lived in the city it was taken for granted that he would be at the party. Not to mention the fact that his wife was a member of the Gregson family.

Tessa had spied the Baldwins once or twice this evening, but fortunately Jason had kept his distance thus far. The very last thing she wanted tonight was any sort of confrontation, for he most certainly would not be happy with having been transferred, and most likely demoted as well.

Her good fortune, however, wasn't to last for long. After dinner and dessert, the dancing started. No expense had been spared for this lavish party – from the open bar to the expensive wines to the beautifully prepared sit-down dinner – and that included the excellent seven-piece live band. They played a wide variety of music, from big band and standards to current pop and rock songs.

Tessa loved to dance, often doing so around the apartment with the music blaring, and she missed having a partner of her own tonight. Kevin and Terence had each taken her for a spin on the dance floor, but mostly she had just remained sitting at the dinner table, wistfully watching all the other couples having fun. Alicia's date Ross – who'd kept glancing Tessa's way on numerous occasions this evening – had asked her to dance once, but Alicia had glared at her with such malice that Tessa had quickly mumbled some excuse and declined.

She was alone at the table – everyone else either on the dance floor or at the bar – when someone sat down next to her. Tessa glanced up in alarm into the smirking face of Jason Baldwin, and immediately tensed up.

He was also wearing a tuxedo, his dirty blond hair slicked back, and she supposed most women here tonight would find him extremely attractive. Tessa, however, couldn't shake off the revulsion she felt at his unwanted presence.

"Good evening, Tessa. You look smashing tonight, by the way." His voice was low and deliberately husky, and each word out of his mouth made her skin crawl.

When she refused to reply or even look at him, Jason persisted. "Where's your husband tonight? I can't imagine any man leaving someone as tempting as you are alone this way." He leaned closer to murmur in her ear, "After all, another man might not be able to resist the temptation and try to steal you for himself."

Tessa subtly moved her chair over a couple of inches, desperate to escape from him but not willing to make a scene in front of this large group of people. "My – husband is out of the country working," she stammered.

It wasn't precisely a lie. Peter was indeed working and currently in Egypt. And technically he was still her husband, at least for a short while longer until the divorce was final.

Jason trailed his fingers up her bare arm, and she quickly jerked it away. He made a low, snarling noise at this obvious display of her revulsion. "So, no one here to protect precious Tessa this evening then, hmm? Your husband has foolishly left a prize like you alone, while your avenging hero Ian is occupied with his current fuck buddy. He's smart, I'll give him credit for that, and with the patience of a fucking saint. But he doesn't fool me one bit. His shipping me off to that bloody hotel wasn't just a punishment for breaking his little rules – it's because he wants to fuck you himself."

"What?" Tessa's head jerked swiftly back in Jason's direction, not at all certain she'd heard him correctly or believed a word he said.

Jason chuckled. "Ah, got your interest now, do I? I suppose you're attracted to him, aren't you? Most women are with his sort of money and power. But you're way out of your league with him, little girl. A man like Ian would take what he wanted from you and then move on to the next woman without missing a beat. Trust me, you'd be much better off with me. I'd hang onto a prize like you for a long time."

Tessa's anger was slowly beginning to overtake her fear. "And what would your wife have to say about that?" she snapped.

He looked at her in amusement. "Ah, so the sweet little kitten does have claws after all. I'd love to make you purr, little kitten. But don't worry about my wife – she tends to turn a blind eye to my little – er, friendships."

Tessa shook her head in disgust. "That's horrible. And I'm not interested in being your friend. Or ever speaking to you again for that matter."

His good humor faded rapidly, his fingers clamping viciously around her upper arm. "Someone is getting very brave, isn't she? But your would-be knight in shining armor wouldn't dare sweep in to save you tonight – he won't show his hand in front of all these people and especially to his very charming companion. So I'd advise you to be a little nicer to me, kitten."

"Or what?" she challenged defiantly. "You wouldn't dare try anything in front of all these people, either – including your wife."

Jason's handsome face contorted into an ugly, snarling mask. "You little bitch. It's all your fault that I'm stuck down in fucking Scotts Valley. Do you know I have well over an hour's drive each way every day? You'll pay for that one of these days, Tessa, and pay dearly."

She jerked her arm away. "Go to hell. And leave me alone. I'm not interested in you, and you ought to be ashamed of yourself, being a married man."

"You're damned lucky there's so many people here tonight," hissed Jason. "Otherwise I'd be teaching you that lesson you need to learn so badly."

"It sounds like you're the one who hasn't learned his lesson, Jason. Perhaps Mr. Gregson ought to ship you to another continent next time."

Tessa whirled around at the sound of the familiar – and very, very welcome – voice of Andrew. He was standing behind her chair and glaring icily down at Jason.

Jason grimaced. "I was wondering when Tessa's guard dog would show up. Your boss send you over here to do his dirty work for him again?"

Andrew's mouth tightened grimly as he and Jason continued to glare at each other. "That's none of your business, Jason. And neither is Tessa. In fact, she's promised me a dance that I've come to collect on. Oh, and I believe Mrs. Baldwin is looking for you so you'd best run along back to your own table. Tessa – if I may?"

Tessa surged to her feet and gratefully placed her hand on Andrew's proffered arm. Without a backwards glance, she allowed him to guide her onto the dance floor. A slow song was playing as Andrew held her lightly at a casual distance from him.

"Thank you," she told him in a meek voice. "I – he was saying –."

"I can imagine what he was saying, Tessa," stated Andrew rather matter-of-factly. "You're not the first female employee he's harassed, after all. Jason Baldwin is a menace and no one was happier than I was when Mr. Gregson kicked him out of headquarters."

Tessa attempted to lighten the mood by joking, "Maybe we should have had a farewell party for him – without his being in attendance, of course."

Andrew never laughed, and really didn't smile, either, but she was certain she saw the corner of his mouth tilt up slightly. "That's the general idea, yes. Your husband wasn't able to attend this evening?"

Tessa was a bit taken aback by this abrupt change of topic, and hesitated before replying. She figured that since she had told her co-workers the truth about her marriage that she owed Andrew the same consideration. "Peter and I – aren't together any longer, Andrew. Our divorce will be final in a few weeks."

She didn't think she'd ever seen Andrew shocked – or speechless – but apparently her news had had that precise effect. It took him a little while before he told her in an oddly gentle voice. "I'm so sorry, Tessa. When did this happen?"

"September. I – I haven't said anything until very recently. The only ones in the office who know are the rest of the team. I just – couldn't' -" her voice lapsed off weakly.

"You just don't believe in broadcasting all the details of your personal life around the office," finished Andrew in his usual brisk manner. "And I've always appreciated that, Tessa. But you should have told us sooner. I'm sure you could have used the moral support."

She gave him a small smile. "I suppose I've just grown used to depending on myself. Well, and Peter, of course, but now it's just me."

Andrew frowned. "We've never really discussed this sort of thing, but where's your family? Aren't they around to help you through this?"

Tessa shook her head. "There's no one. My mother died when I was still a teenager. Peter was all I had and now he's left, too."

Andrew looked dumbfounded and stumbled a bit, stepping on her toe. "Sorry," he murmured as she uttered a low yelp of pain. "I'm not a very good dancer, I'm afraid. Thank God this is a slow number."

"It's okay," she assured him. "You can step on my toes for the rest of the evening if it means I don't have to see Jason again."

"Yes, well, not to worry. I think he's got the message loud and clear. Mr. Gregson was adamant that I get you away from him, and assured me he'd make certain Jason stays away after that."

Now it was Tessa's turn to be startled. "Mr. Gregson sent you after me? Has – is that why you've always seemed to be nearby whenever Jason was bothering me?"

Andrew shrugged. "Mr. Gregson didn't want a repeat of what happened with Sarah to occur with any more employees. So, yes, I was asked to keep a discreet eye on him. As for this evening – well, Mrs. Baldwin is in attendance as are Mr. Gregson's parents. He wanted to make sure there wasn't any sort of potentially ugly scene."

"Oh. Of course."

Tessa tried to mask the disappointment she felt at this revelation. Somehow, she'd assumed that Ian had sent Andrew to rescue her because he was worried about her personally. But of course it made all the sense in the world that his real concern was for his family, and to make sure they weren't embarrassed or upset with Jason's very blatant flirting.

The song ended at that moment and Tessa took a step backwards as Andrew released her. "Thank you for the dance, Andrew. I hope your girlfriend doesn't mind."

He made a dismissive motion with his hand as he escorted her back to the table. "Not to worry. Even if Isobel was here tonight, she wouldn't care. But she despises these sort of events so I'm usually here alone."

"She's an artist, isn't she?" Tessa had only met Andrew's long-time girlfriend once, when she'd run into the couple at a coffee shop near the office. She had been startled to meet the pierced and tattooed Isobel with her purple-streaked hair and funky clothes, never in her wildest imagination having pictured the straight-laced Andrew with someone like her.

"Yes, she's a sculptor. And when the inspiration hits, she can work for hours and hours at a time. When I left tonight she'd been at it since noon, and will probably keep on working until three or four in the morning." He shook his head in mild disgust.

"My mother was like that, except she could literally go for two or three days at a time without any sleep."

Tessa wasn't sure who was more shocked at the words that had just slipped so unthinkingly out of her mouth – herself or Andrew. She *never* talked about her mother, except perhaps to

Peter and then only sparingly. It had just seemed like the most natural thing in the world, sharing confidences with Andrew, and she had zero idea why.

Andrew stood by her chair as they reached the table and regarded her curiously. "Your mother was an artist?"

"No." She shook her head. "A writer. At times a brilliant one but in later years she mostly wrote a bunch of gibberish."

When she didn't offer up any additional information, Andrew tactfully changed the subject. "Well, thank you for the dance, Tessa. I see some of your tablemates starting to return, so I doubt Jason will bother you again tonight."

She smiled at him gratefully. "I'll probably be leaving soon, anyway, it's getting a little late. Thank you, Andrew. I'll, um, see you on Monday."

He gave her a little nod. "Bright and early as usual. Good night, Tessa."

Kevin and Terence arrived back at the table mere seconds after Andrew left, with Kevin gaping in astonishment.

"Were you really dancing with the Ice Man?" he asked in disbelief. "My God, I think I might have just witnessed one of the seven signs of the apocalypse."

Tessa smiled indulgently at his usual high drama. "He was just being nice. Though he could admittedly use a few dance lessons."

Kevin gave an eye roll. "And a personality transplant. Maybe surgery to remove that stick wedged up his ass, too. At least he looks halfway decent in that tux and he actually bothered to style his hair tonight."

"So what you're saying is that there's hope for him?" teased Tessa.

"I wouldn't go that far," sniffed Kevin. "Ooh, here's the girls. I'm dying to hear what they've got planned for the rest of the evening. You *have* to go with us, Tessa."

"Go where?" she asked in confusion.

As Gina, Alicia and Shelby returned to the table with their dates, they were chattering excitedly about the round of clubs they wanted to make after leaving the party. Marisol and her husband had left after dessert since their younger child was ill with a cold, and they felt obliged to get home and tend to her. Terence did not appear terribly thrilled at the idea of going clubbing with a group who were all a dozen or more years his junior but Kevin was doing his best to sweet talk him into it.

Tessa, meanwhile, was trying desperately to think up a valid excuse for not joining them. Not only did the thought of drinking heavily and dancing with a bunch of groping strangers repel her, but she simply didn't have the money to pay for cover charges and drinks. The cash tucked away in her clutch would barely cover her cab fare home, but she was too proud to admit this to her co-workers. Instead, she decided to play the sympathy card.

"I'm sorry, it sounds like a lot of fun, but – well, I'm just not ready for all that," she confessed almost tearfully. "It's still too soon after my breakup with Peter, you know? You guys understand, right?"

Kevin put his arm around her shoulders. "Oh, honey, of course we do. God, we don't mean to be insensitive."

"You're sure, Tessa?" asked Gina. "Maybe it might get your mind off things if you joined us."

"You can ride with Alicia and me," offered Ross. "We'll even drop you off at your place afterwards."

Alicia gave him a not so subtle look of displeasure before smiling at Tessa with an almost sickly sweet expression. "Sure, we could do that. It'll be fun, Tessa."

Tessa shook her head, standing as she picked up her clutch. "Thank you all for thinking of me, but I'm afraid I wouldn't be much fun. You guys go have a great time and I'll see you all on Monday. Don't get *too* crazy, okay?"

Kevin gave her a hug goodbye, and this time she did have to turn her head away, for his potent cologne was now mingled with the strong scent of vodka. "You want one of us to walk you out?"

"No, thanks. I'll be fine. I'm sure there are plenty of cabs right outside the front entry." She smiled and waved good night to everyone at the table before exiting the ballroom.

Tessa was waiting for the attendee to retrieve her coat when she heard an achingly familiar voice from just behind her.

"You're leaving already, Tessa?" asked Ian Gregson in his deep, crisp British accent.

She whirled to face him, her heart thudding rapidly when she realized he was standing mere inches from her. "Yes, sir. I, um, the others are going to head out to some clubs and I wasn't really in the mood to join them, so I figured I would just go home."

Ian frowned. "A wise move. Some of your co-workers have been drinking a bit too much this evening so I'm relieved to see that you're being sensible at least."

"Here's your coat, miss."

Tessa turned but before she could take the coat Ian had already done so and was holding it open for her.

"Allow me."

She was torn between being embarrassed at how old and worn her coat was, and enjoying the little thrill that traveled up her spine at his gallantry. She closed her eyes briefly at the feel of his big, powerful hands glancing over her arms and shoulders as he helped her into the coat.

"Thank you, Mr. Gregson," she murmured, turning to face him once again but keeping her gaze downcast this time.

"Your husband wasn't able to attend this evening?" he inquired politely.

Tessa paused yet again this evening at the mention of Peter. But, after finally telling her co-workers and supervisor the truth, she couldn't in all good conscience not be honest with her boss at this moment.

"Um, no. That is – my husband and I – we aren't together, sir. We're in the process of getting a divorce."

She didn't know who was more shocked – Ian at her announcement or herself at his reaction to the news. He was staring at her in obvious disbelief, and Tessa could swear his tanned skin had paled a shade or two.

"Divorce." His voice was barely above a whisper. "You're – you're getting a divorce."

Tessa frowned, completely perplexed by his odd behavior. "Yes, sir. We, um, separated in September but the divorce will be final next month."

"Christ." He ran a hand over his face, giving his head a shake as if to clear his thoughts. "I'm so sorry, Tessa. I had no idea or I certainly wouldn't have been so rude as to ask about your husband."

"No, it's fine," she assured him. "I didn't tell anyone at the office until very recently. Andrew just found out tonight himself."

"Ah, well that would explain things." He gave her an assessing look. "Are you all right, Tessa? Especially considering the unexpected encounter with Jason this evening. I'm very sorry you had to be subjected to his appalling behavior yet again."

"I'm okay, thank you. Andrew came to the rescue again. It seems that one or the other of you is always there to make sure Jason doesn't bother me."

Ian smiled. "Yes, well, that's the plan after all."

Tessa felt her knees grow weak at the force of his dazzling smile. She couldn't ever remember him smiling at her in quite *this* way before. She could feel the awareness that flared up between them like an electrical surge, and very nearly had to put her hand against the wall to support her suddenly wobbly legs.

"Well, thank you, sir. For watching out for me and all, that is. I'd better be on my way now. Good night."

His hand grasped her arm firmly. "Let me see you out."

She let him guide her down the wide, sweeping staircase that led from the mezzanine level where the ballroom was located down to the lobby. "I don't want to keep you from your guests, sir. I'll be fine," she assured him, while still being thrilled at his concerned attention. Even through the fabric of her coat she could feel the warmth of his hand around her upper arm, and she longed to lean into his big, hard body, to rest her head on his broad shoulder and feel his arm slide around her waist and hug her close.

"I'm not worried about my guests. They can look out for themselves for a few minutes while I see you safely on your way. Do you have your valet ticket?" he asked.

Tessa shook her head. "No, I don't own a car, sir. I took a cab here."

"Then we'll get you a cab."

They had reached the front doors of the hotel, which Ian held open for her as she stepped outside. The night air was biting cold and she shivered as she belted her raincoat about her.

Ian gave her a brief, assessing glance. "It's freezing out tonight with these winds, Tessa. You should have worn a warmer coat."

"I don't have – I mean, you're right," she stammered, refusing to admit this was the only coat she owned but she feared he had already suspected that.

His mouth tightened with displeasure. "Let's get you that cab so you can get inside and keep warm."

He motioned over a valet who was extremely eager to provide assistance to the regional director. An idling taxi pulled up directly in front of Tessa mere seconds later.

Ian opened the back door and handed her inside. "Hold on just a moment, Tessa. I need to speak to the driver."

She watched curiously as he walked over to the driver's window and spoke to him in a low voice. Tessa's eyes widened in surprise as Ian reached into the pocket of his tuxedo trousers and drew out a money clip. He peeled several bills off and handed them to the driver before walking back around to Tessa's side of the car.

"The driver has instructions to walk you to your door and make sure you get in safely. And the fare has been taken care of, you're not to worry about it," he told her firmly.

"Mr. Gregson –" she started to protest, until she saw the steely look in his eyes. "You don't – thank you, sir. That's very kind of you."

"It's my pleasure, Tessa, the least I can do. Now, you get home safely and I'll see you in the office on Monday." He hesitated, still holding her door open, and then added, "I'm sorry again to hear about your divorce. I hope you'll let me know if there's anything I can do to help you through this difficult time."

Tessa gulped and stared up at him, touched by his kindness and generosity. "I appreciate the offer, sir. Good night."

Ian closed the door to the cab and stood watching as it pulled away. Tessa felt a warm glow spread through her whole body, and couldn't help the smile that teased at the corners of mouth. It was almost a certainty that he had only been acting out of concern for one of his employees, but for tonight at least she could pretend it was because he was as attracted to her as she was to him.

***

Ian remained rooted in place for long seconds after Tessa's cab had disappeared from sight. He stood there so long, in fact, that the same valet who'd hailed the cab asked if he needed anything else. Pulling himself out of his daze, Ian almost brusquely shook his head before striding back inside the hotel.

Tessa was getting a divorce. After all this time, she was going to be a free woman. Free to date other men, to be pursued by other men, and – most importantly – free for *this* man to finally claim her for himself.

He paused at the foot of the staircase that would take him back up to the ballroom, where the party was still in full swing, reluctant to be around so many people right now. He badly needed a few minutes alone to ponder the startling news he'd just received, so he made his way to the small, intimate bar tucked in a back corner of the hotel. The bar was rarely ever crowded, and most patrons didn't even know it existed, but it definitely suited his needs at this particular moment.

Ian ordered a snifter of brandy from the very attentive bartender, who apparently recognized him, his greeting a respectful "Good evening, sir." He was grateful to see that the bar was nearly empty, and settled himself into a small, darkened corner of the room where he could be alone with his chaotic thoughts for a bit.

God, he had feared for so long that this day, this opportunity, would never come along. He wasn't enough of a bastard to have actively wished that Tessa's marriage would one day be in trouble, or that she and her husband would decide to part ways. And there was no way – no *possible* way – that he would have ever tried to seduce her away from her husband. But now he couldn't deny his joy at knowing she was unattached, and finally within his grasp. However, the tricky part was just beginning – figuring out how to pursue her without scaring her off or coming on too strong.

Ian sipped the fine brandy slowly, savoring the taste on his tongue and the way the expensive liquor warmed his throat. As he did so, he considered all of the obstacles still in his way at this point and how to navigate around them. He was fairly certain that Tessa hadn't already begun seeing other men, based on the facts that she had attended tonight's party alone, and then wisely declined to accompany her inebriated co-workers to some club. Tessa was also too fine, too loyal, to enter into another relationship so soon after her marriage ended. She had seemed sad tonight, especially when she'd quietly admitted that she and her husband had split, and Ian guessed she was having a difficult time in getting over the breakup.

She was still far too young for him, of course, the age difference between them a good fifteen years. But Tessa was very mature and composed for her age, not seeming in the least bit frivolous or silly like the other girls on the team. As for himself, he was just a few months from his fortieth birthday but thought he didn't look half bad for his age. He worked out frequently and with even more intensity that he had a decade ago; ate a healthy diet and didn't overindulge in alcohol; and generally took excellent care of himself. He had never been vain or egotistical – not like that horny bastard Jason – but at the same time he didn't miss the interested, assessing looks he received from women wherever he went.

And perhaps it was wishful thinking on his part, but he didn't believe Tessa was completely immune to him as a man. She was so sweetly, adorably shy that he couldn't picture her ever trying to flirt with him or attract his attention – not like that very obvious and annoying pair Gina and Alicia. But there had definitely been times when he'd caught Tessa's very blue, wide-eyed gaze upon him and he could swear there had been something there – awareness, attraction, adoration. It had given him hope that one day those discreet little glances might deepen into something far more serious.

His cock hardened immediately as he recalled how beautiful and utterly tempting she'd looked this evening. Her dress and shoes were obviously inexpensive, especially when compared to so many of the other women at the party who'd been garbed in designer clothing. But Tessa had still managed to outshine every other female present tonight. The sapphire blue color of her dress had been perfect for her gleaming ivory skin and thick golden hair, a fact that he stored away for future reference. The strapless bodice of the dress had bared a delectable amount of cleavage, just enough to let his rather filthy imagination run rampant. His hands had itched to plunge inside the neckline of her dress and cup her full, lush breasts, to see for himself if they were as firm and round as they looked.

Ian had felt badly for her when he'd noticed she was at the party alone, never having imagined at the time that she and her husband were divorcing. He had wanted nothing more than to approach her on multiple occasions this evening and ask her to dance, to luxuriate in the rare opportunity to hold her closely against his body and be able to touch her. But he'd had to restrain himself, knowing full well how it would look for him to single out one of his employees. The only women he'd dared to dance with this evening had been Rebecca, his mother, and his cousin Charlotte.

Thank God Rebecca wouldn't be a problem when he began his pursuit of Tessa in earnest. The lovely brunette banker was an old friend and business associate, and any romantic involvement between them existed only in the gossip columns. Ian was one of the very, very few people who knew that Rebecca had been carrying on a secret affair for almost a dozen years with a very prominent – and very married – member of the U.S. Congress. Ian had never judged her, or attempted to offer his advice, but had always thought it foolish and naïve for a woman as beautiful, intelligent and accomplished as Rebecca to waste her best years on a man she could never be seen with in public. They rarely discussed her affair with the man, but Ian knew she was hopelessly in love, and hadn't given up hope that the politician would eventually divorce his wife upon retiring from public office one day. Personally, Ian found Rebecca's choice to not only be morally wrong but also tragically sad.

Still, her clandestine love affair had made her available to act as his escort – and vice versa - on numerous occasions, with the clear understanding that they were only friends. It had been convenient for him, especially when his obsession with Tessa had begun to grow to such an extent that it had been impossible for him to even consider having a romantic or sexual relationship with anyone else.

No, Rebecca would be genuinely happy that he had found someone and would support him all the way. Ian wondered a bit grimly if he could expect a similar type of understanding and acceptance from other friends and his family. His parents, for one, would be sure to think Tessa too young and too gauche, but he had rarely allowed their opinions to influence his important life choices, and he certainly wasn't going to let that change now. Not when he was this close to finally snaring the girl of his dreams.

He would have to move slowly, he thought, to gradually let her know of his interest. He would also have to deal very soon with the added complication of her being his employee, especially given his very strict rules on that same subject. And particularly since he had just made a very emphatic point to Jason that he wouldn't tolerate any form of sexual harassment in his office. The last thing Ian was prepared to do was give Jason even the tiniest bit of ammunition to protest his unwanted transfer out of regional headquarters. The bastard wouldn't hesitate for a moment to call Ian the worst sort of hypocrite and demand that he, too, be disciplined for breaking the rules.

Ian almost snarled when he recalled the sight of Jason once again daring to put his filthy hands on Tessa this evening. He'd been keeping a close eye on his cousin's husband all evening, not trusting the little shit to behave himself. And when he'd seen Jason sit down next to Tessa and start whispering in her ear, he'd had to exercise incredible self-control to stop from marching over there and breaking the scum's jaw just as he'd promised he would. And because he simply couldn't afford to make a scene in front of all these people– one that would have greatly upset his family and, more importantly, betrayed his attraction to Tessa – he'd been forced to send Andrew to handle the problem.

But he hadn't been able to resist the opportunity to finally be alone with Tessa, even for a few minutes, when he'd spotted her leaving the party a short time ago. He'd followed her discreetly from the ballroom, intending only to wish her a good night, but then she'd walloped him with the shocking news of her divorce. God, if he hadn't been obliged to see Rebecca home – and if his parents weren't staying at his house for the duration of their visit – Ian was not at all sure he could have stopped himself from taking Tessa home himself. Or, if she had been agreeable, taking her to his house and persuading her to spend the night. Fortunately, he'd remembered his obligations in time, not to mention the continued need for discretion among his employees.

No, he and Tessa were going to have to be very, very discreet, at least until he could persuade her to quit her job. Ian was fully prepared – and very much looking forward – to supporting Tessa and taking exquisite care of her.

He would start, he thought rather dourly, by getting rid of that appalling coat she'd been wearing this evening. He would gladly buy her a dozen others, ones that were far more worthy of her stunning beauty. And that was just for starters.

As he finished his brandy, Ian made a mental note of all the ways he planned to spoil and indulge Tessa once she was truly his. The first step, though, was going to be the slow seduction of his golden girl, treating her like a princess the whole while, and making her feel protected and cherished at every turn. With that in mind, he took his phone out and pressed the most frequently used number on the speed dial.

"It's me," he said when the call was answered after just one ring. "Yes, I'm on my way back up now, a small matter I had to attend to. Now, remind me please what dates in January you'll be on vacation. All right, that's what I thought. Make a note for Monday for us to discuss who'll be filling in this time while you're away. I have an idea and I don't intend to be talked out of it."

Ian ended the call, pocketed the phone, and strode confidently out of the bar. The very first step in what would be his extremely pleasurable wooing of Tessa had just been taken.

Chapter Seven

January

"Mr. Gregson's office. How may I assist you?"

As Tessa attended to the caller on the other end, she still couldn't quite believe that she was actually filling in as Ian's PA this week, even though this was already nearing the end of the fourth day. She'd been astonished when Andrew had first approached her with the news a few weeks ago.

Tessa had blinked at him in disbelief. "Excuse me. You want me to do what?"

Andrew had sighed with barely contained impatience. "You heard me. I'll be out of the office the second week in January, and it's been decided that you'll be filling in for me during that time."

She had still not quite believed what she was hearing. "But – you've never had me fill in for you before. It's always been Marisol or Gina or sometimes Alicia. Even Kevin once or twice."

Andrew hadn't been in an especially good mood that day, and had dismissed her concerns brusquely. "Well, consider this your turn. I assume you have no objections to the assignment?"

"Oh, no. Of course not. I'd be honored to fill in for you, help out while you're away. I just hope I don't screw something up," she'd confessed nervously.

Andrew had given a roll of his eyes, which usually meant his patience was wearing extremely thin. "You'll be fine. It's not brain surgery, after all. And of course you'll need to spend several days learning my routine and what will be expected of you."

That had been the understatement of the year. Tessa had been wide-eyed and slack-jawed – not to mention exhausted and emotionally drained – at the end of her week long training session with Andrew. But at least spending so much time with him had greatly allayed her fears about working for Mr. Gregson, for she had realized that nothing about Andrew's job was really all that difficult or complicated. And of course she'd took copious notes on top of the multi-paged and extremely detailed list of information Andrew had left for her.

Mr. Gregson had still been away for the holidays - visiting his family in England - during her training period. In a way, that had been a relief for she'd been able to learn the ropes without the added pressure of his presence. But then, when he'd arrived back in the office on Monday morning – her first day of filling in for Andrew – her nerves had almost consumed her with the fear that she would fail miserably, or anger him in some way. So far, she was rather astonished to realize that nothing could be farther from the truth.

Ian had been graciousness personified these past four days, and so easy to work with that she'd found herself breathing a huge sigh of relief. He was patient and kind, and always exceedingly grateful for her assistance. Tessa had been thrilled at his appreciation and acknowledgment of her hard work, and she made sure that everything she did for him was completed to perfection.

And of course it had been the sweetest sort of torture to work in such close proximity to him. Several times she'd found her hands trembling in reaction simply from standing across his desk as he signed a report she'd prepared. She had watched him discreetly from beneath her lashes, taking in every strong, masculine feature of his face, noting how his finely tailored dress shirts stretched across the breadth of his shoulders and emphasized his toned, muscular torso. Once she'd almost swooned at his arousing scent – a perfect combination of his light cologne, soap and pure maleness. And on more than one occasion she'd had to resist the urge to sway against him, or run her hands through his hair or over the firmness of his jaw.

Each night this week when she'd arrived home, she had been alarmed to realize how aroused she was – her breasts full and heavy, her nipples peaked, her sex wet and swollen and oh, so needy. She'd had increasingly explicit dreams about Ian, not able to recall too many specific details, but it had only taken the lightest stimulation of her nipples and clitoris upon waking to come long and hard. Her young, healthy body was almost starved by now for affection, and she craved physical contact almost more than she did food and sleep.

But of course she didn't dare to so much as touch Mr. Gregson, or betray her ever growing physical attraction to him in any way. She was the epitome of professional decorum, always careful to keep her conversations with him brief and businesslike, and never discuss anything personal with him. Andrew had, after all, put the fear of God in her about even considering such a thing.

"Do *not*," he'd warned her ominously, "ask him how his evening was, or what he had for lunch, or anything at all that doesn't have to do with work. He's not one for idle chatter, and sticks to his schedule religiously."

But Tessa hadn't been able to keep her pulse rate from accelerating any time she was near Ian, or all the other ways her body reacted to him involuntarily. Earlier today she'd cursed beneath her breath to realize her nipples were hard and poking very noticeably against the thin fabric of her blouse. And, unfortunately, she was pretty sure he had noticed, too, since she'd been placing a steaming mug of tea on his desk at the time. She had made a hasty exit, and had struggled to control the reaction of her treacherous body for the rest of the day.

She couldn't believe how quickly the past four days had flown by, and she wished that Andrew was taking two weeks off instead of just the one. Of course, he'd sent her several emails, both to check in and also to remind her of the various tasks she needed to do. Tessa realized that even when Andrew was on vacation he was really still at work.

The reactions of her co-workers had been mixed when they'd learned she would be the one to fill in for Andrew this time. Marisol, who most often subbed for him, was actually relieved because she'd been battling a nasty case of bronchitis for over two weeks and was worn out. Gina had seemed a little miffed at the news but not overly concerned. Kevin had teased her about moving up to the big time, while Shelby had shuddered at the very thought of having to train so closely with Andrew for a whole week. And Alicia had been downright catty about it, wondering how Tessa was going to cope with such a high profile assignment given her lack of experience and education.

It was nice to be away from the rest of the team this week, to have all this space and privacy, and to finally know what it felt like to work at the top level of this company. She would miss it a lot when she had to return to her small cubicle on Monday.

And she loved being able to take care of Mr. Gregson in subtle little ways – hanging up his suit jacket; preparing his tea the way he preferred – Darjeeling blend with one lump of sugar, which, very coincidentally, was exactly the same way she took hers; answering his phone and managing his appointments. And he always smiled his thanks whenever she did something, making her feel like a million dollars.

She'd spent the better part of this afternoon preparing a complex spreadsheet that Mr. Gregson needed for a late afternoon meeting. She'd finished printing it out mere minutes before he had to leave, noticing with a grimace that the printer was now flashing a low ink warning. Since she had a slew of reports to print out first thing in the morning, it seemed that she would need to change the printer cartridge before leaving for the day.

Tessa had just finished collating and stapling a dozen copies of the spreadsheet when Ian emerged from his office, shrugging into his suit jacket.

"The copies are all ready, Mr. Gregson. Just let me put them in a folder for you."

She reached into a file drawer and extracted an empty folder, then neatly slipped the papers inside.

Ian took the folder and slid it into his leather briefcase. "Thank you, Tessa. An excellent job as always," he told her with a warm smile.

She smiled back, the pleasure of his compliment making her feel like the most special girl in the world. "I hope the meeting goes well, sir. And the dinner reservations are all set. I just called the restaurant a few minutes ago to confirm everything again."

He reached across the desk and gave her a light squeeze on the shoulder. "You've been doing a marvelous job filling in for Andrew. I've barely noticed he's gone. Except," he added with a wink, "you look far better sitting behind that desk than he does."

Tessa stared up at him, too flustered by his teasing to think of an intelligent reply. "Um, thanks" was all she could think of to mumble.

Ian chuckled. "I didn't mean to make you uncomfortable. Or blush. But it seems I've managed to do both so I'd best head out before I say anything else. Have a pleasant evening, Tessa, and I'll see you tomorrow."

"Good night, sir."

She groaned softly after he left, burying her face in her hands in mortification. God, could she be any more of an idiot when he was around? It was obvious that her shyness and tendency to blush at the drop of a hat amused him, and she guessed her very perceptive boss was aware of her silly crush on him. She was going to have to do a much better job of managing her reactions to him.

But that was proving to be extremely difficult, given the close proximity they'd been working in this week. Tessa had seen facets of both his work and private persona that she had never before been given the opportunity to observe. She'd already known that he was a man who was always in complete control, who commanded and received respect from everyone around him, but who also treated each person fairly and with the same amount of respect they gave him. But she had never seen him like this – like a king managing his vast empire, dealing smoothly and efficiently with telephone calls, meetings and correspondence without missing a beat. He was precise, organized, and highly efficient, the sheer amount of work he managed to get through each day staggering. Ian was not a man content to rest on his laurels, or rely solely on others to take care of things for him. He worked harder than anyone else in this office, even though he could have easily delegated a great deal of his responsibilities to his very qualified management team. Tessa was in awe of his strict work ethic, and how he refused to take advantage of his family's name and prestige by shirking his duties. He was extremely intelligent, with most of the conversations she'd heard him engage in way over her head, and about subjects she had very little knowledge of, mostly involving finance and marketing. She had also heard him speaking in at least three different foreign languages – Spanish, French, and Italian – and wondered with some astonishment if he knew any others.

And she had also seen a much lighter-hearted side of him this week, too. He'd been in an excellent mood all week, looking relaxed and well rested, and had smiled and laughed more in the past few days than she could ever remember him doing before. Of course, up until this week she'd had little to do with him day to day, mostly just seeing him walk past her desk or observing him conducting meetings when it had been her turn to set up the conference room.

Ian's manner towards her had been mildly teasing, almost – well, flirtatious at times, though Tessa figured that had to be her overactive imagination playing tricks on her. Ian Gregson did not flirt – he was far too dignified and regal for that sort of behavior, and he most certainly didn't flirt with silly little admin assistants like herself. She told herself that he was simply being kind, and probably felt sorry for her after learning about the divorce.

The divorce that was going to be final very soon now. Tessa had tried very hard not to dwell on that fact, or that she hadn't corresponded with Peter since Christmas. She knew this was his way of cutting her loose for good, for giving her that much needed push to stand on her own and not depend on anyone else to take care of her.

She'd spent Christmas alone, for Kevin had gone out of town to visit his family and she really didn't have any other friends who might have invited her. Julia had tentatively suggested spending the holidays with her family down in Carmel, but Tessa had refused, especially since she'd had to work the day before and after the holiday.

Being alone hadn't been so bad, anyway. She'd spent the day watching movies, reading a book, and making herself comfort food. But she'd missed Peter terribly, and hadn't been able to completely hold back the tears at the end of the day.

She had spent New Year's Eve alone, too, even though Kevin had returned by then and urged her to attend a party he and Terence were hosting. She hadn't felt in the least like celebrating anything, and instead had taken the time to write down any number of New Year's resolutions – the top one simply reading *Be Happy.*

Tessa frowned as she recalled another resolution a little further down the list – this one involving finding a cheaper place to live before the lease expired in April. She'd already started to do some research and had been appalled at the skyrocketing cost of rents in San Francisco. Unless she lucked out and found some fabulous deal, she was most likely going to have to settle for a shared rental with two or more roommates, or consider moving out of San Francisco and having to commute. But she still had a little time before having to get serious about moving, so she pushed that troubling thought out of her head and returned her focus to work.

It was drawing close to five-thirty before she finished and began shutting down the computer and tidying up. And then she remembered about needing to change the ink cartridge for the printer and groaned. The printer that Andrew and Mr. Gregson used was a much more expensive, high-tech one than she was used to, and she'd kept her fingers crossed all week that nothing would go amiss with it.

Fortunately the directions on the package for the replacement cartridge were fairly straightforward, and she was able to install it without much trouble. But then, as she went to dispose of the old cartridge, she realized it had leaked and that she now had black printer ink smudged all over her hands and on her blouse as well.

"Crap!" she muttered loudly, grateful that no one else was around to hear her outburst. Not only had everyone else left by now, but these offices were set far apart from all the others down their own private hallway.

Almost without thinking, Tessa dashed into the private washroom in Mr. Gregson's office. She doubted he would mind, especially since she didn't want to risk getting ink on any other surfaces in the office. She scrubbed her hands thoroughly, relieved to see the ink had all washed off. Then she turned her attention to her badly stained blouse.

'Oh, no!' she thought in dismay as she saw the black blotch that covered far more of the fabric than she'd initially noticed. Not only was this silvery gray blouse one of her favorites, but she'd just recently had to discard two other items from her already limited wardrobe – a sweater that she'd snagged on something and torn an irreparable hole in, and a blouse that had simply become worn and frayed from so many washings. She'd stretched her budget far too thin after buying the dress and shoes for last month's Christmas party, and certainly couldn't afford to buy anything new for some time to come.

Tessa bit her lip uncertainly, for the stain would be almost impossible to get out, especially given its location along the side of her torso. How the ink had landed in that particular spot was a puzzle but if she had any chance at all to salvage the blouse she was going to have to do some serious – and swift – scrubbing.

Quickly, she unbuttoned the blouse and stripped it off, shivering a little as she stood there in a pale gray lace bra and her navy skirt. She pumped some liquid hand soap directly onto the offending stain and dampened it before scrubbing the fabric almost desperately.

"Darn it!" she cursed, as the ink stain seemed to be spreading rather than disappearing. Not willing to give up hope just yet, she applied more soap and continued trying to wash the stubborn blotch away. But after a third application of soap, Tessa had to regretfully admit defeat. The stupid ink stain wasn't budging and she was going to have to throw out the blouse. She could try to have it dry cleaned, of course, but that would likely cost almost as much as the bargain rack blouse was worth.

She was wringing the water out of the garment since she still had to wear it home, stained or not, when she froze in horror at the sound of Ian's deep voice as he walked inside his office.

"Are you still here, Tessa? It's well past time for you to have called it a day. What – "

His voice trailed off abruptly as he caught sight of her framed in the doorway of his washroom. Tessa felt like a deer trapped in a hunter's scope, knowing she ought to move or look away but too shocked to do so. He stared at her in stunned disbelief, his gaze raking over her nearly nude torso, her full breasts almost spilling out of the fragile lace bra.

Horrified, she clutched the damp blouse to her chest, her cheeks on fire as she glanced away and began to babble almost incoherently. "I'm – I'm so sorry, Mr. Gregson. I – ah, got printer ink on my blouse and I was just trying to rinse it out. I didn't know you'd be returning and, oh, God, just let me put – "

"Look at me."

Startled, she responded immediately to the commanding tone of his voice, one that didn't allow for disobedience. She raised her gaze to his and gasped when she saw the barely controlled lust on his handsome face – eyes blazing, nostrils flaring, his cheeks darkly flushed. She was petrified and enthralled at the same time, and dimly became aware of how badly her legs were shaking.

"Come here."

Another of those brief, succinct commands. He was a man of a few words but they were more than enough to make himself understood. Slowly, her gaze remaining transfixed on his, she walked across his office until she was standing a few inches away, still holding her ruined blouse up to cover as much of her breasts as possible.

But Ian apparently had other ideas, for he clasped both of her wrists, forcing her to release the blouse as it fluttered to the carpet. His eyes took in every inch of her bare skin, lingering on the heavy swell of her breasts, and Tessa closed her eyes in embarrassment as she felt her nipples harden in reaction.

"No. Look at me. Open your eyes and look at me, Tessa." Another command from him that she didn't dare resist.

She was starting to tremble all over as she forced herself to open her eyes and meet his intense, burning gaze. Without breaking eye contact, he backed her up until she was standing against a wall of the office, effectively trapped between it and Ian's tall, powerful body.

He drew both of her arms above her head, then pinned her wrists against the wall with just one of his big hands. He used his other hand to caress her cheek, his thumb brushing gently over her lips and causing her mouth to gape open in surprise. His hand continued its downward path, brushing over her collarbone and shoulder, traveling down her arm and the side of her ribcage and then, ever so slowly, back up her abdomen until it stopped just below her breasts.

"Christ, look at you."

His voice was guttural, barely recognizable, and filled with so much raw need that Tessa was nearly swooning.

"Ah, God." That was her voice, more like a long, drawn out moan, as his hand cupped one swollen breast. His thumb expertly manipulated the taut bud of her nipple through the lace of her bra, and his touch was like an electric shock that pulsed through her entire body.

With a low growl, Ian leaned into her, shoving her further back against the wall. His mouth descended towards hers, and her head fell back helplessly as his warm, firm lips caressed a sensuous path from her temple to her flushed cheek to the soft spot just below her ear. His hot mouth continued moving across her throat, to her chin, and then finally to claim her mouth in a blistering, domineering kiss.

Tessa felt as though she'd been in a dreamlike sleep state for twenty four years, and was just now awakening into the real world. The few times she'd been kissed in her life had never come close to anything like this – this sensation of drowning, of being devoured – and she realized faintly that this was the first time she had ever truly been kissed. Ian's mouth was hungry and demanding, his tongue parting her lips with ease and thrusting possessively inside her mouth.

He released his grip on her wrists and she instinctively wrapped her arms around his neck, pulling his body closer into hers and silently urging him to take even deeper possession of her mouth. She was growing dizzy from the almost brutal demand of his kiss, and was only vaguely aware when he began to slide a bra strap off her shoulder. It wasn't until his hand closed over the bare, warm flesh of her breast that she realized what he'd done, and then she was far too overwhelmed with the pleasure his touch brought to care.

"Ohhh. Oh, please, yes."

Tessa didn't realize the high, desperate whimpers had come from her lips. Ian's long fingers were splayed over her breast, the tips rolling her nipple, plucking it to an even harder peak. He swore softly beneath his breath but otherwise didn't speak, his mouth nuzzling again at that tender spot beneath her ear. With one hand still fondling her breast, he used the other to lift her leg, wrapping it around his hip. This movement brought their bodies flush against the other, allowing Ian to nestle his immensely swollen cock into the juncture of her thighs. At the same time, he reclaimed her lips in another of those all-consuming kisses, his tongue now ravenous as it plundered her warm mouth.

She was rapidly threatening to overload on sensation as her entire body was being stimulated at once – by his hot, hungry mouth eating at hers like a starving man; his hand at her breast, twisting her engorged nipple between thumb and forefinger, the pleasure traveling directly to her womb; and the feel of his hard, thick penis rubbing against her cleft, where she was wet and needy and far more aroused than she had ever come close to being before. With each movement of his groin against hers, she could feel the friction against her ultra-sensitive clit, even between the layers of their clothing. He was surrounding her with pleasure, using his mouth, his hands, his cock, and it was suddenly too much for her as a very unexpected orgasm rippled through her body.

Ian stilled as he lifted his mouth from hers, murmuring in awe, "My God, Tessa. Christ – you're so beautiful, darling. I can't believe you just - "

Whatever else he was going to say was abruptly halted by the ringing of his cell phone. Tessa's eyes were tightly shut, too wrecked from what had just happened to even think of opening them yet. She dimly heard Ian curse impatiently as he answered the phone with barely restrained annoyance. As he eased his body away from hers to take the call, she felt suddenly bereft without the hard warmth of him pressed against her.

And then, as the glowing haze of her orgasm began to slowly fade, her mortification returned tenfold. She glanced down and had to stifle a moan when she saw her exposed breast, the nipple still red from his touch. Hastily, she jerked the cup and strap back into place, then grabbed the discarded blouse and pulled it on, her fingers fumbling with the buttons.

Ian's call ended and he gazed at her from the other side of his office. She knew she must look a sight, with her flushed cheeks, mussed hair and stained, wrinkled blouse that she wasn't sure had even been buttoned up correctly. The only thing that helped her retain a bit of her composure was the realization that Ian seemed as shook up as she was by what had just happened. His tie was askew, his hair rumpled, and he appeared to be at a complete loss for words.

He glanced at her, then at the ship's clock on his credenza before grabbing an envelope from his desk.

"I need to go," he muttered brusquely, and then strode out of the office without a moment's hesitation.

Tessa stared after him, too shocked at what had just occurred to even move. Just a few short minutes ago her body had been burning up, every part of her on fire for Ian's touch, the heat of his big body almost smothering her. And now, devoid of all that, she began to shiver almost uncontrollably, shaking in reaction, and she had to wrap her arms about her torso to steady herself.

"Oh, my, God," she uttered in disbelief. "What in the world have I done?"

***

Ian was echoing almost the same exact words as he very nearly ran out of his office, grateful when an elevator arrived almost immediately and even more so when it proved to be empty. On the ride down to the lobby, he forced himself to take several deep breaths, trying to still the frantic beat of his heart. At the same time he swiftly restored order to his rumpled hair and clothing, and offered up a silent thanks that his raging erection had subsided, for there was no way he could have walked across the lobby to meet his associates in that sort of condition.

His meeting had ended earlier than expected, and he'd agreed to have a quick drink with two of his associates before they headed off to dinner. But then he'd realized he had left a report he needed to give someone in his office, and they had been obliged to make a quick stop to retrieve it.

He hadn't expected anyone to still be at the office when he arrived, and indeed the floor had been empty when he'd walked through. But Tessa's purse and coat had still been on top of Andrew's desk, and then he'd heard her voice as he walked inside his office.

What had happened next was still completely surreal to him, like a dream he had yet to wake from. She'd been standing in the doorway of his private washroom, the upper half of her body unclothed except for that rather insubstantial lace bra, and she had been so tempting, so sexy, and so completely desirable that he'd had trouble remembering his own name. Her smooth ivory skin had glowed, her long golden hair tumbling about her bare shoulders, and – oh, Christ – those beautiful, ripe tits spilling out of the low-cut bra. They had been bigger, rounder and firmer than his very dirty imagination could have ever pictured – or hoped for – and he'd been instantly, violently aroused.

Ian hadn't been able to stop what happened next, any more than he could have stopped breathing. He'd waited too long, denied himself for far too many months, and couldn't wait even one more day to have her. He'd barely recognized the dominant, forceful commands that had come out of his mouth, but Tessa had responded instinctively to them, obeying him without hesitation.

He'd fallen on her like a starving man, kissing and touching her with absolutely no finesse, grinding himself against her like a horny teenager. He'd never been so hard in his life, had never felt his blood pump so hot, or had the need to fuck like an animal. The sounds she'd made – her groans, the breathy little pants, her husky words of encouragement – had only served to make him harder.

And then, with astonishing, jaw dropping swiftness, she'd come – her body quivering in reaction. He'd never been with a woman who could orgasm that quickly, and certainly not without far more stimulation. His head was still spinning with the recollection of how she'd looked and sounded when she had climaxed, and he was hard again.

"Damn it!" he cursed, for the elevator was nearly at the lobby level. He had to forcibly remove all thoughts of Tessa from his mind as he exited the elevator and located his associates.

If one of the men hadn't called his cell – wondering what was keeping him – God knows what might have happened next. Christ, he'd been so far gone, so consumed with pleasure and need, that he had little doubt he would have taken Tessa then and there – on his sofa, his desk, or the floor – maybe all three. It had shaken him badly, for he was always, *always* in control of his emotions. Except, it seemed, when it concerned his startlingly responsive, sexy as sin, golden girl.

He felt like an ass for having just walked out on her like that – without an apology or explanation or even an acknowledgment – but he'd been in panic mode by then. The very last thing he'd wanted to happen was for his associates to come upstairs looking for him, and so he'd made a hasty departure before that could happen.

But it was probably all for the best, since he badly needed some time to compose himself and think about what had just happened. One thing was for damned sure – he could no longer keep his attraction towards Tessa a secret, not after the way he'd dry humped her against the wall and come within minutes of fucking her senseless. God damn it, this was *not* the way he'd wanted things to unfold, to let her know of how he felt about her. He had intended to woo her gently, to take things slowly and show her exquisite tenderness and patience. But all it had taken was one glimpse of her nearly naked breasts and his carefully planned seduction of her had been escalated at breakneck speed.

Ian agonized all during dinner about where things went from here, barely touching his food or saying much of anything. He was vaguely aware that the others at the table were regarding him oddly, asking if he was all right, and he mumbled some excuse about being a bit under the weather.

He had difficulty falling asleep that night, his body hard and throbbing when he recalled how soft Tessa's lips had been, how sweetly passionate her response. It had been far too long since he'd been with a woman, resorting to jacking off in the shower to find some temporary relief. But now that he'd finally touched and kissed her, he knew no one else would ever do.

As he eventually drifted off into a restless slumber, he still had no idea of what he was going to say or do when he saw her again tomorrow. He should be annoyed that a sweet, shy girl like Tessa had him feeling as rattled and uncertain as an adolescent boy, but instead the realization only brought a smile to his lips as sleep finally claimed him.

Chapter Eight

In the five years she had worked for the Gregson Hotel Group, Tessa had never truly considered calling in sick – even when she'd been so ill with the flu she could barely lift her head off the pillow. But today she seriously toyed with the idea, even as she dragged herself out of bed and started getting ready.

Even if she had somehow been able to get the damned ink stain out of her blouse, Tessa knew she'd never be able to wear it again. At least not without remembering in explicit, excruciating detail everything that had happened last evening in her boss' office. Her cheeks still burned with embarrassment as she recalled the way she'd responded to his kisses and expert caresses, how she'd moaned in arousal, and, most shocking of all, how she'd had an orgasm right there on the spot, her body evidently so starved for physical contact that it had taken less than five minutes for her to go off like a skyrocket.

'Oh, God, he must think you're some kind of man-hungry slut,' she despaired as she searched through her ever-diminishing wardrobe for something to wear. 'Letting him touch you like that, moaning like you're in a bad porn flick. How in the world am I going to face him today?'

Tessa had barely slept a wink last night, tossing and turning as she worried about the consequences of last evening's fiasco. It was all her fault, she thought wildly, for using his private washroom and then foolishly deciding to strip off her blouse in what had been a futile attempt to get it clean. She should have just used the ladies room in the office, or at the very least had enough sense to close the door to Ian's private washroom.

He would unquestionably be angry with her, that much was for certain. The look on his face when he'd stormed out of his office had been ferocious, and she only hoped he'd had the opportunity to calm down overnight and deal with this awful mess in a rational manner.

She chose one of her oldest outfits – a black turtleneck sweater and a black and white checkered wool skirt. The skirt was a little loose since she'd lost some weight, but after unintentionally exposing herself yesterday she was anxious to present a conservative image this morning. She wore minimal makeup and considered pulling her hair back into a knot but ran out of time.

During the bus ride to work, Tessa continued to fret about what Mr. Gregson was likely to say or do after their encounter in his office. It was possible that he was as horrified by his impulsive actions as she was about hers, and that he would very tactfully say nothing, acting as though it had never happened. They would finish out the week with her working for him, and then it would likely be a cold day in hell before she was ever asked to fill in for Andrew again.

That was actually the best case scenario. In other, less desirable ones, Mr. Gregson would give her a severe reprimand, arrange for her immediate transfer to another department or location, or, in the absolute worst case, terminate her employment.

Tessa honestly didn't think Mr. Gregson would go so far as to fire her. He was a kind and fair man, and knew she was on her own now. She simply couldn't see him putting her out of a job.

No, the first and second options were the most likely, and she feared he would in fact arrange for her to be transferred as soon as possible. Of course, her co-workers would immediately begin to speculate that she must have screwed something up big time while filling in for Andrew to suffer such a swift and severe punishment. They wouldn't guess that what had almost been screwed was Tessa herself.

The bus left her off a couple of minutes earlier than usual due to the "Friday lite" traffic. She was grateful for the extra time to get to her desk and somehow compose herself before Mr. Gregson arrived.

The first thing she noticed when she arrived at her temporary office was the damned printer. Tessa glared at it darkly, thinking it and its faulty ink cartridge the root of all evil.

But then she felt a huge sense of relief when she booted up the computer and looked over the master schedule for today. By some fortunate stroke of luck, Mr. Gregson wouldn't be arriving at the office until almost noontime. He had a breakfast meeting with the same group of worldwide business associates he'd met with yesterday, followed by a conference he was addressing at the Gregson Hotel up on Nob Hill. Those two appointments would take up most of the morning, giving Tessa some badly needed time to compose herself.

The morning went by quickly as she downloaded and printed a stack of reports, updated some weekly spreadsheets she was in charge of preparing, and answered several emails. She was surprised when she glanced at the clock and realized it was almost noon, and then the butterflies in her tummy really kicked in for Ian ought to be arriving any minute now.

But as the minutes ticked by and he didn't appear, she assumed he'd just gone to lunch or had a personal appointment. There was *no* way she was going to call or text him to see where he was and when he might be arriving in.

Her stomach growled, reminding her that she'd barely eaten any dinner last night, far too shook up to have an appetite, and that so far today had only been able to stomach some tea and half a protein bar. But she honestly didn't think she could keep any food down right now, as edgy and nervous as she felt.

It was past one o'clock before Ian made an appearance, and her heart almost stopped beating when she saw him striding down the hallway towards her desk. God, he looked magnificent, she thought almost desperately, so incredibly handsome and sexy in a charcoal gray suit and burgundy tie. He was as poised and regal as ever, betraying no sign of the passionate, aggressive lover she'd seen all too briefly last evening.

Their gazes locked and held until he inclined his head towards his office. "I'd like to speak with you in my office please, Tessa."

She shot to her feet in agitation. "Yes – of, of course sir."

Tessa clasped her hands in front of her, anxious to still their trembling, and preceded him inside his office. She'd been mentally preparing herself for this moment since last night and just hoped she wouldn't do something foolish, like start to cry.

But what she absolutely hadn't prepped herself for was the way Ian swiftly shut and locked the door behind him, and then swept her into his arms. She gasped in surprise, her hands drifting up to rest on his upper arms as he gazed down at her with an almost desperate look in his eyes.

"Just tell me," he pleaded, "that you don't regret what happened last night. And that whatever this is between us – that you feel it, too."

Tessa was astonished at his impassioned words, the very last sort of thing she had expected him to say. Despite her shock, she was still able to whisper, "No. I – I don't regret it. And yes – I feel it, too."

"Thank God."

And with those fervently uttered words, he took her mouth in a hungry, possessive kiss, his arms banding about her so closely that she could hardly breathe. She slid her arms inside his suit jacket, holding on to him tight, and a groan rose up from her throat as he continued to plunder her mouth with his seeking tongue.

She heard him give a soft chuckle as he finally released her mouth and murmured in her ear, "Easy, darling. We don't want the whole office to hear you."

Tessa gazed up at him in bewilderment. "What?"

Ian smiled at her tenderly, tucking a strand of hair behind her ear. "You're very vocal when you're aroused. You didn't know?"

She was horrified, not realizing how loud her moans of pleasure must have been, and shook her head. "No, I had no idea. Oh, God, I'm sorry. How embarrassing."

He threaded both of his hands into her hair, holding her head still as his eyes bored into hers. "I'm not complaining, love. In fact, those little sounds you make are extremely sexy and a tremendous turn-on. And when I take you to my bed, with all of this beautiful hair spread out on my pillow, you can moan as loudly as you like. In fact," he added huskily, as he kissed his way down the side of her neck, "I look forward to exploring a hundred different ways to make you moan in pleasure."

"Mmm." She sighed with delight as he kissed her again, his mouth moving on hers more slowly this time, lingering, savoring the taste of her. She was very quickly becoming addicted to his masterful kisses, loving the way he held her so tightly in his strong arms, and the hunger he displayed with each embrace. She hadn't had the opportunity as yet to process the mindboggling notion that this dynamic, brilliant man was for some reason attracted to her. But for now, Tessa didn't let herself think about that, and instead gave herself up completely to Ian, kissing him back with every pent-up ounce of passion in her body. She was wild for him, desperately needy, clutching the fabric of his shirt in her hands as she tried to get even closer to him.

Ian was gasping for breath as he gently eased her away from him, his eyes wide with astonishment. "Christ, Tessa. Have a care, darling. I'm a lot older than you are, after all, and not at all certain that I'll be able to keep up with you." He ran a long finger over her trembling lips. "What a passionate little thing you are. I would never have guessed that someone as shy and sweet as you was really a tigress in disguise."

She felt her cheeks flame in embarrassment and glanced away. "I'm sorry," she whispered. "It's just – been a long time for me. I didn't mean - "

"Hush." He placed two fingers over her lips, silencing her. "I wasn't complaining, love. Far from it. My God, you're probably going to wear me out very quickly but it will damned sure be worth it. And," he added severely, "I don't ever want you to apologize for anything. Especially not for wanting me. Understood?"

She nodded and he removed his fingers before taking her hand in his.

"Let's sit over here, shall we? In separate chairs, I think," he said dryly. "We have a few things to discuss and if you're within arm's reach talking is going to be the very last thing on my mind."

Ian led her over to the sitting area in one corner of his expansive office, urging her to sit in one of the large leather chairs while he took a seat a safe distance away on a sofa.

"How are you today, Tessa?" he asked gently. "I'm arriving at the office a bit later than I'd planned, and I've been worrying about you all morning.

"You have?" she asked in surprise.

"Yes, quite worried after what happened last evening. Especially since I ran out of here like the place was on fire. I can't even imagine what you must have thought of me when I did something like that."

Tessa picked nervously at a piece of lint on her skirt. "I thought – well, that you probably regretted what had happened and - "

"No." His denial was emphatic. "Not even the slightest regret. What happened, Tessa – it's what I've wanted for a long time now."

Startled, she glanced up at him. "How long?"

"Forever, it feels like. Specifically, though, two years and four extremely long months. In other words, darling girl, I've wanted you from the first moment we met. You've been my obsession, my one desire, ever since you started working here. And I never imagined that I could be in a position to tell you how I felt. Not when you were a married woman."

Tessa stared at him in disbelief. "All this time? I can't – I mean, I never even thought you noticed me, I always assumed I was just one of your employees. And not a very important one at that."

Despite his vow not to touch her, Ian reached over and grasped her hand firmly in his. "I noticed you every damned day. Too much. I've memorized almost every article of clothing you own, noticed that you drink the same blend of tea that I do, and that you tend to wrap a strand of hair around your finger when you're trying to concentrate on something. I think it's gone far beyond noticing you, darling, and moved into obsession." He raised her hand to his lips. "And in my opinion, you're the most important employee I've ever had."

She was dazzled by his impassioned speech, and by the almost desperate way he gripped her hand. "I don't know what to say. I just never imagined a man like you would ever be attracted to someone like me."

"Why ever not? Tessa, you are beyond beautiful, enough to tempt a saint. Not to mention sweet, kind, and loyal. I can't imagine any man *not* being attracted to you." Ian gave her hand a quick kiss before releasing it. "Now, we can talk about my no longer secret infatuation with you a little later. I have to be on a conference call in a few minutes and there are things we need to discuss first."

At her nod, he continued. "First, I would be very pleased if you'd consent to have dinner with me this evening. Around seven o'clock?"

"I'd love to have dinner with you," she replied in delight. "But should we? I mean, aren't you afraid someone might see us together? That's – we're not really allowed to – "

"Well, that's another matter entirely. But don't worry about anyone from the office seeing us out together tonight. I'll make certain our privacy is guaranteed. So, it's a yes then?"

Tessa smiled. "It's a definite yes."

Ian beamed at her. "I adore how you never play games, how honest you always are. It's a refreshing change from all the pretense and social niceties I usually have to navigate through. But since you've already mentioned the subject of our working together, it goes without saying that for the time being at least we need to keep our – er, attraction for each other strictly between us."

She nodded emphatically. "Of course. I wouldn't dream of saying anything to anyone. I'm usually pretty closed-mouthed about my personal life anyway. That's why it took me so long to tell anyone here about my divorce."

"I know I can count on you to be discreet, Tessa. And we'll discuss the matter in more detail over dinner, hmm? Now, two last things and then afterwards I'd like for you to order a quick lunch for both of us, then help me set up the conference call. Are you on birth control?"

She blinked, a bit taken aback by the question. "Um, yes. I have an IUD."

Ian seemed relieved by her answer. "Good. I'm – well, I've always been extremely careful over the years in my relationships, not that there have been all that many. I get tested every year when I have my annual check-up, and I can promise you that I don't have any nasty communicable diseases I could possibly pass on to you."

"I wouldn't have even imagined it," she told him earnestly. "And I know you'd never lie to me."

He leaned over and gave her a quick kiss. "Christ, you're sweet. So damned sweet. And you're absolutely right – I will never, ever lie to you, Tessa. But if you're protected and you trust me – I'm hoping you won't mind if I don't use a condom when we're together." He whispered huskily in her ear, "The first time I slide deep inside of you, I want to feel every delicious inch of you bare against me."

She gulped, feeling her nipples peak at the sensual image his words evoked. "Oh, God. I want that, too."

Ian shut his eyes tightly and groaned. "You are the most tempting, irresistible – Jesus, let me finish before I do something to make you moan again." He sat back on the sofa, his hands clasped firmly together. "Now, one final thing, love. The reason I was late getting back to the office today was because I made a stop at Neiman Marcus." He paused to fish a business card out of his jacket pocket and handed it to her.

Tessa glanced at the card, which bore the name and title *Marlene Brennan, Personal Shopper*. "I don't understand."

"I've used Marlene's services several times since moving to San Francisco. Strictly to buy gifts for the female members of my family," he clarified. "I'm not in the habit of purchasing personal items for the women I've dated in the past. You'll be the first."

She frowned. "You bought me something?"

"No. At least, not yet. I took the liberty of selecting a few things for you, things I would very much like you to wear to dinner this evening. But," he added firmly, "it's entirely up to you, Tessa. If it makes you feel uncomfortable, I'll understand."

Suddenly self-conscious about her inexpensive, well-worn clothing – especially when compared to his elegant designer suit – she plucked at a pulled thread on her skirt. "It's not that. It's just – no one has ever really given me things before."

Ian regarded her quizzically. "Not even your parents? Or your husband?"

Tessa shook her head. "Money has always been – well, something of a problem. So I'm not used to receiving gifts."

He smiled. "Well, then, I will definitely look forward to spoiling you frequently and thoroughly. Starting with tonight."

She gave him a shy smile in return. "You don't have to buy me things. I don't expect or need that."

"I know that, darling. That doesn't mean you don't deserve to be pampered a bit, though. I'm guessing from the little I know about you that you've had a rough go of it. Let me take care of you, Tessa. Care, not control," he emphasized. "The choice will always – *always* - be yours."

Tears shimmered in her eyes at how good he was to her, how kind. "I don't know what to say."

"The word is yes, darling girl. At least to this one small thing. Just go see Marlene and look at the things I had her set aside. If you don't like them then you're more than welcome to choose something else. Or nothing at all. I just want to spoil you a little bit."

She noticed how the heel of her black pump was scuffed and starting to wear away. "All right, I'll go look. I don't want to embarrass you at dinner tonight with what I'm wearing. But you really don't need to buy me anything. I can just go home and change, I'm sure I have – "

"Stop it." His voice was firm and she didn't dare argue further with him. "You could never, ever embarrass me, Tessa. You're likely to be the one embarrassed by me. Everyone is sure to wonder what a gorgeous young girl like you sees in an old man like myself."

"No!" she burst out. "You're not old at all! And you're so handsome and wonderful and – and splendid."

Ian looked extremely pleased at her outburst. "You think I'm splendid?"

"Yes," she told him earnestly. "And – thank you. For arranging whatever it is you did."

"You ought to leave the office a bit early today," he suggested. "Say around three o'clock or so. I'll plan to meet you at the store around six-thirty and we'll go to dinner from there."

Tessa frowned. "That seems like a lot of time just to try on a few clothes."

He winked at her. "Well, perhaps there might be another small surprise or two involved. Now, we need to get back to work, darling. Though I have no idea how I'm going to get a damned thing done when all I can think about is spending time with you tonight."

"I'll order lunch." She stood and started towards the office door. "Would you like some tea, sir?"

The title slipped automatically from her lips, as used as she was to calling him that after more than two years. Ian chuckled and caressed her cheek.

"If you keep calling me that," he teased, "I'll start to think you want a very different sort of relationship than what I have in mind. Not that the idea isn't enticing in certain ways."

Tessa blinked. "What idea?"

Ian pressed a quick kiss to her forehead. "You are beyond adorable. And surprisingly naïve for a woman who's been married. I'll explain it to you another time. And yes, love, tea would be perfect."

She beamed at him. "I'll go brew it while ordering lunch, then I'll get your conference call set up."

He grinned. "You've been taking excellent care of me this week, Tessa. So much that I've barely noticed Andrew isn't here. In fact, maybe I ought to suggest he extend his vacation since I like having you around so much."

Impulsively, she reached up and kissed his cheek. "Same here."

Ian growled, then held her head still for another deep, hungry kiss. When he finally lifted his head, it was to mutter in her ear, "How in hell have I kept my hands off of you all this time?"

***

Marlene Brennan had worked as a personal shopper for going on twenty years, and in the retail fashion business for even longer. She had assisted socialites, businesswomen, politicians and celebrities, nearly all of them well dressed and well groomed, and many of them very beautiful women.

She had also provided assistance to quite a few male shoppers who needed gifts for their wives, girlfriends or other women in their lives. One of those men was Ian Gregson, whom she'd first met when he moved to San Francisco several years ago. Marlene may have been a dozen or more years his senior, and a happily married woman, but that didn't mean she couldn't fully appreciate what a magnificent man he was – tall, powerfully built, with ruggedly handsome features and the ability to wear a suit like it had been made for him. Which, considering several of his suits were Savile Row, was an entirely accurate observation.

Over the years, Marlene had helped the debonair, charismatic Mr. Gregson select gifts for his mother, grandmother, aunts, and sisters-in-law. But she had never been asked to help him choose a gift for any of the women he dated. Until this morning.

Mr. Gregson had been – well, glowing might not be far off the mark. He had looked younger, happier, and more relaxed than Marlene had ever seen him. And he'd been intent on picking out a variety of clothing, shoes, handbags, coats, accessories – quite a lot of it considering the relatively short time he'd spent at the store – and all of it apparently for one very lucky woman.

"I'll send her by this afternoon to try on the blue dress and the Louboutins," he'd informed Marlene. "The Burberry coat as well. And I think the Coach bag will go nicely with the shoes, do you agree?"

Marlene had nodded, impressed by his fashion sense and quick decision making. "Absolutely, Mr. Gregson."

"Once you've confirmed her sizes, then I'd like to have you deliver the other things to my home. And you'll be able to arrange for the other services we discussed?"

Her curiosity had been wildly aroused, anxious now to see this woman who had undoubtedly captivated one of the most eligible bachelors in the city. Ian had seemed almost nervous, certainly anxious that what he had chosen would please this woman, and Marlene only hoped she wouldn't be some haughty diva who was impossible to satisfy.

She was almost shocked speechless, therefore, when the impossibly young and heartbreakingly lovely blonde girl approached her shyly, asking in a timid voice, "Are you Marlene

Brennan? I think you're expecting me – Tessa Lockwood."

Marlene hoped that all of her years in working with customers had given her the skills to conceal the surprise she felt at meeting this young woman. Her sharp, discerning eye immediately pegged the girl's raincoat, shoes and bag as being both well-worn and cheap, and she tried very hard not to automatically assume that this ripe, sexy beauty was a gold digger. It was very easy to see why the girl would be attracted to a handsome, wealthy man like Ian Gregson, but Marlene could also understand why he in turn would be obsessed with this beautiful girl who stood regarding her uncertainly.

Marlene smiled at her reassuringly. "Yes, my dear. I'm Marlene. Welcome to Neiman Marcus, Tessa. Have you shopped here before?"

Tessa shook her head. "No. I've never been inside. It's – everything is beautiful."

Marlene patted the girl's arm. "Well, you're in good hands with me. And as for beautiful things – I think you'll be pleased with the items Mr. Gregson has picked out for you to try on. He has excellent taste, the things are exquisite."

Tessa's cheeks pinkened, and Marlene was startled anew, for in her line of work she seldom saw women blush these days. "I – I told him this wasn't necessary," stammered Tessa. "I don't – I'm not used to anyone buying things for me. This is all – I don't know what to think."

Marlene felt a rush of empathy for the girl, who was clearly out of her league in this very high class environment. "Not to worry, my dear. We're just going into a private dressing room so you can try on the dress he selected for you. If it's not to your taste there are plenty of others to choose from. Do you like shopping, Tessa?"

Tessa nodded. "I do. I, um, used to work in clothing stores during high school. Nothing like this, of course."

Marlene began to guide her toward the dressing room. "Where did you work?"

Tessa looked embarrassed to admit she'd worked at both Forever 21 and Old Navy in the past.

"Well, nothing wrong with that, dear. I started off my retail career selling shoes at Sears," confided Marlene. "And here I am today. We all have to begin somewhere."

She unlocked the door to the spacious dressing room and ushered Tessa inside. As the girl removed her raincoat, Marlene's eyes widened as she quickly inspected Tessa's tall, shapely figure. It was small wonder that Ian Gregson seemed so infatuated with her, given the full, rounded bosom, slender waist and hips, and long legs. The fact that her black sweater and checkered skirt had seen better days didn't matter in the least. Tessa had a body built to entice men, and it made little difference what she wore.

"Let me show you the dress Mr. Gregson was especially taken with. He said he liked you in this particular color."

Tessa's eyes widened as Marlene brought over the elegant dress of electric blue gabardine. It was sleeveless, with a scooped neck and scalloped hem. The garment would fit Tessa's slim but curvy body lovingly while still shrieking class and elegance.

"It's Lanvin, dear," explained Marlene. "From the oldest couture house in France. This is one of my favorite pieces in their current collection. And Mr. Gregson has excellent taste – the color and style will look marvelous on you. Would you like to try it on?"

Tessa touched the fabric almost reverently. "It's lovely. Is it very expensive? I really don't want him spending a lot of money on me."

"He can afford it, dear," assured Marlene. "And I know he very much wants you to have it. Why don't we see how it fits, hmm? Mr. Gregson was guessing at your size, so this is a six we have here, but I can always get a different size if necessary."

Tessa shook her head and slowly began to pull the sweater over her head. "I think a six will be fine."

Marlene frowned as Tessa stripped to her underwear. The black lace bra and panties were mismatched and a bit shabby, and it was obvious from the way her full breasts almost spilled out of the cups that the bra wasn't sized properly. The thigh high black stockings were also starting to pill in several places.

"When was the last time you were fitted for bras, Tessa?" she inquired casually.

Tessa looked ill at ease with the question. "Um, I don't recall. I'm not exactly sure I ever have been."

"No problem. After we try the dress and shoes on I'll fit you. Mr. Gregson also selected some, ah, lingerie for you."

Predictably, the girl's already rosy cheeks flushed a deeper shade and she merely nodded. But then, as Marlene zipped her into the classic blue Lanvin, Tessa's eyes grew big as saucers as she gazed upon her reflection in the mirror.

"Oh. It's beautiful, isn't it? I've never had anything this nice before." Tessa skimmed her hands a little uncertainly over the fine fabric.

The girl's heartfelt reaction touched Marlene, and she felt a sudden tenderness towards her. Marlene didn't have children of her own but she was certainly more than old enough to be Tessa's mother. And after so many years of catering to vain, demanding patrons, it was a refreshing change to be able to really help someone as sweet and innocent as this lovely girl. She could certainly understand Ian's infatuation with her.

"It looks wonderful on you," confirmed Marlene as she straightened the skirt just a bit. "I can see now why he favored this color – it's perfect for your eyes and skin tone. Now, let's try the shoes, hmm? I have three different sizes here to choose from."

Tessa wore an eight and a half, and the nude Christian Louboutin pumps fit her to perfection. Marlene showed her the other items Ian had selected for her to wear this evening – a butter-soft leather handbag in a coordinating shade to the shoes, and a luxurious camel-colored cashmere coat lined in a satiny fabric.

Tessa was seemingly fascinated by the coat, touching the soft fabric. "It looks so warm," she marveled. "It's been so cold these past few weeks."

Marlene wondered if the thin raincoat could possibly be the girl's only coat. There was no other reasonable explanation why she would have worn it on a bitingly cold but otherwise clear day. "Its pure cashmere, dear, and a Burberry. One of the finest coats we sell here. He wanted only the best for you."

Tessa smiled. "He's wonderful, isn't he?"

"I think he feels the same way about you, Tessa," replied Marlene gently. "Now, why don't we get you out of that dress so I can measure your bra size. Then Mr. Gregson has arranged some other – ah, services for you."

A quick check with the tape measure confirmed that Tessa's bra was indeed two full cup sizes too small, which clearly explained why she'd almost been falling out of the black lace garment. While she slipped back into her own black pumps, Marlene handed her a belted smock, the kind used in hair salons and spas.

"You can leave your things here, Tessa. I'll lock the room while you're gone and you can come back and change afterwards," assured Marlene. "Follow me now, we're just going up one floor."

Marlene left her charge off at the in-store salon, where she was to have a blow-out, a mani-pedi, and a makeup application. When Tessa returned to the dressing room nearly two hours later, she looked a bit dazed but even more beautiful – her skin glowing, her blonde hair smooth and shiny, her nails buffed and covered in pale pink polish.

She helped Tessa dress, satisfied with the fit of the pale blue lace bra and panties, and with the new pair of sheer nude thigh-highs. After Tessa was zipped up into the dress and wearing her new shoes, Marlene added the finishing touches – a sapphire pendant suspended from a dainty gold chain and a matching pair of drop earrings.

"These aren't real sapphires, are they?" asked Tessa with what sounded like panic.

"They are, yes. Don't worry, Tessa, they're insured. You won't lose them."

"It's not that." Tessa's big blue eyes grew shiny with tears. "This is all just – a little overwhelming. I feel like Cinderella."

Marlene laughed. "And you look like her, too. You're a beautiful girl, Tessa, and Mr. Gregson is going to be speechless when he sees you. He'll be very pleased."

That seemed to do the trick as Tessa looked to Marlene for

assurance. "You really think so?"

Marlene nodded. "I know so, dear. He was very anxious earlier today for you to like the things he chose. I've rarely see a man take the sort of care he did. Now, come. It's time to dazzle him."

Chapter Nine

Ian discreetly pulled back the sleeve of his shirt to check the time on his Cartier watch. It was still a few minutes before six-thirty, and he hoped that Tessa would be ready soon. He'd been waiting for this moment with ill-concealed impatience ever since she'd left his office earlier today.

After his doubts of last evening, he had breathed a huge sigh of relief after finally seeing Tessa today. In fact, her response to him had been well beyond his wildest expectations. She was shy and uncertain, and he couldn't be too aggressive with her, but he was overjoyed to discover that she was as attracted to him as he was to her. He had never envisioned making this much progress so quickly, and was looking forward to speeding up the very enjoyable process of seducing his golden girl. How many times had he fantasized about this – taking her to dinner and then quite possibly to his bed.

But, no, he couldn't push her. Despite her eager response to his advances and her shy admittance of being attracted to him, Ian could still sense her uncertainty and inexperience – something that seemed odd for a soon-to-be divorced woman. He wondered if Peter had been her only boyfriend, her only sexual partner, which could explain her shyness around other men.

And while he would love nothing better than to bring Tessa home with him tonight and finally make her his, he wasn't going to rush things. The last thing he intended to do at this point was to scare her off and ruin his chances with her. He'd waited this long – surely his patience could last a while longer.

But his good intentions were all dashed to hell when he saw her emerge from the dressing room, Marlene Brennan trailing in her wake. Ian froze as he got a good look at Tessa, and his heart caught in his throat at her beauty.

The blue dress – almost exactly the same shade as the one she'd worn to the office Christmas party – clung in all the right places and made her look svelte and sexy while still shrieking class. Her breasts looked higher and rounder, and he wondered how she looked in the seductive blue lace bra he'd selected for her, as well as the tiny matching panties. His erection began to throb painfully and he groaned in silence, realizing it was going to be a damned long night ahead if he kept up this train of thought.

Tessa was glowing – there was really no other word for it. Her lovely face didn't actually need cosmetics, but the makeup artist had done an excellent job with the subtle application she'd given her. His gaze lingered on the soft pink gloss on her lips and how her eyes seemed even bigger and bluer than usual. Her hair was shiny and smooth, falling in a straight, glossy fall down her shoulders and back. The sapphires he'd chosen to go with the dress were just right, not too large or showy.

She was smiling as she reached him, standing a couple of inches taller than usual with the added height from her new shoes.

"Hi," she said breathlessly.

Ian grinned at her, absurdly proud of how striking she looked and how happy she seemed. "Hi, yourself, darling. You look gorgeous, absolutely gorgeous. I assume you like the dress?"

She pressed a quick kiss to his cheek, and his skin burned from the contact. "It's beautiful. All of it. Thank you so much, I love everything."

He couldn't resist wrapping an arm around her waist and hugging her close. He buried his face in her hair, which smelled like vanilla and spice. "It was my pleasure, love. Especially when I see how happy my little gift has made you. Are you ready to leave now?"

"I just need to get my coat and bag," she assured him, and turned to face Marlene.

Ian took the cashmere coat from the personal shopper and held it open for Tessa. He smiled as she buttoned up the coat and then snuggled the collar more closely around her neck.

"I really love this," she said guilelessly. "I've never, ever had anything so nice before. Or so warm."

He leaned closer to whisper in her ear, "Careful, or I might find myself getting jealous of a coat. Though I admit it's a big improvement over that bloody raincoat."

Tessa laughed, and took the Coach handbag from Marlene. The older woman was also carrying a large paper shopping bag which she handed to Tessa.

"This has all the things you were wearing when you arrived," she explained.

"I'll take that," offered Ian, thinking of how much he longed to burn the damned raincoat that he could see folded on top of the bag. "And I must thank you for taking such excellent care of Tessa. I didn't think perfection could be improved upon, but I believe I've been proven wrong. She looks – breathtaking."

Marlene smiled. "She certainly does. And the two of you make quite an attractive pair if I may say so. You'll certainly have every eye in the place on you, wherever you might be headed this evening."

Ian shook her hand. "My thanks again, Mrs. Brennan. You've outdone yourself. I'm sure you'll be seeing more of Tessa before too long."

"It would be my pleasure, Mr. Gregson," replied Marlene smoothly. "She's been a joy to work with, and I would adore the opportunity to help her in the future."

"Thank you for everything," Tessa told Marlene, giving her a shy hug. "I'm sorry if I was a lot of trouble."

"Dear, I can't remember the last time I enjoyed working with a customer more than I did today," assured Marlene. "You were no trouble at all. And Mr. Gregson is right – you are breathtaking. Now go do me proud and dazzle everyone you see."

As Ian guided Tessa to the elevators, he wanted nothing more than to pull her in close for a long, deep kiss. But he was unfortunately all too aware of the curious pairs of eyes that followed them along, and he chose instead to merely keep a discreet hand on the small of her back. Once inside the elevator – which was occupied, much to his chagrin – he took hold of her hand as though they were teenagers, and received a bright smile from Tessa. Unable to resist her a moment longer, and not giving a damn who was looking, he pulled her against him for a soft, lingering kiss.

When he lifted his head, the elevator was stopping at the

ground floor, everyone around them smiling indulgently, and Tessa's eyes were as shiny as the sapphire at her throat.

"Come along, darling," he murmured, tucking her against his side. "Cinderella's carriage awaits."

The "carriage" was the black Lincoln MKT Town Car that Ian utilized primarily for business purposes, or if he thought he might have a bit more than usual to drink at an event. He introduced Tessa to Simon, the tall, silver-haired Welshman who'd worked as his chauffeur since he'd moved to San Francisco. Simon was quiet, efficient, and extremely discreet – not that Ian was in the habit of engaging in amorous activities in the backseat of the vehicle. He was a firm believer in discretion, and that there was a time and a place for everything. He was too old now and too straight-laced to ever seriously consider having sex in a public place or even his car. The privacy of his own home, or the owner's suite at one of the company's hotels was a different matter entirely. Especially if the blonde beauty currently snuggled against his side was closeted up in the room with him.

He kept an arm about Tessa's shoulders during the short drive to the restaurant. The top of her silky hair brushed up against his nose, and he inhaled deeply of the scent of her shampoo.

"Your hair smells like cinnamon and vanilla," he murmured, then pressed a kiss to her temple. He took a long, shiny strand of her hair between his fingers. "And it feels like silk."

Tessa nodded. "I love how soft and shiny it is right now. I'm such a klutz with a blow dryer that I could never get it to look like this. The stylist wanted to cut some of it, but we didn't have enough time."

"Good." He nuzzled his face into her hair. "I like your hair long."

She patted his arm reassuringly. "It was only going to be a couple of inches, just a trim. I like my hair long, too."

Ian captured her mouth in a soft kiss. "Then I'll take you back to the salon soon when there's more time. Or to any other salon you'd prefer if this one wasn't to your liking."

"It was perfect," she told him. "They treated me like a queen. Or a movie star. But I can't let you keep doing things like that."

"Why not? I told you earlier today that I intended to spoil you, and I meant it."

Tessa looked uneasy. "I just don't feel right letting you buy me all these things. I mean, I know I've worked for you for over two years but – well, we don't really *know* each other."

He tucked her glossy hair behind one ear. "I know that, Tessa," he said gently. "And I certainly don't want to overwhelm you or make you feel uncomfortable. I think perhaps I've just wanted for so long now to be with you, to take care of you, and, yes – get to know you – that I'm probably coming on a bit too strong. We'll take this as slowly as you want to, all right, love?"

She nodded, then gave him an impish little grin. "Well, not *too* slowly."

Ian laughed and hugged her close. "It's all up to you, darling. I'm just your willing servant. Now, you haven't asked me where we're having dinner."

Tessa shrugged. "Anyplace you choose is fine with me. I'm afraid I don't know very much about restaurants in San Francisco, just the few little places in my neighborhood. And I'm guessing we aren't going to Zen Sushi or El Toro Taqueria."

He wrinkled his nose. "Your guess would be correct. I think we'd both be a bit overdressed for either of those fine establishments. No, this evening we're dining at Le Mistral. Have you heard of it?"

She shook her head. "No, I don't think so. Is it French?"

He picked up her hand and kissed it. "*Oui, mademoiselle*. It's very French and very romantic. And best of all, they have private dining rooms so that you and I can – ah, get to know each other."

Tessa had a wistful look on her face. "You speak French, don't you? So does Julia. I heard her talking to Henri the last time she was in the office."

"Yes, though my French is not quite as good as Julia's. I also speak Italian and Spanish and some German and Portuguese."

She used her thumb to trace a little pattern over their clasped hands. "You're so smart and accomplished. I love hearing you talk at meetings. Not that I always understand what's being discussed, but I just like the sound of your voice."

Grateful for the unquestionable discretion of his chauffeur, Ian hauled her against him and gave her a deep, searing kiss. At the sound of her low but audible moan, he reluctantly lifted his head, only to whisper in a husky tone, "I hope you'll like hearing all the things I plan on saying to you when we're alone. And I'll be sure to say them in English so that you understand every single word."

He felt her quiver in arousal against him, and knew that if he slid his hand inside her coat he would find the hardened peak of her nipple.

"It's okay," she whispered back. "Even if I can't really understand you, I think hearing you speak French or Italian would be incredibly romantic. And sexy."

Ian groaned. "I fear that when I take you to my bed I'm going to forget my own damned name, much less how to say it in French."

Simon pulled up to the restaurant moments later, holding the back door open as Ian exited first, then assisted Tessa out. It was a chilly evening, and he smiled indulgently as she snuggled deeper into her new coat.

"I'm developing a serious case of envy for that coat," he grumbled as he opened the door to the restaurant.

She giggled as she preceded him inside. "How can you be envious of a coat?"

He slid his arms around her waist, hugging her back against his chest. "Because it's wrapped around your body, and I'd give anything at this moment to change places with it."

He pressed a little closer against her buttocks, and he knew from the little gasp she made that she could feel the heavy ridge of his erection, even through the fabric of her coat. He was grateful that he was wearing a black wool overcoat of his own, which he quickly buttoned before approaching the host stand, hiding his rather obvious arousal.

Ian patronized this restaurant often enough that many of the staff knew him by name. Tonight the maître d' himself – Victor - greeted Ian, who then introduced him to Tessa.

Victor was far too discreet and well-trained to betray even a hint of surprise at seeing Ian here with a date – and with a woman who was obviously quite a bit younger than he was.

"Welcome to Le Mistral, Mademoiselle," greeted Victor as he shook Tessa's hand. "I can guarantee that you will have the most wonderful meal of your life this evening. Now, if you please, follow me to your table. You are in the Blue Room as requested, Monsieur Gregson."

The Blue Room was a small, private dining room that could hold up to a dozen guests comfortably. Ian had hosted a number of business dinners here as well as entertained family members when they had visited. But for tonight he and Tessa would be the only occupants.

As he took Tessa's coat and hung it on the corner rack, he smiled to observe her as she took in the truly fabulous interior of the private room. A fresco in blues and golds had been painted on the domed ceiling; the walls were papered in a blue and cream stripe; and the thick carpet beneath their feet was of a lush shade of blue. Ian was thankful to note that the large dining table that was usually in this room had been temporarily moved out and replaced with a much smaller, more intimately sized one. It was set with pristine white linens, exquisite blue floral china, gleaming flatware, and fine crystal, the high backed chairs upholstered in a pale blue fabric.

Tessa's eyes were wide with wonder as she turned to him. "This is so lovely. Like a palace. I've never been anywhere like this before."

Her heartfelt confession tugged at his emotions, and he feared he was going to continue discovering just how little Tessa had experienced or been given in her life thus far.

"I'm glad you like it," was all he said in reply. "I entertain business associates here quite a lot and the food is just about the best in the city. And," he added, "there's the extra bonus of these private rooms. I doubt we'd run into anyone from the office here this evening but it's always a possibility."

"Oh." Tessa bit her bottom lip, as though that thought hadn't occurred to her until now. "You're sure it's all right?"

"Yes, it's fine. Not to mention that Victor is extremely discreet and would never dream of telling anyone that I was here this evening. We'll need to talk some about how we're going to have to conduct ourselves around the office, but that can keep.

For now, let's have a seat, shall we?"

The waiter entered the room just after they had seated themselves, and Ian grinned broadly as he greeted the man.

"I was hoping they'd assign you to this table, Roland," he told the waiter. "This is Miss Lockwood, my dining companion. Tessa, Roland is the very best waiter here at Le Mistral. I know he'll take excellent care of us this evening."

Roland, a short, slightly rotund man with an Eastern European accent, told Tessa how delighted he was to meet her and assured her that Mr. Gregson was correct – he would strive to take very good care of them.

Tessa looked a bit uncertain when Roland asked for their cocktail orders, and Ian swiftly came to the rescue. "I'll have my usual, please. As for the lady – let's see. Do you like lemonade, Tessa?"

She nodded, visibly grateful for his assistance. "Yes, very much."

"Then a lemon drop for the lady, Roland."

Roland bustled off to get their drinks and Tessa smiled at Ian in relief.

"Thank you for that. I'm not much of a drinker," she confessed. "Just a little wine or champagne on occasion. Peter – he didn't like keeping alcohol around the apartment."

"Why was that?" Ian inquired curiously.

Tessa paused for a moment before replying. "He grew up with an alcoholic mother who was also abusive. Peter had a rough time of it with her and just couldn't handle having any liquor around as a result."

Ian nodded. "That's perfectly understandable. And you don't ever have to feel pressure to drink if you don't choose to, Tessa."

A busboy entered the room while they waited for their cocktails, filling water glasses and setting out a basket of assorted breads and a beautifully arranged plate of olives, charcuterie, and pates. Roland arrived a moment later with their drinks – the lemon drop in a frosted martini glass for Tessa, and Ian's preferred blend of single malt Scotch in a heavy crystal tumbler.

"Sir, I'll leave the menus for you to look over at your leisure.

Enjoy your cocktails," offered Roland.

Alone again, Ian picked up his glass and clinked it lightly against Tessa's. "To getting to know each other," he toasted with a gentle smile.

Her cheeks flushed fetchingly as she smiled in agreement and took a tentative sip of her drink.

"It's delicious," she told him. "Thank you for suggesting it."

"My pleasure, darling. And while it may taste like lemonade it's a great deal stronger, so sip it slowly, all right?" he cautioned.

She nodded. "Yes, of course. I'm – sorry if all of this is so new to me. I'm sure all the other women you date must be - "

"Stop." He placed a finger over her lips. "First, I believe I already told you not to apologize for anything. And second, despite what you might think, there have actually been very few women I've dated in my life. Especially not in the past two years."

Tessa was gaping at him in surprise. "But there are always photos of you in the newspaper and – and Gina and Alicia are always talking about who you escorted to this event or the other."

Ian shook his head in mild disgust. "Don't believe anything those two shrews say, especially Alicia. I'm well aware of how much they gossip, but I promise you they know next to nothing about my personal life. Suffice it to say that attending a social function with a female friend or acquaintance doesn't always equate to dating her." He reached across the table and took her hand. "I know this is all new to you, Tessa. And while I don't want to ever make you feel ill at ease, at the same time it makes me very happy to know that I'll have the honor of introducing you to a great many pleasures. Both in and out of my bed."

Her lips trembled and her eyes grew wide at his last statement. Glancing down, he had to stifle a groan when he noticed the hard peaks of her nipples poking against her dress, betraying the arousal she felt from his softly spoken words.

"We'd better start looking at the menu," he murmured huskily, and handed her one of the heavy leather-bound books.

Ian was aware of Tessa's distress from the moment she began to scan the expansive and complex menu, with its numerous courses and elaborate descriptions. And when she began to twirl a lock of hair around her finger in agitation, he asked her gently, "Would you like me to order for both of us, Tessa?"

She looked up at him gratefully. "You wouldn't mind? I'm sor – I mean, I'm just not familiar with a lot of these dishes."

"I know." He gave her hand a reassuring squeeze. "And I don't mind in the least, darling." He picked up her hand and brought it to his cheek. "You'll soon learn, Tessa, that there isn't anything I wouldn't do for you."

Her glossy pink mouth fell open in a round "O" of surprise at his quietly impassioned declaration. He was astonished to see the shimmer of tears in her eyes, and his heart ached as one teardrop began to trickle slowly down her rosy cheek.

"You're so good to me," she whispered. "So kind. I don't have any idea how I got this lucky."

"Darling." He reached across and softly kissed each of her eyelids, brushing the tears away with his thumb. "It's not luck – it's fate. You were meant for me all along, Tessa. It just took a while for the stars to align properly. Now, let's take a look at this menu together, hmm? You tell me if there's something I suggest that you don't like."

With her approval, he ordered the lobster salad, a creamy porcini mushroom soup, and the salmon in sorrel sauce, accompanied by a crisp French Chardonnay.

In between courses of the delicious, beautifully prepared food, he subtly tried to engage her in conversation, and to open up a little more about herself.

"Were you born in Tucson?"

Tessa took a small sip of her wine, then shook her head. "No. According to my birth certificate I was actually born in Savannah, Georgia. But I have no memories of the place and my mother never talked about it. Mostly I grew up in the Southwest."

"Do your parents still live in that area?"

There was another pause before she replied, and he sensed she was choosing her words carefully. "I don't know where my father is. I've never actually met him or even know his name. And my mother is dead."

Ian frowned, not sure what disturbed him more – the

information that Tessa had just shared or the sad, almost matter-of-fact way in which she had done so.

"I'm so sorry, love," he told her sincerely. "Was your mother's death recent?"

"No, it was several years ago."

A very young age to find herself without parents, he thought grimly. Ian guessed there was more – a great deal more – that she wasn't telling him, but this was certainly not an evening where he intended to make her talk about sad things. There would be time enough to learn her life's story on another occasion. But there was one question that he desperately wanted an answer to.

"Was Peter your first boyfriend?"

Tessa seemed startled at his question. "Um – yes, actually. Why do you ask?"

Ian ran a finger around the rim of his wineglass. "You seem extraordinarily shy, especially around men. I'm just assuming that you don't have much experience with other men besides your husband."

She gave a slight nod. "Peter is the only man I've ever been with. He – we've know each other since high school. He was the only family I had, but now he's left me, too."

"What?" He was dumbfounded. "Peter was the one to leave? I thought – I just assumed you had initiated the divorce."

"No. Peter left last September for Bahrain to start his new job. It was his idea to split up, especially since I wouldn't have been able to move with him."

Ian could only shake his head in disbelief. "How in the world could he – could any man – just walk away from you? It's inconceivable, Tessa."

"It's not what you think," she told him quietly. "Peter and I – well, it's a very long, involved story. The reasons we married and stayed together – it's complicated."

"Then let's not discuss it tonight," he declared firmly. "Tonight is about getting to know each other better, but not sharing stories that make you sad. I don't ever want to make you sad, Tessa."

She gave him a smile that went right to his groin, and what she said next made him stifle a groan.

"You don't," she assured him. "Being with you here this evening – it's the happiest I've felt in a very long time."

Ian leaned over and kissed her tenderly. "My darling girl, you have no idea how happy that makes *me* to hear. And I intend to work very hard on making any sad thoughts or memories you've ever had disappear as though they never existed. In other words, I'm planning to devote myself to making you happier than you've ever been before."

The rest of the meal passed by without any additional references to Tessa's past. Instead, he focused on learning any number of little things about her – likes and dislikes – such as her favorite color (blue), favorite flavor of ice cream (cookie dough), and favorite movie (the hopelessly romantic *Sleepless In Seattle*). He also discovered that she exercised every day, liked to cook but admittedly wasn't terribly skilled at it, and that of all the places in the world she'd ever dreamed of visiting, Italy and Spain were at the top of her list.

"I suppose you've been to both places," she said wistfully.

"Yes, many times. My family owns a villa in Tuscany, so we've vacationed there for decades. Perhaps you'll let me take you there sometime," he offered.

Tessa's face lit up with delight. "Really? You'd really want to take me to Italy with you?"

Ian smiled at her obvious pleasure at the idea. "Of course, love. If you'll allow me, Tessa, I'd happily show you the world."

She sighed. "God, could you be any more romantic? You're starting to make my head spin with all of this – this splendor."

"Ah, no more wine for you then," he teased. "Besides, it's nearly time for dessert."

He had actually been keeping a careful eye on her alcohol consumption after she'd told him that she seldom drank. When he had poured her more wine, it had only been in small amounts at a time. But aside from her rosy cheeks and the way she appeared to have relaxed a little more, Tessa certainly didn't seem drunk or even tipsy. Which was very fortunate because he hadn't entirely given up hope on the way he wished this evening might end.

Dessert was a trio of mini pots de crème – one each in dark chocolate, caramel and mocha. They fed each other bites with the tasting spoons playfully, as though they'd been lovers for years. Ian sipped a post-dinner brandy while Tessa had wisely passed on more alcohol and was drinking tea instead.

"So how did you come to favor Darjeeling?" he inquired. "It's not as well-known as other blends like Earl Grey or English Breakfast."

"Mrs. Carrington," replied Tessa. "She got me started on it. I had a terrible cold one day, but was refusing to go home until I finished some work. So she brewed me a cup of Darjeeling and insisted I drink it if – let's see if I can remember her exact words – ah, it was something like 'if you're going to continue to act like a mule headed child and stay here in your condition, then the least you should do is have some hot tea.' She watched me while I drank the entire cup, and then forced me to go home, threatening to fire me if I didn't."

Ian laughed heartily at the story. "Yes, that sounds exactly like our Mrs. C. Unfortunately, charm is not one of her better qualities."

Tessa smiled. "She was tough but she made me a better employee. And in her own way, she was kinder to me than almost anyone else in my life had ever been before."

He filed that particular snippet of information away for another time. "How did you come to work at the resort?"

"Through a job placement program at the community college I was attending. After my first year of office tech classes, I had acquired enough skills to get a part-time job. When I finished the program a year later I was lucky enough that a full-time position was open."

"You never thought about continuing your education?" he inquired casually. "Or getting your degree?"

Tessa bent her head as though the question embarrassed her. "I wasn't – well, a very good student in high school. Things came hard for me, actually. I just seemed better suited to working than going to college."

He frowned. "I find that difficult to believe. You're one of the brightest and hardest working employees I've ever had."

She looked incredibly pleased at his compliment. "But that's just office work – clerical stuff. Things like word processing and spreadsheets came easy for me. Other subjects like algebra and biology not so much."

Tessa seemed anxious to change the subject, and he allowed her then to turn the tables and ask questions about him. She learned that he had been a three-time boxing champion at Oxford, and that he still worked out at a gym several times a week to keep his skills sharp; that *his* favorite flavor of ice cream was Haagen Dazs chocolate peanut butter; and that his favorite movie of all time was *National Lampoon's Animal House*. She hadn't believed the latter until he'd begun to recite dialog and recall scenes from the film.

And when he told her that he had been engaged once but that it hadn't worked out, she didn't probe further, merely touching his hand and telling him she was sorry. It seemed that she was no more eager to delve into his past this evening than she was to reveal hers.

He had already handed Roland his AMEX black card and was waiting for him to return with the credit slip when he took Tessa's hands in his.

"Would you do something for me, darling?" he asked. "It's something I've wanted you to do for a very long time."

She looked a bit uncertain for a moment or two, but then nodded emphatically. "Yes, of course I will. What is it?"

Ian cupped her cheek. "Say my name. That's all. All this time it's been 'Mr. Gregson' or 'Sir'. I want to hear my real name on your lips."

Tessa smiled sweetly. "That's an easy request – Ian."

He brushed his thumb over her lips. "I'm looking forward to hearing you say that over and over."

The weather had declined during their nearly three hour dinner, the wind whipping up and dark storm clouds gathering above. Ian kept Tessa snuggled closely against him as they walked towards the waiting Town Car.

He stopped before helping her inside. "Tessa, would you – Christ, I feel like a gangly adolescent asking you this – but would you like to see my home?"

He waited with barely concealed patience for her answer, not at all sure how she would respond. Long seconds ticked by before she finally gave a small nod.

"Yes, I'd love to see your home – Ian."

He was sure he was grinning like a fool as he handed her inside the car, and then told Simon, "Take us to the house, mate."

Chapter Ten

Tessa tried desperately to quell her nerves during the drive to Ian's house. He had caught her a bit off-guard with his unexpected question, and her initial reaction had been to decline the invitation to see his home. But he had looked and sounded so hopeful, almost shy, that she hadn't been able to refuse. Now, however, she kept wondering if she'd made the right decision.

The past twenty-four hours had been like a hurricane force whirlwind, to say the least. So much had happened in such a short period of time that she felt like she was on a crazy carnival ride that just kept on going. Of course, it had all started with Ian's very unexpected reaction to her in his office last evening, followed by his shocking admission that he'd been attracted to her for over two years. Tessa had never, ever imagined that her elegant, debonair boss could actually desire her, much less for all those months when he'd known she was married to another man. She was still having difficulty in processing that bit of news, and wanted to pinch herself every few minutes to make sure she was really cuddled up against his big body in the back seat of his luxurious car.

And her head was definitely still spinning from the swiftness and ease with which Ian had arranged for everything – the clothing and salon treatments at Neiman Marcus, reserving the private dining room at Le Mistral. He was sweeping her off her feet and spinning her around in circles, and she wasn't sure if she wanted to get off the ride or have it continue without end.

Tessa knew that simply agreeing to see his house didn't necessarily mean she'd consented to sleeping with him. Instinctively, she knew Ian would never dream of forcing or coercing her – he was too gallant, too much a gentleman to do such a thing. He was also so incredibly handsome and overwhelmingly male that he would never need to sweet talk a woman into his bed – they would line up eagerly for the privilege. So why was she even thinking about refusing him?

She turned her face into his broad shoulder, liking the feel of his fine wool overcoat against her cheek. His clean, masculine scent filled her senses, and she couldn't resist nuzzling her nose against the warm skin of his throat.

Ian slid his hand to the back of her head, tilting it back for his kiss. Tessa gave a little "mmm" of pleasure as his tongue swept through her mouth, and she wrapped her arms around his neck, urging his head even closer towards hers. He gave a low growl and hauled her onto his lap. He tasted of brandy and chocolate, and Tessa was quickly losing herself in his devouring kisses as they continued for long minutes.

"God, what you do to me," he whispered in a raw voice. "You make me forget my own name with just a kiss."

"It's the same for me," she whispered back.

Ian kissed her again, but this time quickly, gently, and then he reluctantly eased her back onto the seat.

"Not here, darling," he murmured in a low voice. "If this car had a privacy panel it would be a very different matter. But we don't want to shock poor Simon, or give him a show."

Under cover of the dark interior of the car, he slid his hand up beneath her coat and dress until he reached the lacy top of her stocking. She gasped as he caressed her thigh, and then realized belatedly just how aroused she was. She squirmed restlessly beneath his hand, longing for him to slide it further up her leg until he was cupping her aching sex.

Instead, he slowly withdrew his hand, his voice low against her ear. "Shh. I have no intention of making you moan when we have an audience, even one as discreet as Simon. Your pleasure is going to be for my eyes and ears only. We'll be at my home very soon now."

Tessa was trembling in arousal as he stayed a safe distance away, merely linking their hands together casually. To distract herself from the growing need for physical release, she forced herself to look out the window, trying to determine where they were headed. It was obvious from the size and elegance of the houses they drove by that they were in a very affluent neighborhood, and Tessa was fairly certain from the street names that it was the exclusive Pacific Heights area.

Two blocks later, Simon was pulling through a set of wrought iron gates that he'd used a remote control to open and parking on the side of a stately red brick mansion. Because it was so dark and cloudy outside, Tessa couldn't make out too many exterior details, but there was little doubt that Ian's home was a multimillion dollar residence.

Ian helped her out of the car, then went around to the driver's side to speak to Simon briefly. Then he was taking Tessa by the hand and leading her up to the wide front door. He drew out his phone and punched in a code, explaining that he was disengaging the alarm system. He unlocked the door and ushered her inside, and Tessa could only stare in stunned disbelief.

The foyer of his home was nearly as large as her entire apartment, and she swiftly took in as many details as possible – from the high ceilings to the polished oak floors to the wide staircase that led to the upper and lower floors of the grand house. There was beautiful artwork on the walls and a plush Persian carpet covering part of the floor. She had never been inside such a magnificent, elegant home before, and she had barely begun to see any of it.

"Let me take your coat, Tessa," offered Ian, as his hands went to her shoulders. As she unbuttoned it and he helped her remove it, he added teasingly, "I promise to return it to you, despite my jealousy."

She gave a nervous little laugh as he opened an entryway closet and hung both of their coats inside. She left her purse on a long, low table that held a fabulous floral arrangement inside a porcelain bowl with an Oriental design.

She had feared she'd feel cold without her coat, but Ian's home was blissfully warm and cozy, a far cry from her old, drafty apartment. To save money on her heating bill, she usually kept the heater turned off these days, choosing instead to bundle up in multiple layers to keep warm.

"Here, we'll give you the grand tour," said Ian as he took her hand and began to lead her from room to room.

His house reflected his vibrant, charismatic personality in each and every room – from the living room with its dark furniture and huge stone fireplace, to the more intimate library with more books than a person could ever hope to read in one lifetime, to the enormous kitchen with its state of the art appliances, brick wall oven and black granite countertops. There were windows everywhere, and Tessa imagined on a sunny day that the house would be flooded with natural light.

"The views from the back terrace are incredible, even at night, but since it's just begun to rain I'll have to show you the exterior another time," he told her regretfully.

"I'll look forward to it," she told him, trying not to sound giddy with excitement that he was already talking about having her visit again. In fact, nearly everything he had said about their budding relationship thus far seemed to indicate that he intended for it to be a long-term thing and not just a brief affair. But Tessa forced herself not to get too hopeful, especially once Ian fully realized just how naïve and inexperienced she really was. Once he did, it was entirely possible that he'd regret seeking her out and that her lack of sophistication would prove an embarrassment to him.

"Let's go see the other floors," he urged, and led her down the long, winding staircase to the lower level.

"Do you have live-in help?" she inquired. "I mean, this just seems like a really big place for only one person."

Ian shook his head. "I have a housekeeper here about three days a week, and a gardener as needed but no one lives here but myself. It is a very large house for just me, but I happen to value my privacy a great deal. And I have to travel so much for business that I'm simply not here all that often."

"It's a beautiful home," she told him sincerely. "And it still feels warm and intimate despite how grand it is."

He seemed pleased at her compliment. "That's the exact effect I was striving for. Of course, I worked with a decorator when I first bought the place, but I had very definite ideas about what I wanted. Plus, I've collected a great deal of artwork and other items during all my years of traveling and so now they have a permanent place to be displayed."

The lower level of the house was clearly the pleasure center of the home, for it consisted of an immense wine cellar, a home theater, a fitness room, and a billiard/card room complete with its own bar. Tessa was in stunned disbelief that one home could really boast so much luxury and space, never having imagined that people actually lived this way. It made her feel uneasy, for seeing up close what an opulent, privileged lifestyle Ian enjoyed only served to emphasize the vast cultural and economic gaps between the two of them. His world of moneyed extravagance was completely foreign to her, and she feared she could never fit in or feel entirely comfortable with such a lavish way of life.

But she struggled to hide her various insecurities and doubts as he led her back upstairs, and then continued to the upper level of the house.

There were a total of five bedrooms on this level, each with their own attached bath, and each one larger and more beautifully decorated than the last. The final bedroom was located at the end of the hallway, and featured a set of wide double doors at the entrance.

"This is my room," Ian told her quietly, and then opened the doors wide.

Tessa walked inside the enormous room slowly as he flicked on a lamp somewhere. Ian's master suite was easily larger than her entire apartment, kitchen and bath included, and every bit as lavish as the rest of the house. She imagined the view from the bank of windows set against the far end of the room would be breathtaking, and she could envision herself curling up on the wide, padded window seat sipping tea and watching the sun rise. The furniture in here was all dark, polished woods and clean, simple lines, large pieces that nonetheless didn't dwarf the room. Like the rest of the house, there was nothing the least bit fussy or overdone, and it was very obvious that this was a man's room.

Tessa's gaze fell to the imposing four poster bed, easily the largest of its kind she'd ever seen. It was covered in a thick duvet of a pale mocha shade, both luxurious and simple at the same time. She couldn't resist running her hand over it lightly, the fabric soft and almost velvety to the touch.

"Do you like it, Tessa?"

She whirled to face Ian, who was standing just behind her.

He'd removed his suit jacket and tie as she'd been inspecting the room, and her breath caught at the splendid sight of his white shirt stretching across the broad expanse of his chest and shoulders.

Aware that he was waiting for her reply, she nodded and then glanced away abruptly. "It's wonderful, Ian. This is – way beyond anything I could have ever imagined. I've never seen so much – well, I suppose splendor is a good word for it."

Tessa shivered in reaction as he came up behind her, pressing his body against hers and lightly running his fingertips up and down her bare arms.

"I've wanted you here in my house – my room – my bed for so long now, darling," he murmured in her ear, his lips caressing the side of her throat. At the same time, his arms circled her waist, one hand splayed over her belly as he pulled her in closer. "I never imagined it would actually happen, though. Seeing you here now like this – tell me I'm not dreaming again, Tessa."

The pleading tone of his voice startled her, for he sounded almost desperate. She was quick to reassure him.

"You aren't dreaming. I'm really here. But I'm the one who feels like she's in some fantastic dream world," she confessed.

His tongue began to trace erotic little patterns around her ear before he gently nibbled on the lobe. "If you aren't ready for this, I promise I'll understand. I won't ever pressure you, Tessa. So tell me – should I drive you home or will you stay here with me?"

Tessa closed her eyes as her head fell back onto his shoulder, one of his hands now stroking her hip and then up the side of her rib cage. "What – what happens if I stay?"

Ian's voice grew huskier, and was filled with so much raw passion that she felt she might swoon. "Then I do what I've dreamed about doing since the first time I met you – undress you slowly, lay you out on my bed, and then taste and touch every inch of this beautiful body." His hand slid up her abdomen to cup her breast, his thumb brushing masterfully over her erect nipple. "After that I'll slide inside of you, all the way in, and stay there for a long time. Hours, maybe days. After all, I've got two years of unfulfilled fantasies to satisfy."

"Ah, that's so good," she whispered roughly, as his hand squeezed her breast, his fingers plucking the nipple through the fabric of her dress. "Please, Ian."

"Tell me first, Tessa," he demanded. "Will you stay – or should I take you home?"

Tessa cried out as one of his hands slid down to cup her sex. "Oh, God! S-stay! I want to stay here with you."

"Thank Christ," muttered Ian as he kept one arm banded about her waist, while grasping her chin with his other hand. He tilted her head back to meet his blistering kiss, his tongue ravaging her mouth. This kiss had none of the finesse of his previous ones; this particular kiss was all raw hunger, all fevered possession, and Tessa groaned as her arousal built quickly to the boiling point. She tried to turn so that she could touch him, wind her arms about his neck, but his grip around her waist was immovable.

"Let me see you now, love," he whispered unevenly, and it gave her a thrill to hear how hard he was breathing, to know that he was as turned on as she was.

Tessa's eyelids fluttered shut as he began to slowly unzip her dress. She let her arms fall to the sides as he eased the fabric off her shoulders and then down past her hips. Ian gripped one of her arms to steady her as she stepped out of the dress, and she felt his gaze on her nearly nude body like it was a burning thing. Though she kept her eyes closed she could sense his presence strongly, felt him circle around her once, twice, and her cheeks burned to realize how closely he must be inspecting her body.

But she was completely unprepared for what happened next, and her eyes flew open in shocked surprise as Ian knelt at her feet, wrapping his arms around her legs and resting his forehead on her thighs. His dark head was bent, and she was startled to see how much he was struggling for control.

"My God, you are so beautiful, Tessa," he rasped in an almost incoherent voice. "God knows I wanted so badly to take this first time slowly, to savor every second, but now I don't think I'm capable of that. I've wanted you too badly for too long to control myself that way. This first time – I just need to have you, love."

She gasped as his hands gripped her hips and he lifted his head to nuzzle at the dampened crotch of her lacy blue panties. A cry of surprise escaped from her throat as he wrenched the fragile underwear farther down her thighs, and then thrust two long fingers deep inside of her core.

Ian swore softly. "Christ, you're so wet, Tessa. And so damned tight. God, as hard as I am right now I don't know how much longer I can hold back. But I don't want to hurt you, either."

"I don't care," she choked out, her hips moving instinctively with the thrust of his fingers. "I can't wait, either. It's too good, too – ahh!"

With just the smallest flick of his thumb against her clit, Tessa's long-starved-for-attention body burst into a shuddering climax, her legs threatening to give out from under her. And while she was still in the blissful throes of her orgasm, Ian swept her into his arms, tearing the duvet off the bed with one impatient hand and then dropped her onto the mattress.

"Take off your shoes and panties," he told her in a deep, commanding voice, as he began to rather clumsily unbutton his shirt and toe off his shoes. "Leave everything else on. I'll finish undressing you later."

Tessa obeyed, then watched wide-eyed as he unbuckled his belt and shoved his pants off. She was stunned at the sheer size of his erection as it strained against his snug fitting black briefs, and couldn't tear her eyes off of it. He removed his socks and then quickly divested himself of his underwear, baring his truly magnificent body to her gaze.

"Oh, my God," she whispered dazedly at the sight of his powerful, heavily muscled body. He looked like a gladiator, like the prize fighter he had been in his youth, and she doubted a more beautiful man existed anywhere in the world.

And then she was beyond any sort of thought – rational or otherwise – as he climbed onto the huge bed beside her. He rolled her beneath his body, his chest heaving with the tremendous effort he was exerting to keep himself under some small bit of control, and she almost recoiled at the look of smoldering, dangerous passion in his eyes.

"I can't take this slow or easy," he told her harshly. "I want you too damned much. Next time I'll have more control but for now this is how it must be."

Tessa's mouth fell open in shock but for once no sound escaped her lips as Ian surged fully inside her tight, hot core in one powerful thrust. He was unbelievably big, not to mention hard and hot, and she felt impaled by his bare, throbbing cock buried so deeply inside her body.

"Jesus," he uttered rawly. "I could come right now, just like this, without moving an inch. That's what you do to me, Tessa. And as many times as I've imagined this moment, I never dreamed it could feel this good."

He drew her stockinged legs up to wrap around his hips, and she whimpered as this movement drove him even deeper into her body, impossible as that seemed. Ian leaned down and kissed her wetly, open-mouthed, his lips and tongue eating relentlessly at her mouth. So aroused and needy she felt like she might faint, Tessa wound her arms around his neck, groaning beneath his kisses as he began to thrust his heavy cock in and out of her now yielding body.

She felt tears begin to trickle down her cheeks, sobbing softly at the tremendous pleasure he was wringing from her body, pleasure she'd never known she was capable of feeling. The sensation built with each dominant thrust of his body, each time he stroked that magnificent cock in and out of her tight, clenching pussy, until she exploded in a massive, earth shattering orgasm that she could feel in every nerve ending in her body. Moments later she dimly heard Ian give a shout, and then he was coming hard, his big body shuddering repeatedly as he emptied himself deep inside of her.

Tessa wasn't even aware of the heavy weight of his body nearly crushing hers into the mattress as he lay sprawled atop her. Their limbs were entangled, a fine sheen of perspiration covering their skin as they both struggled for breath. She wasn't certain whose heart was beating faster – hers or his – or if the rapid thumps were one in the same. Ian's face was buried in the side of her neck, his hair damp to the touch as she tentatively lifted a hand and began to stroke the back of his head.

He let out a long, low groan as he slowly lifted his head, and her heart gave a little start to see the expression of heavy-lidded passion on his darkly flushed face. Her hand cupped his cheek, almost withdrawing at how hot his skin felt, but then he captured her wrist between his fingers, pressing a lingering kiss to her palm.

"That was – extraordinary," he told her in an emotion-laden voice. "I have never, ever, lost control that way in my life. And my assumption was correct earlier today – right now I don't even know my own bloody name."

She gave a soft laugh, running a finger over his firm mouth. "Well, I remember it – Ian."

"God, what you do to me," he moaned. "You're so sweet, so beautiful, and so very, very passionate. I'm already hard for you again, love."

She was shocked to realize he was right – his cock was still buried snugly inside her body and she could feel him begin to swell and harden.

He tilted her head to the side so he could nuzzle the soft spot just beneath her ear. "But next time I intend to do this right and take it very slowly. At least that's the plan. I can't guarantee I'll have any more willpower this time around."

"It's all right," she whispered to him. "I don't mind. I just want to be with you, Ian, any way you want me."

Her sweetly murmured words seemed to further incite him, as he abruptly sat back on his heels and pulled her upright to straddle his lap. His iron-hewed arms curled around her waist like bands of steel as he took her mouth in yet another devouring kiss.

"Don't say things like that to me, love," he told her huskily. "Especially now when my control is barely in check. You'll find yourself being ravished a dozen times over."

"A dozen? Is that some sort of record?" she teased lightly. She was a little surprised that she could feel this sort of instant, comfortable familiarity with him.

Ian chuckled. "It would be something of a challenge, I think, but as much as I want you it might just be possible." Then he frowned slightly as his thumb brushed over the dried traces of her tears. "God, were you crying, Tessa? Tell me I didn't hurt you. I know I was rough, impatient, but - "

"Shh." She placed a fingertip over his lips. "You didn't hurt me. I didn't even realize I had cried until now. I think – what I felt – it was just overwhelming, you know?"

He looked visibly relieved. "I know exactly what you mean. And now, as much as I'd love to have you again just like this, I'm determined to show a bit more finesse this time. Wait here for just a moment, love. Easy now."

But she couldn't suppress a little whimper as he carefully eased his still-erect penis out of her, and then slid off the bed. Tessa remained kneeling in the middle of the bed as Ian disappeared into his en suite bathroom. She could hear the sounds of running water and then watched him walk back out a few moments later, her eyes hungrily taking in every fabulous, naked inch of his glorious body.

In addition to the unbelievably wide shoulders and powerfully sculpted arms, his chest and abs were so magnificently detailed that it made her mouth water in anticipation of pressing hot kisses along every inch of his torso. Her eyes continued their downward path to the tautness of his stomach and to his strong, muscular thighs and legs before fixating on the intimidating thickness of his cock.

She couldn't quite believe that *that* had just been deep inside her body – that she had actually been able to accept a man like him. He was built like a mythological being, a Greek God like Apollo or Hercules, or the gladiator she'd likened him to earlier. She stared in unabashed lust as he grew even harder and longer beneath her fevered gaze, the velvety head of his penis reaching upwards towards his belly.

His voice was dangerous and low as he approached the bed, a dampened washcloth in his hand. "If you keep looking at me that way, Tessa, I'm going to quickly lose all control again. And we'd just have to keep trying until we finally get to do this my way."

She licked her lips, unable to tear his gaze away from his throbbing dick. After the years of abuse he'd suffered, Peter hadn't been able to tolerate having his penis touched in any way, and so Tessa had never given a man a blow job. But at this moment, all she wanted was to take Ian's big, beautiful cock into her mouth and pleasure him for hours.

"Would you let me – can I - " she pleaded tremulously.

Ian's eyes darkened. "Jesus, Tessa. Don't, at least not now. Before this weekend is over I want that sexy mouth of yours to touch every inch of my body. I'm going to take you in a dozen different ways, and you, darling girl, can gladly do the same to me. But not this time."

She thought she would be embarrassed to have him wash her, but the feel of the warm, damp cloth between her legs was only soothing. He wiped away the sticky traces of his semen that had already begun to dry halfway down her thighs, then set the used cloth aside before sliding back into bed.

She went into his arms eagerly, her young, healthy body already humming with arousal at just being near him. He buried his face in her hair, crushing her against him.

"Just let me hold you for a minute, love," he pleaded. "I need to compose myself so that we don't have a repeat of what happened earlier. God, I think I was a fifteen year old virgin the last time I went off that quickly. Guess that's what comes from over two years of abstinence."

"What?" Tessa raised her head to gaze down at him in bewilderment. "I don't understand. Two years?"

He smiled up at her and nodded. "I haven't been with anyone else for all that time. I just – couldn't. After I first met you and was so instantly obsessed, I naturally attempted to forget about you with other women. But it soon became very apparent that wasn't going to help. In fact, it made things worse."

She stared in disbelief. "But – all those women – the photos, the articles – why would you -"

He brushed a damp lock of hair off her forehead. "Because if I couldn't have you I didn't want anyone else. I preferred to be celibate rather than settle for something less. And I already explained about the other women – strictly platonic. In fact, most of the women I escorted are involved in one way or another with someone else."

Overcome by the realization of just how much he was attracted to her, Tessa couldn't resist pressing a tentative kiss to his lips. It was the first time she had initiated such an action between them, and she dimly hoped that she wasn't making a fool of herself, betraying her lack of experience.

But then Ian swiftly flipped her onto her back, his powerful thighs straddling her hips as he drew her arms above her head and held them pinned in place.

"Enough, temptress. Now, are you ready to begin round number two? If you intend for me to try to make it an even dozen, we don't have any time to waste."

Chapter Eleven

Ian had imagined this particular scenario dozens of times in the past two and a half years – a warm and willing Tessa spread out on his bed, her lush, ripe body bared to his devouring gaze, and her big blue eyes silently pleading with him to take her any way he pleased. But none of those fantasies could come close to the real thing – the gorgeous, nearly-naked beauty who was staring up at him in wide-eyed wonder, her golden hair tumbled over his pillow.

"How beautiful you are," he murmured, as he dipped his head, his lips brushing her forehead. "How many times I've wished for you to be here just like this, and now it's finally come true." His mouth moved to her temple, then to her rosy cheek before sliding around the curve of her jaw and back up the other side of her face. She was already moaning in arousal, making those little noises that were so incredibly sexy, that made his cock swell a bit harder each time she made one.

"I told you earlier that I intended to touch and kiss every inch of you, Tessa," he told her passionately. "Including this." He dropped a kiss on her nose. "And this." His mouth briefly sucked the skin just behind her ear. "And most definitely this delicious mouth."

He took her soft, sweet mouth in a deep, lingering kiss, his tongue tangling with hers until her groans rose to a fever pitch beneath his relentless kisses.

Tessa was gasping when he finally lifted his head, begging him breathlessly, "Please, Ian."

He laughed softly as his mouth moved to caress the side of her throat, then continued its downward path along her collarbone. "Please what, my sweet?" His hands ran up and down her arms, his fingers toying with the strap of her pale blue bra. "What is it that you need, Tessa?"

Her hips were moving restlessly beneath him, her pelvis starting to lift off the mattress, and he knew she was every bit as aroused as he was. "I need – you," she panted "In – inside of me.

Please."

"Shh. Such an eager little temptress you are," he scolded her teasingly. "And when I haven't even begun to touch and kiss you in all the places I've wanted to do for so long. Have some patience, love."

Tessa's head was thrashing back and forth on the pillow as she tried to grasp his hips and pull him to her. "I - I can't," she pleaded. "I'm too – I need to - "

"To come?" he finished for her, his lips moving in a line across the upper curve of her breasts. "I know, darling. You're very, very responsive, aren't you? Has it always been this easy for you to climax?"

"N-n-no," she cried, as he grasped both of her hands in one of his and drew them over her head. "J-just with you."

"Ah, then, I'll have to make sure I'm satisfying you often and thoroughly. You're going to be a greedy lover, I can tell already. Lucky for me, I'm just as hungry for you, Tessa." He traced one finger around the full globe of each breast, feeling her quiver beneath his touch. "You look gorgeous in this bra, Tessa. It makes these fabulous breasts look even bigger and firmer. And it very much makes me want to touch them and taste them. Let me, darling."

He released her hands, then deftly unhooked the sexy, lacy bra and drew it away, baring her ripe, round breasts to his hot gaze. His big hands cupped both of the lush mounds, shaping them, pushing them up until they appeared even fuller.

"God," was all he could manage to croak. Then he bent his head and began to run his tongue over each taut nipple, flicking the erect peak over and over before drawing it in to his mouth.

Tessa's body bowed off the mattress as she clutched his head to her breast, her hands pulling on his hair. "Ohh, ohh. Yes, more, please. It feels so good."

His cock had never felt this hard before, hard enough that it was almost painful, but the very best sort of pain. The whimpers and moans she made as he continued to feast on her breasts tested every ounce of self-control he had left, and he had never wanted anything more than to slide deep inside her welcoming, eager body at that very moment.

She cried out in frustration as he finally lifted his head, but then gasped again as his hands slid down the side of her ribcage to grip her hips, his mouth tracing its way down between her breasts until it reached her belly. His tongue rimmed her navel, then he pressed kisses across her body from one hipbone to the other. His hands preceded his mouth as he worked his way down to the tops of her thighs where she still wore the silky, lace-topped stockings.

"These are so fucking sexy," he rasped, his language turning coarser than normal, for he was too overcome with lust to temper his reaction to her. "I want these long, lovely legs wrapped around my neck while I'm inside of you so that you can feel me buried as deep as I can go." He ran his hands up and down the outside of her legs. "I'll buy you a dozen pair of these stockings so you can wear them under your skirts and dresses every day, and only you and I will know you have them on. Except I wouldn't be able to keep my hands off of you for too long."

One by one he rolled the stockings off, letting them flutter heedlessly to the floor. Ian pinned her hips to the mattress with his hands, holding her still as his mouth finally reached her cleft. She was wet and glistening, the pouty folds of her labia beckoning him to taste her like she was the juiciest of fruits. With a groan, he delved between her legs and rimmed the opening to her body with his tongue, tasting her there for the first time.

Tessa let out a cry of surprise, her hips thrashing wildly even though he held her firmly in place. "Ian, oh, God, I've never – " she managed to utter in a ragged voice.

He lifted his head, startled at her confession. "Easy, darling, I've got you." Instead of his tongue, he slid two fingers deep inside her soaked slit, amazed at how quickly she became aroused. "Tessa, if you don't want me to touch you that way, then I won't. But I'd love to taste you there, to make you come that way. Will you let me try? I promise to stop if you tell me to."

Her head fell back on the pillow and she closed her eyes. "O-okay," she whispered. "It's okay."

Ian kept his fingers thrusting slowly in and out of her tight passage as he kissed his way back up her inner thighs. "Trust me, love. You're so damned responsive, so easy to arouse. Let me do this for you now."

He was exquisitely gentle, his tongue licking at her damp folds with light flutters. As he felt her begin to relax, he deepened the licks, until he replaced his fingers with his tongue, thrusting it deep inside of her body. His thumb found her clit, manipulating it as he continued to eat her out with expert skill.

"Ian!" She screamed his name as her hips moved in sync with the thrust of his tongue and the stimulation of his thumb, the orgasm causing her whole body to tremble in reaction. And while her core was still convulsing around his mouth, he kept at her, determined that her pleasure continue, licking and stroking and sucking her until she came again.

Tessa was dazed and almost incoherent as he finally slid back up alongside her. If his own body hadn't been screaming almost violently for release, he might have let her rest for a bit. Instead, he flipped her over onto her belly as his hands and mouth caressed her back body – traveling from the nape of her neck where her golden hair was damp from exertion; down between her leanly muscled shoulder blades and the curve of her back to the base of her spine. He squeezed the firm, high cheeks of her buttocks before running his tongue up and down the backs of her thighs and calves.

And then, Ian reached the very end of his limits, not able to wait even a minute longer to have her again. He eased Tessa onto her hands and knees, her gorgeous ass in the air as he knelt behind her.

She cried out in shock as he entered her from behind. "Oh! Oh, God, Ian! I don't – "

"Hush, love. It's all right." He pressed a kiss to her nape as he rubbed her hip soothingly. "Am I hurting you this way?"

She shook her head. "No – it feels – so good. You're just – so deep. I can feel you so deep inside me this way."

He groaned, banding an arm around her waist as he moved inside of her experimentally. "And it feels amazing, doesn't it, love? God, Tessa, I need – need to move now, darling. Easy."

Her little gasps as he slowly, carefully, thrust in and out of her made him even harder, and he couldn't hold back, picking up the frequency and force of his movements until he was fucking her like an animal. Tessa's gasps became screams as he pounded into her, and he felt her convulse around his cock just seconds before he came. Ian's head fell back, his eyes tightly shut as he roared like a jungle beast, spilling himself into her as his body shuddered repeatedly.

They collapsed next to each other on the bed, his arm flung over her body as he struggled to regain some small degree of composure.

"Are you all right?" he was finally able to murmur in her ear. "I wasn't too rough with you?"

Tessa turned into him, looping her arms around his neck and wrapping one leg about his hips. "You were amazing," she whispered huskily. "*That* was amazing. I've never, ever felt anything like that before."

Ian groaned, pulling her even closer against him. "God, you're good for my ego," he told her with a low laugh. "I'm just hoping my tired old body can keep up with your hot young one, even for a little while."

She ran her hands over his shoulders and down his chest, pressing a kiss to the base of his throat. "You are *not* old. I wish you'd stop saying that. And your body is – beautiful, Ian. I can't get enough of it."

Her sweetly spoken words threatened to make him hard again, even though he'd just come so thoroughly he had seen stars. He gave her a soft kiss, then brushed damp strands of her hair off her face.

"I've never felt like this either, you know," he confessed. "Never had such spectacular sex, or come that hard. And I've never, ever felt so much like a man before."

Tessa pulled his head down to hers and kissed him. "I'm not very experienced, you know," she told him uncertainly. "I'll tell you about – well, my marriage at some point so you'll understand what I mean."

He kissed the tip of her nose. "Only when you're ready, darling. And I rather like that you're inexperienced. I'd be very, very happy to teach you a great many things. Wait here, I'll be right back."

When he returned from the bathroom with a clean towel, he smiled indulgently to see that she was almost asleep. Tessa made a small sound of protest as he cleaned her up, and then, as he slid into the bed with her, she snuggled up against him and promptly fell asleep.

Ian gave a low chuckle as he covered them both with the duvet, then pulled her close. "Guess we aren't going to try for that record dozen times after all," he whispered to her. "Never mind, love. There's always tomorrow."

***

Tessa woke reluctantly, semi-conscious as she was of being warmer and more comfortable than she'd ever been in her life. As her eyes opened sleepily, she blinked in disorientation, her sleep-fogged brain taking some time to fully realize where she was. She was definitely not in her own bed, for the mattress cushioning her body was much firmer and plusher than her own, and the pillowcase beneath her cheek smelled crisper and cleaner than her own sheets.

And then she had to stifle a little gasp as she realized exactly where she was – curled up trustingly against Ian's warm, muscular body, her arm draped over his torso, and her head tucked next to his. Ian – who less than two days ago had been her rather intimidating, completely out of her league boss – and who was now, by some quirk of fate, her lover.

Tessa's cheeks flushed when she recalled just how intimate they had been – the things he'd said to her, the way he'd touched and kissed her, how thoroughly he'd taken her. As if on cue, she felt an unfamiliar soreness between her legs, the muscles definitely not used to the sort of physical, demanding sex she'd engaged in.

And she was aroused again, simply from lying next to him as he slept. Her breasts felt swollen and heavy, the nipples already peaking, and she knew if she touched her cleft it would be moist and ready, despite her soreness.

Her eyes slowly grew accustomed to the darkness of the room, lit only by the glow of numbers from the digital bedside clock, and from the streetlights that shone in from outside. Tessa still couldn't quite believe that she was really in Ian's bed, or that everything that had happened in the past thirty-six or so hours wasn't actually a dream. She gazed longingly at the handsome face in repose next to hers, his strong, masculine features sexy even as he slept. The lines of his firm mouth were softer now, and she noticed the dark stubble across his cheeks and chin. She was so used to always seeing him clean shaven that it was a surprise to realize how dark his hair really was. Tessa resisted the urge to press a kiss to his cheek, or run a finger over his lips, not wanting to wake him.

And then she belatedly became aware of another urge, and carefully slid out of bed to use the bathroom. Shivering without the heat of the duvet or Ian's body, she looked around furtively for something to wear and decided on his white dress shirt. The rest of their things were scattered haphazardly around the bedroom, and the sight brought a smile to her lips. She knew from the extreme tidiness of his office that he must be something of a neat freak, and that this disarray of clothing was certainly not the norm for him.

She buttoned up his shirt as she padded into the bathroom, one room she hadn't seen yet. Tessa was in awe of its size and extravagance – all black granite counters, marble floors and walls, and modern fixtures. The walk-in shower was enormous, more than big enough for two people, as was the sunken tub. She wondered if he would ever take her in either of those places – hopefully both – and then blushed anew as she realized where her train of thought had led her.

'God, one night with him and you've turned into some sort of nymphomaniac!' she scolded herself.

She took care of her needs swiftly, and then took an extra minute or so to wash off her makeup, making do with the soap she found by the sink. A quick check inside one of the multitude of drawers and cabinets revealed a tube of toothpaste. She squeezed a dab on her finger and gave her teeth a makeshift brushing.

Tessa left the bathroom and walked over to the bank of windows, peering out through the wooden blinds at the dark, stormy night. The grand house was so well insulated that the sounds of wind and rain were barely discernible but from what she could see the storm was quite fierce.

"Is everything all right, love?"

She whirled at the sound of Ian's sleepy, sexy voice. He had risen onto one elbow, the duvet slipping down to bare his arms and chest, and she couldn't help running her gaze longingly over his heavily muscled torso. He was so beautiful, so incredibly strong and – well, just so *male* – that it made her throat close up to look at him.

"Yes, it's fine. I just needed the bathroom. I'm sorry if I woke you," she told him, walking back towards the bed.

"You didn't wake me," he assured her. He smiled as his gaze flicked over her body. "Nice shirt. It looks much better on you than it does on me."

Tessa laughed. "I disagree. I hope you don't mind my borrowing it."

His eyes twinkled at her mischievously. "Not at all. Though now I'm jealous of the shirt, even more so than your coat, because this is actually touching your bare skin."

She placed her hand in his as he extended an arm towards her. "I may not give this back. It smells like you, after all." She turned her face and inhaled deeply of the soft fabric.

Ian smiled. "You like the way I smell?"

Tessa nodded. "Yes, very much. I used to wish I could just bury my face against your chest and inhale your scent."

His thumb brushed over her knuckles before he drew her hand to his lips. "So you were attracted to me at least a little?" he asked thoughtfully.

"More than a little. I confess to having quite a crush on you for a very long time."

Even in the dimly lit room she could see how his eyes darkened at her confession. "Is that a fact? Well, it seems as though both of us spent far too much time pining for the other. We'd better start making up for lost time then, hadn't we?"

Tessa's breath hitched at the barely restrained passion in his voice, and the way his eyes dropped to her breasts. Her nipples were hard and poking against the fabric of the shirt, and all she could offer in response to his very pointed question was a brief nod.

"Take the shirt off. Slowly."

Her fingers were trembling as she did his bidding, unfastening one button at a time until they were all undone. She slid the shirt off her shoulders and let it fall to the floor.

Ian made a feral sound as he threw the duvet off his body, then swung his long legs over the side of the bed on either side of hers, effectively trapping her between his thighs.

His hands swept up to cup her swollen breasts. "Just so you know," he murmured in a husky voice, "I am obsessed with these perfect tits. They can expect to receive a great deal of attention from me."

"Ahh." She let out a long, low moan as his thumbs brushed over her ultra-sensitive nipples. Her moans grew louder as he pulled on the taut buds, twisting them between thumb and forefinger.

"You like that, love?" he rasped. "Your breasts are very sensitive, aren't they?"

"Yes, yes," she cried as he bent his head and took a nipple in his mouth, sucking hard. She slid her hands into his hair, silently urging him to continue. He moved to the other breast, his tongue flicking over the nipple again and again.

Ian buried his face between her breasts, his tongue tracing a line up and down her deep cleavage. His hands slid around her hips to squeeze her buttocks, and then he swiftly hauled her onto the bed. He lay on his back, pulling her astride him, her thighs straddling the outside of his legs.

"I want you again," he told her raggedly. "As you can plainly see. You're not too sore, are you, love?"

Tessa licked her lips as she glanced down and saw for herself just how aroused he was – his long, thick cock pulsing and fully erect, practically begging to be touched. Tentatively, she reached down and ran a hand lightly over his throbbing length, almost recoiling at how hot and hard he was. But even that faint touch was too much for Ian, his breath hissing out savagely as he grasped her wrist, stilling her motion.

"Not now," he bit out. "Christ, you'll have me coming in your hand in ten seconds if you do that."

Tessa used her free hand to caress his chest, loving the feel of his hot skin and hard muscles. "But I want to touch you, too," she pouted. "Just like you did to me earlier."

He captured her other hand, too, holding both of them immobile by her sides. "I want that, too, darling," he murmured. "More than you can possibly know. I've dreamed of your hands on my body, of you kneeling before me, my cock in your mouth." He lifted his head off the pillow, high enough to give each of her nipples a brief lick. "But not now, love. I seem to lose all control when I'm near you."

She began to rock her pelvis back and forth against him, trying to free her hands. "It's not really fair, you know. Maybe I should have just done what I wanted to you while you were sleeping."

He chuckled. "And maybe someone is becoming very bold and needs a spanking because she's such a wicked girl."

Tessa let out a squeal of surprise as he gave her a quick smack on her right buttock. But any further protest she might have made faded away at his next feverishly murmured words.

"Take me inside you, Tessa. I want you on top this time, riding me. Have you done this before?"

She shook her head. "No. Let me, Ian." She lifted her hips, reaching eagerly for his erection.

"Easy, love," he admonished, his hand guiding hers as she positioned the tip of his penis at the slick entrance to her body.

Tessa gasped as he slowly, gradually, fed his cock inside of her an inch at a time, until she was fully impaled. She was unable to move momentarily as she grew used to the feel of being so completely filled.

Ian's hands grasped her hips, his voice gentle. "All right there, love? Am I too deep?"

"No, no," she protested, afraid he would withdraw if she said yes. "You feel so good. It's so good, Ian."

His hands caressed her thighs, her ass, slid up her ribcage to squeeze her breasts. "Move with me now, Tessa. Here, like this."

He guided her movements with his hands on her hips, showing her what he wanted until she was riding him in a near frenzy, posturing up and down on his cock frantically.

"Jesus," he panted, his hips pistoning wildly in an attempt to keep up with her pace. "You're going to kill me for sure, love. I'm very sadly out of practice as I've already told you." His big hands gripped her hips, forcing her to slow down. But by then both of them were breathing raggedly, a fine sheen of sweat misting their bodies. Tessa's moans increased in frequency and volume each time he guided her up and down on his cock, lifting her up until only the tip remained inside her, and then lowering her with maddening, exquisite slowness until he was once again fully sheathed.

"God, those sounds you make," he breathed. "I've never heard anything so damned sexy before. I'm more than tempted to see just how loud I can make you moan."

"Oooh," she whimpered as he rubbed her clit with the pad of his right thumb, while twisting her nipple with his left fingers. Without his hands guiding her movements, she picked up the pace again, grinding against his hand as she felt the now familiar approach of another orgasm. He was stimulating her in too many places at once, overloading her pleasure centers, until it was all too much to take and she called out his name over and over as she quivered with sensation, still riding him hard.

Tessa barely heard Ian swear softly before he clamped down on her hips again, holding her still as he pumped himself inside of her, finding his release. His hands fell limply to his sides as if in surrender, and she slumped down to lay on his massive chest, her hands tangling in his damp hair.

"If you do manage to kill me," he whispered hoarsely a few minutes later, "at least I'll die a very, very happy man."

***

She yawned sleepily as she woke, stretching her arms and legs in opposite directions, luxuriating in the feel of the plush mattress beneath her and the softness of the bedcovers over her. They felt so good, in fact, that she gave in to the temptation and snuggled deeper into the pillow, fully intending to fall back asleep.

But then a low chuckle made her stir again, as did the warm hand caressing her bare shoulder. "You *are* a little sleepyhead, aren't you, love?"

Tessa's eyes flew open to find Ian gazing down at her, his handsome features filled with amusement. She shivered as he ran one long finger over the bridge of her nose down to her lips. His stubble was even darker and heavier this morning, his hair mussed, and she thought how incredibly sexy he looked this way – quite a change from the suave, elegant man who strode through the office with such authority. He looked wilder, rougher, but at the same time softer and more approachable.

"Good morning," she murmured, as his hand cupped the back of her head.

"Good morning to you, too, love," he told her just before claiming her lips in a sweet, searching kiss.

"Mmm." She turned into his arms willingly, rubbing her naked breasts against his chest and loving the indrawn hiss of breath he took at the contact.

"Easy, darling girl." He gently broke the kiss and eased her head onto his shoulder, keeping her wrapped in his arms. "Otherwise, you'll have me waking you up a bit more – uh, enthusiastically shall we say."

Tessa snuggled even closer against him, wrapping her arms around his waist. "I wouldn't complain about that. In fact, you can wake me that way whenever you like."

Ian gave her butt a pinch, eliciting a yelp of protest from her. "What a saucy little imp you've become rather quickly," he teased. "What's happened to the shy young girl who usually blushes when I simply tell her good morning?"

She caressed his steely abs, pressing a kiss to his shoulder. "You turned her into a woman practically overnight," she confided. "A woman who's absolutely obsessed with you."

She gave a cry of surprise as he tumbled her onto the mattress, his big body looming almost intimidatingly over hers. She gulped as she noticed the way his eyes had darkened, and the smoldering look on his face.

"Then we make quite a pair, love, because I've been completely obsessed with you – your face, your body, your sweetness – since the first time I saw you," he said raggedly. "And I'm beginning to fear that my obsession with you is only going to get stronger." Ian gave her a quick kiss before reluctantly sliding out of bed. "But if we don't get up and about now, I fear we'll never leave this bed today. How does a shower sound before I take you out for breakfast?"

Lazily, she buried her face back into the pillow. "Not nearly as good as staying here in this bed with you all day. Why can't we do that instead?"

He laughed heartily, bending over to nuzzle her neck. "Because I'm an old man, darling, and I need food if I'm going to have enough energy to ravish you again. Now, time to get up, you lazy wench."

Tessa shook her head in protest, pulling the duvet over her body. "I don't think I ever want to leave this bed. It's the most comfortable one I've ever slept in."

"It better be, considering what I paid for it. This is a Hypnos mattress, it was handmade and custom designed. I'm glad it passes Sleeping Beauty's high standards," he teased. He tucked a strand of hair behind her ear. "You do like to cuddle, don't you, love? You were practically on top of me when I woke."

She felt her cheeks grow warm as she gazed up at him. "I'm sorry. I didn't know I – um, did that."

"Hush." He gave her a lingering kiss. "Remember, the word sorry is no longer in your vocabulary. And I wasn't complaining Tessa. Far from it. I'd love nothing better than to wake up with you snuggled against me every day. I was just marveling at what an affectionate little thing you are."

Tessa went to him eagerly as he scooped her into his arms and carried her into his opulent bathroom. She was delighted to discover the floors had radiant heating, which helped to keep her nude body warm as Ian turned on the shower taps and gathered up towels.

Once inside the huge granite shower that boasted dual showerheads, Ian wasted no time in pulling her into his arms. He backed her against the wall, his voice rough as he asked, "Is this going to be another first for you?"

She shivered despite the blissful warmth of the shower spray. "Yes."

"Good." He nipped her earlobe teasingly. "You might have to make a list for me."

Tessa groaned as his hands slid down her back to cup her ass. "It might be a long list."

His lips moved down the side of her throat. "I was hoping you'd say that. And I'd be very happy to add anything you might forget to that list."

He released her momentarily so that they could each wash their hair. Tessa was surprised to find the same shampoo and conditioner that the stylist at Neiman Marcus had used yesterday, but didn't question the coincidence.

She had just rinsed out her long hair when Ian came up behind her, his arms wrapping around her waist and his massive erection pressing against the cleft of her buttocks. His soapy hands palmed her breasts, drawing a sigh from her throat, her head falling back onto his shoulder as he tugged at her nipples.

"Let's make sure you're clean all over, shall we?" he whispered in her ear, just before his soap-slicked fingers thrust deep inside her moist, swollen sex.

Tessa feared her legs might have given out from under her had he not been holding her up. "Ohhh." Her breath expelled in a long, low wave as his talented fingers continued to arouse her, his thumb rubbing circles around her clit.

"I love how tight you are," he crooned, slowly withdrawing his fingers only to replace them with the tip of his fully engorged penis. "How it feels like you can't possibly take all of me but yet you do anyway. How this sweet, hot pussy sucks me in."

She whimpered as he eased inside of her one long inch at a time, her breasts being crushed against the slippery granite shower wall, and she felt surrounded by his tall, strong body.

"Ah, oh, God," she cried as he thrust all the way inside of her.

He wasn't gentle with her this morning, and she loved this rougher, more primitive side of him. She braced her palms against the wall as he gripped her hips, pounding into her fiercely. Even above the sound of the streaming water she could hear how hard he was breathing, as well as the words he growled in her ear, praising her, encouraging her, urging her on.

"That's my beautiful girl. Yes, love, ah, you feel so damned good. I could stay buried inside you like this for hours. Come for me now, Tessa, let yourself go. Ah, yes, just like that."

She emitted a high-pitched wail as she came powerfully, this orgasm stronger than any of the others he'd given her so far. She was barely aware when Ian bit her shoulder as he, too, found his release, slapping his hand against the wall to hold himself up.

He insisted on drying her off, even though she feebly protested she could do it herself. He wrapped her up in the same sort of plush, cream colored bath sheet that he'd draped around his own hips.

"I have something for you, Tessa," he said, handing her an incredibly soft pearl gray garment. "The tags are still intact so if you don't like it we can exchange it for something else."

The robe was gorgeous and fit her perfectly, exquisitely warm against her bare skin. "It's beautiful, Ian. I love it," she told him sincerely. "But you've already done too much for me."

"I've barely begun to spoil you the way I intend to. I have some other things for you as well. Come have a look."

As he took her hand, she glanced down and almost fainted when she glimpsed the tag attached to the cuff of the robe. It was La Perla – a label she'd heard Gina and Alicia rave about on numerous occasions – and the price of the robe was $450. That was more than Tessa's food budget plus the cost of her bus pass for an entire month combined, and she was stunned that he would spend so much on her for one simple item.

"Ian." She tugged on his hand. "This is way too much money for just a robe. I can't let you spend this much on me."

In response he merely took hold of the offending price tag and tore it off. Grinning wickedly, he urged her along.

He showed her the drawers and cabinets in the huge double sink where toiletries, skin care products, and cosmetics had been stored for her, everything still in their wrappers and boxes. Tessa recognized some of the brands, especially the cosmetics that the makeup artist had used on her yesterday, while others were unknown to her. All of them looked expensive and high end.

But the real surprise came when Ian led her into his enormous walk-in closet. She had thought Julia's closet jaw-dropping but this one easily dwarfed her friend's several times over. The clothes racks, dark wood drawers, and granite topped counters had obviously been custom built and installed, for the closet was the sort of elaborate set-up that one only saw in design magazines or TV shows about the homes of the rich and famous.

Tessa stared at the rows of carefully hung suits, shirts, trousers, jackets, sweaters and other apparel. Dozens of pairs of shoes were neatly arranged on racks. The built-in drawers undoubtedly held things like socks, T-shirts and underwear. It was a huge space, far more than one person needed, as evidenced by the empty spaces here and there on the clothes racks.

"I didn't have time to select much, just a few things really," Ian was telling her as he walked her over to a partially filled clothes rack. "Once Marlene was able to confirm your sizes she packed everything up and had it delivered here to the house. I – I hope you like them, Tessa."

She was startled at the amount of clothing – far more than a "few things" – that hung from the rack. There were dresses, skirts, trousers, jeans, blouses, sweaters, and jackets. On the shoe rack just below were half a dozen pair of assorted pumps, boots and casual footwear. Tessa didn't need to look at labels or price tags to know that all of it had been very costly.

She'd never, ever, had such beautiful things before, never even let herself imagine she would ever own things as luxurious as these. For her entire life, her clothes had come from thrift shops, discount stores, and when things had been really bad, donations of used items from a charitable group.

Tessa couldn't help the rush of tears that filled her eyes as she tentatively ran her hand over a pair of designer jeans before admiring a gorgeous silk blouse of pale blue.

"Do you like them?"

She turned to face Ian, who stood just behind her, a rather anxious expression on his face. It touched her deeply that he had evidently hand selected all of these lovely things for her, and even more so that he was worried if they were to her liking or not.

Tessa wrapped her arms around his waist, snuggling her face against his bare chest. "How could I not?" she replied tearfully. "I know without even looking at everything that it will all be perfect. You have wonderful taste."

He tipped her chin up, frowning at the sight of her tears. "If you like everything so much, then why are you crying?"

She felt a tear begin to trickle down her cheek. "Because you're so good to me," she whispered brokenly. "I'm not used to anyone doing these sorts of things for me, or trying to take care of me the way you do. I guess I'm just a little amazed."

Ian kissed both of her eyelids. "This is just the tip of the iceberg, you know," he told her solemnly. "I intend to buy you whatever your heart desires, Tessa. I don't ever want you to be deprived again."

She shook her head. "I don't need things, Ian. I'm used to making do with what I have. I hope – I mean, that's not why I'm here with you. Because of your money, I mean. That's just not important to me. So don't expect me to ask you for things because I won't."

"I know that, darling." He combed her damp hair through his fingers. "Which is exactly why you can expect to receive a great many surprises from me. Ah, let's not forget these."

He opened a built-in drawer to reveal half a dozen sets of lacy lingerie, each in a different color. Ian picked up a very sexy bra of black lace and a matching pair of panties.

"I've been imagining you in this particular set since I picked them out," he murmured in a husky voice.

Tessa fingered the lacy cups of the bra, feeling a little shy that he'd personally chosen lingerie for her. "They're beautiful. And I'll wear them for you whenever you want me to."

The smile on his handsome face was positively amoral. ""Well, if I had my preference, I'd keep you dressed in nothing but these skimpy bits – or nothing at all – twenty four seven. But I suppose I need to let you out of my bed once in a while, don't I?"

She giggled, liking this playful side of him. "Don't forget I have a job. And a very demanding boss. Somehow I don't think he'd consider these "skimpy bits" proper office attire."

"You're damned right he wouldn't," he growled, banding an arm about her waist and yanking her against him. "I haven't waited this long for you only to share the sight of this luscious body with anyone else." He cupped her breast through the soft fabric of her robe, his thumb rasping over the nipple. "But that doesn't mean you can't wear these under your clothes, so I can fantasize about how you look in them all day."

Tessa gave a little moan as he continued to fondle her breast. "I'll do whatever you want so long as you keep touching me like that."

His fingers splayed open over her breast before giving it a squeeze. "You are quickly becoming a lusty little thing, aren't you?" he purred. "But I'm afraid you've wrung me dry for the moment, love. Christ, I've never had this much sex in such a short amount of time. You're like a constant aphrodisiac. Now, it's time to take care of other appetites, hmm? Let's find you some clothes so we can head out for breakfast."

She ran a hand up over his pectorals, loving this opportunity to touch his bare skin. "Is it still raining?"

"Absolutely pouring. It eased up a bit during the night, I believe, but a second front is passing through right now. Why do you ask?"

Tessa rested her head on his shoulder, her fingers plucking at the towel wrapped around his waist. "Would you mind very much if we just stayed here today? I'd love to cook breakfast for you. I mean, my cooking skills are pretty basic but I can manage breakfast."

"I don't want you to have to work at all this entire weekend," he declared. "That is – I hope you can stay with me the rest of the weekend. Am I interfering with any plans you'd made?"

She grinned. "Just a hot date with my laundry. And a very fun afternoon at the grocery store. Nothing that won't keep a couple of days. And I really don't mind making breakfast. You have such an amazing kitchen that I'd love the chance to use that stove. Provided I can figure out how to operate it, that is."

"Ah, so now the real truth comes out," teased Ian. "It's my kitchen you're really interested in, not me. I'll tell you what, love. We'll cook breakfast together, all right?"

She raised a brow in surprise. "You know how to cook?"

He shrugged. "Well, I'm no Emeril Lagasse but I can manage some basics. My brothers and I were required to work our way up from the bottom in the company, and for me at least that included a stint or two working in hotel restaurants. My housekeeper usually restocks supplies on Friday, so we'll see what we can put together. Now, I suggest you get some clothes on, love. If you stay in that robe, it will be far too tempting – and easy - for me to slip it off you at a moment's notice."

Tessa tugged playfully at his towel. "Not as easy as it would be for me." Then she squealed as his big hand swatted her bottom.

"Behave," he admonished. "I think we'll both be safer if you dress in here while I go shave. And don't even start looking at price tags. I should have had them all cut off."

"When exactly did you have time to put all these things away, anyway?" she asked curiously.

"I'm afraid I had to leave that task to my housekeeper," he admitted. "Fortunately, Mrs. Sargent is both accommodating and discreet. Though I could sense she was very anxious to ask me several questions about who all these things were for."

"So you don't normally buy things for your overnight female guests?" she asked pointedly.

Ian shook his head. "Except for family members, I have never purchased clothing – much less very fetching lace undies – for a woman. Same thing with overnight guests. The only women who have ever been in this house are Mrs. Sargent and family members."

Tessa was extremely pleased at this revelation. "So I'm a first for you in at least a couple of ways, too."

He held her face between his palms and kissed her forehead. "More than a couple, love. Let me grab some clothes now and I'll go change outside after I shave."

She clasped his wrist. "Wait."

As he gazed at her expectantly, she asked him shyly, "Would it bother you not to shave today? I – um, like you this way for a change. The stubble, I mean. It's very sexy."

Ian grinned as she caressed his cheek. "I don't mind at all, Tessa. In fact, I don't always shave when I'm home on the weekends. And if you find it sexy, then I definitely won't do it today."

She pressed a soft kiss to his cheek. "Thank you."

Sweat broke out on his brow and his eyes darkened. "Christ, I feel like a horny teenager whenever I'm near you. I'd better get my things before I check another item off your list of firsts."

She regarded him curiously as he efficiently selected clothing from the racks and drawers. "What item would that be?"

He winked at her cheekily. "Shagging in the closet."

Chapter Twelve

The quiet, mellow morning was one of the most enjoyable that Ian had ever spent in this big, often lonely house. He typically spent so much time traveling on business, attending meetings or social events that he wasn't actually here all that much.

But he could certainly make a strong case for spending a great deal more time at home provided that Tessa kept him company as she was right now.

They had cooked breakfast together, assembling eggs, potatoes, and bacon, and then finishing off the meal with tea and the scones Mrs. Sargent had bought from his favorite local bakery. It had been a quiet, companionable meal, the two of them gazing out the kitchen windows as the storm continued to bring heavy rain and winds outside. Tessa had been delighted to discover that there was a secluded courtyard just outside of the kitchen's sliding glass doors, and was even more pleased when he'd promised her they could have breakfast out there another time when the weather allowed.

After cleaning up the dishes, they spent a couple of hours in his home office. Ian worked on preparing notes for yet another trip he was taking week after next, while Tessa happily curled up on the sofa with a short stack of books he'd helped her select from his library.

He glanced up at one point and smiled fondly as he watched her unobserved. She was wearing the gray yoga pants and pink thermal sweater he'd bought for her, her bare feet tucked beneath her. She was avidly looking through a thick, glossy book with photographs of Tuscany, wrapping a lock of her hair around her fingers. She was enchanting, enthralling, and he thought he could happily stare at her for hours on end.

She looked up then, as if feeling his gaze upon her, and returned his smile a little shyly. "Hi. Taking a break?"

Ian pushed aside the reports he'd been reviewing. "Calling it quits for the day, actually. I don't want to spend even one more minute of this weekend with you doing work. But speaking of work, we ought to get that issue resolved while we're able to think rationally."

"Okay." She set aside her book as he took a seat next to her on the leather sofa.

Ian picked up her hand, idly brushing his thumb over her knuckles. "You know I've broken all of my rules for you," he began half-teasingly. "In all the years – decades, actually – that I've worked for my family's company I have never dated or even flirted with a female employee."

Tessa gave him an impish smile. "And I'm guessing it wasn't for lack of opportunity. An awful lot of opportunities."

He rolled his eyes at her. "Don't believe all the gossip you hear, darling. I've worked hard to develop a reputation as a cold, unapproachable bastard over the years. It's done a lot to keep most of the overly optimistic females at bay."

She snuggled up against him, her hand creeping under his gray cashmere pullover to rub his lower back. "There's nothing the least bit cold about you," she whispered, her breath tickling his ear. "You're actually really, really hot."

Growling, he yanked her onto his lap. "And you're making me burn for you, my sweet. Careful about playing with fire, hmm?" He brushed a kiss on her cheek. "Now, before you make me forget my damned name again, let's talk about the office. More specifically, how you and I are going to have to conduct ourselves while we're there. At least for the short term."

Tessa frowned. "Short term? I'm not sure I like the sound of that. Are you planning to have me transferred somewhere?"

"No. That's not one of the options I've considered. But we're getting ahead of ourselves just a bit." He brushed her hair behind her ear. "I've told you more than once that I don't want to overwhelm you, Tessa. Nor do I want to control or manipulate you – ever. That's not the sort of relationship I want to have with you."

She nodded. "I know you don't. And that means a lot to me, Ian. It would be so easy for me to just allow you to take me over, to depend on you for everything. But I don't think I'd like myself very much if I let that happen."

"Well, it's nothing you have to worry about because I won't let that happen, either. You're a bright, capable young woman and I fully intend to help you realize that. Now, as I was saying, I've broken all of my hard and fast rules for you – getting involved with an employee. In particular, an employee who works directly for me. We cannot let anyone else find out, Tessa. The repercussions for both of us would be – unpleasant."

"I know," she agreed readily. "I'm good at keeping secrets, Ian. I'm also very closed mouthed about my personal life, even if the rest of the team is pretty much an open book about theirs. Especially Kevin."

Ian grimaced when he noticed the way she wrinkled her nose in distaste. "Yes, I've had the great misfortune of overhearing some of that young man's – er, exploits. I can just imagine some of the tawdry tales he's offended you with."

"It's okay," she assured him. "He's an airhead and – well, kind of a slut – but at least he's always been kind to me. Not like A - "

"Alicia," he finished. "No great surprise there. That one's a nasty, stuck-up little witch. Unfortunately, her parents attend many of the same events that I do, and she's invited along occasionally. I'm not pleased that she knows quite so much about my social life."

"She's pretty fixated on you," Tessa told him quietly. "She's even talked about quitting her job so that you'd be free to date her."

Ian made a small sound of distaste. "It certainly wouldn't bother me in the least if she quit, but there's nothing she could do that would entice me to ask her out. Ever. Alicia is definitely not my type, so put that thought out of your head right now."

"Okay," she agreed happily.

"I appreciate that you've always been the epitome of discretion at the office, Tessa. You're going to have to take even more precautions to make sure no one suspects we're involved. If someone asks what you did on the weekend, for example, or if you're dating someone, you'll have to find a way to diffuse the situation." He hesitated. "I hate to outright ask you to lie, but if it becomes necessary - "

"I'll do whatever I have to in order to protect both of us," she insisted. "And I've become pretty good at avoiding personal questions. Fortunately, the others love to talk about themselves so much that they seldom ask about me."

Ian was beginning to feel a little less worried about what could easily develop into an awkward situation. "All right. I'll count on you to keep everything under wraps and simply avoid discussing your personal life as much as possible. The far more difficult part, I fear, is going to be for the two of us to act as though nothing has changed."

"I know." She began to twirl a lock of her hair through her fingers again. "While we're at the office, you're back to being Mr. Gregson. And we really don't see much of each other during the day anyway. Especially since you travel so much."

"And that's another huge problem." He picked up her hand, forcing her to release the lock of hair. "I've always missed you when I was away, but at least in the past it helped having some distance between us. Out of sight, out of mind, that sort of thing. But now that we've been together it won't be nearly so easy to stop thinking of you. It will be damned near impossible, in fact." He brought their clasped hands to his lips, his voice solemn. "I want you with me all the time, Tessa. Here in San Francisco, living with me permanently, but also traveling with me wherever I need to go."

She made a small sound of surprise and gazed at him wide-eyed. "But how would that be possible? I mean, there's no way to keep that a secret. Plus, I have to work. I couldn't just take time off whenever you had to travel."

"You'd have to quit your job, Tessa," he told her gently. "And if we're going to continue this relationship – something I'm going to do my damndest to make sure happens – then you'll need to do that sooner than later. I don't want to pressure you, it has to ultimately be your decision, but we could be together freely if you left the company."

She gazed down at their clasped hands quietly, her expression almost brooding. "I wouldn't be able to work at all if you want me to travel with you. You'd be – I'd have to be dependent on you to - "

"Support you. Yes, I'm aware. And that is certainly not a problem, love. I'm more than willing and capable of doing exactly that."

Tessa shook her head. "Ian – as much as I appreciate that, I can't do it. I can't just be your – your girlfriend or whatever the correct term is for that sort of arrangement."

He smiled wryly. "The very old-fashioned term you're thinking of is a mistress. And that's not at all what I'm proposing, darling. My thought was to have you travel with me and provide any administrative support I needed. As you know, Andrew rarely travels with me, only a few times a year. The rest of the time I depend on the office staff at whatever hotel I'm visiting to provide assistance. But if you were along I wouldn't need to do that."

She instantly brightened at his suggestion. "So I would unofficially be your traveling PA, something like that. Just not officially an employee of the company."

"Exactly." He smiled to note how pleased – and relieved – she seemed at the idea. "And you can expect to work quite hard during those times. I work long hours, attend far too many meetings, go to incredibly boring dinners. But if you were along to help me – not to mention grace me with your beautiful company – it would make everything a great deal more pleasant."

"That sounds – reasonable," she agreed. "I mean, I wouldn't be earning a salary but I also wouldn't feel like a – a kept woman, or something like that, so long as I could be doing real work."

"I think it's an excellent plan. In addition, I'd like for you to continue doing all of my spreadsheets, whether we're traveling or not. I frankly don't trust any of the others to do them correctly, even Andrew." He gave her a conspiratorial smile. "But don't you dare tell him that, he'd be quite offended. And truth be told, he can be very intimidating."

Tessa laughed. "Not you, too? All of us try to walk on eggshells around him, not wanting to annoy him. Though poor Shelby seems to receive the brunt of his displeasure."

"So, it's settled, then? When you feel the time is right – after we've come to know each other a bit better and you're more comfortable with the idea – you'll give notice?"

She nodded. "Yes. I just need some time, as you said. And I want you to detail for me exactly the sort of things I'd be expected to do as your traveling PA. I want to make sure I'm really doing something valuable, not just fetching you tea and sorting out your papers."

He grinned. "Not to worry, love. I'll find many ways to keep you busy all day long." He bent his head and nuzzled her throat. "All night, too."

Ian gave her a quick kiss, then set her down on the sofa before standing and offering her a hand up. "It's still pouring outside, I'm afraid, so we're stuck here. How does a workout in the gym sound?"

Tessa was more than agreeable and joined him a few minutes later in his small but well equipped home fitness room. Ian usually worked out at the exclusive private club he belonged to, one that boasted two Olympic-sized pools, an expansive weight and cardio room, handball, squash and tennis courts, and a boxing room where he could keep his skills sharpened. But his home gym more than filled his needs on those occasions when he didn't have time to get to his club, or when the inclement weather made it preferable to stay at home.

During his condensed shopping spree at Neiman Marcus yesterday, he'd thrown in a set of workout attire for Tessa almost as an afterthought. But as she walked inside his gym, he silently congratulated himself on his hurried choices.

She wore an exercise bra of dark blue piped in black, with a wide black zipper down the front. The Lycra fabric clung to her breasts lovingly, and sweat popped out on his brow even before he'd begun his workout. The coordinating shorts were even tinier that the ones she'd been wearing that day at the office gym, when that bastard Jason had dared to put his slimy hands on her. The dark blue cotton shorts bared a great deal of her long, shapely legs and cupped the luscious curves of her rounded ass enticingly.

He was thankful that no other admiring eyes were around to see her dressed like this – or, more accurately, barely dressed. Ian made a mental note to buy her some other workout gear that wasn't nearly as skimpy. He shuddered to imagine the reaction she'd receive walking into his club looking like this – all endlessly long legs, ripe tits, and glowing skin.

Over the next hour he tried – *really* tried – to focus on his own workout – lifting weights; doing several sets of crunches on the slant board while hefting a medicine ball; using the pull-up bar before dropping to the floor for as many push-ups as he could endure. But he found it impossible to stop sneaking glances at Tessa every five – or two – minutes, and then having to stifle a groan at the tempting sight she made. As she jogged on the treadmill, her breasts jiggled slightly, the exercise bra not quite as supportive as it ought to be. When she took her turn on the slant board, the waistband of her shorts dipped a couple of inches to reveal her navel. And as she bent over at the waist to stretch her hamstrings – flexible enough that her palms were flat on the floor – the hem of the tiny shorts crept up to bare part of her ass cheeks.

What made these frequent, furtive peeks at her even more alluring was the realization that she wasn't even trying to seem enticing, and that she didn't appear to even be aware of his gaze upon her.

After an hour, both of them were sweaty and fatigued. Ian took a long swig from a bottle of water before handing it to Tessa.

"Had enough for today?" he asked.

She nodded, swallowing a gulp of water. "I'm good. This is so awesome that you have your very own gym. You must work out here a lot."

"I try to get in a workout at least five days a week, but I don't actually use this room very often. The club I belong to is much larger and I like to use their pool and other facilities."

She ran her palm up his arm under the sleeve of his workout shirt. "Is that where you box?" she asked in a husky voice, her big eyes seeming bluer than usual.

Ian stifled a groan as Tessa stepped closer, her breasts

brushing up against his chest. "Yes, that's the place."

She gave his bicep a squeeze while her other hand slid up his chest. "Would you let me – that is, could I watch you sometime? Go through your workout? I've love to do that."

"Of course you may," he replied, pleased at her interest. "But we might need to wait on that a bit, love. Several of my executives belong to the same club and work out there frequently, so I'd have a bit of a tough time smuggling you in."

Tessa rubbed her cheek against his throat. "Hmm, extra motivation for me to leave the company that much sooner, I suppose."

His hands gripped her hips, pulling her close against him, and letting her feel his rapidly hardening erection. "When it's time, I'll get you a membership there so we can work out together. They have classes you might like, too – kickboxing, spinning, yoga."

Tessa ground her pelvis invitingly against his cock, severely testing his already fragile self-control. "I love yoga," she told him, sliding her arms up his chest to clasp around his neck. "Julia has brought me to her studio as a guest a couple of times and her teacher is amazing."

Ian grit his teeth as she pushed her breasts into his chest. "I – ah, didn't realize you saw Julia outside of the office."

"Is that all right?" she asked anxiously. "I mean, she's always been so nice to me and I don't have many friends so - "

"Hush." He kissed her softly. "Of course it's all right. I'd much rather see you going out with Julia than with one of the girls from the office. She's far more grounded and sensible than any of them, not to mention engaged to Nathan."

Tessa regarded him curiously. "What does that have to do with it?"

His hand splayed over the band of bare skin between her exercise bra and shorts. "She's already spoken for, darling, which means she won't be talking you into trolling singles bars looking for men."

She tunneled her hands up beneath his shirt, exploring the muscles of his back. "And why would I want to do something like that anyway?"

He hissed as one of her hands slipped beneath the waistband of his athletic shorts, not stopping until it reached his buttocks. "So that you could find someone closer to your age, perhaps." He shrugged, feigning a nonchalance he damned sure didn't feel. "A hot, gorgeous girl like yourself would only have to walk inside a bar or a club, and you'd be swarmed with interested young men."

Tessa swiftly slid her palms to either side of his face, gazing at him with fire in her blue eyes. "If I was in a room surrounded by a thousand different men, you're still the only one I'd want – the only one I'd see. I don't care about the age difference, Ian. My God, you've got the most beautiful body of any man alive. Why would I ever want anyone else?"

Her passionately spoken words not only touched him profoundly, but aroused him fiercely. "I'm a damned lucky bastard," he muttered. "Though I'll have my work cut out for me keeping up with you, my sweet. Extra workouts, more vitamins, increasing my intake of red meat. I'll need to do all of that and more in order to have enough energy to keep you satisfied."

He yelped as she very unexpectedly gave him a smack on the ass.

"You're making me feel like some sort of sex fiend," she pouted prettily. "I can't help it if you turn me on."

"Are you turned on now, Tessa?" he breathed in her ear. "Tell me, love, are you wet?"

She groaned as he cupped her buttocks and ground himself against her cleft. "God, yes!"

His tongue traced around the dainty shell of her ear. "And are your nipples hard?"

The little laugh she gave was positively wicked, and he was rather shocked at how quickly she'd shed her inhibitions. "Why don't you find out for yourself?" she challenged in a naughty voice.

"Jesus, Tessa." He didn't have to look down to realize his erection was already tenting his shorts. His gaze fell instead on the lush mounds of her breasts straining behind the snug fitting exercise bra. Her nipples were definitely hard, poking against the slick fabric, begging to be touched.

His fingers toyed with the pull tab of the bra's zipper. "I admit to having an ulterior motive in mind when I picked this particular item out."

Her breathing had grown choppy. "What – what kind of motive?"

Ian began to lower the zipper very slowly. "This kind."

Tessa was trembling as he finished unzipping the bra, her breasts bursting free to tumble into his waiting palms. She let out one of those erotic, drawn-out moans as he squeezed her breasts then tugged at her nipples.

"Oh, oh, that's so good!" she cried. "Please don't stop."

"God, darling, you make me crazy with those little sounds you make," he groaned, bending his head to take one of her nipples in his mouth. He circled the hard tip with his tongue before sucking the entire areola into his mouth.

He was so focused on lavishing attention on her breasts that he wasn't aware of her hand slipping down between their tightly fused bodies. At least not until she began to tentatively palm his throbbing cock, a light touch that nonetheless almost had him exploding on the spot.

"Tessa." This time he was the one who moaned, long and low.

"Let me."

He was helpless to resist her as she pushed his shorts down past his hips, freeing his pulsing erection.

"Fuck." The harsh curse hissed out from between his tightly clenched teeth as her warm, smooth hand closed around his cock. He sensed her uncertainty, the hesitant way she tried to please him, and he placed his shaking hand over hers.

"Like this. Long, slow strokes. God, yes, just like that. Easy, love. Christ, what you do to me."

She picked up the rhythm quickly, her hand stroking his cock until he was groaning, thrusting eagerly in sync with her motions. Then she startled him again by sinking to her knees, the tip of his penis mere inches from her full, lush mouth.

"Is this how you pictured me?" she breathed seductively. "How you've wanted me?"

His hands gripped her shoulders tightly as she continued to

stroke his erection. He made a raw, dangerous sound deep in his throat as he gazed down and saw what a decadent, carnal picture she presented – tendrils of blonde hair escaping her ponytail to curl about her flushed cheeks; her blue eyes huge and round as they stared up at him wantonly; her lips full and trembling, eager to suck him off and give him untold pleasure. She still wore the unzipped exercise bra, her ripe tits fully bared to his gaze, the nipples hard and pointed. She looked like sex incarnate, the most tempting, irresistible beauty he could ever imagine, and she was his – all his – to do with as he pleased.

"This is exactly how I pictured you," he murmured hoarsely. "Except you're even more beautiful, more tempting."

"Tell me how to please you, what you like."

Ian honestly didn't think he could do it – instruct Tessa in the finer points of giving him a blow job – at least not without coming hard within the first few seconds. But somehow he managed to do just that, telling her what he liked, praising her efforts, groaning when she learned all too quickly how to bring him to the very edge. At his guttural, brusque instructions, she ran her tongue up and down the length of his penis before closing her lips over just the tip and sucking hard. Her tongue circled the broad, plush head of his cock, licking up the thick beads of pre-cum, before taking as much of him as she could inside her mouth. His hands fisted in her hair, pulling it free of the ponytail, as she sucked him eagerly, as though she'd been doing this forever instead of mere minutes.

Ian's legs were shaking, and he was dimly aware of being more aroused then he'd ever come close to being in his entire thirty-nine years. At the last minute, when he was perilously close to losing it and coming hard down her throat, he jerked himself out of her mouth and took a step back.

"Together," he uttered rawly. "We'll come together."

They quickly stripped off their remaining articles of clothing before he lifted her in his arms and carried her over to the closest wall, slamming her up against it. Tessa barely had time to wrap her legs around his waist before he plunged inside of her with one savage thrust.

The blood was roaring in his ears so loudly that he could

barely hear the little gasps she made as he pounded her against the wall, holding her up as though she weighed nothing. He was crazy with lust, so consumed with the driving need to possess her, that any sort of rational thought was impossible. As if from a great distance, he heard her give a high-pitched cry and then her tight, slick pussy was clenching around him like a fist as she reached her climax. The shout he gave as he came mere seconds later was more like a bellow, echoing around the room.

Tessa was shaking in his arms as he gently eased her to her feet, wrapping her in a fierce embrace.

"God, please tell me I didn't hurt you," he begged. "I didn't mean to lose control that way, to be so rough with you."

She shook her head as her arms banded about his waist. "You didn't hurt me. And I like that you were a little rough, that I can make you lose control a bit."

"Did you now?" he asked, amused. "I think if I let you, darling, you could turn me into a wild animal. Once again, I'm not certain I could even spell my name right now."

She shivered in his arms. "I'm cold. Can we get into a hot shower, please?"

He grabbed two towels from a shelf in a corner of the room and wrapped one about her shoulders. "Of course, love. But what if we make it a hot bath instead? That way," he murmured wickedly against her ear, "we can check off one more item from your list of firsts."

***

Tessa seemed quiet and pensive the rest of the afternoon and evening, as though something was troubling her. But Ian tactfully didn't push or pry, sensing that she was having an inner struggle with some matter.

He'd taken her again during their bath, but it had been a far cry from the frantic coupling they'd shared in the gym. He'd taken his time with her in the huge sunken tub, petting and soothing her with soft kisses and exquisitely gentle caresses. Their lovemaking had been slow and tender, but she had still been so wrung out afterwards that he'd had to physically lift her out of the tub and dry her off, as though she were a small child. Tessa had been sleepy, clearly not used to the multiple demands he'd made on her body in less than twenty four hours, and he'd laid her down carefully in his bed. She'd been asleep within minutes and he had watched her for almost half an hour before forcing himself to leave the room.

The fierce storm had finally ebbed, and he'd taken her out to dinner, this restaurant far more casual than Le Mistral. It was a charming Italian café not too far from his house, and the owners knew him well. Ian chatted with them briefly in Italian, and introduced them to Tessa.

Over a shared Caesar salad, platters of steaming, fresh pasta, and a bottle of red wine, he'd studied her with some concern. Even her appetite was off tonight, as she ate only sparingly and drank more water than wine. She looked beautiful, of course, wearing one of the outfits he'd bought her – skinny black jeans, a dark blue sweater that skimmed over her lush breasts, and black high-heeled ankle boots. Her cheeks were still flushed becomingly from her nap, not to mention all the sex they'd been having, and she was damned near irresistible. The restaurant was crowded, and Ian's perceptive gaze didn't miss even one of the very interested male glances that fell Tessa's way. At one point he reached across the table and took her hand in his, sending out a silent message to anyone looking that this one belonged to him.

He longed to ask her what was wrong, if there was something he could do for her, but continued to keep quiet. Instead, he only made occasional small talk over dinner, giving her the space she so obviously needed, and tried to tamper down his unsettled feelings. He was more than half afraid that Tessa was having second thoughts about all of this – about him, them – that she was realizing he was in fact too old for her or that she wasn't ready for another relationship so soon after being divorced. She was likely agonizing over how to tell him, especially given the fact that he was her employer and she didn't want –

"Ian."

He glanced up at her softly spoken word. She was worrying her bottom lip to keep it from trembling, and he saw the sheen of tears in her eyes. He took a swig of wine, needing the fortification. "What is it, love?"

She slid her hand over his, giving it a squeeze. "I want to tell you everything. About my mother. And my marriage. And, well, about me. I'm ready."

He felt an overwhelming sense of relief at the exact time a wave of empathy washed through him. He squeezed her hand back reassuringly. "All right, darling. Let's go home and you can tell me whatever you like."

Chapter Thirteen

"My mother was bipolar. I didn't know that's what her illness was called until I was about eleven or so, when I was old enough to ask questions and do some research. Up until then all I knew was that sometimes Mom was happy and liked to do fun things, but other times she was very, very sad and didn't get out of bed most days. As I got older, the sad times started taking her over more and more, until that's all there was."

Tessa paused to take a tiny sip of the brandy that Ian had insisted she drink. She'd never tried the stuff before, and while the first couple of sips had made her shudder, there was no denying that the undoubtedly expensive liquor was beginning to warm her up.

"Mom was a writer," she continued. "She actually had several books published and the royalties she got helped support us for a while. Then she started falling deeper into depression and could barely function most days, much less write. And when she did try writing during her manic episodes, it was just a bunch of nonsense, nothing that made sense or that she could ever hope to have published."

Tessa and Ian were sitting in his library, one of the coziest rooms in his house. He'd started a fire since she had felt chilled, and he was now sitting on the opposite end of the sofa, giving her the space she needed as she visibly struggled to tell him about her life.

"You never tried to find your father?" he inquired gently.

She shook her head. "There was really no place to even begin to do that. One of the few times in my mother's life when she was actually lucid enough to talk about it, she admitted that I'd been conceived during an especially manic period of her life. The – the research I did later referred to it as hypersexuality. In other words, she slept with a lot of different men in a very short period of time. Any one of them could have been my father."

Ian gave a brief nod. "And I'll just assume she never bothered to learn any of their names?"

"Yes, you'd be correct with that assumption. So, no, there's absolutely no chance of ever learning who my father is. It was just my mother and I, since she'd lost contact with all of her family as well."

He touched her cheek softly. "Was there no one else then to help you, Tessa? No friends, neighbors, a doctor perhaps?"

"No. We moved around – a lot. When Mom got into one of her manic phases, she'd be full of all these plans, ideas for a new book, and most of those times she'd decide we had to move somewhere different so she could find inspiration. We lived all over the Southwest – Arizona, New Mexico, southern California, west Texas. We'd move at least once a year, sometimes as many as three or four times."

He frowned. "That couldn't have had a positive effect on your schooling."

Tessa gave a bitter little laugh. "It was absolute hell, as one could imagine. I was always the new girl in class, having to play catch up with what all the other kids were learning. I was constantly getting used to a new teacher, a new book, a different way of learning. My grades suffered, and it was usually a struggle just to keep up. And my mother certainly wasn't any help with studying or schoolwork. When she was manic she'd actually encourage me to skip school so that we could go out and have fun that day instead. And of course when she was down – well, she couldn't even look after herself, much less take care of me."

Ian gave her hand an encouraging squeeze. "I'm assuming that due to all your moving around that it was difficult to make friends. Is that why you had no one to help you?"

"Partly, yes. I was shy to begin with, so it took me a long time to make friends. And just when I'd finally begin to settle in, my mother would uproot us again and I'd have to start over. So there were never any long term friendships, people I could count on. And then, as I got older, I'd start hearing horrible stories about foster care, especially for kids my age. I was afraid that if I approached a teacher or a doctor and told them about my mother that they would separate us – that I'd wind up in foster care and my mother in some sort of mental institution. So I – I began to look after her as soon as I was old enough."

"What?" Ian looked and sounded shocked. "How is that even possible, Tessa? How old were you?"

She shrugged. "Maybe seven or eight. When she was in one of her down phases, I'd try to get her to eat, encourage her to get up and about. I learned early on how to look after myself – fixing meals, getting to and from school, even doing the laundry. I was terrified someone would take me away, Ian. My mother might have been sick, but she was all I had."

"Take another sip of your brandy, darling," he urged. "I'm sure this all must be upsetting for you to relive."

Tessa drank a bit more before continuing. "Things got tougher as I grew older and my mother got sicker. When she was manic she'd usually be able to find some sort of job – waitressing, a cashier, a hotel maid. There was never much money, barely enough to keep us going. But when she was down, she couldn't work, basically just slept most of the day. We – we lived on welfare during those times, sometimes in homeless shelters, sometimes in our car."

He visibly paled before drinking down the rest of his brandy. "My God, Tessa. To think of you in a place like that – being homeless. Christ, I want to wrap you up in my arms and never let go of you," he told her fervently.

"I didn't mean to upset you," she said softly. "It really wasn't as bad as I know it must sound."

"No, I'm guessing it was far worse and you'll never admit to me just how bad it really was," retorted Ian. "But I won't press you for more details right now. Go on."

Tessa began to twirl a lock of hair between her fingers, betraying her agitation. "As soon as I was old enough I got a job. Fortunately I matured early so I looked two or three years older than I really was. At thirteen I bluffed my way into working at a summer day camp. Some of the kids attending the camp were older than I was. Then I got after school jobs, mostly at fast food restaurants or shops at the mall."

"Thirteen. Bloody hell, you were still a child." He shoved a hand through his hair, mussing it, clearly displaying his distress. "But it's beginning to sound like you never really were a child."

"No, I wasn't," she agreed solemnly. "But at least I was able to earn enough to keep us out of homeless shelters. I worked one job after school and another on weekends. My schoolwork suffered even more, but I made sure to pick easier classes that I could keep up with. No calculus or chemistry for me, I'm afraid."

Ian hauled her against his side, as though unable to keep from touching her a moment longer. "It doesn't matter, love. You're the brightest, most brilliant girl I've ever known."

Tessa sighed. "I always felt stupid in school. Except in my computer classes. I knew early on that I wouldn't even try to go to college, and instead worked on improving my computer skills so that I could get a good job. I had always figured on taking care of my mom, you see, hoped that once I graduated from high school and got a real job that I could finally get her some help, get her on the kind of medication that might allow her to have a normal life. But I ran out of time."

She started to tremble then, finding the next part of her story the most difficult and painful. She took another fortifying sip of brandy, not even flinching from the burn this time.

"I had turned sixteen a few months earlier, but had only received my driver's license two months before," she continued. "By that time, my mother wasn't even getting out of bed most days, much less driving the car. We were living in Tucson then, had moved there in January. It was October when it happened – on a Wednesday, of course. Because almost every bad thing that's happened in my life has been on that day of the week."

Tessa hid her face in her hands, struggling to find a way to resume her story. The next part of her tale was by far the most difficult, the most gut wrenching, but it had also been the catalyst that had set so many other things in motion.

She kept her eyes downcast and fought hard to prevent her voice from breaking. "When I was driving home that evening from work, I could smell the smoke in the air. I pulled up in front of our apartment building and it – it wasn't there anymore. There had been a fire earlier in the day and the entire building was destroyed. When I got there a fire truck was still on site making sure the flames were under control." She raised tear filled eyes to Ian, her jaw wobbly. "My mother – she didn't make it out, Ian. Most other residents weren't at home at the time, and the few who were heard the smoke detectors and got out. My mother – she was probably too deep inside her dark place to pay attention, probably didn't even hear the alarms or the sirens or smell the smoke. She was – gone. Everything was gone – our furniture, our clothes, dishes. All I had left were the clothes I was wearing, my purse and school books, and the car."

Tears were running freely down her cheeks now as she whispered in a broken voice. "I should have been there with her. I knew how bad off she was, how far into the darkness she'd fallen. I could have saved her, could have - "

"Stop it." He crushed her against him, lowering her head to his shoulder and holding her while she wept. "Hush, love. Don't do this to yourself. I'm guessing you've blamed yourself for years, but it wasn't your fault. Your mother was very ill from the sounds of it, and you were at work when the fire started. Working to help take care of her, I might add. So stop feeling responsible, Tessa. It was just a terrible accident."

Ian continued to rock her gently in his arms, as though she were a child, until her sobs began to subside and she was calm enough to continue telling her story. She didn't resist when he refilled her brandy glass, and obediently took a swallow.

"So what happened to you after that?" he prodded gently. "You were what – sixteen? Were you forced into one of those foster homes you had heard awful things about?"

Tessa shook her head. "No. There was a Red Cross volunteer on site the night of the fire, and she arranged for most of the residents to stay in a motel for a few days. It was pretty confusing that night so no one really bothered to ask how old I was or anything. I stayed in the motel for a week, and the Red Cross arranged for vouchers for stuff like food and clothes. But I knew it would only be a matter of days before someone figured out I was underage and had nowhere to go. One of the girls I worked with on the weekends – Michelle – heard about what happened and convinced her mother to let me stay with them. Michelle was one of the few friends I had, though I didn't know her all that well since we went to different high schools. But she'd always been nice to me, and I was desperate at that point, so I agreed."

"Go on," encouraged Ian. "What happened then?"

"I moved in with Michelle, her mother and younger sister. Her mother didn't seem all that happy to have me there at first, but when she learned she'd get a monthly foster care check that made things a little better. But it was – well, kind of a nightmare living there. The three of them fought constantly – screaming matches, name calling, horrible, awful fights – and they seemed to happen almost every day." Tessa gave a little shudder. "As sick as my own mother was, she never once yelled at me or called me the sort of terrible names Michelle's mom used. But I wasn't even at the house all that much between school and two jobs, and it was better than being homeless."

"So you stayed there until you turned eighteen?"

"No." She gave another shake of her head. "I stayed there for just a few months, until Michelle's older sister moved back home. Along with her boyfriend and their two small children. Both of them had lost their jobs, been evicted from their apartment, and had no money. So all of a sudden the house – which only had three bedrooms – went from having four people living there to eight. And what had been a nightmare for me became a living hell. Now there were five adults all fighting with each other, plus two screaming kids. Michelle and I had to move out of her bedroom so her sister and her family could use it. I wound up sleeping on the floor of the room Michelle had to share with her younger sister. Even then I kept telling myself it was better than living in my car."

The expression on Ian's face had become deadly serious, his mouth a grimace. "I'm going to assume that wasn't precisely the case, though."

"It wasn't. The sister's boyfriend – he was – a real creep, no other way to put it. My skin would crawl from just being in the same room with him, so I made sure I avoided him like the plague. Unfortunately, he was – attracted to me, made some very unwanted advances, said some really disgusting things to me. I was on the verge of leaving the house for good just so I wouldn't have to see him again."

Ian made a low, snarling sound. "If you're about to tell me that piece of filth touched you - or worse- I swear that I will hunt him down like the animal he is and beat him to death."

She laid a hand on his arm, soothing his barely controlled rage. "No. It never got that far. But Michelle's sister overheard some of the stuff the creep said to me, and she went a little crazy, accusing me of trying to steal him away. Her mother got involved and took her daughter's side, then basically told me to get out because I was disrupting the household and I couldn't stay any longer. Michelle tried sticking up for me, but her mother threatened to toss her out, too, so I just left. Believe me, sleeping in my car was an improvement over having to live in those conditions one more day."

Ian shut his eyes, and didn't speak for several seconds, almost as though he were silently counting to ten to keep his rage in check. "Christ. You actually slept in your car, Tessa? There was nowhere else for you to go? Wouldn't a foster home – no matter how awful – have been a better solution?"

"I truly didn't think so at the time, no," she replied honestly. "I'd read some real horror stories and talked to kids at my school about the kind of homes teenagers were usually placed in – mostly group homes where you lived with recovering addicts or kids just out of juvenile detention. There were other stories, too, about girls who'd been raped or abused. I decided to take my chances on my own."

He ran a hand down his face, as if unable to believe what he was hearing. "How did you manage? I mean - "

"The school term was still going on so I was able to use the showers in the gym during the week. Weekends I had to – er, improvise some. I did laundry at a laundromat. I qualified for free school lunches and made that my main meal, and just ate what I could afford the rest of the time. I made sure I moved my car around a lot when I parked for the night so I wouldn't look suspicious always staying in the same neighborhood. And I always parked in good areas that were well lit. The weather in Tucson is pretty warm all year round so being cold at night was never an issue."

"God." He surged to his feet and began to pace around the library. His entire body was tense and almost shaking, and he kept clenching and unclenching his fists, as though he longed to hit something.

"If it's any consolation," she told him meekly, "I only lived that way for about four months."

He spun around to face her, his handsome face livid with rage. "Four *hours* would have been too long for you to live like that. I feel – sick, Tessa. Bloody sick at the thought of you all alone and helpless. Jesus, anything could have happened to you out there. You could have been raped, robbed, murdered."

"I know," she admitted reluctantly. "I never slept especially well those months, was always cautious to make sure no one bothered me."

"What changed after those hellish months?" he rasped. "Please, for God's sake, tell me things got better after that."

"They did. And what happened after that was Peter. My hus – my ex-husband. He – well, there's really no other way to say this. He saved me, Ian. In more ways than you can possibly imagine."

Ian refilled his brandy snifter and drank half the contents in one gulp. "Continue, Tessa. I'm sorry if I seem upset but – Christ, to think of you all alone that way." His voice trailed off as he shuddered.

"It's okay, honestly." Tessa found it a bit odd that she was the one offering *him* comfort under the circumstances. But then, she already knew how the story ended.

"I'd known Peter for a little over a year," she related. "He and I both worked at Old Navy after school. Well, saying I knew him might have been a stretch. I knew his name, said hello in passing, and spoke to him on occasion when I had a question about something in his department. He was quiet, like me, and very introverted. A real loner." She was relieved to notice that Ian had stopped his frantic pacing and seemed calmer.

"Because our shifts at the store didn't end until late, we usually walked out to our cars together. It wasn't something he ever offered to do, it just sort of evolved into that. Anyway, one night we got out to our cars and mine had been broken into. Fortunately, anything of value I had was in my purse which I had taken with me so nothing was stolen. But, well, it was all just too much for me to take and I started crying. And of course, it happened to be another Wednesday."

"So Peter – he helped you?"

"He did." She nodded in assent. "We stopped somewhere for coffee and I told him everything that had happened in the last few months – the fire, living at Michelle's, sleeping in my car. He didn't say much, but told me to follow him when we left. We wound up at his house. The house itself was in pretty bad shape, but it was on a big corner lot and there was some space in the back that was sheltered where he told me I could park every night. He figured it would be safer there and he could keep an eye on me."

Ian was still frowning. "Why didn't he just invite you inside?"

"Because if my life had been difficult, Peter's had been one of constant torment. His mother was a chronic drunk, a really horrible woman, and he refused to even let me meet her, told me I didn't need any other negative experiences in my life. He'd sneak me inside when she left the house or was passed out drunk so I could use the shower or bathroom, would bring me food and just sort of look out for me. It wasn't perfect but at least I felt a little safer and not quite so alone."

He leaned back against a low table that held a marble chess set, his feet crossed at the ankles as he sipped his brandy. "And how long did this new arrangement last?"

"Just a few months. Until Peter graduated from high school and turned eighteen."

Ian raised a brow. "What happened then?"

"He married me."

***

Ian was damned glad he hadn't chosen that particular moment to take a sip of brandy because he most certainly would have choked on it. When Tessa had told him rather uncertainly at the restaurant that she wanted to tell him about her past, nothing in the world could have prepared him for all of the terrible things that had befallen her in her relatively short life thus far. But this latest revelation – while certainly not terrible – might have been the biggest shock of them all.

He stared at her in disbelief. "So exactly how old were *you* when this marriage took place?"

Tessa looked down at her lap where she was clasping and unclasping her hands in agitation. "Seventeen," she murmured, her voice barely above a whisper.

"Seventeen. Why, Tessa? Why couldn't you have waited until you were a little older? Were the two of you that much in love?"

Her gaze flew up to meet his at this question, and she shook her head in denial. "That – that's not it at all. We rushed to get married as soon as possible so that Peter – so that he could be legally responsible for me. The social worker assigned to my case finally figured out that I wasn't living at Michelle's any longer – even though her mother kept cashing the support checks. So Peter offered to get married in order to – well - "

"To save you. Yes, I understand now." Ian heaved a sigh. "So you didn't marry for the usual reasons, then?"

"We weren't madly in love, if that's what you mean. Peter was kind to me, we became best friends, but it was never a romantic relationship. And we never intended to stay married. Peter had always planned to pack up and leave Tucson as soon as he turned eighteen – too many awful memories there for him. But he stayed – for me – first so I could finish high school, turn eighteen and be considered a legal adult."

"And yet you remained married for quite a long time after that." His curiosity was growing by leaps and bounds.

"Yes." She took another sip of her brandy. "Peter enrolled in community college that first year and we moved into a shared rental. *That* was another disaster. We were in such a hurry to find a place that we could afford that we didn't bother to find out much about our roommates." She managed a small smile. "You know how you told me your favorite movie is *Animal House*?"

Ian nodded, quite certain he wasn't going to like where her question was leading. "You aren't going to tell me your roommates were like the characters in the movie, are you?"

"Worse. It was the nonstop party house, people coming and going constantly, no privacy, everyone helping themselves to food and things that Peter and I bought for ourselves. We ended up stashing things in our room, buying a padlock for the door, and spending as little time as possible there. We'd signed a lease for a year, couldn't afford to break it, and didn't have enough money saved to put down on another place anyway."

"So you toughed it out for a year?"

Tessa wrinkled her nose in distaste. "Somehow, yes. We each worked two jobs, took a third over summer break, and saved every penny until we had enough to get a little place of our own the following year."

"Why did you stay together after that first year? What changed?"

She heaved a little sigh. "Peter felt responsible for me, even though he had no real obligation. He told me he wouldn't have been able to live with himself leaving town knowing I'd be trying to fend for myself with no money, no real marketable job skills, no family to help out. So we decided I'd enroll in the office technology program at community college and get my certificate. He agreed to stay in town for the two years of the program, until I could get a good enough job to support myself. In the meanwhile, he received a scholarship to the University of Arizona and decided he might as well get his degree to have something to fall back on if his journalism career didn't work out."

"So you remained married another year so you could help him finish his degree?"

"That's it exactly," she agreed. "By then, we'd been married for four years and – well, we'd just grown used to being together, I suppose. When Peter got the job offer up here in San Francisco, I transferred, too. I didn't have especially fond memories of Tucson so I welcomed the opportunity to leave."

Ian offered up a brief smile. "Just about the only good thing to come out of this whole mess, wasn't it? Your ex-husband's job brought you into my life – even though I've had to wait an eternity for you."

Tessa returned his smile a bit timidly. "Yes, that was a good thing as it turned out. And I do love San Francisco. It's very different from any other place I've lived."

"You're leaving out the final piece to this puzzle, Tessa. Why did Peter ask you for a divorce after so many years – how many was it?"

"Seven. We'd been married a little over seven years when he got the job in the Middle East. I wanted to go with him, but he set his foot down. Told me it was time we stopped fooling ourselves that we could ever have a normal marriage, that it was time for me to finally start living."

Ian looked perplexed, even as he took a seat next to her on the sofa. "What exactly does that mean? I know you said you didn't get married for the usual reasons, but surely after seven years - "

"No. We never had a truly romantic marriage, or anything remotely near a normal relationship. Peter – he had a lot of issues. He only told me part of what happened to him but – well, he was badly abused as a boy and never really dealt with those issues."

"The alcoholic mother, I presume?"

Tessa had a sad look on her face. "Unfortunately, she was only the tip of the iceberg. His father left them when Peter was about six, but evidently he'd been violent towards both of them. But the real problems began when his mother's younger brother moved in. He – he was a pedophile, Ian, and abused Peter for years – sexually abused him."

He was slowly starting to see where this sad tale was leading. "That's terrible, darling. His mother did nothing to help?"

"She didn't believe him, called him a liar and a troublemaker. Apparently, she depended on her brother to help with expenses so she turned a blind eye to what the bastard was doing to Peter. The abuse went on for several years until the uncle got caught trying to molest another child and was shipped off to prison."

Ian's jaw clenched in anger. "A fitting place for the scum of the earth like him. I assume he's still rotting away there?"

"Most likely, yes. But that wasn't much consolation to Peter, considering the damage that had been done. Peter had great difficulty being intimate. We were married for almost three years before we finally managed to have sex. And it was never easy for him. He – he couldn't really bear being touched, especially in a sexual way."

He stroked her hair lightly. "That must have been difficult for both of you. You're such an affectionate little thing, Tessa. I can't even imagine how hard that was for you."

"Peter used to tell me that I should – oh, God, this is embarrassing." She took a deep breath. "When he wasn't able to – um - "

"Get an erection?" he supplied.

Tessa's cheeks flushed as she gave a short nod. "Yes. He, uh, had a lot of difficulty with that or with, um, keeping one long enough to - "

"It's all right, love," he assured her. "I get the idea. So I assume that you two didn't – weren't intimate very often?"

"No, we weren't. I got to a point where I didn't want to pressure him, or make him feel worse. As it was, he used to actually suggest I find someone else, another lover, someone who could – well, take care of me that way."

Ian took her into his arms, pressing a kiss to the top of her head. "I know without having to ask that you never even considered that idea. No matter what the state of your marriage I don't think you'd have it in you to be unfaithful. With Peter's permission or not."

"You're right. I never even gave it a serious thought. Normal marriage or not, I always thought of Peter as my husband as well as my best friend. I wouldn't have been able to live with myself if I had done something like that."

He eased her head onto his shoulder, still stroking her hair. "So he decided to set you free after all that time. He knew that he could never give you what you needed and that you'd never cheat on him. After all the good deeds he did for you, Tessa, the last might have been the kindest one of all."

"I didn't get that at first," she admitted. "All I could think about for the first couple of months was how alone I was. And of how terrified I was that I'd become like my mother."

Her last confession startled him anew, and he tipped her chin up. "What in the world are you talking about, Tessa? Why are you afraid of something like that? Mental illness isn't hereditary."

"I know that. And I've never had a manic episode like she did, nothing like that. But – the other – the darkness. Sometimes it gets so hard, Ian. I have to fight it off, to keep myself from falling under like she did. When Peter left – and all the times before when he'd be away for weeks at a time on assignments – I'd have to force myself to keep going, to not let the depression take me over."

Tessa was weeping quietly, and he felt like his heart would shatter into a thousand pieces at the sound. He cuddled her close, knowing how she liked that, and tried not to feel helpless as he soothed her.

"Tessa, darling, it's hardly a surprise that you'd feel sad and, yes, depressed at times. My God, what you've had to endure in your life – most people never experience even a fraction of those sorts of hardships." He kissed her softly, tenderly. "You might think you're weak, or not especially bright, but to me you're the strongest, smartest, most capable person I've ever known. I am in complete awe of you, love."

She wrapped her arms around his neck and snuggled a little closer. "Thank you," she whispered. "For listening to me and understanding."

"I will always be here for you, Tessa," he told her earnestly. "You're never going to be alone again. Or frightened. And definitely not homeless. I can't even process that idea yet – it makes me want to hit something when I think about it. But you can be damned certain nothing or no one is ever going to hurt you again, so long as I'm alive and kicking."

She fell asleep in his arms not long afterwards, emotionally exhausted from everything she'd just told him. He carried her upstairs to his room and undressed her carefully, leaving her clad only in the black lace bra and panties she'd obviously worn to please him. But as beautiful and tempting as she was, he kept his libido in check, for this was not a night for amorous activity. Not when she was so vulnerable, so in need of comfort and support. Instead, he covered her with the duvet, brushing her hair back with a tender hand, before returning to the library.

It was a long time and two more snifters of brandy later before he felt the least bit sleepy. What Tessa had just told him – the sad picture she'd drawn for him of her life – made him feel sick at heart when he tried to imagine how lost and lonely she'd been. Unbidden, images of her at various points in her life flitted through his mind – one of a small, innocent child left to fend for herself while her mother was too deeply mired in depression to even get out of bed; the next of a shy, lonely adolescent girl beginning her first day at what was her third new school that year, desperately trying to catch up with the lessons; and the last – and most disturbing image – that of a teenaged Tessa, alone and forced to sleep in her car because she had no family or friends to take her in.

And yet she'd come through all of that without any obvious emotional scars, save for the shyness she still exhibited and her fear of succumbing to the dark depression that had ultimately been responsible for her mother's death. She had taken the required steps to acquire a good job, to support herself and make certain she would never again be a victim of poverty. And throughout the telling of her story, Tessa had never once complained about the lot life had dealt her, or expected sympathy because of it. It was remarkable, really, what she and her soon-to-be ex-husband had made of themselves, given their unfortunate upbringings. From what he'd surmised, Tessa and Peter had both worked hard to support themselves with multiple jobs and had lived a very frugal lifestyle.

And learning about the abuse Peter had suffered as a boy, and the subsequent effect it had had on his relationship with Tessa explained quite a bit. Peter's seeming inability to be intimate with his gorgeous young wife made it clear to Ian why Tessa was so inexperienced sexually.

'Christ,' he thought in some amusement, 'she's practically a virgin, mate.'

He felt nothing but empathy for what Peter had suffered, and great appreciation for how the boy had helped out an innocent young girl, but he was also selfish enough to feel elation that he – and not Tessa's ex – would be the one to bring her true sexual fulfillment.

Ian finished the last of his brandy, made sure the fire was doused, and went upstairs to bed. Tessa was sleeping peacefully, her cheeks flushed becomingly as he undressed and slid into bed beside her. And as she turned towards him automatically in her sleep, his heart sang with the joy of finally having her exactly where he'd always dreamed of for so long.

***

Tessa's hands were a little unsteady as she unlocked the door to her apartment. She'd rather foolishly hoped that Ian would agree to just drop her off and not expect to come inside, but she really ought to have known better. Ever since she'd told him about her past last night, he'd seemed extra protective, even more solicitous of her, and when she'd told him just now that he really didn't have to see her inside the look he had given her was almost scathing.

"Don't be silly," he'd told her firmly. "Tessa, after hearing how you've had to struggle for so many years I'm not expecting that you'll be living in a penthouse somewhere."

But she honestly didn't think he had any idea of just how humble her tiny apartment was. Ian was used to Georgian brick mansions and Tuscan villas and staying in the owners suites of luxury hotels. Not a dark, poorly insulated and shabby little set of rooms inside an old building located in a not so nice part of the city.

Tessa offered up a silent thanks that at the very least the place was as clean and tidy as possible. After the shocking turn of events in Ian's office last Thursday evening – which now seemed as though it had happened three months ago as opposed to a mere three nights – she'd been so rattled and unable to sleep that she had cleaned the entire apartment from top to bottom.

But no amount of cleaning or tidying could hide the fact that the apartment was cramped, with scuffed wood floors, only one window that let in filtered light, and a rather odd assortment of mismatched furniture that she and Peter had acquired from a variety of sources over the years – garage sales, thrift shops, ready-to-assemble pieces, and even things that had been left in front yards with a FREE sign attached to them. The apartment couldn't have been any different from Ian's own splendid, elegant home and Tessa was very uncomfortable having him here.

He was silent and unsmiling as he walked inside, his big, broad-shouldered body dwarfing the place and making it seem even tinier than usual. She knew that steely-eyed gaze of his that never missed a trick would be quick to pick up on the cheap furniture, lack of space, and the cracks in the wall. If he had been even two inches taller his head would have brushed against the low ceiling.

"When is your lease on this place up?" he asked briskly.

She tried to interpret the rather closed-off expression on his face but quickly gave up and answered him. "In April. Peter's been sending me a little money every month to help with the rent, but I'll need to find something more affordable very soon."

Ian frowned. "What's the rent?"

Tessa told him and didn't miss his startled reaction. "I know it sounds like a lot for such a small place but, well, that's what rents are like in San Francisco these days."

"I'll pay off the lease for you," he offered abruptly. "I don't have my checkbook with me but I can bring a check to your landlord tomorrow. I don't want you staying here even one more night, Tessa."

She shook her head. "I can't let you do that, Ian. Not that I don't appreciate the thought but – I just can't. Until we're ready for me to travel with you and work as we discussed, I have to earn my own way."

"That's ridiculous," he scoffed. "You can still keep working until you decide it's time to give notice – which I trust will be much sooner than later. That's not a valid reason why you can't move in with me right away. If you're concerned someone will see us arriving at work together, I can arrange for a separate driver for you or just get a taxi to take you to the office."

Tessa laid a hand on his arm gently. "No, Ian. This needs to be on my terms – please? I'm not ready for that – to just move in with you so quickly. You've told me more than once that you don't want to overwhelm me. So – don't. Please."

"God, I'm sorry, darling." He swiftly took her into his arms. "You're absolutely right. I told you that I wanted to indulge but never control you and I meant every word. I'm just so anxious to have you with me all the time. Especially after seeing this neighborhood you live in. Forgive me, but there were a few too many unsavory characters we passed on these last few blocks for me not to fear for your safety."

"I know." She rubbed his back as if to reassure him. "But I always lock my doors, never go out at night alone, and keep aware of what's going on. The building even has its own laundry room so I don't have to go out for that."

"It's not just the area." He waved a hand around the room. "This place – I'm sorry, Tessa, but it's just – depressing. There's a crack in the ceiling, mold in the corner, a draft coming in through the window. I intend for you to live like a princess from now on, not a peasant or a pauper."

Tessa shrugged. "I know it's not much but it's actually a lot better than some places I lived in with my mother. We had some pretty awful living conditions over the years. If you think this place is bad, you'd really want to start hitting something if you could see some of the others."

He ran a hand through his hair in agitation. "Christ, I'm going to have nightmares about that, I swear. Every time I let myself imagine what it was like for you - "

"Then don't," she admonished. "Let's start forgetting about my past and focus on the future. I – I just need a little time, Ian. Okay? I mean, just a few days ago you were my boss – *only* my boss – and I had zero idea that you even thought of me in that way. And now you want me to move in with you and travel everywhere and take care of me. I mean, it all sounds like some sort of wonderful fantastic dream but, well, my head is kind of spinning when I try to take it all in."

"Shh." He lowered her head to his shoulder. "You're right, of course you are. I'm just so used to being in complete control of everything around me that I need to step back just a bit and give you a little space."

Tessa nodded. "It's just – ever since Peter left I've been completely on my own for the first time in years. Even when my mother was at her sickest, in her deepest depression, I could still tell myself I wasn't alone, could fool myself into believing that she'd come through for me if I really needed her. And then when Peter offered to marry me so I wouldn't have to go into foster care- well, it was easy to just depend on him after that. I got too complacent, letting him handle the finances and make most of the decisions. It just felt good to let someone else take care of me for a change."

"That's completely understandable," he soothed her. "In fact, it seems like a very natural reaction given all of the hardships you'd endured over the years."

"When Peter moved out in September, it left this huge hole in my life. I had to start figuring out how to rely on myself again, and not to depend on another person. I've just really started to do that, Ian. And as much as I want to be with you, I'm not sure I should be letting myself depend so completely on someone else."

Ian clasped her face between his hands almost desperately. "I am not letting you go, Tessa," he bit out harshly. "If it's space you need for a while, I'll give it to you, even if it means leaving you in this place for a time. But I'll do whatever I have to in order to keep you with me in the long term."

"I'm not going anywhere," she murmured, sliding her hands over his. "I want to be with you, too, more than anything. But I don't want to feel weak or helpless again, or worry that I can't look out for myself if necessary. Can you understand that?"

He touched his lips to her forehead. "Of course I can. And with that thought in mind, let me offer you a different alternative. If you'd rather, Tessa, you could go back to school, earn your college degree. I'd still want you to live with me, but if it made you happy I'd gladly support you going to college. Even if it meant I couldn't have you traveling with me like we discussed. At least you'd have the security of that degree, knowing that you could always fall back on it to get a job if necessary."

She was touched by his offer, and placed a hand on his chest. "Thank you, Ian. I'm not sure if that's what I want but it's nice to know I have the option. I'll give it some thought. And I *will* move in with you, sooner than later. I just need a little time to process all of this. Is that – is it okay?"

He gave her a bone-crushing hug. "It's more than okay, love. And if I start acting too domineering I want you to promise you'll tell me, hmm?"

Tessa smirked. "You mean like earlier today when you got upset about the clothes?"

Ian had the good graces to look properly chagrined and nodded reluctantly. "Yes, damn it, like that."

After dinner at a very good Japanese restaurant where they'd shared sushi and sake, they had stopped at Ian's house in order for Tessa to pick up her things. And had promptly become engaged in what had threatened to become their first real argument.

At issue was the clothing and other things he'd bought her, things he'd fully expected her to take to her apartment and use. After all, he'd explained, he intended on buying her a great deal more, with or without her approval, so she might as well make use of the items he'd already purchased.

"But I can't wear any of these things to the office," she'd explained gently. "Gina and Alicia and the others would recognize these labels – especially the red soles on those Louboutins – from the other side of the room and wonder how I was able to afford them. If we're going to keep things discreet between us at work, no one can suspect I have a new man in my life. Especially not one who can afford to buy me a seven hundred dollar skirt or a three hundred dollar blouse."

Ian had scowled. "I thought I'd cut off all those bloody price tags. And I wanted you to have some nice things for the office, darling. Not to mention," he'd added with a wink, "I owe you a blouse since you ruined one of yours on Thursday. Thank God for leaky printer cartridges. Otherwise, I'd still be in the very beginning stages of the extremely involved plan I had to seduce you. That faulty cartridge sped up my game plan by at least three months."

They'd argued back and forth a bit longer, until he'd rather sullenly agreed with her reasoning. He was somewhat mollified when she consented to take the lingerie, loungewear and toiletries he'd bought, reasoning that no one would be able to tell what she was wearing underneath her clothes, or determine what brand of shampoo she'd used.

Ian had growled. "You're damned right no one else is going to see those skimpy bits you've got on beneath your clothes. Especially that bra you have on right now. Christ, it makes your tits look even bigger than they are. Or like they're going to fall out of the cups if you breathe the wrong way."

Tessa had giggled, despite the stormy expression on his face. "Should I remind you that you were the one who bought it for me?"

He had pulled her into his arms, his good humor restored. "Perhaps we should just let you try everything on before we buy more things. Mmm, my very own private fashion show, with you as the only model. Remind me to call Marlene and set that up."

But as they walked down to the garage to get into Ian's imposing black Range Rover – one of four vehicles he owned – he'd become pissy all over again, this time due to the old, well-worn raincoat that Tessa had been buttoning up.

He'd glared evilly at the coat. "You really have to wear that bloody thing? Do you have any idea how much I hate the sight of that particular garment?"

Tessa had fiddled with one of the buttons. "I'm sorry if it offends you, but aside from a couple of sweaters and an old sweatshirt it's the only outerwear I own. Not counting the three thousand dollar cashmere coat you just bought me. Or that cute leather bomber jacket that cost - "

He'd placed a hand over her mouth, cutting her off. "I get the picture. You can't walk into the office decked out in designer garb or that coven of witches you work with will suspect you've got a rich sugar daddy taking care of you." He'd rubbed her back comfortingly. "I just hate to see you having to wear the same things week after week, love. I want to lavish all the beautiful clothes and shoes and jewels you never had before on you. But I know I have to be patient. You're trying to be the sensible one here, and I'm overreacting."

"It's all right," she'd told him with a kiss. "I understand how you feel, even though labels or designers don't matter in the least to me. It's you I want, Ian, not the things you can give me."

He'd pulled her into his arms at that point, kissing her hard. "God, I really hit the jackpot when I found you, didn't I?" he'd murmured.

Tessa had thought the subject of her coat closed until he'd pulled out of the garage.

Ian had glanced over and given the coat one final grimace. "You can keep it for now, but mark my words. The day you move in with me permanently and quit your job, we're having an official raincoat burning party. And I get to do the honors of tossing the damned thing into the fire."

Chapter Fourteen

Late January

"What time is His Hotness due in today?"

Tessa forced herself not to flinch or otherwise betray her reaction to Gina's casual inquiry. She also had to bite her tongue to stop herself from automatically replying to the question by informing everyone that Ian's Town Car was even now pulling up to the curb downstairs, and that he would be striding through the office within the next few minutes.

She knew this, of course, because he'd just sent her a quick text with that very message. Within the first week of their new relationship, he'd presented her with a brand new, state of the art smartphone. Ian had been appalled to notice how old and outdated her cell phone had been, and the one he'd replaced it with was linked directly to his own.

"My private cell phone," he'd clarified, "and not the one I use for business. Only a very few people even have this number so we don't need to worry about anyone from the office reading texts or emails we send each other."

And he had very quickly made it a habit to send her regular and frequent messages, especially over these past few days when he'd been away on business. He'd flown out last Sunday afternoon on the corporate jet to visit properties in the Pacific Northwest – Portland, Seattle, Vancouver and Victoria. It had been the first time they'd been separated since becoming lovers, and the time apart had been agonizing for Tessa. She hadn't imagined she could miss him so much after being together for such a short period of time, but the separation had been awful. The only things that had gotten her though the last four and a half days had been all those texts and emails, and his nightly phone calls.

She knew his plane had landed last night, for he'd called her on the way home from the airport. He'd called her again as she was getting dressed for work this morning, largely to ask her in a sexy voice what set of undies she was going to wear today so that he could imagine her in them all day. Just the sound of his deep, cultured voice had been more than enough to arouse her, and she'd almost had to change out of the lacy black panties she'd put on when they quickly grew damp.

"You have no idea how much I'm looking forward to seeing you again, darling," he'd told her huskily. "I may lock you in my bedroom all weekend. After being celibate for over two years now I can't even go four days without you."

Tessa knew the feeling all too well. Sex with Peter had been so infrequent and so frustratingly unsatisfying that she hadn't known what a normal, healthy sexual relationship was really like. But even after such a brief time with Ian, her body craved him almost constantly. She wasn't sure how she was going to hold back the urge to fling herself into his arms when he walked through the office any minute now.

"Ah, and he's arrived," murmured Kevin in a hushed tone. "What suit is it today, Gina?"

Gina glanced up as Ian began to walk past their cubicles. "It's the black pinstriped Dolce & Gabbana. He must have a hot date tonight, usually only wears that one on special occasions."

Tessa couldn't hold back the small smile that crossed her face, first from knowing that Ian's "hot date" was with her, and also from realizing that he'd worn that particular suit especially for her.

They had both been fresh from a very intimate shower they'd taken after a workout in his home gym. It had been last Sunday, the day he'd had to fly out on his trip, and he'd invited her to help him pack. Tessa had happily agreed, liking the idea of doing things for him, and also enjoying the opportunity to familiarize herself a little with the contents of his extensive wardrobe.

At his instructions, she'd located the various drawers where his socks, underwear, and workout clothes were stored, and handed him several sets of each. He packed everything with the expertise of a longtime world traveler into his Bottega Veneta suitcase, along with a fully stocked toiletry case that he always kept ready to go.

"Suits next, darling, then shirts and ties. Which suits do you fancy the best?" he'd asked.

Tessa's gaze had been drawn automatically to the elegant black pinstriped one. He didn't wear that one very often, but she could easily imagine how handsome and sinfully sexy he would look in it.

"This one's my favorite," she had told him. "So maybe you shouldn't take it with you."

Ian had cocked his head to one side, regarding her curiously. "And why is that, love?"

She had stalked towards him then, her eyes glued to the wide expanse of his bare chest, the towel wrapped around his waist his only article of clothing. She'd been wearing a beautiful little robe he'd bought her, of champagne silk that ended at mid-thigh and felt decadent against her skin.

Tessa had run her fingers lightly up over his ripped biceps to the rock hard muscles of his broad shoulders. Her lips had begun to trace a path across his pecs. "Because I don't want any other women to see how hot you look in it. Especially since I won't be there with you," she had murmured huskily.

Then, before he could stop her, she'd sunk to her knees and ripped away his towel, exposing his massively aroused penis. The curse he'd uttered as she'd taken him into her hands had been guttural, but he hadn't offered up any resistance as she had stroked him persuasively.

"You're getting awfully good at this," he'd croaked, as one of her hands pumped his cock while the other reached back to give his swollen balls a light squeeze.

Tessa had given him an impish grin. "You know what they say – practice makes perfect. But I really think I need to keep practicing, don't you?"

Ian's breath had expelled in a long, drawn-out hiss as she'd taken him into her mouth. As she had continued to suck him eagerly, he'd fisted his hand in her wet hair, holding her head still as he thrust into her warm, willing mouth.

After he came minutes later, he'd hauled her up into his arms and whispered naughtily in her ear, "I think you've perfected that particular skill as well."

And then he had proceeded to untie the belt of her silky robe, cupping her breasts, before dropping to the floor and returning the favor she'd just bestowed on him – using his considerable oral skills to bring her to a stunning orgasm.

Tessa squirmed a little in her desk chair as she remembered just how hard she'd come, and then realized her panties were getting soaked all over again at the recollection.

She was able to pull it together just enough to murmur a subdued "Good morning, Mr. Gregson" along with the others as he passed them by. Any disappointment she felt at knowing he couldn't make any sort of direct eye contact with her, or single her out in any way in his greeting, was quickly dispelled a couple of minutes later when her new phone pinged, signaling an incoming text.

Tessa kept the phone tucked into a pocket of her purse, where she could easily take discreet little peeks at it without any of her co-workers noticing. She forced herself not to smile or betray her reaction in any other way, but couldn't stop the warm feeling that spread throughout her body as she read Ian's text.

Good morning, love. Wishing I could give u a big kiss right now. Can't wait 4 tonite.

She waited until she was sure no one else was watching and tapped out a reply.

Morning to u 2. Txs for wearing my fav suit. U look very sexy.

There was a prompt reply. **Txs 4 wearing my fav undies. Counting minutes till I can take them off u.**

She had to fight off the urge to giggle as she replied. **Yes but I might have 2 take them off cuz they're kind of damp.**

Ian didn't respond for almost ten minutes, and she'd almost given up hope that he would when the familiar ping sounded. This time she couldn't hold back the smile that stretched across her features.

Sorry on a call. Sounds like u need 2 keep spare undies with

u. We'll buy more tomorrow.

Kevin looked at her curiously as she forced her attention back to her computer screen. "You look like you're in a good mood, sweetie. Whatcha smiling about?"

Tessa tried her hardest to seem nonchalant. "Oh, just thinking about an episode of *Modern Family* I caught last night. This really hilarious scene where the gay couple had these oversized stuffed animals strapped to the roof of their car."

Kevin's face instantly lit up. "I know exactly what scene you're talking about. The stuffed gorilla keeps rocking back and forth like it's trying to hump the elephant. Priceless, isn't it?"

That fortunately distracted him – sadly, it didn't seem to really take much to accomplish that – and he was riffing about other TV shows for the next half hour. Meanwhile, Tessa continued to feel a little thrill each time she got a flirty text from Ian. It was almost like they were high school sweethearts, exchanging naughty messages during English class. Except that she'd never had a real boyfriend in high school, and had certainly never been carefree enough to text flirt with one. So she allowed herself this indulgence now, this feeling like she was sixteen again and flirting with the really hot guy she'd had a mad crush on for two years. She allowed the indulgence because she'd never had the opportunity before, had never really been sixteen or even a teenager, had never known the sweetness and innocence of a first love.

The work day flew by quickly, as it usually seemed to do when Ian returned from a trip. Andrew was delegating tasks to the team right and left, no doubt as quickly as his boss was passing them on to him. Tessa had three complex spreadsheets to update plus two new ones to create, and immersed herself in her work.

She was so engrossed in what she was doing that at first she paid no attention to what Gina and Alicia were yakking about. Tessa honestly had no idea how the two of them got any significant amount of work done, given the frequency and length of their conversations. But then she caught the tail end of a question Gina was asking, and found herself listening discreetly for Alicia's reply.

"…didn't bring a date to the ballet fundraiser? Not even his little ballerina friend?"

Tess knew they were discussing Ian, and an event he'd attended last week. It had been, as Gina mentioned, a fundraising cocktail party for the San Francisco Ballet, of which Ian was a patron. He had been reluctant to attend without Tessa, but had glumly acknowledged he couldn't very well take her along. Yet.

"This is why you need to move things along, darling," he'd admonished. *"Why you need to resign and move in with me – so that I can take you with me to these dreadfully boring events and show you off to everyone."*

She hadn't been able to resist teasing him just a little. "But if they're so boring, wouldn't we be better off finding something more – er, fun to do?"

He'd given her a light smack on the ass. *"Cheeky little devil. Yes, you're right, but there are some events I just can't shrug off, I'm afraid. However, if you were with me, then they wouldn't be nearly so boring."* He'd whispered in her ear then, causing a shiver to run up her spine, *"I'd probably try to find ways all evening of copping a feel. That would certainly make things a damned sight more interesting."*

Tessa bit her lip to keep from groaning at the memory, especially when she recalled what had happened next. She distracted herself from her wayward thoughts by casually eavesdropping on the rest of her co-workers conversation.

"No, he was definitely there solo according to my mother," confirmed Alicia. "And didn't stick around very long, either. Plus, his date for the Christmas party – remember the banker in the Elie Saab gown? – has apparently been seen out with a new man."

Gina grinned. "So does this mean His Hotness is back on the market? Maybe it's time for you to finally turn in that resignation and go for it, girl. Oh, but you've got Ross now, don't you?"

Alicia sniffed. "Seriously? You think Ross can hold a candle to him? *Nobody* is on the same scale as the boss man, *nobody*. Besides, when he showed up without a date last week the speculation was running rampant that he has someone else but that she isn't local. If he keeps attending these events on his own, then we'll know it's true."

'Not necessarily' was on the tip of Tessa's tongue. She and Ian had discussed the matter of his past dates, and he'd explained in some detail about each of the women he'd escorted to functions over the last couple of years. Rebecca – the banker – was carrying on a clandestine affair with a married politician; Erica – the news anchor – was married but her husband was severely disabled and rarely left their home; and the ballerina – Gabriela – an ethereally lovely, waifishly slim portrait of delicate femininity was actually a lesbian. She kept that fact a carefully guarded secret for fear that it would have a negative impact on her career.

But despite the fact that his relationships with all three women were strictly platonic, Ian had declared he wouldn't escort any of them again. Until such time as Tessa was able to arrive on his arm, he would attend as few events as possible and those selected ones alone. She longed to throw that fact in Alicia's snotty face, but continued to keep a lid on her emotions.

Fortunately it was time for the roommates to leave for lunch, and it was blissfully quiet once again. Tessa was so focused on her work that she didn't hear her phone pinging. It was three texts later that she finally paid attention and hastily grabbed her phone, tapping out a swift reply to Ian's messages.

Sorry lost in your spreadsheets. This last one is tuff.

His reply came within seconds.

Need some help?

She couldn't suppress a wicked grin as she answered. *With the spreadsheet or my wet panties?*

Long seconds later his reply pinged. *I think u have discovered the fine art of sexting. Tonite u might discover the equally fine art of spanking.*

Tessa clapped a hand over her mouth to keep from giggling, conscious that Shelby and Marisol were nearby. She couldn't resist typing back. *OK I'll behave.*

Ian's reply was swift. *Damn. Not the answer I wanted.*

Mischievously she replied. *But u can still spank me. Sir.*

When she had teasingly called him that at work one day last

week, he'd explained to her later than evening about BDSM and dominant/submissive relationships.

"The submissive – most often the female in the relationship – is supposed to address the dominant as Sir or Master. So when you call me that, it makes me feel a bit uncomfortable. If you have to address me in the office, let's try to keep it to Mr. Gregson, hmm?"

She'd toyed with the lapel of his jacket before asking him quietly, "That – that isn't the sort of relationship you've ever had, is it? Or want to have?"

"God, no," he'd replied fervently. "I've never been interested in any of that stuff. Nor would I ever consider marring even an inch of your perfect skin with a whip or a rope. And I would never, ever, order you around or demand your obedience. That thought doesn't appeal to me in the least. We're going to be equal partners in this relationship, Tessa. Both in and out of bed."

As usual, whatever he said was so overwhelmingly romantic that she'd felt like swooning in his arms. Tessa was still having to pinch herself on a continual basis, in disbelief that someone as wonderful as Ian was really interested in her. She'd been half-afraid that all he'd wanted was a quick roll in the sack, and that as soon as they had slept together he would get bored and break things off. But it seemed her fears were completely unfounded, for everything he'd said had indicated he expected their relationship to be a long term one.

Ian had an afternoon meeting and then a conference call, so the frequent, flirty texts came to a halt. But as it drew closer to five o'clock – the time she was due to meet him – Tessa couldn't help the flutters of excitement that shimmied through her body. She remained quiet as her co-workers chattered about their weekend plans, and when Shelby asked her directly what she had going on, she kept her reply intentionally vague.

"Oh, you know, the usual stuff. Sleeping in a bit, maybe catching a yoga class, just relaxing."

She was relieved that she didn't actually have to lie, because she did plan to sleep in and spend some time relaxing. The fact that she planned to do both with Ian was not something her coworkers needed to know.

Tessa wasn't at all surprised to see the black Town Car parked in the exact location that Ian had texted her. She knew he hated these clandestine meetings, having to sneak around so no one from the office would see them together. And he'd been fairly patient so far, but Tessa knew his natural tendency to control would take over sooner than later and he'd be pressuring her to quit her job and move in with him. She was probably ten kinds of an idiot for not automatically giving in to him and doing exactly as he wanted. She couldn't imagine too many other women in her position resisting Ian for very long. But she just needed some time to feel more comfortable with him, more secure that she wasn't going to embarrass or disappoint him in some way, as well as feeling more confident in her own abilities to take care of herself and not just let Ian assume entire responsibility for her.

Simon was standing by the side of the car as she approached, a polite smile affixed to his otherwise impassive features. He gave her a nod as he opened the back door for her. "Good evening, Miss Lockwood."

Tessa smiled a bit uncertainly, not able to keep herself from worrying if the rather starchy Simon considered her a golddigger. Or a slut. Or both. She shook off her hopefully unfounded fears and merely replied, "You, too, Simon. Thank you."

And then any fears or doubts she might have been harboring were swiftly dashed away as Ian's hand closed firmly over her arm, pulling her into his embrace as she slid onto the seat.

"Christ, I missed you," he rasped, and then his mouth took hers in a raw, open-mouthed kiss, his tongue sweeping through her mouth demandingly.

Tessa clutched the lapels of his black wool overcoat and kissed him back hungrily, as starved for his touch as he so obviously was for hers. Neither of them noticed Simon discreetly starting up the car and pulling out into the very congested downtown commute traffic.

They were both breathing hard when Ian finally lifted his head, and Tessa was startled to realize she'd somehow managed to climb onto his lap. But when she started to ease off of him back onto the seat, his big hands clamped down on her hips, holding her in place.

Her cheeks flushed, she whispered to him urgently, "Aren't you afraid Simon will notice?"

Ian grinned, shaking his head. "Not in the least. Simon is very discreet, as I've mentioned before, and he also knows I'm quite fixated on you. So you can keep this very delectable bottom of yours right where it is."

Tessa sighed in bliss and lowered her head to his shoulder in surrender. "Okay." She turned her head and pressed a kiss to his cheek before murmuring softly, "I really missed you, too."

His arms tightened about her in reaction. "I trust you're going to show me exactly how much as soon as we get inside the house," he replied in a low, urgent voice.

She bit down on the inside of her cheek, stifling a gasp as his hand worked its way under the hem of her black skirt, squeezing the flesh of her inner thigh. "I'm not sure I can wait that long," she told him, trying very, very hard not to moan as his long fingers traced the crotch of her panties.

"I can tell," he breathed in a low voice. "You're very aroused, aren't you, love? Have you been like this all day?"

She nodded, closing her eyes in ecstasy as he slid one finger beneath her soaked underwear and began to stroke the moist folds of her labia. "Ever – ever since you called me this morning," she confessed breathlessly.

Ian's tongue traced around her ear while his finger continued to tease her drenched slit. "And I've been hard and aching for you all damned day, imagining how you look in these skimpy black lace bits. Stockings, too, I see." His hand slid back down to the top of her leg where her silky black thigh-highs ended.

Her body suddenly felt overly warm, her breasts swollen and achy, and she squirmed on his lap, her bottom brushing against his thick, fully erect cock. "Please," she whispered shakily, not quite sure what she was asking him for.

But he knew, apparently very well, because this time he slid two fingers under the band of her panties, plunging them as deep inside of her as he could manage, given their somewhat limited space.

"Shhh," he urged in a hushed tone, as a low moan began to escape her throat. "If I agree to take care of you here, love, than you have to promise to be very, very quiet. Knowing how shy you are, you'll never be able to look Simon in the face again if he hears you come."

Tessa gave a quick nod, and then fisted her knuckles against her mouth. Stifling the sounds of her pleasure proved an almost impossible task, however, especially when Ian's talented fingers brought her to a swift, stunning climax. Still, she remained silent, the very thought of Simon hearing her beyond mortifying.

This time when she slid off his lap, Ian didn't protest, merely taking her hand in his.

"Thank you." She leaned over to whisper in his ear. "I'll, um, return the favor later."

He chuckled before whispering back, "We're not keeping score here, love. But I'll certainly take you up on your very inviting offer before the weekend is over. Quite possibly before this night is."

For the remainder of the drive to his house, they were on their best behavior, their linked hands the only parts of their bodies touching. They talked about work, his trip, the weather forecast for the weekend which was supposed to be pleasant and warmer than was the norm for this time of year.

Tessa's interest was piqued. "Can we have breakfast out on the terrace? I don't mind if it's a little cool in the morning, do you?"

He smiled at her indulgently, as though she were a little girl who'd just asked for a new doll. "Not at all, darling. Especially since the terrace is nicely sheltered from the wind. Not to mention all the patio heaters I have outside."

She beamed at him. "So, it's a date, then? Will you let me cook for you again?"

Ian brushed his thumb over her lips. "If that gives you pleasure, then, yes, of course. But you're going to spoil me very quickly if I allow you to keep doing things like that."

"I like doing things for you," she told him guilessly. "And you deserve to be spoiled, especially after everything you've done for me. Has no one ever done that for you?"

"Spoiled me, you mean?" He shook his head. "Not that I've lived a deprived lifestyle by any means. But my parents were determined that my brothers and I not grow up to be pampered, snobbish brats so we weren't overly indulged as children. As far as another woman spoiling me – I can honestly say that you're the only one who's ever offered to do so."

Tessa smiled in delight. "Once again I'm very happy that I was the first for you in some small way."

Ian's expression was one of incredible tenderness, so much that it made her heart soar. "Tessa, you have no idea how many firsts you've already given me. When the time is right, I'll tell you exactly what they are."

They arrived at his house moments later, not giving her an opportunity to quiz him on his mysterious comment. And then, almost the very second the front door was shut behind them, she wasn't given the chance to do anything but submit willingly to his very urgent desires.

"Hurry," he urged, leading her up the stairs to his room. "It feels like four years since I've had you instead of only four days."

Clothes were shed in between hungry, passionate kisses, a trail of coats, shoes, shirts, and other garments left in their wake as they stumbled into his bedroom. Tessa still wore her lingerie and shoes as he all but flung her onto the bed, while he was splendidly nude save for his snug-fitting black briefs. Her blue eyes grew round and huge as he swiftly divested himself of his last remaining article of clothing, baring his truly magnificent body to her eager gaze, the sight of his massive erection causing her to pant in anticipation.

She hadn't expected him to be gentle, given the near-desperation of his kisses, but she still cried out in shocked surprise as he fisted one hand in her panties, yanking them down her legs, just before surging as deep inside of her as possible in one masterful stroke.

"Ah, ah, oh, my God," she wailed, feeling the head of his cock battering against the tip of her womb. "Ian – oh - "

Her voice trailed off as he began moving inside of her roughly, his voice low as he uttered a series of brusque instructions.

"Lift your legs up onto my shoulders. Yes, like that. God, that's good."

"That's it, love, wrap those beautiful long legs around my neck."

"Ah, Christ, you're so damned tight. I'm not going to last long this first time."

Just when Tessa didn't think he could possibly fill her even one more inch, couldn't get any deeper inside of her, he slid his hands beneath her buttocks and lifted her several inches off the mattress. At his first hard thrust from this position, she came instantly, sobbing out his name as the pleasure rocked through her body.

He continued his hard, almost brutal thrusts until she heard him curse vividly, "Jesus, fuck," and then he was coming uncontrollably, his body jerking over and over. Tessa gazed up at him, spellbound by his erotic male beauty – his dark hair damp with sweat, his eyes tightly shut as he continued to spill himself inside of her. Even as she felt the hot, sticky bursts of semen begin to trickle down her inner thighs, he was still coming, still filling her with his seed.

He groaned as he collapsed on top of her, crushing her much lighter body into the mattress as he buried his damp face against the side of her neck. She stroked his head soothingly, her lips touching his temples and brow. They remained just that way for several minutes, until the weight of his heavily muscled body was too much and she began to gasp a little for air. Ian quickly slid off of her onto his side, drawing her close.

"Sorry, sorry," he murmured, his hand tilting her head back. "I didn't hurt you, did I? Not just now, but, well, before when - "

"No." She gave him a brief kiss. "You didn't. But I think I might have seen some stars there for a few minutes."

Ian chuckled. "I know the feeling, love. Except I think I was in another solar system entirely. God, the way you make me lose all control, Tessa – that's never, ever happened to me before."

She ran her hand up and down his arm, squeezing his bulging bicep along the way. "It's hard to imagine you ever losing control. At the office you're always in total command, everyone's more than a little intimidated by you."

He captured her roving hand, running his tongue over the knuckles. "Ah, but I don't have a mostly naked, entirely tempting goddess to entice me into losing control there. Well, I do, but you're not - "

"Mostly naked there," she finished. "Except for one very embarrassing time."

He laughed in recollection. "I have to keep the door to my washroom closed most of the time, you know. Otherwise, every time I look in that direction all I can see is the vision you made standing in the doorway that night, these gorgeous breasts almost spilling out of that bra. Speaking of which."

Tessa gasped as his hand slid up her bare hip past her ribcage to squeeze one breast. In the next moment she'd been tumbled onto her back and he was straddling her thighs, his gaze locked hotly on her breasts still encased in the black lace bra.

He dipped a finger into her deep cleavage. "I've been imagining you all day long in this bra, you know," he told her huskily. "But no fantasy is quite as remarkable as the real thing. Let me see you now, Tessa."

He unhooked the bra with ease and peeled the cups away, baring her full breasts. Their groans were simultaneous as he filled his palms with her warm flesh, his fingers plucking the nipples into even harder peaks. She whimpered as his caresses grew more aggressive, his fingers twisting and pinching the nipples, his large hands palming her breasts roughly.

"Do you like this?" he asked in a voice that demanded a reply.

"Y-yes," she breathed. "S-so good."

Ian slid down her body, his lips tracing a hot path from the base of her throat down between her breasts. Then his tongue was licking a slow, deliberate circle around one reddened nipple, as her back bowed off the mattress, her hands clutching at the sheets.

"Easy, love," he soothed her, stroking her hip. "You're so

responsive, Tessa, so naturally uninhibited."

"Ummm." She sighed in bliss as his mouth closed over her nipple, sucking it until she was squirming. He shifted his lips to the other breast, while his hand slid down over her quivering belly into the soft nest of her pubic hair. Two long fingers thrust deep inside her slit, where she was still sticky from his very recent orgasm.

"You're all creamy from my cum," he purred in her ear, his thumb brushing over her clit and making her thrash wildly beneath him. "It feels as though I've marked you, claimed this tight little pussy as my own." His fingers thrust as deeply inside her as they could reach. "And you are mine, Tessa, make no mistake about it. You belong to me now, and I've no intention of letting that change."

"Yes, yours," she sobbed as he continued to arouse her, the thrust of his fingers and the rasp of his thumb twin assaults on her already over-stimulated senses. She cried out almost plaintively as he brought her over the edge yet again.

"Beautiful," he murmured, holding her tight. "You're magnificent when you come, Tessa. It makes me want to see how many times I can bring you that sort of bliss."

She felt limp and replete, almost boneless as her arms twined loosely around his neck. "Okay," was all she could manage in response.

Ian gave a low laugh. "Perhaps just one more, hmm? Then I'll get us fed so we can keep our strength up. After all, our weekend has barely begun."

Tessa was so lightheaded and sated from her most recent orgasm that she didn't think it was possible for her to even move, much less make love again. But then Ian was gently rolling her onto her side, his hard body spooning her, and she gasped when he eased inside of her from that position.

"All right there, love?" he hummed, even as he lifted her leg to wrap around his hip. "You're not too sore, are you?"

"Mmm, no." She expelled a breath as he slid in and out of her, gently this time, as though he were savoring each slow, careful thrust.

"You feel so good, Tessa," he groaned. "God, I've never felt this much before, felt like I could keep fucking you for hours. It's perfect, you're perfect."

He grasped her chin and tipped her head back just far enough so he could kiss her long and hot, his tongue sweeping lazily through her mouth until she was mindless with the pleasure.

Her climax this time was as gentle and tender as his lovemaking had been, but no less satisfying. Ian held her within his arms for a long time after he came, until they were almost falling asleep.

After a leisurely shower, they dressed in comfy loungewear and picked up their discarded clothing from the hallway and stairs. Ian ordered in Chinese food for them, from a restaurant that was light years better than the greasy takeout places in her neighborhood. They ate in the kitchen, sharing a bottle of perfectly chilled Chardonnay, before settling in to watch a movie in the library.

Mrs. Sargent had stocked their favorite ice cream flavors for them – Ben & Jerry's cookie dough for her, Haagen Dazs chocolate peanut butter for him.

Ian grinned as Tessa licked ice cream off the back of her spoon. "Remind me to add whipped cream to next week's shopping list. Maybe some chocolate or caramel syrup, too."

Tessa wrinkled her nose. "The ice cream is rich enough for me. I'm not sure I want to spoil the taste with that other stuff."

He leaned over and licked a dab of ice cream off the corner of her mouth. "Ah, but it isn't for the ice cream, love," he teased. He trailed a finger around one of her breasts. "I think this would taste even more delicious with some syrup drizzled on it." His hand drifted over her belly to cup the juncture of her thighs. "And I could get very inventive with a can of whipped cream."

Her head fell back against the sofa, her spoon clattering to the floor as he rubbed her clit through her yoga pants. "Sounds – ah, messy. We might – ooh – get the sheets sticky."

His tongue traced over her lips, his mouth cool from the ice cream. "That's the plan, darling."

***

Tessa stared in some dismay at the amount of clothing, shoes, lingerie, and other accessories that had been strategically hung up and arranged around the oversized dressing room. She hadn't realized that they had picked out quite so many items for her to try on while perusing the various racks earlier in the day.

She turned to face Ian, who'd taken a seat on the wide, padded bench that took up most of one wall of the room. "I can't possibly need all of these clothes," she told him firmly. "It will take me hours to try everything on."

He raised a brow at her expectantly. "Well, then, you'd best get on with it, hadn't you? I made dinner reservations for seven-thirty so there's not much time to waste."

Tessa frowned, glancing at the wall clock. "But it's not even one-thirty, we have hours yet."

Ian smiled meaningfully. "Ah, but I have other plans for you this afternoon as well. And you'll likely need both a hot shower and a long nap afterwards."

She felt her cheeks grow warm at his very pointed words. He'd made love to her again last night after carrying her upstairs to bed, but she'd been too sleepy and a bit on the sore side this morning for anything more than some cuddling. To her delight, the weather had been pleasant and sunny, and they'd been able to enjoy breakfast out on his secluded flagstone terrace. The gardens and backyard decks of his house were as beautifully designed as the interior, and Tessa was looking forward to exploring them in more detail with the approach of springtime in a few more weeks.

By mid-morning they'd arrived at Neiman Marcus, and meeting with Marlene who seemed very pleased to be helping them again. Tessa had struggled not to feel lost as Ian had taken her by the hand, examining an endless assortment of clothing for her to try on. Marlene had followed in their wake, tagging each item as they went along and taking copious notes besides.

Ian seemed to have an innate sense for the styles, colors and fabrics that suited her best, and she was more than happy to follow his suggestions. On the rare occasions that she didn't like something he chose, he adhered to her wishes immediately. And if she spotted an item that caught her fancy, he instantly agreed with her choice. The one thing he strictly forbade her to do was even glance at a single price tag.

To give Marlene and her staff adequate time to assemble all of the items, Ian had whisked her off to the in-store restaurant for a quick lunch. Tessa hadn't missed the way the mostly female patrons eyed him admiringly, and she couldn't blame them in the least. He was so handsome, so compelling, that she couldn't take her eyes off of him even for a minute. Ian did everything with a masterful touch, whether it was directing his division of the company, choosing clothes for her, or ordering their lunch. She envied him his easy confidence; the way he commanded respect and attention – both male and female – without much more than a glance; and the natural charisma that drew admiring looks even when he went out of his way to be discreet.

He was clean shaven this morning, but she knew that his five o'clock shadow would start appearing sooner than later. He wasn't wearing a suit since it was a Saturday, but the perfectly pressed gray wool slacks and black fisherman's sweater worn over a crisp white shirt were still elegant and classy, giving him the look of a 1940's cinema star – a Cary Grant or Clark Gable. Tessa was glad she'd worn one of her new dresses – a gorgeous Donna Karan burgundy wool wrap-front paired with taupe Jimmy Choo heels. The chic, expensive outfit made her feel worthy of being seen with Ian, and also of fitting in with the other well-dressed store patrons.

Marlene had raved about her outfit when they'd arrived this morning, complimenting the color and fit.

"But then with your hair and skin tone you can really wear almost any color," the personal shopper had acknowledged. "Not to mention the fabulous figure you have." Then, in a hushed tone for Tessa's ears only, she'd added, "It's small wonder he's so crazy about you, dear. He can't keep his eyes off of you for very long."

It was on the tip of Tessa's tongue to reply that the feeling was mutual, but Ian had called her over at that point to look at a selection of cocktail dresses.

Now in the dressing room, Tessa glanced around in confusion.

"I don't even know where to begin," she confessed.

Ian gestured at the far end of the room. "Just begin down there, darling, and work your way across. If there's something you don't like, you can leave it on the rolling rack they brought in."

She sighed. "Okay, here goes. But I'm telling you right now – there is *no* way you're buying me all of this stuff."

He gave her an indulgent smile. "We'll see."

Tessa was very aware of his gaze upon her as she stripped off the burgundy dress and stood there in her lacy lingerie – a sumptuous bra of blush colored lace and matching lacy panties that bared half of her ass, along with the sheer lace topped thigh-highs that Ian seemed to be fascinated with. She heard him mutter something indecipherable under his breath and glanced his way inquisitively.

"Something the matter?" she asked, reaching for the first dress on the rack.

His gaze was fixated on her breasts as he shook his head slowly. "Not one damned thing, no. You look – Jesus, it's going to be a bloody long afternoon watching you dress and undress."

She gave him a cheeky smile. "Hey, this was your idea. *I* wasn't the one who picked out enough clothes to fill two closets."

Ian scoffed. "Darling, what's on these racks won't even make a dent in the space set aside for you in my closet. Correction, *our* closet, At least it will be when you move in. And you'll need all of these things plus a great deal more when you start traveling with me."

Tessa shook her head in disbelief, even as she zipped up the Roland Mouret dress of jade blue wool. "This is an obscene amount of stuff. I've never needed more than a few blouses and skirts and a handful of dresses before."

He gave her a quick look-over in the classy dress with its asymmetrical neckline and fitted waist before nodding in approval. "That one for sure. The color is perfect for you. And yes, I'm aware you've made do with a limited wardrobe before and think all of this is unnecessary. But if you're going to live in my world, darling, you'll have to get used to this sort of thing. Like it or not, you'll be somewhat in the public eye, certainly photographed when we attend events, and dressing well is something of a requirement."

She gave a reluctant nod "I understand. And I don't want to embarrass you, Ian. I already feel awkward and completely out of your league. I'm sure everyone is wondering what in the world you see in me."

"Tessa." He beckoned her over and she walked to stand between his spread legs, his hands resting on her waist. His voice was stern but gentle as he told her, "You could never embarrass me. I've told you that already. And it's absolutely no secret what I see in you – the most gorgeous, sexy and enchanting woman I've ever known. On the contrary, they're all wondering what a hot young thing sees in this old man."

She opened her mouth to protest but he shushed her with a finger pressed to her lips. "Let's not have this debate again, hmm? I'm absurdly proud to have you with me, Tessa, and I can't wait until we're able to be seen together everywhere. Now, best move this sexy little tush along and torture me some more with the sight of you in these lace bits."

She squealed as he gave her a swat and hurried to change into the next outfit.

After almost an hour, it seemed she'd made barely a dent in the dozens of items hanging on the racks, not to mention trying on the coordinating shoes, scarves, belts and jackets. Marlene popped in every so often to check on the progress, offer up an opinion, fetch a different size if needed. As the second hour drew to a close, Tessa was relieved to see that only one more dress remained.

"Last one," she sighed, zipping up the navy cap-sleeved Michael Kors sheath. "I need a cup of tea after this. Maybe one of those strawberry scones left from breakfast, too."

"Ah, but you forgot about these. You still have to try this little pile on," he reminded her, holding up an exquisite pink lace bra.

There were at least a dozen or more bras, chemises, and other articles of couture lingerie resting on the padded bench to his right.

"Oh." She had in fact forgotten about the intimate apparel he'd also selected and forced herself to stifle a yawn. "Can't I just – um, you know, look these over and kind of guess what will fit right?"

Ian shook his head, handing her the frothy pink lace bra. "After all, this is the part of the fashion show I've been looking forward to the most."

Tessa took the bra from him a bit hesitantly, not missing the heated expression in his gaze. But she only nodded, unhooked the blush colored bra she'd worn here and replaced it with the new pink one.

She couldn't suppress the gasp that rose up from her throat as he pulled her between his spread legs again, then ran a finger over the tops of the lacy cups before slipping under one of the satiny straps.

"Beautiful," he rasped. "We'll definitely take this one."

She was extremely aware of his rapt attention as she continued to try on the remaining items, her nipples seeming to harden a bit more each time she changed into the next piece. She was grateful that she'd kept her own panties on, for she would have soaked through any new ones she tried on – and wouldn't *that* have been humiliating when it came time to check out.

She was down to the third to the last item – a sheer, lacy black chemise with attached garters that ended at the top of her thighs. It was Jenna Leigh and came with a matching black thong that she chose to leave on the hanger. But Ian had other ideas and held the insubstantial piece of silk and lace out to her insistently, his hazel eyes blazing.

"We want to be sure and get the full effect, love. Let's see how it looks with this." His voice was raw and barely audible.

She took the tiny garment from him uncertainly. "Um, but there's a problem, you see. I'm, uh, well – sort of - "

"Wet?" At her nod, he smiled in the most carnal manner she'd ever seen. "Ah, well, that could get a bit embarrassing, I suppose. I'll tell you what – since this flimsy little bit of nothing isn't really going to cover anything up anyway, just take off your panties. I'll be able to visualize the whole picture quite nicely."

It was beyond ridiculous for her to start feeling shy at this point – given that he'd been avidly watching her in various stages of undress for more than two hours – but Tessa felt her whole body heat up as she slowly peeled her very damp panties off. Ian made a twirling motion with his index finger, and she turned around slowly in a full circle.

When she faced him again, her pulse was racing madly, her breasts swollen and tight, and little rivulets of moisture were beginning to trickle down her inner thighs. "Do you, ah, like it?" she asked, pulling the very short hem of the chemise an inch or so lower.

Ian's gaze shifted reluctantly from her near-naked body to the crotch of his trousers, where an extremely impressive erection was tenting the fabric. "Does that answer your question?" he rasped. "I – ah, think perhaps the fashion show should wrap up now, love."

But Tessa's eyes were fixated on the sight of his massive erection, unable to tear her gaze away. She licked her lips as she sank to her knees in front of him, his widespread legs on either side of her frame.

"You poor thing," she murmured in a decidedly seductive voice that sounded foreign to her. "Ooh, we really must do something to take care of you. After all, it's not like you can just walk out of here in this condition."

"Tessa -," he began to admonish sternly. But then his head fell back against the wall with a low gasp as her hand tentatively stroked his throbbing cock.

"Let me," she whispered, reaching for his zipper. "Let me take care of you, Ian."

"Oh, Christ," groaned Ian as she drew out the thick, hard length of his penis, the tip already oozing thick droplets of pre-cum.

"Mmm," purred Tessa as she licked the pearly beads off his cock, just before taking him fully into her mouth.

"God. Fuck," he snarled as she sucked him eagerly, his hips moving in an instinctive rhythm with her mouth.

She lifted her head, his cock slipping from between her lips while her hand continued to stroke him with the long, smooth motions she knew he liked. "Shh," she warned him mischievously. "If Marlene or one of the others hear you come, you'll never be able to look them in the face again."

Ian growled as she teased him with the very same words he'd cautioned her with yesterday. "Come up here, then," he commanded. "If you're determined to take care of me, let it be mutual. Another rule I'm apparently breaking for you – shagging in a public place."

She giggled as she straddled his lap, positioning the tip of his cock at the entrance to her drenched core. "And here I thought you were the one corrupting me," she joked.

"Wanton little minx," he growled, squeezing the firm cheeks of her ass as she carefully lowered herself onto his erection. "You're going to get us kicked out of this store."

Tessa bit down on the inside of her cheek to stifle the moan she would have otherwise emitted as his cock filled her completely. As she began to ride him, she bent down and whispered in his ear, "No way would they kick you out after all the money you've spent. Besides, the door is locked."

He groaned against her neck before pressing hot, fevered kisses along her throat, collarbone, the upper curves of her breast. Almost frantically, he jerked the strap of the sheer, lacy chemise off her shoulder, exposing one round, lush breast. As his mouth closed roughly over the nipple, muffling the moans rising up from his throat, she buried her face against the top of his dark head in an effort to silence her own sounds of passion.

She was close, oh so close, and could tell by the ferocity of his movements beneath her that he was, too, when a discreet knock sounded on the dressing room door. Tessa froze, but Ian evidently didn't hear anything since he continued to piston his hips at a frantic pace. Then came the carefully modulated sound of Marlene's voice.

"How are things coming along in there?" she asked. "Getting close to finishing up?"

Tessa had to shove a fist into her mouth to keep from laughing at Marlene's very unintentional double entendre. Ian's mouth was still busy suckling at her breast so she forced herself to reply in a rather high, thin voice, "Um, yes, thanks. Nearly done now."

There was a long pause, during which Ian remained blissfully unaware of what was going on and continued to ram his cock inside of her, bringing her ever closer to climax. Finally, Marlene murmured, "Well, just let me know if you need anything" at the precise moment Tessa's orgasm ripped through her. Ian followed her moments later, his mouth clamping so fiercely on her breast as he did that she grimaced in pain.

He was panting like he'd just run the 400-yard dash, his hair mussed and a little damp as he stared up at her in a daze. "I swear to Christ you're going to kill me," he wheezed. "And in a public place to boot. You make me forget everything else when I'm inside you, Tessa."

She smiled, tenderly brushing his hair back into place. "So much that you didn't hear Marlene asking if we needed anything."

He looked shocked, and then his cheeks grew red, something Tessa guessed happened to him very rarely. "Uh, do you think she - "

"Heard us? I don't think so, especially since your mouth was – um, otherwise occupied."

He glanced down at her still-exposed breast and frowned when he noticed the mark around her areola. "Did I do that? Does it hurt?"

"No, it's fine. I'm just so fair skinned that I tend to bruise easily."

Ian reluctantly pulled the strap of the chemise back up, covering her breast. "You'd better get dressed, love. Never mind about trying on the other things, we'll just take them. I'm not sure I'd survive watching you for even one more minute."

She gave a little wiggle, feeling his semi-hard cock still buried inside of her. "Hmm, feel like putting that theory to the test?"

He pinched her bare buttock – hard. "Not here, no. Besides, I think I'll need some reinforcement before I'm ready to go again – an extra-large protein shake, a couple of handfuls of vitamins, the biggest, rarest steak the restaurant has available. And that nap I mentioned to you earlier – I'll definitely need that whether you do or not."

Tessa ran a finger over his firm mouth. "You seem to be going to an awful lot of trouble for me."

He nuzzled his face into her cleavage. "Trust me, darling. It's the best sort of trouble."

Chapter Fifteen

February

Sasha Fonseca glanced up from the conversation she'd been having with one of her students as half a dozen others filtered inside the already packed yoga studio. It was nearly time for her Sunday morning class to begin, and the popularity of her grueling Vinyasa practice never ceased to amaze her.

She nudged the petite woman standing next to her. "Isn't that your friend over there? The pretty blonde in the purple top? You brought her to class with you a couple of times."

Julia looked in the same direction that Sasha was pointing, and was more than a little taken aback to see who her teacher was talking about. "Yes, that's definitely Tessa. I had no idea she was going to be here today. I'd better go say hi."

Because the room was so crowded, Julia didn't dare move her mat for fear she wouldn't be able to find another spot. As it was, Tessa seemed to have nabbed one of the very last spaces, stuck back in a corner of the jammed room. She looked more than a little flustered as she rolled out her mat, her cheeks flushed and wisps of blonde hair escaping her rather messy braid.

"Hey, it is you," greeted Julia, dropping down into a squatting position. "I didn't know you were planning to come today. You should have called me and I would have picked you up."

Tessa's gaze flew up to hers in alarm, and she looked almost guilty. "Oh, Julia, hi. Um, sorry, I – I was running really late and didn't even know if I'd be able to make it here in time. And I thought you were in New York."

Julia nodded. "I was, trying on wedding gowns and going quietly insane finding a bridesmaid dress that my sister would actually approve of. But I got in late yesterday and really needed some yoga to decompress."

Tessa seemed unnaturally distracted and merely nodded, offering up a nervous smile. Tactfully, Julia patted her on the arm and stood. "Well, class is about to begin so I'll catch you afterwards, okay?"

As tough as the class was, demanding her powers of concentration be at their peak, Julia still couldn't help but wonder what had brought Tessa here this morning. She knew her friend was on a really tight budget, and was surprised that Tessa had been able to afford the class. SF Flow was pretty much the top yoga studio in the city, and the cost of even a single class was pricey.

At Sasha's instructions, everyone turned to face the back of the room for the next sequence. Julia glanced in Tessa's direction, noticing for the first time the stylish new yoga apparel the blonde was wearing. The gray cropped pants and purple racerback tunic were from the new Prana collection the studio had just received in less than two weeks ago. Julia frowned, knowing that the outfit would have cost well over a hundred dollars, and recalled how Tessa had fretted over spending too much on her Christmas party dress.

Julia temporarily forgot about Tessa as the class got progressively tougher. During the time she'd spent in New York, she had admittedly overindulged in food and alcohol, and hadn't been able to squeeze in even one yoga class. Combined with her jet lag, she was really feeling the burn as Sasha pushed her students harder and harder. Sweat poured down her forehead and trickled along her spine, and she kept telling herself it was good for her, to detox all the poisons she'd ingested on her trip. With each sun salutation, each arm balance, and all the twisting poses, she visualized making up for every bite of cake, every spoonful of cream sauce, and – damn her – every shot of tequila that Lauren had dared her to bolt.

By the end of the ninety minute class, Julia felt wrung out, but definitely in a good way, and resolved to drink a ton of water, and subsist on salads, grilled fish and veggies for the next week. Especially if she hoped to fit into the gorgeous Badgley Mishka wedding gown she'd decided on.

She hurried over to Tessa, anxious to chat her up a bit. But the blonde was already rolling up her yoga mat – which Julia recognized as a Manduka, the most expensive brand the studio sold – and stuffing it into a chic purple-print carry bag.

"Hey, do you want to get coffee?" offered Julia. "Nathan should be waiting for me outside and I know he'd love for you to join us. We can give you a ride home later."

"Oh." Tessa looked rather disconcerted by the offer. "Um, normally I'd love to but I – ah, I'm sort of meeting – someone."

Julia grinned. "You little devil. You have a new boyfriend, don't you?"

Tessa's cheeks were already flushed pink from the exertion of the class, and they deepened to a much brighter shade at Julia's frank question. "Ah, I – I guess that's what – yes, you're right. I do." She looked down at her bare feet shyly. "I'm just – it's pretty new, so - "

"You can't really talk about it yet," finished Julia. "I get it, honey. But I think it's great. You really deserve some happiness. So, go meet your new guy and we'll have coffee another time."

Tessa looked relieved. "Okay, thanks. I'll give you a call this week."

Julia watched her friend dash out of the studio hurriedly, wondering who this new boyfriend was and hoping that he was treating Tessa right. But at least the existence of a new man in her life explained why she was suddenly able to afford yoga classes plus the new clothes and equipment. Julia hoped he wasn't some sleazy creep who was just using Tessa, dazzling her with nice gifts and expensive dinners. She knew Tessa was rather naïve about men, despite the fact that she'd been married for seven years, and kept her fingers crossed that she wasn't in over her head.

Julia spent a couple of minutes chatting with Sasha before grabbing her things and heading out to meet Nathan. Her superhot fiancée was lounging against the side of the building, his thick dark brown hair still damp from the laps he'd just swum at his health club's indoor pool. Nathan had played water polo during high school and college and still liked to get a vigorous swim in a few times a week.

"Hey, baby." He pulled her into his arms and gave her a quick but still semi-dirty kiss.

"Hi." She snuggled close as he took her yoga bag from her, slinging it over his own shoulder as they walked down the block to one of their favorite cafes.

"You look a little sweaty. Did Sasha kick your cute little ass again?"

Julia nodded. "Always. I swear I don't know where she comes up with some of her moves. If you think I'm flexible, you ought to see her in action. She's like Elasticgirl, or whoever that character is from *The Incredibles*."

Nathan squeezed her ass cheek under cover of the thigh length cardigan she wore. "You're plenty flexible for me, baby. Especially last night. I, uh, didn't know you could actually get into that sort of position."

She raised a brow. "Complaining?"

"Oh, hell, no. You can get, ah, all bendy and twisty like that anytime. Hey, was that Tessa I saw leaving the studio? I was just getting out of the car when I saw her turning the corner."

Julia nodded. "That was her all right. Sounds like she has a new boyfriend. I just hope he's a good guy and treats her right."

Nathan stopped in his tracks, a frown on his handsome features. "Wait a second. Now that you mention it, I did notice her getting into a car. And – holy shit."

She shook his arm. "What? What is it? And why are you grinning like an idiot?"

He chuckled, shaking his head. "That sneaky sonofabitch. Let's just say I've got a very good idea of who Tessa's new boyfriend is."

Her eyes widened in surprise "Who? Did you see him? What kind of a car is he driving? God, don't tell me it was a pickup truck. Or a Prius. I'm not sure which one would be worse."

Nathan was full out laughing now. "Oh, not even close, baby. No, your friend was getting into a vintage Jaguar E-type. It's a very expensive and very rare car. In fact, there's only one person I know of who owns a car exactly like that one. I even rode in it once – en route to the new hotel site in Napa."

It took Julia a moment or two for his words to register, and then she gasped, clutching his arm so tightly that he winced. "You mean – Tessa's new boyfriend is – is Ian?"

He was grinning from ear to ear. "Yup. He denied being attracted to her when I brought the subject up once, but when you're right, you're right, baby."

"I knew it!" she squealed. "Didn't I tell you, Nathan? I knew he had his eye on her the first time I saw them together." Then a sudden thought instantly sobered her up. "You don't think – I mean, Tessa never told me why she and her husband broke up. You don't imagine she and Ian were having - "

"No." Nathan's denial was emphatic. "I know Ian pretty well after all. He would never mess around with a married woman. Trust me, he and Tessa were not having a sordid affair. That is not why she and her husband are divorcing. I think this relationship with Ian is very new."

Julia nodded. "I think so, too. She seemed really nervous to see me there today, like she expected I was still in New York."

"Well, if she's still working for Ian it goes without saying they want to keep this quiet. And you, my little devil, are not to breathe one word about this to anyone. Got it?" he told her sternly.

She reached up and gave him a smacking kiss. "Yes, I've got it. And I won't say a word to anyone." She took Nathan's arm and placed it around her shoulders as she leaned against him. "God, they make a really gorgeous couple, don't you think?"

Nathan smiled wickedly. "I'm guessing she's keeping him, uh, busy. There's a pretty big age difference between them, after all. He's probably keeping his fingers crossed that he'll be able to keep up with her."

"Oh, I don't know about that," replied Julia airily. "Ian looks like he keeps himself in very, very good shape. Though Tessa did look a little, um - "

"Well fucked?" he whispered in her ear. "Kind of like you do this morning?"

Her cheeks flushed. "You are so bad," she whispered back as they entered the crowded café. "But, yeah, now that you mention it, she might have looked like she'd just tumbled out of bed. And she did say she was running late."

"Told you." He was grinning as they got in line to place their orders. "Hmm, Ian and I will have to compare notes sometime, see which one of us is getting more action."

Julia gasped in outrage. "Oh, my God, don't you dare! You wouldn't seriously do that, would you?"

"Relax, baby." He rubbed her low back soothingly. "What goes on in our bed stays there, okay? No matter how many times my buddies try to pry details out of me. I would never in a million years tell anyone how much you like it when I start - "

She clapped a hand over his mouth. "Quit while you're ahead, Nathan. And you'd better take that last photo of me off your Facebook page. You know exactly which one – your disgusting friends have already given it a bunch of likes."

"Okay, I'll take it off," he acquiesced reluctantly. "It's just so cool that all of my buddies are really eating their hearts out now. The consensus is unanimous that I've got the hottest girl by far among the whole group."

Julia just glared at him, pulling his phone from the side pocket of his track pants. "I'll order for us while you delete that photo. Now."

Over breakfast, they chatted about their upcoming work weeks – due to be busier than ever with all the projects they had going on; about the wedding plans that were quickly starting to take over their lives; and about Julia's very recent trip to New York. She'd spent almost a week there, accompanied by her mother, sister and girlhood friend Angela. They had all met up with Julia's Aunt Madelyn as well as Nathan's mother Alexis, who'd been overjoyed to be invited to the girl-getaway. Madelyn, the head buyer at Bergdorf Goodman, had arranged for Julia and her two bridesmaids – Lauren and Angela – to select their gowns for the June wedding.

"So your sister was even more of a pain in the ass than you feared?" asked Nathan.

Julia nodded. "Way worse than I expected. In fact, she was in a really bad mood for almost the entire trip."

He smirked. "When exactly is Lauren in a *good* mood?

Anything in particular that got her pissed off this time?"

"Now that you mention it, things seem to get noticeably worse after we ran into her boss the first morning out at breakfast. She was actually okay at dinner the night before, but as soon as Ben stopped by our table she just seemed – I don't even know how to explain it."

Nathan took a sip of his coffee. "Bitchier? More terrifying? And you didn't tell me you'd finally met Ben the Bastard."

Julia frowned. "He's actually a really nice guy. Not to mention totally Lauren's type. Not the tattooed, pierced rocker type but the other kind she goes for – the chiseled, outdoorsy hunk with three-day stubble."

"You think there's something going on there? Though I'd truly feel sorry for the dude, especially given the way your sister flies into these rages whenever she mentions him."

She shook her head. "Lauren made a point of telling me that Ben has a live-in girlfriend. And there is *no* way my sister would ever hit on a guy who's already taken. She'd figure it was his loss if he preferred someone else over her."

Nathan grinned. "Wouldn't that be something, though? Your twin having a thing for a guy and not being able to do anything about it? There may be some justice in this world after all."

Julia scooped up a dollop of foamed milk from her cappuccino, licking it off her fingers. "You know, the more I think about it, Lauren wasn't necessarily just in a bad mood. She seemed – now don't laugh at this, okay? – kind of - well, sad and depressed."

He gaped at her in disbelief. "Baby, I'm not laughing but those two words sure as hell don't fit the Lauren McKinnon I know. Now Angela, she's the fucking poster child for sad and depressed, but your sister is still the ballsiest babe I've ever met. There's a reason she scares the shit out of almost everyone who meets her."

"I just can't put my finger on it, Nathan, but there's something off there. I know my sister – she's literally the other half of me, don't forget. And you might have something there about Ben. I've never seen Lauren as moody and – God, almost vulnerable after he stopped by our table."

Nathan squeezed her hand. "You seem to have pretty good instincts about this stuff, baby. After all, it looks like you might have been right about Ian and Tessa."

"*Might* have?" She arched a perfectly plucked brow at him. "Oh, no, there is no "might". I *know* I'm right, there's way too much circumstantial evidence to support my cause. And if I'm right, you owe me a pair of very expensive new shoes."

"Crap. I forgot all about that stupid bet," grumbled Nathan. "I have *so* got to remember not to make any bets with you when a) I've had a little too much to drink, and b) you've just blown me so hard I can't walk straight. Besides, I'm going to require more than circumstantial evidence before I shell out eight hundred bucks. And why the hell do you need more shoes anyway?"

Julia batted her lashes at him flirtatiously. "Because this really hot architect I know is building me this awesome waterfront house in Tiburon, complete with the biggest walk-in closet I've ever seen. I don't have nearly enough stuff to fill it up."

"I knew I shouldn't have let your father talk me into making that damned closet so big," he replied darkly. "And you haven't won yet, baby. I need more proof before I whip my credit card out."

She gave him a dangerous smile. "Leave it to me. I'll get you all the proof you need."

***

Ian knew that Tessa would already be in the conference room setting up for the architect's meeting due to start in less than an hour. He had far too much work to get through today, did not have even ten minutes to spare for anything not already on his packed schedule, and yet he still found himself walking in the direction of the conference room where he knew she would be. He'd mumbled some harebrained excuse to Andrew about where he was going, and received a disapproving frown from his by-the-book PA. But it had seemed like an eternity since he'd been alone with Tessa, even though in reality it had only been three days ago.

He'd convinced her to stay over at his home on Sunday night rather than bringing her back to that god-awful apartment of hers. Still intent on keeping their relationship a carefully guarded secret, he'd sent her off to work on Monday in a taxi while Simon had driven him to the office as usual. And even though he and Tessa had only been together for just over a month's time, he was already at the end of his rope with this very unsatisfactory arrangement they had. He wanted her with him constantly, sleeping in his bed every single night, and was extremely displeased with this elaborate pretense they had to keep up.

Thank God there was a long weekend beginning tomorrow, when they would be spending some quality time together. Tomorrow, Friday was Valentine's Day, and the President's Day holiday three days later. Tessa was taking a vacation day tomorrow, but he had a morning meeting that would be impossible to re-schedule. But once the damned meeting was over he was whisking her off to the Gregson resort in Lake Tahoe for the holiday weekend – three and a half days of skiing, relaxation, and a whole lot of sex.

The phone calls and texts they'd exchanged since Monday morning weren't nearly enough to make up for not having her in his arms, and he badly needed to see her alone, even for a few minutes. Ian realized this was uncharted territory for him – this almost stalker-like behavior he was engaging in – but he couldn't help this obsession he felt for her. He was taking a risk, of course, with so many people in the office this morning, but he was more than ready to throw caution to the wind just for five minutes with her.

'Jesus, mate, you're acting like a thirteen year old schoolgirl,' he chastised himself. 'What the hell are you going to do when you're away from her for two bloody weeks?'

Less than a week from now he had to fly to London for a mind-numbing series of board meetings and other matters that required his presence at worldwide headquarters. Under normal circumstances, he'd actually be looking forward to spending some time with his parents and brothers and the rest of his family. But the very thought of being away from Tessa for so long was eating away at him, and he honestly had no idea how he was going to bear the separation. If she hadn't been so stubborn, she would have quit her job by now and be spending the full two weeks in England with him.

But even as that thought crossed his mind, Ian knew in all fairness that Tessa simply wasn't ready for that. She was still so shy and uncertain around him, still getting to know him really, and it wouldn't be especially considerate to overwhelm her so completely by having to meet all of his family at once. He knew she was terrified of embarrassing him, and that she didn't feel worthy to be seen out in public with him – two ridiculous matters he was determined to resolve sooner than later. If he brought her to meet his family now – when she was very much like a skittish, frightened fawn – she could very well decide to end their relationship, fearful that she could never be what he needed.

Ian wasn't going to do a damned thing to risk losing her at this point, not after he'd longed for her for so many months. What he *was* going to do – in a very persuasive manner – was convince his surprisingly stubborn little love that if he had her with him permanently she would be *all* he would ever need. His plans for this coming weekend revolved around convincing her of just that.

As he approached the conference room, he frowned in irritation to realize she wasn't alone. He recognized the rather whiny, nasally tone as Kevin's and stopped in his tracks, quite intentionally eavesdropping on the conversation the younger man was having with Tessa.

"Got any hot plans for Valentine's Day tomorrow?" asked Kevin cheerily. "Or the long weekend?"

There was a pause before he heard Tessa reply, her answer thankfully vague. "Oh, nothing specific. Just relaxing, maybe a yoga class, the usual."

"Well, that just won't do," declared Kevin. "It's not right that a hot babe like you doesn't have a date for Valentine's Day. And don't feed me that BS about not being ready to move on. It's been months, Tessa, way past time for you to get out there and find a new man. Maybe several of them."

Ian was furious, outraged, to hear that little shit trying to convince Tessa – *his* Tessa, god damn it – that she ought to be dating other men – *lots* of other men. He had to clench his fists to keep from slamming one into the wall, and counted to ten instead to calm himself down.

"Thanks for thinking of me, but I'll know when the time is right," Tessa replied casually.

"Well, maybe I can change your mind. One of the attorneys who works with Terence is recently divorced and on the prowl. And let me tell you, sweetie, he is H-O-T. Looks just like Ryan Gosling. Or is that Ryan Reynolds? I always get those two mixed up. Anyway, he saw the photo that Terence took of you and me at the Christmas party and he is *very* interested in meeting you. His name is - "

Ian had had quite enough, and chose that moment to enter the conference room, his strides long and purposeful. Kevin and Tessa looked up as he all but burst inside, and the expression on his face must have been murderous judging from the looks on their faces.

"M – Mr. Gregson. Can I – ah, help you with something?" stammered Tessa.

Ian glared pointedly at Kevin. "Yes, I need to review some data on one of the spreadsheets before our meeting. Kevin, would you excuse us please?"

Kevin looked as though he was about to faint – or piss his pants – but merely gulped and nodded. "Uh, sure. I need to get back to work anyway. See you after the meeting, Tess."

Ian drummed his fingers on the table impatiently until Kevin slinked out of the room. Mere seconds later he was quietly shutting and locking the door, and then he very nearly flew across the room until he was jerking Tessa into his arms.

"Just so we're perfectly clear," he bit out, each word enunciated slowly, "you are *not* going on a date with any lawyers, doctors, or anyone else that little fucker offers to set you up with. You are not "getting out there" to find a new man. Because you already have a new man in your life, and he's damned sure not willing to share you."

"Ian - " Whatever she was about to say was quickly swallowed up by the fierce, desperate way he kissed her. She whimpered beneath the force of his lips and tongue, especially when his hand slid down her back to cup her ass. Tessa clutched the lapels of his suit jacket as he ground himself against the cleft of her thighs.

They were both gasping for air when he finally lifted his head, half-afraid he'd come in his pants if he continued to dry hump her a second longer. He slid his hands into her thick, glossy hair instead, gazing into her huge blue eyes, and frowned when he saw the way her lips were trembling.

"Did I frighten you?' he asked in concern, making sure to keep his voice low, belatedly aware that anyone could try to enter the room and wonder why it was locked. "God, please tell me I didn't do that, darling."

Tessa's hands were resting lightly on his chest. "No. You just – ah, surprised me. I didn't expect you to walk in like that and then – well, we're at the office after all."

He pressed a kiss to her forehead. "I know. This is possibly the most insane thing I've ever done, there are dozens of people on the other side of that door. If any one of them suspect we're locked in here together - "

Her hands smoothed down his lapels, adjusted his tie. "It would be very bad, wouldn't it? So we should really look at that spreadsheet so we can - "

Ian chuckled. "Ah, my beautiful, naïve girl. There is no spreadsheet. At least none that I have a question about. I just needed an excuse to get rid of that little – pimp, for lack of a better word. And I wanted a few minutes with you. It's been three entire days since we've been alone."

Tessa sighed, resting her head on his shoulder. "I know. I've missed you, too."

He held her against him gently, his hand stroking her back. "This is quickly becoming an obsession for me, Tessa. *You* are becoming my obsession. I think about you constantly, can't focus on work half the time. These days and nights away from you are just too damned hard. It's not nearly enough to see you around the office briefly, or exchange texts or phone calls. You need to - "

"To quit my job and move in with you," she finished. "I'm working on that, I promise. Please be a little patient with me, Ian.

I promise it won't be very much longer."

He sighed. "I find when it comes to you that I have no patience whatsoever. At least not in terms of how long I have to wait before I can see you again. I've never craved anything like I do you, love. It's a feeling of utter desperation at times."

She nodded. "It's the same for me. I can't even begin to think about next week when you have to leave for London."

"Well, trust me, I have, and I'm damned sure not looking forward to it, to say the least," he growled.

"At least we have this long weekend coming up," she consoled him.

Ian hesitated. "Would you consider – that is, I've got this bloody dinner tonight with those German tourist board members. But I was hoping you'd be agreeable to spending the night? I can have Simon pick you up at your place and bring you to the house. The thought that you'd be there waiting for me when I got home – I can't tell you how much that would mean to me."

"Yes." She agreed easily, without the slightest fuss or argument, a trait he adored about her. "I'll spend the night – happily. Just tell me what time to expect Simon."

Ian grinned broadly, his good humor instantly restored. "Probably around eight, but I'll text you with the exact time." He gave her a quick kiss. "Thank you, darling. I'm just – especially needy for you today. The thought of having to wait until tomorrow night to have you again was driving me mad."

"Well, we can't have that, can we?" she teased. "Especially after you terrified poor Kevin that way. I'd hate to think of you fixing that glare on anyone else today."

His phone buzzed at that moment and he dug it out of his pocket impatiently. "Andrew," he mouthed to Tessa before asking brusquely, "What is it? Yes, I'll be right there. No, everything's fine now."

He ended the call and pocketed the phone, shaking his head. "At times I wish he wasn't quite so damned efficient. I have an overseas call I need to take. I'll see you at the meeting shortly, hmm?"

Tessa nodded. "Of course." Then, as she glanced over at the massive conference table, an odd expression crossed her features.

He regarded her curiously. "And what does that particular look mean?"

She looked away hastily, as though embarrassed by her train of thought, and resumed setting up for the meeting. "Oh, nothing, just something silly. You'd – ah, better go take that phone call."

Ian waved a hand dismissingly. "It's only some annoying clerk from the London offices calling to go over the schedule of meetings with me. He can damned well cool his heels for a minute longer. Now, I want to know what this silly thought of yours was. That look you had on your face – as though you were remembering something."

Tessa fidgeted, clearly ill at ease with this topic. "It was just – kind of a strange dream I had once. A few months ago, actually. I don't even remember most of it."

"Liar," he taunted. "You know you need to tell me about it now. My curiosity won't be appeased until you do."

She was completely flustered now, refusing to look at him as she reluctantly replied, "I was – God, this is really embarrassing."

He leaned back against the table, crossing his arms and raising a brow. "I don't have all day, Tessa. Out with it now."

She began to twirl a lock of hair around her fingers. "I was laying on the table. On my back. With – ah, with my arms and legs spread out."

Ian was instantly intrigued. "Nude?" At her nod, his voice deepened. "Bound?"

Her eyes flew up to his. "Not exactly. I mean, it felt that way but the bonds were – well, invisible, I guess."

"And were you alone in the room during this dream?"

"No." She shifted from one foot to the other in agitation. "Er, you were here, too."

His smile deepened. "Was I naked?"

"God." She closed her eyes. "No, you – you were dressed. Except for your jacket and tie."

He stepped in close to her, trailing his fingers up and down her arms. "And what was I doing to you? Was I touching you?" She nodded and he pressed on. "Kissing you?"

"Yes."

"Where? Here, perhaps?" He touched her full, lush mouth. "And I think of course here."

His hands cupped her breasts, squeezing them lightly. Tessa gasped, even as he slid one hand down to gently cup the juncture of her thighs.

"And here. Was I kissing you here?"

Her cheeks were a deep, rosy pink as she uttered a small moan. "You were – just about to. Then I woke up."

"Well, that's a pity, isn't it?" he murmured in her ear. "Perhaps we can re-enact your dream sometime, only this time it won't end nearly so abruptly."

Tessa looked around the room wildly. "You're not serious, are you? I mean, I'm not sure I could really do – *that* here."

He slowly removed his hands from her body and stepped back to put some much needed distance between them, unable to walk back to his office with his fully engorged cock tenting his trousers. "I was thinking of this weekend actually. The bed we'll be using at the resort is a four poster – one post for each of your limbs. Does that idea excite you, Tessa – being bound that way? Would you allow me to do that?"

Her eyes grew even bigger and rounder, her lips slightly parted. His gaze dropped briefly to her breasts, and he swore softly beneath his breath as he noticed how her nipples were poking against the fabric of her blouse.

"Yes," she told him breathlessly. "I think – yes, I'd like that. You can do – whatever you like."

"Jesus." His pulse rate ratcheted up by several beats as she gazed at him with an expression of unabashed, naked desire on her face. "You make me want to spread you out on that table right now, just like in your dream, and fuck you until neither one of us can summon a single coherent thought." He forced himself to walk over to the door. "And if I don't leave now to take that phone call I might just act on that impulse."

Ian was thankful to notice that no one was loitering in the hallway outside the conference room – not that any of his employees would have dared to inquire why the door might have been shut. No one questioned his authority here or at any of the hotels under his direction. He was the unequivocal leader, the "boss man" as he'd heard himself referred to on occasion, and the amount of power he could wield over his share of the family empire – if he so desired – was staggering. But Ian had learned a long time ago to never, ever abuse that power, to treat every employee with respect, and not act like some feudal lord of the manor. There was a very fine line that had to be walked in his position, and he prided himself on never crossing over it.

Though if anyone in this office began to suspect that he was carrying on a very personal and very passionate relationship with one of his employees, there would certainly be hell to pay. As he listened with barely controlled patience to the employee from the London headquarters drone on about the series of board meetings he'd be attending, Ian was rather appalled at the complete lack of control he'd just displayed. He was damned lucky no one had come looking for him, or tried to enter the conference room when he'd been locked inside there with Tessa. But then, ever since he'd revealed his attraction to her and they'd become lovers, he seemed to be losing a bit more of his ironclad control every day. That was what she did to him – a girl fifteen years his junior; a sexual innocent despite her marriage of several years; and the only woman who'd ever come close to making him go crazy with lust, enough so that he'd just taken a very unwise risk, not particularly giving a damn if they were discovered.

And then she'd made everything ten times worse by telling him in that sexy as hell, breathy voice that he could do whatever he wanted to her. God, did she have any idea – even the slightest – what that sort of confession did to a man? Especially a man who already panted after her constantly, as though she were a mare in heat.

By the time the architect's meeting was ready to begin a short while later, Ian had regained full control of his wayward emotions, assuming his formal Managing Director persona once again. He forced himself not to glance towards the back of the conference room where he knew Tessa would be, and instead walked directly towards the other extraordinarily beautiful woman in the room.

"Julia. How are you this morning?" He greeted the always

smartly dressed interior designer with a firm handshake. He knew that she had befriended Tessa over these last few months and was exceedingly grateful for the kindness she'd shown her.

Julia gave him a rather odd smile, her expressive green eyes twinkling with a hint of mischief. "I'm very well, Ian, thank you. And I owe you a huge favor after you arranged for the wedding coordinator at your Pebble Beach resort to call me back. Not to mention mysteriously finding an open date for us in June."

He winked at her. "It's all in the way you ask the questions, my dear. And I'm very happy to be of help."

"Nathan and I are actually heading down to Carmel this weekend to visit my parents, so we've set up a meeting at the hotel. Do you have any special plans for the long weekend?"

He was instantly on alert at Julia's super sweet tone, not to mention the way her rose-glossed lips curled into a smirk. "Ah, yes, I'm actually headed to Lake Tahoe. The skiing is supposed to be quite good this weekend." He intentionally didn't mention that he was bringing Tessa along with him.

Julia wrinkled her pert little nose. "Hmm, not much of a fan of the snow. Something about being cold and wet just doesn't appeal. But I hope you enjoy your weekend, Ian. By the way, is Tessa working the meeting this morning? I have something I need to ask her."

Ian forced himself to remain impassive as he replied. "Yes, I believe I saw her here earlier setting up. Was there something you needed for the meeting, Julia? I'm sure Tessa can take care of it for you."

Julia shook her head. "Oh, no, nothing like that. It's not really business related. We – well, one of Nathan's clients gave us four tickets to see *The Book of Mormon* next weekend and I wanted to see if Tessa would like to go with us." She lowered her voice as she added, "Nathan and I were thinking of setting her up with one of his friends. After all, she's way too young and pretty to stay at home every weekend, don't you think?"

Ian froze. If he didn't know better, he'd swear that the innocent-looking Julia was quite deliberately trying to provoke him, or at least goad him into reacting. He wasn't sure how she would know, but he had a very strong feeling that she suspected there was something going on between him and Tessa. He knew the two women had run into each other at their yoga studio last weekend, but he'd been extremely careful to park a block or so away when he'd picked Tessa up so as not to be seen.

His right hand curled into a fist as he waged an internal struggle to remain calm. "You should – ah – discuss that with her, Julia."

Julia smiled brightly, looking too much like a cat who'd swallowed the canary to put him at ease. "I believe I will. Oh, there she is. Oops, better go rescue her from Jake the Snake. God, that man does not understand the concept of taking no for an answer, does he?"

Julia actually had the audacity to give him a saucy wink just before sauntering off in search of Tessa. Ian's steely gaze followed her progress, his mouth tightening in mingled annoyance and anger as he noticed how closely Nathan's associate architect Jake was standing next to Tessa. And when the prick actually dared to put his hand on Tessa's lower back as he murmured something in her ear, Ian was about five seconds away from losing it.

"Nathan."

Julia's fiancée – and the lead architect on the new hotel project - was at Ian's side in an instant, a look of concern on his face.

"Is there a problem, Ian?" he asked.

"Two of them actually." Ian inclined his head towards the back of the room. "You need to call your boy Jake off. At once. And tell him I have a very strict hands off policy when it comes to my – employees."

Nathan gave a curt nod. "I'll take care of it. What was the other problem?"

Ian glared at Julia, who was even now approaching Tessa with a perky smile. "Your very charming but extremely nosy fiancée. Tell Julia that if she persists in playing with fire that someone besides herself might get burned."

Julia waved at both of them cheekily before returning her attention to Tessa, elbowing Jake aside at the same time. She had an extremely satisfied smile on her face.

Nathan sighed. "Aw, hell. I think I've got to go shoe shopping with her after work."

Chapter Sixteen

Tessa couldn't help the rather awestruck reaction she had as Ian drove up beneath the porte-cochere of the hotel. The mountain lodge in Lake Tahoe was of a much different design than either the opulent high-rise hotel in San Francisco, or the sprawling Mission-style resort in Tucson, the only other two Gregson properties she'd ever set foot in. Situated high on top of a mountain, the lodge was majestic and grand with its stone façade and high windows. Pristine banks of carefully groomed snow surrounded the property on all sides. Tessa had read on the lodge's website that it offered ski-in/ski-out accommodations, as well as a ski valet and highly rated ski shop on premise. She had never been on skis before, and the only time she'd ever seen actual snow had been one winter years ago when she had lived in Sedona with her mother. She knew Ian was an accomplished skier, and that he had plans to get her out on the slopes this weekend, a prospect that she was admittedly a little nervous about.

The drive up from San Francisco had been smooth and relatively traffic-free. Ian had rushed home as soon as his meeting had ended, and was behind the wheel of his sturdy, four-wheel drive Range Rover by late morning. It had been just past three o'clock when he'd exited the highway for the lodge.

Tessa was more than a little amazed at the way the hotel staff mobilized so swiftly, evidently having been informed to expect Ian and his guest. In quick succession, a valet had taken his car keys, a bellhop unloaded their luggage, and the doorman held the massive front doors leading to the lobby open for them. Ian kept a hand on the small of her back as they walked through the sprawling lobby with its vaulted, wood beam ceilings, flagstone floors, and imposing stone fireplace. Tessa didn't miss the way almost every single person passing through turned and stared at him, the admiration evident on both female and male faces. She was beginning to get used to the effect her handsome, debonair lover had on people, how he attracted attention no matter where they went, and also how he seemed to be so completely nonchalant about it. For her part, she couldn't help the thrill she felt at knowing this magnificent man was really hers, and that for reasons she couldn't really fathom as yet, he'd chosen her out of the thousands of other women around the world who'd give anything to be by his side right now.

The pretty brunette desk clerk who checked them in appeared to be as susceptible to Ian's charm as anyone else, staring up at him with unabashed interest as he signed in and took the card keys to the owner's suite. Tessa gave the brunette a tiny frown before sidling up closer against Ian's side, silently staking her claim. He smiled down at her, dropped a kiss on top of her head, and slid an arm around her waist. Tessa's frown quickly changed to a very satisfied smile, and she was pleased to note that the clerk was suddenly all business, averting her gaze as she finished the check-in process.

Tessa's jaw dropped open again as the private butler assigned to their suite opened the double doors and ushered her inside. She could hear Ian speaking to the man in a low tone as she stared in disbelief at the splendor of the lavishly appointed rooms.

Here, too, were the vaulted wood beam ceilings, and a huge stone fireplace, though these floors were covered in a thick, plush carpet. Floor to ceiling picture windows offered a breathtaking view of the snow-covered mountains outside, and French doors opened out to a private patio where she could see a fire pit and hot tub. The furnishings were a combination of rustic comfort and understated luxury.

A quick inspection of the suite revealed a spacious living room, separate formal dining area, and a fully equipped kitchen. There were two bedrooms, each with their own en suite bathroom. The suite was easily large enough to live in comfortably for days or weeks at a time, and it suddenly dawned on her that this was exactly the sort of opulent lifestyle she could expect to live when she moved in with Ian permanently. And as thrilling as that idea was, it also gave her renewed cause for concern, bringing to the surface all of her fears and insecurities that she just didn't fit into this world of privilege and extreme wealth.

"Does this meet with your approval?"

Tessa turned to face Ian, who was just now closing the door to the suite. Her heart caught in her throat as she thought of how handsome he looked, how mouthwateringly sexy. He was more casually dressed than usual, clad all in black – wool slacks, a turtleneck sweater and a heavy leather jacket worn in deference to the cold weather. He looked dangerous and sophisticated at the same time, an irresistible combination.

At his urging, she'd dressed in a similarly casual manner – dark skinny jeans, black cashmere sweater, black ankle boots and a black knit cap pulled over her ears. Tessa didn't want to think about how much money such a seemingly laid back outfit like this had cost, though she knew from performing a quick Google search that just the little cashmere cap had cost over a hundred dollars.

She walked over to Ian, sliding her hands up his chest to clasp around his neck. "Are you referring to this room or to yourself? Because if it's the latter, I would have to say a very emphatic yes."

"Is that right?" he asked lazily, his hands sweeping down the sides of her hips to cup her buttocks. "Well, I'd say you also have my wholehearted approval. Especially the way your gorgeous arse looks in these tight jeans."

Tessa smiled, burying her face against the strong, warm column of his neck and inhaling deeply. "Mmm, you smell even better than usual. Must be the added touch of the leather."

He kissed her temple, his hand keeping her head pressed to his shoulder. "Would you like the butler to unpack for you, or would you prefer to do it yourself?"

She looked up at him in surprise. "He would do that – actually hang my clothes up and put my shoes away? Not to mention unpacking all my – ah, more personal stuff. I think I'd rather do it myself, actually."

He grinned, giving her a playful chuck on the chin. "To answer your question – yes, Tyson would certainly be happy to perform that task for you. You'll begin to see as we travel together that each of our hotels offers this sort of private butler or concierge service for occupants of the larger suites. You'll need to get used to them doing things for you and letting yourself be pampered. It's one of the many perks you'll enjoy as my companion."

"Okay. It's just – well, it might take some getting used to. I never thought I'd let a complete stranger – a male one at that – unpack my underwear for me," she admitted shyly.

"Ah, well, that I understand. You could consider packing all of your lacy bits in a separate bag from now on, and simply instruct the butler not to touch that one." His lips caressed the soft spot behind her ear. "In fact, I'd probably prefer that. Hell if I want another man to touch your lingerie."

Ian lifted his head and took her firmly by the hand. "Come, let me give you the grand tour. I gave Tyson instructions to bring up an afternoon tea service in a few minutes, so we don't have much time."

As he showed her around the grand suite, she belatedly noticed the beautiful vases of roses arranged in several different locations – the showy red ones on the coffee table; the delicate pale pink blooms in the dining room; a gorgeous arrangement of rich apricot blossoms filled the master bedroom with their fragrance; and the exotic lavender bouquet that had been placed in the en suite bathroom.

Tessa sniffed appreciatively of the last bouquet, which Ian told her were officially called sterling silver roses.

"How beautiful they are," she murmured. "Did you arrange for all of these?"

He smiled, seeming pleased at her reaction. "I did, yes. I didn't know which color you preferred so I ordered several different ones. Of course, red roses are traditional for Valentine's Day but – well, the lavender ones in particular reminded me of you."

Tessa touched the delicate petals with care. "And these just happen to be my favorite of all of them. Thank you, Ian. Once again you're spoiling me rotten."

"Ah, and the weekend is just beginning. I have a whole string of surprises planned for you." He wrapped his arms around her waist, pressing his chest to her back, his voice husky in her ear. "Happy Valentine's Day, my love."

She caressed his hands where they rested just above her belly. "I'm sorry my little gift to you was so – simple. I had no idea what to get you since you already seem to have everything."

"Shh. I already told you that having you here with me is the best gift I could ever hope for. And a batch of homemade cookies is icing on the cake, so to speak. Especially since they're my favorites."

She had fretted over what to buy him for Valentine's Day, knowing that she couldn't possibly afford to buy him anything extravagant, given that he wore two hundred dollar Hermes ties, had a library bursting at the seams with first edition volumes, and a well-stocked wine cellar where the cost of even a single bottle would likely make her shudder.

But she did know he liked snickerdoodles, since Mrs. Sargent had left a bakery bag for them after a recent shopping trip. Fortunately, they'd been easy to bake, given her tiny kitchen and limited cooking skills, and Ian had seemed genuinely thrilled when she had presented him with the festively beribboned bag filled with three dozen cookies.

Having skipped lunch, they both ate hungrily of the sumptuous afternoon tea service that Tyson delivered to their room. Tessa couldn't quite stifle a yawn, however, despite the twin jolts of caffeine and sugar her system had just received.

"Sleepy, are we?" asked Ian in amusement.

She clapped a hand over her mouth. "Sorry. It's just – well, we didn't get much sleep last night what with - "

"I know," he interrupted. "I hope I wasn't too – that it wasn't - "

"No." She shook her head firmly. "You were perfect. It was perfect. I needed you just as badly, Ian."

Tessa had been waiting for him in the library when he'd returned home just after ten o'clock the previous evening. By now she was becoming used to the hungry, almost desperate way he made love to her, the blatant carnality of his kisses and caresses, the all-consuming manner in which he possessed her body. But when he'd strode boldly into the library last night, she'd been left breathless and unable to even think with the fierce, primal way he'd taken her right there, bent over the arm of the leather sofa. He'd tossed off his suit jacket and unzipped his trousers before yanking the hem of her robe up past her waist and literally ripping the fragile silk and lace panties from her body. He'd surged into her with one powerful thrust, wrenching a cry from her throat and leaving her helpless to do anything but willingly submit to his domination of her body. They had both climaxed within minutes, the entire encounter having taken place without either of them uttering a single word. She had been shaken to the core at such a display of raw, undisguised passion on his part, and astonished that her body could so readily respond to his without even the slightest amount of foreplay.

He'd carried her upstairs to his bed then, and this time had made love to her with exquisite thoroughness, prolonging the ecstasy for what had felt like hours. And then he'd woken her again towards dawn, already imbedded deep inside of her, and wrung another shattering orgasm from her exhausted body.

She was grateful she'd taken the day off from work, because she'd been far too drowsy and pleasantly sated to do more than give him a sleepy kiss as he'd left for the office just before eight a.m. She'd slept until ten, a rare luxury for her, and had had to scramble a bit to shower, dress, and eat breakfast before he arrived home.

But Ian still didn't look convinced at her assurance. "That first time – in the library – I was like a rutting bull, Tessa. No finesse, no control. I was - "

"Wild." She swiftly straddled his lap, twining her arms around his neck. "Like a beast. Or a barbarian." She nipped his earlobe lightly with her teeth before whispering, "And I loved it. I like it when you lose control."

He growled, shoving his hand up beneath her sweater and roughly groping her breast, making her gasp as his fingers slid inside her bra cup to pinch the nipple. "You make me lose control just by being in the same room," he rasped. "It's never been that way for me before, not even close."

"Good." She caressed his cheek, which was just beginning to

show some dark stubble as the day began to draw to a close. "I like that I'm the only one who can make you do that. And," she added playfully, "let's make sure to keep it that way, hmm?"

He gave a short laugh. "Darling, I've told you on multiple occasions that you're far more than I can handle as it is. Why on earth would I notice other women when I have all my heart desires right here?"

The sweet, wildly romantic things he seemed to have a knack for saying made her feel all gooey inside. Still, she couldn't resist teasing him a bit more. "So you're telling me you didn't notice the way that very pretty front desk clerk was checking you out?"

Ian frowned. "Unless you had just mentioned it, I wouldn't have been able to remember if the clerk had been a man or a woman. That's how little attention I paid. But since we're on the subject, I should mention the very interested stares you were receiving from the valet. And the bellhop. Not to mention the doorman. Ah, and I'm forgetting the dozen or so – at least – admiring males who were staring at your very sexy body as we walked through the lobby."

"I didn't notice any of them," she murmured. "Nowadays, the only man I ever notice is you."

He smoothed her sweater back down over her belly. "Well, let's make sure to keep it that way, darling," he said, teasing her with her own words from just moments before.

A knock sounded on the door to the suite, and he deftly lifted her off his lap. As he stood, he gave her a little wink. "That will be the next in the string of surprises," he told her as he walked towards the door. "And this one is for both of us."

The next surprise he'd arranged was a couple's massage. Ian had whispered to her as the two masseurs were setting up their tables and equipment that he'd specifically requested a female to work on Tessa and a male on himself, adding that he wasn't about to let another man put his hands on her, whether it was in a clinical manner or not. The folding massage tables were set up over by the grand picture windows so that they could look outside at the snow falling as the sun gradually began to set. One of the masseurs turned on the state of the art sound system and some relaxing classical music filled the room softly. A candle was lit and the subtle fragrance of bergamot scented the air, lending to the atmosphere of complete relaxation.

Tessa had never enjoyed the pure luxury of a massage before, and couldn't suppress a little moan or two as the masseur found a tight spot here and there. She turned her head in the direction of Ian's table, and gave him a sleepy smile as their eyes met. She thought blissfully that she could easily get used to this sort of pampering, and wondered if he indulged in massages on a regular basis.

When the massage ended an hour later – far too soon for her liking – she felt boneless and limp and so relaxed that Ian had to help her tie the belt of her robe.

"Hmm, I hope the next surprise is a nice long nap," she mumbled sleepily.

He chuckled, wrapping her in his arms and dropping a kiss on her forehead. "I didn't realize I'd worn you out quite so badly last night. I can loan you some of my vitamins," he teased. "And you might want to consider ordering an extra-large portion of protein with your dinner this evening. Speaking of which, our reservations are in just over an hour and I'd like to have a cocktail with you first. Trust me, you'll like where we're going."

Tessa yawned, stretching her arms wide. "Umm, okay. But it's not my fault if I suddenly start nodding off. That massage was incredible. I've never felt that pampered before."

"That was the general idea, darling. To have you feeling relaxed and pampered all weekend long. Though I didn't intend for you to be quite this relaxed," he retorted. "Perhaps I should order you a triple espresso – or two." He leaned forward to murmur huskily, "After all, I plan to keep you awake for hours tonight. Another part of the surprise."

She couldn't help trembling just a little at his heated words. "I can't wait," she told him a little dazedly. "Maybe we should just get room service and, ah, stay in."

He grinned at her, shaking his head. "And ruin all of my plans? Hardly, love. Besides, the anticipation will enhance the pleasure ten times over. Trust me on this. Now, time for the next surprises. Come with me."

Ian led her into the master bedroom, where several boxes of varying sizes had been laid out on the huge four poster bed. She looked at him expectantly, not sure what she was supposed to do next.

"And where did all these just materialize from?" she inquired. "They weren't here earlier when I unpacked my things."

But he only gave her a mysterious smile before telling her, "I'd like you to wear all of the items you'll find in the boxes to dinner this evening. I'll leave you in here while I change in the other bedroom."

Tessa regarded him curiously. "There's plenty of room in here for both of us, you know."

Playfully he tugged at the belt of her robe. "Yes, but if I watch you put on some of the items you'll find in the boxes we'll never get out of here this evening. You might not even get to order room service. Let's just say it will be much safer all around if I use the other room."

His rather cryptic words suddenly made perfect sense as she removed the lids from each box and spied their contents. Her mouth dropped open in a round "O" as she drew out the gorgeous bustier of cream silk and lace shot through with red satin ribbons. There was a matching pair of tiny cream silk panties tied with red satin ribbons on the sides, and sheer, silky stockings that would attach to the bustier's garters. She now understood why Ian was changing in a separate room.

She gasped when she drew out the beautiful cocktail dress from the largest box. It was of red lace, with an off the shoulder sweetheart neckline. The label read Marchesa but of course no price tags were attached to anything. She shuddered to imagine how much it had cost.

She struggled a bit with the back hooks of the bustier but eventually managed to get them all fastened. Once she pulled on the panties and hooked the stockings to the garters, she glanced at herself in the bathroom's full-length mirror, her eyes widening at the image that stared back at her. The wired bustier pushed her breasts up into even more generous proportions than usual, until they were nearly spilling out of the low-cut garment. The undergarment nipped in at the waist, making it look tiny, and the silky stockings made her legs look longer than ever.

The alluring red dress fit her perfectly, as did the red patent leather heels. The final two boxes held a stunning bracelet of rubies and diamonds, and a matching pair of drop earrings. Tessa touched up her makeup and brushed her hair until it shone, placed a few items into her clutch bag, and then tentatively walked into the living room.

Ian was sending a text and didn't hear her come in, so she was able to look him over at her leisure. He was wearing a dark gray suit and a crisp white dress shirt opened at the neck, but no tie. His five o'clock shadow was more prominent now, giving him a dangerous look. He was so sexy, so mouthwateringly male, that her new panties immediately grew damp as she imagined running her hands up his body or pressing a kiss to his cheek.

He looked up then, and his gaze upon her was so smoldering that she could almost feel it burning into her skin. He stuck the phone in his jacket pocket and walked towards her, never breaking eye contact. He threaded a hand into her hair, tilting her head to one side, and brushed a kiss on her cheek.

"Hello, beautiful," he told her huskily. "You look sinful."

She toyed with the open neckline of his shirt for a moment before unbuttoning one more button. "So do you." She nuzzled her nose against the exposed skin of his throat. "And you smell even better."

He trailed his fingers up her bare arm. "I assume everything else fits – er, adequately?"

Tessa smiled. "It does, yes. Though I almost had to call you in to help me fasten up one of the – ah, items."

Ian's hands grasped her hips, yanking her up against him. "I trust you were able to take care of the matter yourself?"

At her nod, his gaze dropped to her cleavage, which was partially bared by the cut of the dress. She whimpered as he traced along the neckline of the dress, his long finger brushing her bare skin.

"I can't wait to see you in it," he rasped. "I'm guessing it makes your gorgeous tits look even bigger than they already are." He replaced his fingers with his lips, kissing the exposed upper curves of her breasts. "I almost bought you the necklace that matched the other jewelry, but then decided I didn't want anything to mar the perfection of these magnificent breasts."

"Please." The throaty moan escaped her lips as he brushed his thumb over her nipple. Her hands clutched handfuls of his shirt as she tried to mold her lower body against his.

"Easy, love." He dropped a kiss on the bridge of her nose before taking her firmly by the hand. "Remember what I told you earlier – anticipation only enhances the ultimate pleasure. So, come now. Time to start anticipating what's to come."

***

The cocktail lounge was on the top floor of the lodge, and offered up a stupefying view of the snowcapped mountains. They sipped one of the special Valentine's Day cocktails – a pomegranate margarita – and took turns feeding each other salted almonds and mini-pretzels.

As she popped an almond into his mouth, Ian clasped her wrist, holding it still as he sucked her finger between his lips. Then it was his turn to feed her a pretzel, and she mimicked his actions by licking his index finger suggestively.

His eyes darkened. "Are you imagining something else in place of my finger inside your mouth right about now?" At her nod, he removed his finger and brushed his thumb over her lips instead. "Naughty girl."

"I like being naughty with you."

"Jesus." He shifted a bit awkwardly in his leather chair. "You're making me forget all of my good intentions, you little flirt. Finish your drink now, love, it's nearly time for dinner."

Once again Tessa marveled at the way the wait staff at the very upscale hotel restaurant catered to Ian, very obviously knowing exactly who he was, and going out of their way to make sure he had a satisfactory dining experience. They easily had the best table in the place next to the window that afforded another fabulous view of the mountains.

He had taken her out to equally posh restaurants often enough over these past weeks that she was more at ease with scanning menus and ordering. They shared a Caesar salad that the waiter hand tossed tableside, as well as an order of black truffle risotto. She chose the sea bass for her entrée while Ian ordered a beef filet, giving her a wink as he did that made her squirm a bit in reaction. He was not so subtly passing along the message that he needed the red meat for what was yet to happen tonight.

He ordered champagne – a Ruinart Brut Rose – and she was delighted to discover it was pink as the waiter poured it into flutes.

"For Valentine's Day," Ian told her. "I hope you like it, my love."

As Tessa took a sip, she realized this was the second time this evening he'd called her "my love" as opposed to simply "love", and wondered at the significance – if any – at this slight change. But she soon forgot about it as the meal progressed, far too intent on listening to him, gazing at him, desiring him. Everything he did, no matter how subtle or seemingly insignificant, seemed to arouse her this evening – the way his long fingers held his champagne flute; the movements of his strong jaw as he carefully chewed a bite of food; not to mention the glimpses she was afforded of his tanned throat and the very beginnings of the dark ribbon of hair that bisected his chest. She knew he hadn't worn a tie very intentionally and could only assume – or, rather hope – that he was planning for this to be the night they played out the fantasy dream she'd described to him.

The deepening hunger she felt must have been obvious in the way she kept staring at him, for he took her hand in his at some point and drew it to his lips.

"That look on your face – God, you have no idea what it's doing to me," he told her in a husky voice.

"Oh." She glanced down at her plate, suddenly shy. "Sorry. I just – I guess I just like to look at you."

"Hush. Don't look away from me, Tessa. Ah, there's my girl," he crooned as she lifted her gaze to his. "I wasn't complaining, darling. Far from it. I love that I can put that particular look on your face – the one that tells me how much you want me. It's so honest and open. I don't ever want you to pretend with me, or try to hide your emotions. Understood?"

She nodded, spellbound by his deep voice and the way his hazel eyes glittered almost dangerously. "I won't," she breathed. "And I do want you, Ian. So much that it's all I've been able to think about all day. It's – too much at times, I think."

"No." He shook his head emphatically. "Never too much. You have so much passion, Tessa, far more than we've even begun to uncover as yet. I knew it the first time I kissed you, when you came so easily and so quickly. We're really just beginning to awaken you sexually. But I'll warn you now – I'm the only man who'll be assisting you in that particular endeavor."

She cupped his cheek in her hand. "I don't want anyone else, just you. You know that."

"Do I? Sometimes I'm not always certain. That's still one of my greatest fears, you know," he admitted. "I'm terrified that you'll wake up one morning and realize you've made a huge mistake, that you'll want your freedom to meet other men, *younger* men, play the field a little and have the sort of fun girls your age ought to be doing. You never had the opportunity to do that, after all, and I'm worried that you'll regret passing it all up."

"Why in the world would I want to do that?" she asked in bewilderment. "That doesn't sound like much fun to me."

"Try telling that to your friends," he replied darkly. "Yesterday it felt like some sort of bizarre conspiracy theory was unfolding – one that involved all of them setting you up with other men."

Tessa was startled at the note of desperation in his voice, the way he looked and sounded so insecure – he, the most confident, self-assured man she'd ever met. "If you're worried about what Kevin said – please don't be. He means well but he's a total airhead most of the time. I hardly ever take what he says seriously. And," she added gently, "I have no intention or any interest in letting him fix me up with anyone."

"It wasn't just Kevin. That was bad enough but then scarcely an hour later I had to bite my tongue when that little scamp Julia asked my opinion about setting you up with a friend of Nathan's. How did you manage to fend off that very persistent little mischief-maker anyway?"

"What?" Tessa couldn't believe what she was hearing. "Julia? She didn't say one word to me about meeting any friends of Nathan's. This was at the office yesterday you're referring to? All she really talked about was the new pair of shoes Nathan was going to buy her."

A slow smile spread across his face, and he shook his head in exasperation. "I think I've been had by a very devious interior designer. And I believe Nathan is quickly discovering he's got his hands full with that little devil he's engaged to. Not to mention several hundred dollars poorer after buying the aforementioned shoes."

She was more perplexed than ever now. "I really have no idea about any of that. But I've got no interest in dating other men. Why would I when I've already got my Prince Charming?"

Her answer seemed to please him tremendously, as well as relieve any doubts he might have still been harboring. "Well, every princess deserves a prince, darling. And I'm going to work very hard to make sure you're every bit as pampered and cherished as a queen."

She let him coax her into sharing dessert, even though she was already full from the superb meal. He fed her bites of warm chocolate lava cake and salted caramel ice cream, while they both sipped coffee – an espresso for him, a foamy cappuccino for her. She didn't drink coffee very often, but was already beginning to feel a little drowsy from all the champagne and rich food, and decided the extra caffeine would be a wise idea. There was no way she was going to fall asleep before they had the opportunity to play out her fantasy.

"Are we going back to our room now?" she asked hopefully as he finished signing the guest check.

"Impatient, are we?" he asked in amusement.

"Yes," she replied in a breathless voice. "The – ah – anticipation is getting to be more than I can bear."

He slid his hand to the back of her head and brought her mouth to his for a soft kiss. "Good. I want you wild with need, so aroused that you'll come at the lightest touch."

Tessa groaned. "I'm already there."

"Are you wet?"

"God, yes," she whispered. "So much that I think I might leave a spot on this chair."

Ian closed his eyes, muttering something beneath his breath, before standing abruptly and pushing his chair back. "Let's go," he said roughly, stepping around the table to pull her chair out. "Otherwise, I'm going to kiss you right here in front of all these people and it will take an awful lot to make me stop."

She was certain he would take her back to the suite after that, but gave a little sigh of frustration when they stopped at the piano bar in the lobby instead. He noticed the little huff she made as they sat at one of the tables and smiled at her.

"Remember what I told you earlier, love? The anticipation builds the pleasure," he reminded her gently. "Don't pout, Tessa, it won't sway my decision. Trust me, darling, this will all be worth it in just a very short while. Meanwhile, relax and enjoy the music for a bit, hmm?"

He ordered them each a brandy, the Camus label she know he preferred. She still found the taste of the fine liqueur a little bitter for her liking but nonetheless sipped her drink daintily. Ian held her hand loosely in his as they listened in companionable silence to the vocalist and her accompanying pianist. Several couples in the bar were dancing in the small space in front of the piano as Ian pulled her to her feet and out onto the dance floor.

He held her close, one arm banded about her waist, the other hand clasping hers where it rested on his shoulder. He danced as smoothly and effortlessly as he seemed to do almost everything, and it was the easiest thing in the world for her to follow his lead.

"I wanted to dance with you so badly at the Christmas party," he murmured close to her ear. "Especially when I saw you there all alone. But of course, I couldn't, not without revealing my hand – and my feelings – to everyone else there that night."

"Including your date, of course," she replied teasingly.

He gave her waist a little squeeze. "Behave. I've already explained to you about Rebecca. And you were the woman I wanted that night, not her. When you told me as you were getting ready to leave about your divorce – you have no idea what I felt to learn the news. I couldn't go back to the party for a while – I needed some private time to fully absorb the reality that you were finally going to be free."

She nestled the top of her head beneath his chin as they kept dancing to the next song. "You were so kind to me that night – getting me a taxi and paying for it. But I just figured you were only looking out for one of your employees."

"No." He rubbed his cheek against her head. "I wanted to be the one to take you home that night, to take you home with *me*. Instead, I sat in the bar of the hotel and began to plot exactly how I was going to seduce you. It was all going to start with you filling in for Andrew during his vacation. I think I gave the old boy quite a shock on that Monday when I shared the news."

She laughed. "That must have been something to see. Andrew doesn't shock easily. I always wondered, you know, why I was never asked to substitute for him before then. I just assumed you didn't think I was capable."

"Not even remotely close to the truth," he assured her swiftly. "The real truth is that I didn't trust myself having you in such close proximity. I'm not sure I could have remembered you were a married woman – or gave a damn – after a while. And you are far more than just capable of doing the job, Tessa. You did a brilliant job filling in for Andrew, far better than any of the others ever did."

She was ridiculously pleased at his praise. "That means a lot. And I'm very glad to know it wasn't my ineptitude that made you reluctant to have me fill in. Speaking of Andrew, there's something else I've always meant to ask you about him."

Ian grinned playfully. "He's not gay, even though he may act like an uptight bastard most of the time."

She gave him a little swat on the arm. "That's not what I was going to ask you. And I've met his girlfriend so I already knew he wasn't gay. Isobel is – well, very different from our Andrew. The saying about opposites attracting could have been invented with the two of them in mind. No, what I was going to ask you concerns – well, Jason, I'm afraid. And why Andrew always seemed to be around when - "

"When that prick was trying to harass you," finished Ian.

"Why do you think that happened, Tessa?"

She shrugged. "I always assumed it was because you didn't want another sexual harassment lawsuit on your hands."

"Wrong. Oh, not that the possibility wasn't a valid concern. But my primary motivation was to make damned sure that son of a bitch kept his filthy hands off of you. And it worked for the most part, until that day in the office gym."

Her cheeks grew warm when she recalled that very unpleasant encounter. "You sent him away because of me, didn't you?"

"Yes," he replied, without the slightest hesitation. "I would have gladly shipped him to the Arctic Circle if I could have, anywhere to keep him away from you." His hand squeezed hers a little tighter. "I'll never allow him to harass you again, Tessa. Not Jason nor any other man. What's mine I protect. And you are mine, aren't you, love?"

In response, she touched his cheek and pressed her lips to his softly. He groaned beneath her kiss, and she quickly forgot there were other people in the room. All she was aware of was the warmth and hardness of his body pressed against hers, of the gentle caress of his lips on hers, and of the stirring lyrics the vocalist was crooning. The song was Alicia Keys' *If I Ain't Got You*, and the beautiful words about not wanting or needing anything else if she couldn't have the man who held her against him so tenderly made tears shimmer in her eyes. She turned her face into his chest, her heart so filled with emotion that she feared it might burst.

"Come, darling," he whispered to her. "I think the anticipation has finally reached the boiling point."

They were silent as they made their way back to the suite, his hand at the small of her back their only physical contact. Once inside the suite he led her directly to the master bedroom, where in their absence the thick duvet had been turned down and a soft bedside lamp left on.

"Let me," he urged, his hands on the zipper of her dress.

She didn't resist as he carefully eased the delicate lace fabric off her shoulders and down past her hips. As she would have stepped out of her shoes, he gripped her by the ankle firmly.

"Not yet," he instructed. "I want to see you first. I've been trying to picture how you'd look in this very fetching ensemble all night long."

Tessa forced herself to keep her eyes open as Ian's heated gaze roamed over her body. But it was nearly impossible to stop her pulse from racing or her legs to keep from shaking when she saw the raw, almost feral desire stamped on his face. His hands clamped tightly around her waist as he gazed down at the decadent display of her breasts as they very nearly overflowed the bustier.

"You look – " he swallowed with some difficulty, his voice cracking a little. "You look like a naughty Valentine, all cream lace and red satin." He slid his hands up beneath her breasts, squeezing them through the wired bodice. "Like an extremely desirable, very fuckable Valentine. And if I hadn't already committed to fulfilling your fantasy this evening, you can be damned sure we'd be satisfying about a dozen of mine instead."

She gasped as his thumbs brushed over her nipples. "There's – there's always tomorrow night," she replied in a thin, high voice.

Ian smiled dangerously. "I like the way you think, darling. Maybe you'll consent to wearing this fetching garment for me again, hmm?"

"Yes, yes," she breathed. "I'll do anything for you, Ian. Anything at all."

He grasped her chin roughly and kissed her, a savage, open-mouthed kiss that left her struggling for air. "This probably isn't a good time to tell me something like that," he hissed. "Not when you look like every forbidden fantasy I've ever had about you come to life. So let's get on with this before I forget I'm a gentleman and go back on my word."

Ian dropped to his knees, holding her steady as she stepped out of the shoes. His fingers trailed up either side of her silk-stockinged legs, until they reached the frilly garters attached to the tops. He unhooked each side before carefully easing the delicate hosiery off her legs. He hooked his thumbs in the side of her panties, but before he peeled them off her body he nuzzled his nose into her damp cleft.

"I can smell how aroused you are," he groaned, his hands

squeezing her buttocks before removing her drenched underwear. "Small wonder, given how wet you are. Ah, if you wear this for me again tomorrow, we'll have to buy new panties, won't we?" He stood and moved behind her where he slowly began to unhook the bustier. "Or perhaps we'll just buy a whole new set like this one. Black this time, I think. As you know, I like you in black lace."

The wired undergarment fell away, leaving her nude and so aroused she feared she would come at even the slightest touch of his hands on her body. But instead of touching her as she longed for, he merely led her over to the bed and indicated she should lay down.

"You know what comes next, Tessa," he told her in a deep, seductive voice. "After all, it's your dream we're bringing to life tonight, isn't it? Show me what you want, love."

She watched through half-lidded eyes as he carefully removed his suit jacket without ever taking his eyes off of her prone body. Just like she remembered from her months-old erotic dream, her arms and legs began to move in opposite directions into a spread-eagle position. As she continued to watch him, he walked over to the dresser and opened the top drawer to remove something. When he approached the bed, she saw he was carrying several long strips of red satin fabric.

With almost maddening slowness, he bound each of her wrists and ankles to the bed, making sure the satin strips were securely fastened.

"Not too tight?" he asked her as he stood.

She gave an experimental tug before shaking her head. "No, they're okay."

"Good. We want this to be pleasurable for you, but never painful. Let me look at you like this. Ah, what a delectable picture you are, Tessa – naked, spread and bound for my pleasure. You are what every man craves, what they dream of. Only you are so much more beautiful than any dream could possibly be."

She closed her eyes, her lower body already starting to bow off the bed, so desperately aroused and needy for his touch that her skin felt like it was on fire. "Please," she whispered weakly.

"Yes, love. I intend on pleasing you very well. Look at me now and tell me, Tessa – is this how it was in your dream? Except, of course, that you're lying on a very comfortable bed instead of a cold, hard table."

She gazed up at him, almost recoiling from the naked passion in his eyes. "Yes," she murmured. "Everything's the same except – your shirt. You need – undo two more buttons, I think. Then, yes, it's just like in my dream."

He complied, his shirt gapping open now to reveal more of his beautifully muscled chest. She longed to touch him, to run her hands over every inch of his hard, sculpted body, but the bonds she'd asked for prevented her from doing so.

And then Ian was beside her, sitting on the bed as he bent his head and kissed her softly. His mouth took hers again and again in a series of long, leisurely kisses. She groaned beneath the pressure of his warm, firm lips, and the feel of his tongue sweeping thoroughly through her mouth over and over. He grasped her jaw between his long fingers, holding her head still as his kisses grew deeper and more demanding, and she felt dizzy from the continued force of his attentions.

Tessa was gasping for breath as his lips finally began to move down the side of her throat, caressing the tender flesh beneath her ear. She gave a little squeal of surprise as he sucked hard on that spot, marking her, only to soothe the sharpness of the love bite a moment later with his tongue.

Ian took his time with her, seeming in no rush whatsoever, and it was both torment and exquisite pleasure for her simultaneously. He lingered over her breasts, lavishing attention on them until she was moaning loudly and moving her pelvis restlessly beneath him. His tongue laved each nipple with maddening slowness before he closed his lips around the areola and sucked hard. His hand cupped the other swollen globe, his fingers plucking at the nipple and coaxing it into an even harder peak. She could feel each lick, each tug, each squeeze of her flesh all the way down to her womb, and she wondered wildly if he could possibly make her come solely by stimulating her nipples.

By the time he finally lifted his head from her breasts, she was so fully aroused – every nerve ending in her body so highly stimulated – that it only took the tiniest flick of his thumb on her clit for her to climax wildly. She felt the satin bonds pull tight as her body bucked up in reaction, and she sobbed his name as the tremors continued to rock her from head to toe.

Ian's big hands bracketed her hips, holding her down on the mattress as the bonds continued to strain. "Poor darling," he crooned. "I made you wait too long, didn't I? Let's see if we can make it up to you somehow."

He kissed his way down her torso, his dark head disappearing between her legs, and proceeded to wring several more orgasms from her seemingly insatiable body, using his lips, tongue and fingers to bring her over the edge more times than she could keep track of. She was so aroused that she could feel the pearly drops of her vaginal fluids trickling down the insides of her thighs and still he kept at her, until her arms and legs were quivering uncontrollably and she feared she might pass out from the pleasure.

And when his thumb began to circle her over-sensitized clit one more time, her head thrashed back and forth on the pillow as she pleaded with him weakly, "No more. Please. I can't, Ian. It's too much."

He slid back up her body, kissing her softly and letting her taste the muskiness of her own juices on his lips. "All right, love," he acquiesced. "Shall I untie you now?"

She was too wrung out to do more than nod, and he deftly unfastened each of the soft satin bonds. As the last strip was untied, she rose up on her knees and slid her arms around his neck, pulling his face down to hers for a kiss.

"Thank you," she whispered. "My turn to return the favor tomorrow night."

He chuckled, holding her close against his half-bared chest. "But the pleasure was mutual, love. And if you plan to tie me down you'll need something much stronger than these scraps of fabric. I wouldn't be able to control myself if you touched me that way. As it is, I have no idea how I've managed to stay in control this long."

She slid her hand down between their bodies, her palm

opening over the massive swell of his erection. The groan he made was the sexiest, most erotic sound she'd ever heard. "Then come to me, Ian. Don't hold back any longer. "

He tore his shirt off, the rest of the buttons flying haphazardly around the room, before unbuckling his belt. Tessa ran her hands greedily over his naked chest, pressing fevered kisses to his heavily muscled chest and rock hard abs as he yanked the rest of his clothing off. In two swift movements that left her gasping, he tumbled her onto her back and thrust deep inside of her, burying himself in her soft, yielding body as far as he could possibly reach.

Tessa wrapped her arms around his neck and locked her legs around his hips, holding him as close to her as she could, and glorying in the feel of his hard, thick cock thrusting in and out of her with increasing ferocity.

"Ah, God, it's so good," she cried, the tears tracking down her cheeks as he continued to move in her body with long, powerful thrusts. She buried her damp face against the side of his throat, her lips caressing his skin as she tried to pull him even closer against her.

She gave a little cry of protest as he lifted his chest from hers, sweat pouring from his body as it mingled with hers. He captured both of her hands in one of his and drew them over her head, holding them in place as he continued to fuck her with ever increasing speed. The look in his eyes was smoldering and dangerous as he stared down at her, his lips parted as his breathing grew ragged.

"I want to watch you when you come," he told her in a guttural voice. "Look at me, Tessa, don't close your eyes. I want to see it when the pleasure takes you over, see how much I can make you feel. You have no idea what it does to me, knowing I can give you that, my love."

She struggled to keep her eyes open as he'd bid her, half-afraid of the intensity she saw burning in his gaze. Maintaining eye contact became increasingly more difficult as he kept stroking his big cock in and out of her body, until she felt yet another orgasm approaching, and knew this one would be by far the strongest of them all.

She was beyond rational thought, was all feeling right now, and as the orgasm hit full force she could only sob out her pleasure, the words tumbling from her lips as naturally as breath. "Ian, ah, oh, God, I'm going to c-come again! Oh, God, I love you!"

Her eyes did shut then, her body too consumed with sensation to even be aware of her actions. Dimly, as if from a great distance, she heard him groan loudly just before pistoning his hips into her body at a breakneck pace, his thrusts almost savage. When he came, he gripped her by the hips as he reared back onto his haunches, and emptied himself fully inside of her. She peeked up at him through half-lidded eyes, enthralled at his spectacular, primitive male beauty – a fine layer of sweat covering his entire body; his dark hair damp and disarrayed; his eyes tightly shut as he continued to fill her with his hot, sticky semen.

And then he was grasping her under the arms, pulling her up to straddle his lap while remaining embedded inside of her. She almost cried out at the ferocity of his gaze, and at the way he fisted a hand in her hair, holding her head still.

"Say it again."

She knew exactly what he meant. "I love you," she whispered, cupping his face between her palms.

Ian's own eyes filled with tears, and she brushed one away with her thumb, staring at him in disbelief.

"God, do you have any idea how long I've wanted to hear you say those words?" he uttered brokenly. "I never, ever, dreamed you would actually do it, though. I've loved you since the day you walked into my office, Tessa. I am completely, insanely in love with you, my darling girl, and you have just made me the happiest man on earth." He kissed her softly. "And I have never, ever, told a woman that before. So you see, you are my first in many ways as well – my love."

"Ian." She was overcome with a whole flurry of different emotions right now – amazement that this proud, regal man had actually been brought to tears by her whispered confession of love; disbelief that he'd loved her that long; and then there was simply all the love she felt for him, the tenderness and the passion. Everything combined was almost too much to take, and she felt like pinching herself to make sure this wasn't another dream she had conjured up.

But she was reminded – in a very, very pleasurable way - that he was all too real, and that what had happened was definitely not a dream. He made love to her again, this time with a gentleness and devotion that brought tears to her eyes. A long time later, they were physically and emotionally exhausted, and finally drifted off to sleep, both whispering "I love you" to the other as they did.

Chapter Seventeen

The international terminal at San Francisco Airport was teeming with people, even at this early hour. Ian had already checked his luggage for the flight to London, and was delaying the moment he had to enter the security line for as long as possible, knowing that Tessa would not be able to proceed past that point. Taking a commercial flight was not something he typically did, for he utilized the corporate jet for the majority of his business travel. But since he would be away for just over two weeks and remaining in London the entire time, he'd decided the company plane could be put to better use by his executives and high level managers who also needed to travel frequently on business.

Wanting to spend every possible minute together until his departure, Tessa had stayed overnight at his house and risen at a very early hour this morning to accompany him on the drive to the airport. Simon was at present circling around the terminal until she re-emerged, and then he would drive her to the office. Or, at least, within a couple of blocks so that no one would notice her alighting from Ian's car and putting two and two together.

"You're certain you won't stay at the house while I'm away?"

Tessa nodded as she smoothed down the lapels of his black wool overcoat. "I'm sure, yes. If I'm going to give notice to my landlord soon, then I'd better use this time to start packing things up and cleaning. I'll have to decide what to keep and what to donate. I want to ask my landlord if any of the other tenants might need some things."

He gave the belt of her raincoat a little tug as he tightened his arms around her waist. "Well, if I get a vote you know what item will be on the top of my donation pile."

She grinned up at him. "I thought you had other plans for this, plans that included a fireplace and a book of matches."

Ian eyed the much-maligned raincoat dubiously. "You're right. I'm not certain there would be any takers if you tried to give it away. Even thrift stores have certain standards."

Tessa gave him a playful swat on the arm. "Hey, it's not that bad. Besides, it's not for much longer, you know."

"I know." He tucked a strand of hair behind her ear. "You'll also get to work on that letter of resignation while I'm away?"

"Yes, I promise. Will you tell Andrew the real reason I'm leaving?"

Ian considered her question for a moment or two. "Most likely, yes. If anyone can keep a secret, he can. Not to mention he's paid a pretty penny to be discreet. And, of course, he probably already guesses that there's something going on between us. It's rather terrifying at times how nothing escapes that boy's attention."

She nodded. "He's terrifying, all right. Wouldn't it be something to have him and Mrs. Carrington in the same room together some time?"

The look of mock horror on his face made her giggle. "God, that would truly be a battle of wills for the ages, wouldn't it?" he asked. "I wouldn't even know which one of them to bet on."

For long seconds after that they just held each other, two lovers who were postponing the moment they would have to part for as long as possible. It was Tessa who finally, reluctantly, lifted her head from his chest and gazed up at him sorrowfully.

"I guess you'd better go," she said slowly. "And I shouldn't keep Simon waiting any longer."

"Simon doesn't mind," he assured her gently. "He knows I'm mad about you. But unfortunately, you're right, it is time. Now, give me a kiss good-by, darling, and I'll call you as soon as I land."

Tessa kissed him with an almost desperate hunger, her arms clinging to his neck as he groaned beneath her lips. Tears shimmered in her eyes as he lifted his head.

He cupped her cheek in his hand, his thumb brushing away her tears. "I've got to go. Dream of me, will you, love?"

"Every night," she whispered. "You, too."

Ian smiled, the look of love on his handsome face causing her heart to ache. "Darling, don't you know? I've dreamed of you every night since we met. I'm not going to stop now."

With one last, quick kiss, he picked up his laptop bag and walked away towards the security line. She watched him for another minute or two before turning away hastily, not wanting to burst into tears in the middle of a crowded airport.

Simon tactfully didn't comment on her teary-eyed state when he assisted her inside the Town Car, and was mostly silent during the drive back into San Francisco. But as they drew closer to the office, his deep, gentle voice startled her a bit.

"He's head over heels in love with you, too, Miss Tessa," he said kindly. "I've never seen him this way with another woman, not even close. And you're definitely the only person who's ever seen him off at the airport before."

Tessa sniffled. "Oh. Well, thank you for telling me, Simon. And I – I love him very much. I hope – that is, I know how all this must look to you. I mean, he's so distinguished and handsome and – well, rich. And I'm just an ordinary office employee, no one special."

"You're special to Mr. Gregson," declared Simon. "And he's an excellent judge of character. If he thought for one minute that you were some type of fortune hunter, he wouldn't have bothered with you. He told me soon after the two of you began seeing each other that he was crazy about you, and not just because you're a very pretty young lady. He said that your real beauty was deep inside of you, and that your kindness and goodness were what really drew him to you."

Tessa felt a warm glow spread through her at Simon's words. "He really said that?"

"He did, Miss Tessa. And he meant every word. And he's absolutely correct. You're a good girl, I can tell, not like all the others who would only be after his money or his looks. You truly care for him, too – for the man he is inside and not just the image he projects. You two make a lovely couple."

Impulsively, she reached forward and squeezed him on the shoulder. "That's so kind of you to say," she told him tearfully. "It will help me get through these next two weeks without him."

Simon gave her hand a reassuring pat. "Trust me, my dear, you're the best thing that's ever happened to him and he knows it. He's the happiest I've ever seen him. I hope you realize he would do anything for you, absolutely anything."

"I do, yes. And the feeling is mutual."

As instructed, Simon let her off a short distance from the office and in a very discreet manner. Before she began to walk away, he reminded her yet again to get in touch with him if she needed anything during Ian's absence.

"I'll be visiting my sister and her family up in Oregon for about a week," he told her, "but I'll be back in town next week. Even if I'm not around I can easily arrange for anything you might need."

Tessa thanked him but assured him she'd be fine, that she was used to taking care of herself and wished him a pleasant vacation. Then she was off to work, where she hoped to keep busy enough over the next two weeks so that she didn't feel like crying nonstop.

She knew that if she didn't want to endure any more painful separations like this one that she would have to remain firm in her resolve to resign. But it was one thing to know it, and quite another to actually accept it. As much as she loved Ian and wanted to be with him all the time, she couldn't quite let go of the feeling that she needed to depend on herself and not simply rely on him for everything. That had been what had eventually happened with Peter, and when he'd left it had felt like her whole world had caved in.

And, if she was being completely honest with herself, she was still having doubts that her relationship with Ian would last. Her misgivings had nothing to do with her own feelings. No, those were rock solid and she couldn't imagine ever loving another man the way she did him. Rather, it was her fear that he would tire of her, that perhaps having a much younger girlfriend was only a novelty for him, and maybe something of an ego booster (not that someone as undeniably hot as Ian needed to pad his self-esteem by any means). What if she became an embarrassment to him once they went public with their relationship – if he determined that she simply wasn't refined or educated or mature enough to live in his world full time?

He would never abandon her, or leave her to fend for herself.

That she knew without a shadow of a doubt. He was too good of a person, too much a gentleman, to ever even think of doing something like that. No, if he ever decided to end things between them he would make sure she was taken care of, settled with a good job and a place to live. But there would be nothing at all he could do to heal the gaping wound in her heart that a breakup like that would cause.

As the workday ended and she headed to the office gym for her workout, Tessa forced herself to stop being such a pessimist. Ian had made his feelings for her very clear, and she ought to be doing cartwheels of happiness right now that such an incredible man was in love with her. Instead, she was letting herself fall back into her old, bad habits and starting to imagine the worst. If she was going to get through the next two weeks without her lover, she was going to have to keep as busy as possible and, more importantly, maintain a positive attitude and not succumb to the depression that often hovered on the edges of her emotions.

The workout helped block out a lot of the insecurities and worries that tormented her, as did the call that came through from Ian shortly after she arrived home. He sounded tired, and she knew it was already the middle of the night in England. Even though she longed to keep him on the phone, she didn't prolong the conversation when he bid her good night.

She kept herself busy the rest of the evening by starting to inventory her kitchen and living room, beginning the process of packing up the apartment. By the time bedtime rolled around, she was sufficiently tired to actually fall asleep fairly quickly.

But the next morning – which happened to be a Wednesday – started out on a sour note when she discovered her period had started. One of the major side effects of the IUD she used for birth control were the heavy, painful menstrual cycles she suffered through. Her periods were also irregular, making it difficult to pinpoint when they were due to occur.

She'd tried using the pill - several different brands in actuality – but had experienced rather severe allergic reactions to each one – terrible headaches, constant nausea, a red, itchy rash. The nurse practitioner at the free clinic had steered her towards the IUD as an alternative method but Tessa wasn't so sure the side effects with it were much better.

Making sure her purse was well stocked with tampons, Tessa swallowed two Tylenol with her breakfast to lessen the pain of the severe cramps she knew would follow shortly. Her period would last for well over a week, with more of the killer cramps and heavy bleeding, enough so that she always felt a little weak and dizzy as a result. She tried to lay low during her cycles, cutting back on her exercise routine, trying to get some extra sleep, and eating as well as she could.

The timing of her period with Ian's absence was just about the only positive note. She was reluctant for him to see her this way, especially when she felt bloated and uncomfortable and on edge. Her periods also tended to make her weepy and depressed, and she knew she'd have to force herself more than usual to get through the days.

It didn't help a bit that things at the office were slow. Not only was Ian away for two weeks, but several of the other managers were either traveling on business or attending a conference somewhere. However, it seemed that Tessa was the only one of her co-workers who wasn't pleased at the lack of work assignments. The others took full advantage of the lull by arriving late and leaving early, taking longer than usual lunch hours, and spending the better part of the day gossiping, searching the Internet, and making personal calls. Of course, Andrew was still very much on top of things, and they had to exercise at least a little caution. But Tessa was quietly convinced he knew exactly what was going on, and was making very careful notes of who was slacking off. Determined not to take advantage of her relationship with Ian, she kept to her normal schedule and routine, and strove to work as hard as possible.

And she couldn't help feeling just a little bit smug when Alicia shared the latest rumors about Ian and his love life with the rest of them. The speculation that he had a new girlfriend was apparently really running wild now, given the facts he'd been a no-show at several important events lately, and that his other two former escorts – the news anchor and the ballerina – had been seen out with other men.

"Most everyone seems to think this mystery woman is someone back home in England," Alicia informed them with a little sniff of displeasure. "They think he met her when he went home for the holidays, because it was very soon after his return that he stopped being seen in public with other women."

"Hmm, so he was probably looking forward to this trip big time," chimed in Kevin. "Two months is a long time for someone like His Hotness to go without a woman."

Tessa had to bite back a retort that Ian had actually gone two *years* without a woman – if she could truly believe what he'd told her about being celibate. And while she still had her doubts that someone as virile and sexual as he was could really go without sex for so long, she also knew he was too honest and moral to lie to her about something like that. Besides, there was always such a desperate, urgent hunger in the way he took her that it was easy to believe he'd abstained for such a long time.

Rather than put herself through a grueling workout in her weakened physical state, Tessa elected to take a restorative yoga class at SF Flow instead. The unlimited monthly membership that Ian had surprised her with had been one of her favorite and most cherished gifts, and she loved the luxury of being able to take classes whenever she wished.

She knew Julia took a 6:00am class at a different studio during the week, so she didn't worry about running into her apparently very nosy friend. She did see Sasha as she arrived, since the curly-haired teacher also taught classes in the evening. Tessa had heard from other students that Sasha was not only the most popular teacher at this studio but also one of the most sought-after in the entire city. She wasn't the least surprised to see the throng of students crowding into the larger of the two practice rooms where Sasha's class was held.

"Hey, I'm not used to seeing you here in the evenings," Sasha told her. "But why aren't you going to my class? Restorative is way too easy for you, Tessa."

Tessa grimaced and placed a hand on her belly. "It's that time of the month, I'm afraid, and it's pretty awful. I figured it would be a good idea to take it a little easy."

"Ah, absolutely," agreed Sasha. "No inversions on your cycle, okay? Backbends, handstands, not a good idea. If you have bad cramps, try drinking some chamomile tea. I wish I wasn't already so booked up tonight with classes or I could try to squeeze you in for a massage. That would do wonders for you right now."

"I actually just had a massage over the long weekend," recalled Tessa wistfully. "My first ever. It was really amazing, something I could get used to."

Sasha nodded. "It's a good addiction to have. Maybe we can set up an appointment for you sometime. Take it easy in class, okay? I'll see you soon."

It didn't surprise Tessa that her teacher was also a massage therapist. During class, Sasha made a point of going around to as many students as possible and making adjustments to their bodies while in poses. Tessa could tell by the knowledgeable way in which Sasha touched her that she was extremely familiar with human anatomy, and her touch was both skillful and soothing. Tessa wondered anew if Ian already had a massage therapist he saw on a regular basis, and made a mental note to suggest that they could possibly use Sasha's services if he didn't.

She felt relaxed and less uncomfortable at the end of the class, a sensation that remained with her during the bus ride home. It was only as she opened her mail box that the all too familiar feeling that something bad was about to happen returned.

The thick manila envelope bore the return address of a local law firm, and Tessa almost dropped the packet in revulsion. She postponed opening the envelope for as long as possible, and didn't even mention its arrival to Ian when they spoke on the phone late that night. With the eight hour time difference between San Francisco and London, it was already very early in the morning for him and well past normal bedtime for her. Still, she gladly gave up the extra sleep in order to hear his voice, to listen to him recount what had happened the day before, and to have him tell her how much he loved and missed her. Determined to remain positive, Tessa didn't mention her painful period or how many times during the last day and a half she'd had to fight off the depression that threatened to engulf her in its darkness.

But once their conversation ended, she stared for long minutes at the offending envelope, knowing she'd never be able to sleep until she opened it.

She'd known without even looking at the return address that the envelope contained the divorce papers. She didn't get a lot of mail in general, and certainly nothing as thick and official looking as this packet. Sighing, Tessa slid the papers out of their envelope and took a quick glance at the top page.

Well, it was over. Officially so, even though her marriage to Peter had in all honesty never really begun. They had been best friends, roommates, confidantes, but never lovers or partners, not in the true sense of the word. Now that she knew what it truly felt like to be in love, to experience sexual fulfillment, and, yes, to finally feel like a woman, Tessa could accept her seven years with Peter for what they had really been – a means to an end; a safe haven for her; and a dysfunctional mess that should never have been permitted to go on for as long as it had.

Still, she cried for a while, because it was never really easy to let go of something that had been part of your life for so many years. And then, she pulled up her email account on the rather ancient old laptop Peter had scrounged up for her way back in high school, and began to compose the letter she ought to have sent him weeks ago.

Dear Peter,

It's been a few weeks since we were in touch and a lot has happened during that time. First, though, the divorce papers arrived today so I guess it's really official – we're no longer married. I just finished having a good cry over it but I can honestly say – finally – that you did the right thing by making this happen – for both of us.

There's – well, I've met someone, Peter. I know you always wanted that for me, but I still can't help feeling a little bit guilty about it. He's a wonderful man, treats me like a princess, and I'm going to be moving in with him soon. As you know, the lease on this place is up pretty soon so I guess the timing is working out well.

He's older than I am by quite a bit, but it's not for the

financial or emotional security that I'm with him. I'm honestly, completely, and ridiculously in love with him, and I hope you'll be happy for me. I told him everything – about my mom, the whole mess I was in when you saved me, and about us. He's not only been good to me but good for me as well, and I'm hoping he'll be the one to slay the rest of the dragons, the few that you didn't already kill for me.

I hope you know how much I still love you, Peter, and how much I always will. You were there for me in my darkest times, and I will never, ever forget that. I hope we can continue to be the best of friends, and that you will keep in close touch. And, most of all, I hope that someday you can finally find the peace that you need so badly – that you'll meet someone who will slay all of your dragons.

With much love,
Tess

Wiping away her tears, she dragged herself into the bathroom and got ready for bed, hoping that between her emotional state and her physical condition that she would sleep soundly. As she started to shut down her laptop, she was astounded to see a new message had popped up, and even more surprised to note that it was from Peter. He never replied to her emails so quickly, and she surmised he must have been online when her message had been delivered to him.

Hey, Tess,

What you are doing up so late? I'm the insomniac, remember? But in all seriousness – yes, I knew the divorce was going to be final today and was thinking of you the whole time. Guess I was just too much of a coward to email you first.

I can't tell you how happy I am to hear you've found someone, Tess. You deserve to have a normal, healthy relationship, and to be loved and adored more than anyone else in the world. I'm just sorry I couldn't be the man to give you that kind of love, because I know I'll never meet anyone half as wonderful as you.

Would I be wrong in guessing that this new, older man in your life is your boss? I might be going out on a limb here but I remember that Christmas party you dragged me to a couple of years back. I never told you this, didn't want to make you feel uncomfortable, but I saw the way he kept watching you all night and giving me the evil eye (just kidding!) If it is him, I think you've made a very wise choice. He'll take good care of you, Tess, give you all the things I never could. Oh, I'm not talking about stuff like cars or houses or clothes. I know you don't give a shit about any of that. The things I'm talking about are romance and normal sex and maybe having a baby one day. I always wanted those things for you and I'm glad you're finally going to have them.

One last thing, because I'm starting to lose it here myself. I've begun therapy, Tess. Once a week I Skype with someone in the States, someone who specializes in my sort of issues. And while I've got a long, long way to go, I'm hopeful that one day I'll be able to slay my own damned dragons.

I love you, too, Tess and we will always be best friends. Take care and be happy, and please do keep in touch.

Love,
Peter

She was crying again as she finished reading his message, but this time they were tears of joy.

***

Two Weeks Later

By his calculations, he'd been awake for more than twenty-four hours, given the time zone difference and the number of hours he'd been either waiting in airports or actually in flight. Ian was exhausted, especially since he'd had precious little sleep on the very long flight home from London. Since he had changed his flight at practically the last minute, there hadn't been any seats available in either first or business class, and he'd been forced to fly coach. For a man of his height and bulk, falling asleep in the restricted space had been all but impossible, especially when coupled with the crying child in the seat behind him and the very chatty couple in front of him. He'd considered the wisdom of taking this last minute flight a dozen times over during the rather hellish journey, but each time he questioned his decision he didn't regret it. How could he, when it meant he would see his beloved Tessa that much sooner than planned?

Wanting to surprise her with his early arrival, he hadn't told her about his change in plans. He'd made up some excuse for why he wouldn't be able to call her as usual this evening, and she sweetly hadn't questioned him further. But now that his flight – the departure having been delayed by more than two bloody hours due to heavy fog at Heathrow – had finally landed, he was making a beeline to her apartment, so that he could sweep her up and take her home with him. He knew she wouldn't mind being woken at this late hour, even though she would have to get up early for work in the morning. And he'd already written off the possibility of actually having sex with her, since his own exhaustion would probably impair his ability to perform, even given their long separation and how damned much he'd missed her.

A quick glance at his phone showed that it was actually already morning, half past midnight to be exact. As he exited the plane and walked towards baggage claim, he hit the speed dial for Tessa's cell phone. He knew she kept it by her bedside to use as an alarm, and was therefore concerned when it went to voicemail after several rings. Frowning, he tried it three more times in quick succession with the same result.

As he located the number for her landline, he tried not to panic, telling himself that perhaps she'd simply forgotten to charge her cell phone. But when the landline also went to voicemail repeated times, he couldn't control his agitation, and the dreadful feeling that something was wrong. After all, didn't Tessa always claim that bad things happened to her on Wednesdays? And though it was barely the next day, this was in fact that very day of the week.

Ian was relieved and grateful to find Simon waiting just outside of the terminal, and left the luggage for his chauffeur to handle as he got inside the car. He tried both of Tessa's numbers again, and this time didn't even attempt to control his panic.

"Something's very wrong," he told Simon as the older man slid behind the wheel. "Tessa isn't answering either of her phones. She hasn't been in touch with you, has she?"

Simon shook his head as he pulled away from the terminal. "No, sir. Haven't seen or heard from the young lady since the day you left town. When did you speak with her last?"

"Last night. A text or two earlier today. Or was it yesterday? I'm so bloody mixed up with these damned time zones that I don't even know what day it is. Christ, Simon, where is she? Why isn't she answering the phone?" Ian raked a hand through his already rumpled hair.

"I'm headed directly to Miss Lockwood's place now, sir," assured Simon calmly. "Would you like me to call my contact at the police department during the drive – just to see if they're aware of anything – ah, amiss in her area?"

Ian closed his eyes, not wanting to imagine any one of a dozen horrible things that could have happened to Tessa – being robbed, raped, stabbed, God knew what else in that questionable neighborhood she lived in. "Yes, please, Simon. And thanks, mate."

While Simon made his call, Ian tried like hell not to overreact. There could be a perfectly logical explanation as to why Tessa wasn't answering either of her phone lines. There could be a power failure in the area, which would account for why her landline wasn't working, and why she hadn't been able to charge her cell phone. Or maybe there had been some sort of gas or water main leak in the neighborhood, and all of the residents had had to be evacuated temporarily. Or just perhaps –

"Sir." Simon's voice intruded on his thoughts and then Ian was listening in horror at what his chauffeur was very reluctantly telling him. "I'm afraid Miss Lockwood's apartment building – well, there's been a fire, Mr. Gregson."

***

The scene surrounding the two block radius near Tessa's apartment building was utter and complete chaos. Ian pushed his way past barricades, completely ignoring the shouts of the police officers who had undoubtedly been told to keep all but essential personnel out of the area. He didn't give a flying fuck if a dozen strong men tried to make him leave – no one was going to prevent him from finding Tessa.

He and Simon had smelled the thick, acrid smoke in the air blocks away, could see the flashing lights and beacons of all the emergency vehicles. Simon had been able to obtain some additional information from his contact at the police department – the man evidently was both a neighbor and a fishing crony – but the data hadn't helped ease Ian's fears in the least. There were no casualties reported, at least not yet, but several residents of the building had been taken to the hospital. Initial reports indicated that the fire had started on the uppermost floor of the building – the fifth – while Tessa's unit was on the second. It was that bit of news that gave Ian the most hope that she'd found her way out of the building unharmed, but nothing was going to fully appease him until he found her.

A task which was going to be a near impossibility from the looks of it. There were emergency vehicles parked haphazardly all along the street – fire trucks, police cars, ambulances – and dozens of people running to and fro, shouting at each other, with no one person seemingly in charge of controlling the scene. The fire was still burning, filling the air with thick black smoke, and the heat from the flames was stifling.

A young Asian policewoman made a rather feeble attempt to get Ian to vacate the area. "Sir, you really can't be here, I'm afraid," she told him, trying to sound authoritative. "Emergency personnel only. You'll have to leave this area at once."

He shook his head. "Not until I find someone. I'm looking for a young woman, mid-twenties, tall, blonde hair. Have you seen anyone fitting that description?"

"Sir, I really have to insist – "

"Please." He turned the full measure of his charm on the pretty young policewoman. "Please, officer, I'm desperate to find her. Do you have any idea where they took the people who had to be evacuated?"

The policewoman hesitated before giving a slight nod. "I'm not positive, but I thought I overheard someone saying they were taking the residents into the Chinese restaurant down the street. You can check there, but then you've really got to leave."

Ian gave her a dazzling smile. "Thank you, officer. I truly appreciate it."

And then he was off, running as fast as his weary, jet-lagged body would move, trying to stay out of sight before another emergency responder noticed him and tried to get him to leave.

Ian was not an especially spiritual man, but he offered up every prayer he could remember from his youth as he hurried along. The very thought that Tessa could be injured – or worse – was not something he could bear to think about. If he were to lose her now, when they'd really just found each other, he wasn't sure he'd want to go on living either.

The Chinese restaurant in question was closer to two blocks away than one, but he didn't care and offered up a silent thanks as he walked inside the dimly lit establishment. Inside, the chaos continued, as the victims of the fire seemed to be either shouting or crying, and in at least half a dozen different languages. A couple of individuals carrying clipboards with Red Cross badges clipped to their collars were bustling about, attempting to calm as many people as they could. Ian considered approaching one of them to see if they knew if Tessa was here, then gave up and went to look for her himself.

He'd very nearly given up, the despair he felt sapping the little energy he had left, when he finally spotted her.

She was sitting by herself at a little corner table, her hair wildly tangled and her face streaked with tears and soot. Someone – presumably the Red Cross – had given her one of those ultra-light space blankets, which she was huddling inside of, her body shivering with cold – or more likely fear. Beneath the unsubstantial blanket, she wore only a pair of sleep shorts and a flimsy tank top, and her feet – Jesus – her feet were bare and dirty. She looked so forlorn and terrified that he wanted to weep. Instead, he pushed past all the other people milling aimlessly about until he was kneeling in front of her.

"Thank Christ," he muttered hoarsely, taking her face between his hands. "God almighty, Tessa, tell me you're all right."

She gasped, her hands drifting up to cover his as the ridiculous excuse for a blanket fell away from her body. "Ian. Oh, my, God, how are you here? How did you find me?" Her voice was hoarse, either from crying or smoke inhalation.

He stood and lifted her into his arms, letting the blanket fall to the floor as he cradled her against his chest. "I'll always find you, my love. Now, let's get you out of this hell hole and take you home."

He carried her out of the restaurant while somehow still managing to dig his phone out and pressed the speed dial for Simon's number. He answered on the first ring.

"I've got her, mate. Yes, unharmed so far as I can tell. Meet us on the southwest corner of the block, past the barricades. Be there shortly."

He stuck the phone back in his pocket and hefted her a bit higher in his arms, scarcely noticing her weight. He would have gladly carried her for miles, crawled through the actual fire, or walked over broken glass, just as long as she was safe.

"Ian," she murmured huskily. "Put me down. I'm too heavy for you to carry."

"Hush, darling. It's no bother at all and you are not walking a step on these filthy sidewalks in bare feet. Ah, there's Simon."

Faithful, devoted Simon was standing anxiously by the side of the car as they arrived, holding the back door open.

"Give Miss Lockwood to me, sir, while you get inside," offered Simon. "I've left a blanket on the back seat."

Ian quickly shifted Tessa to Simon's waiting arms, giving his loyal chauffeur an appreciative pat on the back. "You think of everything, mate. Thank Christ you were here tonight."

He slid inside the Town Car as Simon gently set Tessa down on the seat next to him. Ian wasted no time in covering her shivering, scantily clad body with the much more substantial wool blanket, and then pulled her onto his lap as Simon started the car.

"I want you to be seen by a doctor," he told her firmly. "Tonight. Simon, would you take us to the University Medical Center, please?"

"No," she protested weakly. "Please, Ian, I just want to go – home. The paramedics checked me out and aside from being in shock I'm okay."

"Tessa – I would be much happier if you'd agree to this," he argued. "Your voice – you must have inhaled a lot of smoke."

She shook her head before resting it wearily on his shoulder. "Not so much. My voice – I think it's like this from crying so much. I was so scared, Ian."

"Christ, and I was terrified, Tessa, absolutely fucking terrified. I kept calling your phone numbers and when I didn't get an answer, I started imagining all sorts of terrible things that could have happened to you. God knows this wasn't one of them."

Tessa began to cry, burying her face against his chest, and he rocked her gently, murmuring to her in a soothing voice. Her hair reeked of smoke, her face was grimy with tears and soot, and her body still shook uncontrollably within his arms. He rubbed his cheek against hers, uncaring that his skin, too, was now smudged, or that his suit would also begin to smell of smoke. The only thing he cared about was making sure Tessa was safe and well, to offer her comfort and shelter, and most of all, his love.

By the time they reached his house, he was almost numb with exhaustion and was grateful for Simon's assistance in bringing Tessa inside. She was nearly collapsing in shock and fatigue herself, but he made himself strip off their clothing before lifting her into a hot shower. While she sat slumped over in helpless surrender on the built-in bench, he shampooed her hair and soaped up her body, washing away all traces of soot and smoke. The water was almost scalding hot, but still her body felt chilled to his touch and he forced himself not to panic, hoping it was only shock that was responsible for her continued shivering.

After toweling both of them off, he wrapped her in her robe while tiredly searching around for some night clothes. He cursed softly as he realized the few nightgowns he'd bought her were all sheer, lacy confections that would do absolutely nothing to warm her up. He managed to dig out a pair of her yoga pants before grabbing one of his own sweatshirts and some thick athletic socks.

Ian dressed her as though she were a little girl, a task made that much more difficult by her limp, uncooperative limbs. He tucked her into bed before belting on his own robe, then ventured downstairs to pour them each a brandy. He practically had to force the first few sips down her throat, until the liquor finally seemed to have its desired effect, warming her up enough so that she was able to drink the rest of it down on her own.

He slid into bed next to her, cuddling her still trembling body close, and stroking her hair comfortingly.

"Ian, I - ," she began.

"Hush, love. Not now. We're both exhausted. Sleep now and we'll talk in the morning."

She nodded, her eyelids drooping. "Okay." She was unable to stifle a yawn as she whispered, "I love you."

He kissed her forehead. "And I love you more than life itself, Tessa. Let's rest now, my love."

Chapter Eighteen

Tessa was groggy and disoriented when she woke in the big bed alone, and it took her a minute or two to get her bearings. She was startled to notice the time on the bedside clock – ten-thirty a.m. – and tried to remember what day of the week it was. When her brain was functioning enough for her to realize it was a Wednesday, she gave a little squeak of alarm and flung the covers back, in a total panic that she could have overslept this badly on a workday. Why hadn't her alarm gone off? And why was she waking up in Ian's bed in the middle of the week? Andrew must be having an absolute fit right about now given her unexcused absence. She looked around frantically for her phone or her purse so she could call him.

And then it hit her. Her phone and purse were gone. Consumed, no doubt, by the fire that had viciously ripped through her apartment building last night. Everything was gone – clothes, furniture, dishes, keepsakes. It was like the cruelest sort of déjà vu, for something this awful to happen to a person not once but twice in a lifetime.

Tessa sat down on the bed limply, too dazed and dispirited to move. Last night's disaster had brought back far too many painful memories, ones she'd tried to repress for a long time. When she'd stood across the street from her apartment building as the flames moved through it, gutting it cruelly, she'd been reluctantly pulled back to that terrible night in Tucson. The night where she'd lost absolutely everything, including her poor, helpless mother, and when her life had been forever altered.

She wrapped her arms around herself, shivering a bit despite the oversized sweatshirt she wore that smelled like Ian. She still didn't know how he'd come to be there last night, swooping in like a knight on horseback to rescue her, but she offered up a silent prayer for her good fortune. And while she knew this time would be different, that she wouldn't be all alone and homeless and scared, that knowledge didn't lessen the terror she still felt or the sense of empty despair.

She forced herself to wash up a bit, grimacing at the rather wild condition of her hair. She vaguely recalled Ian taking her into the shower, and assumed he'd washed her hair. Undoubtedly she'd fallen asleep with it still damp, which would account for its out of control waves this morning. She rummaged through the vanity drawers until she found a hair clip, and pulled her thick locks up into a messy ponytail.

Ian was in his home office when she ventured downstairs, and she could hear him talking to someone on the phone. Not wanting to disturb him, Tessa walked into the kitchen and plugged the electric kettle in to brew some tea. There was a crisp white bakery bag on the counter that she knew contained Ian's favorite scones, but her stomach rebelled at the thought of food, even something as plain as the breakfast treat. She got one of the oversized white ceramic mugs that she loved from a cupboard and carried her steaming cup of tea as she went to find Ian.

He was just finishing up his call when he noticed her hovering in the doorway and beckoned her inside the room urgently. He disconnected the call and came to her, setting the mug aside as he cradled her close against his chest.

"Are you all right, Tessa?" he asked quietly, the concern evident in his voice.

She wrapped her arms around his waist, inhaling deeply of his wonderful, comforting scent and shrugged. "I don't know how to answer that. Right now everything seems like a bad dream, one that I've unfortunately had before. I can't – think straight, Ian. It's just too much, you know?"

He kissed the top of her head. "I know, love. Let's sit over here while you have your tea. Did you eat anything?"

"No, I'm not the least bit hungry."

Ian frowned as she curled up on the sofa, and he handed her the steaming mug of tea. "You need to eat, darling. After all, you've just gone through a tremendous shock."

She shook her head. "Maybe later, all right? Not now. I just – can't."

"All right," he relented gently. "But one thing I won't take no for an answer on is the doctor's appointment I made for you. It's at three o'clock today, and I'll drag you there kicking and screaming if I have to. I won't be satisfied until you've been thoroughly checked over."

Tessa sighed. "All right, you win. But I really, really need to call the office before anything else. I'm sure Andrew is not especially pleased with me right now."

"Don't worry about Andrew," assured Ian. "I sent him a quick text last night and called him when I got up this morning. He doesn't expect you in until Monday."

She gaped at him in astonishment. "Um, what exactly did you tell him?"

He took her hand in his. "The truth, darling. All of it. No point in lying to him, he's like a bloody hound dog sniffing out a clue at times. You can't get anything by that boy, he's far too clever for his own good."

Tessa stared down into her mug. "He – he's trustworthy, right? I mean, he won't - "

"He won't say a word," confirmed Ian. "Andrew has proven his loyalty to me – and to you, I might add – time and time again over the years. He might be a royal pain in the arse most of the time but there's no denying his devotion." He brought her hand to his lips. "And he's very supportive of our relationship. Cheeky bastard actually had the nerve to tell me he's known from the very beginning that I fancied you."

In spite of herself, Tessa couldn't suppress a giggle. "Well, not much gets past him, that's for sure."

Ian brushed his thumb over her knuckles. "I also told him to expect your resignation on his desk very soon. He's not especially pleased about that, swears you're the only truly dependable one among the team, but understands why it has to happen. And he's quite happy that you'll eventually be traveling with me as my PA. Of course, he has ulterior motives there."

Tessa smiled. "It will save him some work, I'm sure. Work he can delegate to me."

"Spot on, love." He placed an arm around her shoulders, easing her head against his chest. "Are you up to talking about what happened last night, or do you need some time?"

She buried her face against his chest. "All the time in the

world won't make it easier, so I might as well get it over with. But before I do – how on earth did you happen to be there last night? Your flight wasn't due in until this evening."

Ian gently massaged the back of her neck, working on a stiff spot until she felt like purring. "The board meetings wrapped up a day earlier than expected. I confess to having pushed the agenda along a bit each day in the hopes that we could eliminate a day. I was desperate to see you by then, even by a few hours, and changed my flight. Which turned out to be the flight from hell."

Tessa listened in sympathy as he told her about the mishaps he'd encountered during the flight – the long delay for takeoff, more turbulence than expected, the cramped seat in coach, his noisy neighbors.

"None of that matters," he told her firmly. "I'd have flown home in an aircraft carrier or on a World War I prop plane in order to see you a day early. The only thing I really curse is the delay in leaving London. If we'd taken off on time I would have been able to pick you up and have you here at the house well before the fire started."

She shrugged. "In the end, does it really matter? Whether I was there or not, all of my things were destroyed. Again."

He twirled a loose tendril of her hair around his finger. "At least you wouldn't have experienced the trauma I'm certain you must have felt at running for your life. Can you tell me exactly what happened – how you got out?"

Tessa took a deep breath before nodding. "I'd gone to sleep a little earlier than normal. I – well, I figured the sooner I fell asleep the sooner it would be today when you'd be coming home. Silly, I know, but - "

"No." He kissed her cheek. "I was counting the hours until I could see you again, so I understand. Continue, love."

"The smoke detectors woke me up. I know most everything else in the apartment is old and dilapidated but at least those worked. Very loudly, too. Then there was banging on the door, and the firefighters were hustling me out of there. I didn't have time to grab my phone or purse or even shoes." She stroked her hand over his chest, covered in a navy cashmere pullover. "I'm sorry about the phone. I know it was expensive."

"Shush." He hauled her onto his lap. "A phone is replaceable. All of the things you lost in the fire are. You, however, are completely, irrevocably irreplaceable. When I couldn't reach you on the phone, I imagined all sorts of dreadful things had happened to you. And when Simon and I learned about the fire, when I was running around in a panic trying to find you – all I could think about was making sure you were safe and unharmed." He tipped her chin up to meet his gaze, which was so filled with tenderness that her own eyes filled with tears. "Nothing else matters if I don't have you, Tessa. All of this – the house, cars, *things* – it's all meaningless if you aren't here with me."

"And you know it's the same for me," she whispered. "I've only ever cared about you, and not the things you give me."

He smiled, trying to lighten the mood. "Ah, but now you're going to have to let me give you more things. I've been busy making all sorts of arrangements so far this morning. Your replacement phone will be delivered this afternoon. Andrew is having a new ID badge sent over by messenger later today. And I made an appointment for tomorrow for you to get your driver's license."

She kissed his cheek. "You think of everything, don't you? Thank you. I'm not sure I can remember much of anything right now."

"Leave it to me then, love. I've told you more than once – there's nothing I won't do for you."

Tessa forced a lightheartedness she certainly didn't feel right now. "Well, looks like the fire did cheat you out of doing one thing you've threatened to do for a long time now."

He looked at her quizzically. "And what exactly would that be?"

She chuckled. "Tossing my raincoat into the fireplace. I'm just assuming it burned with everything else."

***

"You're certain you'll be all right if I go into the office? I'm going to make it an early day. God knows I've still got the worst case of jet lag I can remember having in recent years."

It was Thursday morning, and Ian was getting dressed for work, buttoning up his shirt as she watched him from the bed.

"Yes, I'll be fine. And I'm going to work tomorrow, not Monday," she insisted. "The doctor told us yesterday that I'm physically fine so there's no reason for me to just sit around here an extra day. I'd much rather keep busy, it – well, helps me to forget a little."

"All right," he agreed gently. "So long as you don't overdo. Physically you may be fine, but you've suffered a tremendous emotional trauma, Tessa. You don't get over that in a couple of days."

"Okay, let's put it this way. The sooner I get back to work the sooner I can resign."

Ian grinned as he finished buttoning his shirt before leaning down to give her a lingering kiss. "Good thinking, darling. Though I'm still a bit miffed you allowed Andrew to talk you into four weeks' notice. Two should have been sufficient."

She shook her head. "I feel guilty enough as it is. A month is barely enough time for him to find a replacement and have them trained. And he's been good to me in his way, as well as taken very good care of you."

He sighed. "Fine. But it's not going to be one damned day longer, understood? Especially since that wily bastard will still be able to delegate work to you. Now, what time is Julia coming over?"

It had surprised her yesterday when Ian had suggested she call Julia and tell her about the fire. And she had been almost speechless when he'd also urged her to share the news about their relationship.

"Are you sure?" she'd asked worriedly. "I mean, it won't be much longer until we can go public with it. Should we be taking a risk like that?"

"It's fine," he'd assured her. "I trust Julia – and Nathan – implicitly. Both of them will understand the need for discretion, and since they don't work directly for us the chance of them accidentally telling anyone is extremely unlikely. And," he'd added tenderly, "you need your friends around you right now, darling. Julia is cheerful, nosy little wench that she is, and she might be able to help you through this. I'll try to overlook the fact that she'll be gloating about being right about my feelings for you."

Julia had been initially shocked and then deeply concerned when Tessa had told her about the fire, wanting to know if she needed a place to stay, clothes, money, anything. And then she'd chuckled with glee when Tessa had broken the news about her relationship with Ian, not sounding in the least surprised.

"I was wondering when you two would finally fess up about it. Of course, I've known for over a year now how he felt about you. You'll have to tell me all about it. And it goes without saying that your secret is safe with me."

Julia had rearranged her work schedule so that she could spend the better part of the day with Tessa, offering to take her to lunch and shopping, and help her keep her mind off the loss she'd suffered.

"Julia will be here at ten. We're going to the DMV first to get my replacement license and then to lunch and shopping," she told Ian.

He nodded. "Make sure you get whatever you need, all right? Better yet – just hand Julia that credit card I gave you. I have no doubt she'd make good use of it on your behalf. Apparently she's got quite the shopping addiction."

Tessa smiled. "I don't need much, really. Just a few basics to tide me over for the next few weeks at work. You've already bought me more clothes than I could wear in several years."

"That's a matter of opinion, darling. With some of the traveling we'll be doing this summer you're going to need some different pieces to augment your wardrobe. But that's for another day. Now, come give me a kiss so I can head into the office for a bit."

She rose up on her knees by the edge of the bed, the duvet falling away from her body. She had begun sleeping in the nude when she was with Ian, his body heat more than enough to keep her warm at night. She loved snuggling up against his big, hard body, entwining her limbs with his, and falling asleep in his arms. His heated gaze fell on her high, lush breasts, the pale apricot nipples peaking instantly beneath his regard.

"Christ, I'd love nothing better than to tumble you back on these sheets and slide inside of you for a few hours," he rasped. "You're so beautiful, Tessa. Like a goddess – Aphrodite, I think, the goddess of love and beauty. Except that even she would have been jealous of you."

She sighed, twining her arms around his neck, her nipples brushing up against his shirt. "Yes, but only because she would have wanted you for herself. And you're *my* man, no one else can ever have you. "

Ian grinned, his hands spanning her waist. "Getting possessive, are we? Good, because I feel the same way about you."

She kissed him softly, almost teasingly, but it was still more than enough to make her groan and want more. "Thank you for last night," she whispered. "You were so – perfect. You always know exactly the right things to say and do."

He'd made love to her last night with almost heartbreaking tenderness, his kisses and caresses achingly sweet and gentle, treating her like she was some precious, fragile being. Tessa knew he'd held back, had denied himself so that he could focus solely on her needs, and it had been so exquisite that she had wept in his arms afterwards.

"It was my pleasure, love," he replied sincerely.

Tessa caressed his smooth shaven cheek, inhaling deeply of his clean, masculine scent. "Tonight, though, will be for you. I know you held back last night, even though you must have wanted more."

"Hush." He placed a finger over her lips. "Darling, what you don't realize is that I'm deliriously happy to have you any way I can. Whether it's slow and sweet like it was last night, or hard and dirty, it's always the most intense feeling in the entire world for me. And, yes, I did hold back – I always feel like a rampaging beast when I'm near you – but that was what last night called for. But it was every bit as wonderful, Tessa, every bit as satisfying."

She pressed closer against him, her lips caressing the strong column of his throat. "For me, too. But I want to give you what *you* need tonight. I want you to take me however you like. I want," she told him huskily, staring deep into his eyes, "to surrender."

"Jesus." He stared at her open-mouthed, his eyes wide and his skin flushed. "Do you have any idea what those sort of words do to a man? Tessa – my God – you are the greatest treasure any man could ever hope to find in one lifetime." He touched her cheek almost reverently. "But I've told you before. I won't be your master, nor give you orders. This is and always will be an equal partnership, in every way."

"I know that," she murmured. "That doesn't mean I can't give you this now and then, can't give myself over to your control for a night. I know you would never, ever abuse that sort of trust, and that you could never, ever hurt me. I need this, Ian – need to give myself to you freely, without limits, without rules."

He closed his eyes tightly for long seconds, his hand sliding into her hair and holding her head still. Then he nodded and opened his eyes, and she gasped at the searing passion she saw reflected in their hazel depths. "All right, then. I accept your gift – gladly. And I promise that there will be every bit as much pleasure for you as there will be for me." His hand slid down over her shoulder to her breast, cupping it before his thumb brushed over her nipple. At her gasp, he abruptly withdrew his hand.

"God, if I start touching you now I won't be able to stop. Here, better cover up so that I can think straight."

Tessa took the La Perla robe he handed her and belted it around her body as she slid out of the bed. "I'll be looking forward to tonight," she told him in a breathy little voice.

Ian groaned and pulled her into his arms. "Not half as much as I will, love. I'm thinking I'd better stop at the gym and work off some steam first – box a few rounds, swim a few dozen laps. Otherwise, I fear you're going to regret giving me carte blanche with your body."

She laughed, the sound muffled against his chest. "I doubt that very much."

"I was planning to take you to a very elegant steakhouse this evening – Harris'. Is seven o'clock all right with you?" he inquired.

"Yes, perfect. What should I wear?"

He gave her a quick kiss before stepping back, shrugging into his suit jacket. "I'll leave that up to you, love. My only request is that you wear one of the new sets of lingerie we just bought. The lavender set – you know which one I mean?"

Her cheeks pinkened as she pictured the gorgeous demi-bra of sumptuous satin and lace, and the matching pair of tiny, lacy panties. "Yes, I know."

He winked at her. "Good. Those, plus stockings, of course, and high heels. The rest I'll leave up to you. Now, I'd better go before I decide to blow off three separate meetings and start the festivities early. I'll see you this evening, love."

Tessa tried hard not to feel lonely and bereft as he left the room, knowing full well he had important matters to attend to at the office. It had been an extra special treat spending all of yesterday with him, but she acknowledged with a bittersweet resignation that every day couldn't be like that.

She took her time showering and getting ready, fretting a bit over what to wear. Fortunately, she and Julia weren't going anywhere fancy, just the DMV and then to a shopping mall where she needed to buy some things for work. Since all of her office wardrobe had burned in the fire, she would have to purchase a few pieces to get her by for the next few weeks. Now more than ever – when she was officially living with Ian – they would have to exercise extreme discretion at the office. And that meant keeping the lavish, extensive wardrobe of beautiful designer clothes he'd bought her strictly for after work use. She would need to stick to the same sort of inexpensive clothing she'd always worn to the office so that Alicia, Gina and the others didn't get suspicious.

Deciding to go with comfort rather than high fashion, Tessa chose a pair of black cigarette pants, a black and cream striped sweater, and black ballerina flats. The black Prada satchel wasn't even half full after she put her new wallet, phone, brush, lip gloss and house key inside. Most of the day to day stuff she carried around with her had been inside her old purse, another casualty of the fire.

Julia arrived promptly at ten, just as Tessa was putting her breakfast dishes into the dishwasher. As usual, the petite designer was dressed to kill – today in a gray cashmere sweater dress that clung to her curvy body, and a killer pair of black stilettos with a T-strap. Tessa had never seen Julia looking anything less than perfectly put together, and realized the only time she'd ever seen her in something other than a dress or a skirt had been in yoga class.

The very first thing Julia did was to give Tessa a fierce hug. "I'm so sorry, honey," she told her sorrowfully. "What a horrible, horrible thing for you to have to go through. But you're lucky you managed to get out of there without any apparent injuries that I can see."

Tessa nodded. "I'm fine, just a little shook up. Ian practically dragged me to see a doctor yesterday, even though I told him I was fine."

Julia grinned. "Get used to it, honey. He might be on the reserved side, but your man is definitely used to being in charge. And you couldn't have picked a better man to take care of you, Tessa. Ian is a real prize, one in a million."

"I know," admitted Tessa readily. "He's the most wonderful man in the whole world, and I still have to pinch myself something like a dozen times a day to really believe he's mine."

Julia gave Tessa's hand a squeeze. "Well, believe it, girl, because you snagged yourself a real winner. And I'm not talking about his money or his position. I mean the man he is inside – how kind he is and how well he treats people. If I hadn't already been head over heels in love with my Nathan, I'd probably have gone after Ian myself," she teased. "Then again, I saw the way he looked at you during that very first meeting I attended, and knew right off the bat that no other woman would ever do for him."

Tessa couldn't help beaming with delight. "Really? I just never imagined that someone like him – God, he's so perfect – would ever notice me."

"Oh, honey, he noticed you all right. I told you that when we had lunch together the first time but you didn't believe me. I'm glad everything worked out. Especially," she added mischievously, "since I got this fabulous pair of Manolo Blahniks as a result."

Tess smiled. "I can't believe you made a bet with Nathan about whether Ian was really the new boyfriend I told you about. But I am glad you won the bet."

Julia gave her a conspiratorial wink. "I tend to win most of the bets I make with Nathan. Let's just say it all has to do with the timing. Now, as much as I'm dying to get the grand tour of this awesome house – God, from what I've already seen I might just move in here with you – we'd better get going."

Julia's silver BMW sedan – which she told Tessa had been a Christmas present from Nathan – was parked right outside. The women spent a busy but pleasurable morning and early afternoon getting Tessa's new driver's license, and then hitting the mall for lunch and shopping. Tessa was glad she had Julia, with her innate fashion sense, along for the somewhat abbreviated shopping spree.

"I don't need much, just a few pieces to get me through the next few weeks until I quit work," she explained. "And I don't want to spend very much, especially if they aren't things I'm going to wear again."

Julia shook her head. "That's where you've got it wrong. There's no reason at all you can't mix low and high end pieces, and keep wearing the stuff you buy today. Look, this blouse here – it's on sale for thirty five dollars but it would look fantastic with those pants you have on. And I already know those are Stella McCartney which probably cost around four hundred bucks."

"For these?" squeaked Tessa in dismay. "Oh, I'm going to have to talk to Ian again. I don't want him spending that much money. You're sure? For one pair of pants?"

Julia chuckled. "Uh, huh, pretty sure. And don't fight it, honey. The man is absolutely crazy about you so let him spoil you rotten. Let's face it, Tessa – he's going to do it anyway so you might as well just accept it and count your lucky stars."

But Tessa couldn't help fretting over how much money he must have already spent on her, and worrying about what else he planned to buy her. As a result, she adamantly refused to purchase anything besides two skirts, half a dozen assorted blouses and sweaters, two dresses, one pair of plain black pumps, and an inexpensive purse. Everything was either on sale or from a clearance rack, and no amount of coaxing from Julia could convince her to buy even one more thing.

"This will have to do," insisted Tessa as they walked out of Macy's – which had fortunately been holding a huge storewide sale. "I don't want to spend any more of Ian's money, especially if what you're telling me is true about these pants."

"Look," Julia told her gently, "if it's any consolation, Nathan told me once what he guessed Ian's net worth to be – considering the salary he probably pulls in and the percentage of the company he owns."

She named a figure that nearly sent Tessa into a catatonic shock. She'd known he was wealthy, but not *that* wealthy. It was almost inconceivable that he could be worth anywhere near that much.

"So he can easily afford to buy you whatever you want without it even making a dent in his bank account," assured Julia. "Most women wouldn't blink an eye about accepting stuff from him. But I already know – that's not you."

"No. But it sounds like I'll need to get used to that sort of thing," sighed Tessa. "Especially once I start traveling with him and attending events. I'm just terrified that I'm going to embarrass him."

"Not possible," insisted Julia. "You've always been so gracious and helpful at our meetings. You'll handle yourself just fine at whatever party or banquet he takes you to. But you do need to dress the part, honey. Ian's right about that. If you think those two cats you work with can be vicious bitches, the society snobs you'll meet will be licking their chops ready to cut you into little pieces. So you'll have to make sure you look fabulous every single time. Fortunately, you're young and gorgeous and have a killer bod so the rest is easy."

Tessa smiled at her gratefully. "You're so sweet. Would you –

I mean, I know you're super busy with work and wedding plans but – well, I need a little advice about what outfits to wear for certain occasions."

Julia clapped her hands in glee. "I'd love to help you with that. After you give me the grand tour of the house, we'll take a peek at your wardrobe. Anything in particular you need an outfit for?"

Tessa felt her cheeks grow warm when she remembered Ian's instructions for tonight. "Um, well, Ian's taking me out to dinner tonight – to Harris Steakhouse. I've never been there and don't know the right thing to wear."

"I do," declared Julia. "We had dinner there in January with some clients. I'll find the perfect dress for you."

Julia was true to her word. After Tessa showed her around the house – with Julia oohing and ahhing over an antique table or a magnificently framed landscape or a priceless Oriental vase – she brought her into the walk-in closet.

Julia clutched the doorway in mock astonishment. "Oh, my God, Tessa. This is – awe inspiring. You have to let me take pictures of this set-up. Nathan and I are still finalizing the designs for my closet in our new home and this will definitely give me some amazing ideas. Oooh, look at those built-in drawers."

After Julia had snapped a dozen or so photos with her phone, she turned her attention to Tessa's clothes. With something akin to reverence, she ran her fingertips lightly over several garments, then gave a little purr of pleasure when she spied the racks of neatly arranged shoes and bags.

"Oh, honey, he's bought you some gorgeous things," she crooned. "Did the personal shopper you told me about pick all this stuff out?"

Tessa shook her head. "Actually, Ian chose most of it. He's got wonderful taste, doesn't he?"

"My God, that's putting it mildly. Tessa, he's got a gift. Everything is absolutely perfect for you – the colors, styles, all the accessories. It will be the easiest thing in the world to put outfits together for you."

For tonight's dinner, Julia helped her select a sophisticated sheath dress in a luscious shade of violet, pairing it with cream, peep-toe Louboutins. Ian had recently bought her another coat, this one of cream wool with large jeweled buttons that Julia insisted she wear tonight.

And Julia almost squealed with delight when Tessa showed her the drawers filled with exquisite, couture lingerie. Tessa carefully withdrew the gorgeous lavender bra and panty set Ian had instructed her to wear.

"He picked all these out for you, too?" inquired Julia.

Tessa couldn't help feeling a little embarrassed to admit the truth. "Um, well, yes."

Julia laughed. "Well, they do say that still waters run deep. Underneath all that proper British decorum, our Mr. Gregson has a naughty side, doesn't he? And I'll just bet he's a real tiger in bed. Though he'd have a hard time keeping score with Nathan. That man is – well, let's just say stamina is never a problem for him."

Tessa couldn't help giggling at her friend's bawdy talk. "Well, Ian is pretty – um, enthusiastic, too. Even though he always jokes about trying to keep up with me, it's really the other way around."

Julia smirked. "Sounds like we've both got our hands full with horny men, hmm? Trust me, it's a good problem to have."

**

Tessa's co-workers showered her with empathy and support when she arrived back at the office on Friday. In addition to the rest of the team, almost every other employee on their floor – from the receptionist to the highest level executives – made it a point to stop by her desk and extend their sympathies for what had happened. She was deeply touched by all the offers of help that were given as well – did she have a place to stay, did she need clothing or shoes or blankets, did she need any financial assistance? Tessa was almost in tears by the outpouring of kindness and support, and assured everyone that yes, she was fine, that she was staying with a friend and had enough clothes and other supplies. She almost felt remorseful at having to hedge around the truth, but while she was still employed by the Gregson Group no one could know that the "friend" she was living with was really their boss, and that he had already showered her with more clothes than she knew what to do with.

The other members of the team had already taken the initiative to gather up some things for her. Marisol – ever the practical one – handed Tessa a bag filled with basics like toothpaste, deodorant, razors and shampoo. Gina had gone through her closet and picked out a few blouses, sweaters and scarves that she thought Tessa could use. Shelby and Kevin had pooled their funds to buy her a gift card at Macy's so that she could buy some of the things she needed. Only Alicia was empty handed, though she did tell Tessa in a falsely sweet voice to let her know if she needed anything.

Tessa felt guilty accepting the things but realized it was necessary in order to keep up the charade, so she merely thanked all of them profusely.

Getting back to work a day earlier than planned turned out to be the best decision she could have made, for it was so busy that she didn't have time to dwell on her recent trauma. With both Ian's and Andrew's blessings, she had elected not to tell the rest of the team about her impending resignation just yet. Word would get out soon enough, since Andrew was already hard at work searching for her replacement.

It was so busy, in fact, that Gina and Alicia didn't have time to indulge in one of their usual gabfests until mid-afternoon, when the frantic pace of the workday had finally begun to ease up just a bit.

"Oh, my God, it's been so crazy today that I forgot all about the news my mother gave me this morning," Alicia began breathlessly. "She and my father were out at dinner last night with some friends from their club when they saw His Hotness. They were all at Harris Steakhouse and evidently the Boss Man was there with his new amour."

Tessa's fingers froze in midair poised over her keyboard, and she forced herself not to betray even the slightest reaction to Alicia's gossip. She'd been dreading this moment of revelation all day, and had expected Alicia to bring up the subject long before now. Ian had warned her that it was extremely likely the news would travel very quickly to Alicia, once her parents had spotted him at the restaurant last night.

She'd been instantly concerned when he had rather casually mentioned that Alicia's mother and father were seated a few tables away with two other couples.

"Aren't you worried?" she'd whispered urgently. "Alicia talks to her mother every single day and the subject is sure to come up."

Ian had shrugged, not seeming in the least concerned, and had merely taken a sip of his wine. "Not especially, no. They won't have the nerve to actually walk over here and say hello, particularly if I continue to ignore them. And you've never met her parents, have you?"

She'd shaken her head. "No. Alicia meets her mother for lunch quite a bit but she's never brought her back up to the office."

"Then there's no problem," he'd replied in a calm manner. "All she'll be able to tell Alicia is that she saw me here with a young, beautiful blonde who I appeared to be extremely taken with. Alicia is such an egotistical little witch that she'd never begin to imagine that you were the woman I spent the entire evening staring at like a lovesick boy."

He'd taken her hand in his, bringing it to his lips, and smiled fondly as her cheeks had flushed rosily. He had insisted on taking the seat next to her, instead of across the table, and so their shoulders had brushed up against each other continually during the meal.

The pre-dinner cocktail and glass of wine she'd already consumed had given Tessa a heady sensation of boldness as she leaned closer against him.

"Maybe we should really give her mother something to gossip about then, hmm?" she'd murmured in his ear, sliding her hand up his muscular thigh beneath the table.

He'd hissed as her fingers brushed teasingly against his crotch before clamping his fingers around her wrist. "Not just her but the entire restaurant," he'd growled. "And you are entirely too tempting, my love. Especially since I know what you're wearing underneath that dress. Did Julia help you select what to wear?"

Tessa had nodded. "She said to tell you that you have wonderful taste in clothing, a gift in fact."

"Did she?" He'd leaned over and given her a soft, lingering kiss on the lips. "I agree that I have exceptional taste – after all, I chose you, didn't I?"

Gina and the others were all ears at Alicia's big news, instantly clamoring for more details.

"Another brunette, I take it?" asked Gina. "He does seem to favor them."

Alicia shook her head. "Uh, uh. A blonde this time. And young. My mother said she's at least ten years younger than he is, maybe more."

"Ooh, His Hotness is doing some cradle robbing, is he?" cooed Kevin. "Well, he's such a stud it's little wonder he needs a piece of sweet young ass. An older woman probably doesn't have the stamina to keep up with him."

Tessa couldn't help the flush that seemed to spread throughout her entire body at Kevin's ribald comment. At fifteen years Ian's junior, she was constantly amazed at his sexual prowess and at the way he wore her out in bed.

Last night had been a revelation. Given free rein to take her any way he chose, Ian had twisted and contorted her body into sexual positions she hadn't dreamed existed. Tessa fidgeted in her chair and felt her panties grow damp when she remembered how he'd dragged her to the edge of the bed – her back on the mattress, her long legs locked at the ankles around his neck, as he'd fucked her while standing on the side of the bed. He'd been so deep that way, had been able to thrust into her so hard, that she'd very nearly blacked out for a few moments.

Gina waved a hand in dismissal at this bit of news. "Probably just a quick fling. I doubt he'd be serious about a much younger woman."

Alicia made a little sound of displeasure. "Not according to what my mother said. Apparently the Boss Man was completely enraptured by this woman, and totally ignored everyone else in the place. My father wanted to go over and say hello, but when he saw the pair of them were – how did my mother so charmingly phrase it – ah, yes, "canoodling" – he decided he'd better stay put."

Shelby giggled in her high, chirpy manner. "What does that even mean – canoodling? Were they eating noodles or something?"

Kevin rolled his eyes and gave Shelby an indulgent pat on the head. "Can you really be that dumb?" he muttered, half under his breath. "No, sweetie pie, they weren't eating noodles. More like eating face. You know – kissing, cuddling, that sort of thing."

"Oh." Shelby nodded in understanding. "I get it now. But – really? Somehow I can't picture Mr. Gregson actually, uh, engaging in PDA."

Tessa, too, had been in something resembling disbelief when Ian had seemed to be touching her constantly during their meal – caressing her cheek, holding her hand, giving her a series of sweet, soft kisses. He'd acted very much like a man in love, and one who didn't give a damn if the entire world was watching. His affectionate, attentive behavior had made Tessa almost swoon with desire, and made her fall even deeper under his spell.

Kevin grinned wickedly. "She must be some real hot piece of booty to get him to loosen up a little. Lucky bitch."

Alicia grimaced. "You said it, I didn't. And to top it off, my mother said Blondie was dressed to kill. Louboutins – that lavender Moschino dress I was coveting at Barneys – a triple strand pearl choker. Whoever she is, the girl's got great fashion sense."

'Or a rich boyfriend with great fashion sense' added Tessa to herself. But it gave her a great feeling of satisfaction to realize that the beautiful dress she'd worn to dinner last night had been on Alicia's own wish list. Almost maliciously, Tessa wished she had the nerve to wear the dress to the office one day and flaunt it in her co-worker's face.

She heard her cell phone ping, signaling an incoming text, and gave it a discreet peek, knowing it had to be from Ian.

Hello, luv. Sorry I've been so busy today. Just wanted to say

I love u and that last night was amazing. I'm still recovering.

Tessa bit down hard on the inside of her cheek to stifle a knowing smile. If Ian was still in recovery mode, she couldn't even imagine what to call her own condition. Upon waking this morning after a night of true rapture in his arms, she'd been a little dismayed to discover not only the whisker burns all over her breasts and belly, but her reddened nipples, a dark purple hickey on her right hip, and a soreness between her thighs that went way beyond tenderness.

She tapped back *Ur not the only one. Might B a day or 2 b4 I can walk straight.*

His reply came quickly. *Poor baby. I know I was too rough with u. That's what u get when u unleash a wild beast.*

Tessa was glad to see her co-workers were all distracted by Alicia's news and were nosily trying to figure out who Ian's mystery blonde was. Their preoccupation allowed her to focus on sexting back and forth with her very lusty lover.

It was worth it. Tho a hot bath might help. And we might have 2 stick to oral only for a day or 2.

She slapped a hand over her mouth to suppress a giggle at his response. *Well that would be just terrible wouldn't it. But u can always use more practice.*

She stole a glance at the group, satisfied that they were still yakking away. *FYI, the cats out of the bag. Alicia's mom told her all about u and your mystery blonde.*

Ah, no surprise there. Is Alicia in super bitch mode?

Tessa's shoulders shook with barely suppressed mirth. *More than ever especially since she wanted the dress I had on last night.*

She couldn't begin to do it justice. Lavender is one of your best colors. Especially that very fetching bra.

Glad u liked it. Oh, apparently we were spotted canoodling over dinner.

Good thing no one noticed how I was canoodling u under the table.

She stifled a groan as she recalled *exactly* how he'd done just that – his long fingers slipping up under the dress and then beneath the crotch of her panties. She'd had to dig her nails into her palm to keep from moaning right there in the restaurant.

Maybe I'm not 2 sore 4 a repeat performance 2night after all.

There was a longer than usual delay before his reply. *But I might need a transfusion first. U wiped me out, luv. Especially that last time.*

Tessa bit down on her lip and tried very hard not to squirm as his text called forth the very pleasurable memory of the third and final time he'd taken her last night, or – in actuality, about three a.m. this morning. He'd flipped her onto her belly, keeping her torso pressed into the mattress with a hand against her lower back, before urging her onto her knees with her ass in the air. Kneeling behind her, he'd slid so deep inside her body that she'd cried out in half pleasure, half pain. He'd been relentless, commanding, the dominant lover she'd enticed him into being, and she had shattered into a thousand pieces from the orgasm he'd wrung from her body.

A smile played about her features as she slowly tapped out her reply. *U can do that again anytime. Carte blanche whenever u like.*

But it was his response a moment or two later than brought forth a burst of laughter, one that caused her co-workers to look over at her in surprise. Red-faced, Tessa tried valiantly to shrug it off. "Uh, just a friend of mine trying to cheer me up by sending me a dirty joke. But don't even ask – I'd be way too embarrassed to share."

When she was certain they weren't paying attention to her, she snuck another peek at Ian's most recent reply and grinned.

Calling the doctor's office now to schedule that transfusion. Maybe a Viagra prescription 2. U r going to kill me u know.

She couldn't resist tapping out one final retort. *At least we'll have fun trying.*

Chapter Nineteen

Late April

"Nathan and I are really looking forward to seeing the two of you tonight. And we're so flattered to be celebrating Ian's fortieth birthday with you. I have to say, honey, that he is *the* hottest forty year old I've ever seen. Whatever he's doing to stay in shape, tell him to just keep it up."

At Julia's comment, Tessa could hear Nathan in the background, sounding very indignant at the way his fiancée was complimenting another man. Julia called out to him, "But you know I love you best, baby. Besides, the birthday boy is only interested in one girl and it's not me."

"Sorry." Julia offered an apology as she resumed their phone conversation. "Some men just get so bent out of shape at the littlest thing, you know? Just because I can admire another man's goods doesn't mean I want to sample them."

"Good," retorted Tessa teasingly, "because my man isn't giving out samples to anyone but me."

Julia laughed. "That's the attitude, girl. You guard that man like a tigress. Not that you'll ever have to worry about Ian noticing other women. He's head over heels about you, it's very obvious."

"I'd better let you go," offered Tessa. "I know how busy things are for you these days with the wedding only two months away. I'm just glad you can make it to dinner tonight."

"Wouldn't miss it. You and Ian are two of our very favorite people. Before I go, tell me – what dress did you finally decide on?"

Julia had stopped by the house last weekend and helped Tessa set aside two different dresses. She'd assured her that either one would be equally suitable – and equally stunning – for the very elegant restaurant where they would be celebrating Ian's birthday.

"The black one," replied Tessa. "He, um, likes me in black."

"Yeah, I'll just bet he does," teased Julia. "Especially that very sexy set of undies you bought to go with it. That's the nice thing about buying lingerie – it's really a present for both of you. Nathan calls it the gift that keeps on giving."

Tessa couldn't help giggling in delight before bidding her friend good-by. As she ended the call, she was still laughing, even as Ian strolled leisurely into the kitchen.

He smiled at her inquiringly. "Someone is in a very good mood this afternoon. Any particular reason?"

She set her phone down before flinging herself into his arms. "I'm always in a good mood these days. And especially today, when I have a very special birthday surprise planned for you."

Ian grinned, his strong arms banding about her waist. "It's not one of those singing telegrams, is it? Because I do tend to embarrass easily."

Tessa ran a finger over his lips and shook her head. "That's definitely not it. This surprise is more – um, private. And I doubt anything can really embarrass you, especially what I have planned."

He raised a brow. "Well, if it's anything like the surprise you gave me earlier today, I'm very, very sure that I'm going to like it. A lot."

She cupped his cheek in her hand. "That wasn't a *planned* surprise. I just couldn't help myself after seeing you at the gym this morning. God, I'm getting hot all over again just thinking about it."

Today was Saturday, and they had just returned to San Francisco late Thursday night after Tessa's first official business trip as Ian's PA. The trip had been a short but hectic one, cramming in visits to hotels in New Orleans, Atlanta, Palm Beach, and Naples, Florida. With such a packed schedule, neither of them had had much free time to fit in a decent workout on the trip, so they'd spent more than two hours at the gym this morning making up for lost time.

After swimming laps – Ian of course had managed nearly twice as many as she could do – and some weight training, he'd strapped on his boxing gloves and sparred a few rounds with one of the trainers. Tessa had watched him in action for the very first time and hadn't been able to tear her eyes off of him. His sleeveless T-shirt had bared his powerful, beautifully defined shoulders and biceps, and it was evident even to her – who knew next to nothing about boxing – that he was extremely skilled at his chosen sport. He'd made the trainer – a fit, well-built man at least a decade younger that he was – work hard, and Ian had seemed in complete control the entire time.

Seeing him that way – all hard muscle, barely leashed power, completely dominating – had aroused her to the point where she'd barely been able to keep her hands off of him. In the closed, somewhat limited confines of his classic Jaguar during the drive home, she hadn't been able to resist touching him – running her hands over his arms, his thigh, leaning over at a stop sign to press a kiss to his cheek. He'd teased her that he was liable to crash his beloved car into the side of a building if she kept it up, but he'd also been breathing heavily, his cheeks darkly flushed, and a very impressive erection had tented his athletic shorts as they arrived home.

Once inside the house, she'd sunk to her knees right there in the foyer, pulling his shorts down past his hips and freeing his magnificent cock. Despite his half-hearted protests that he really ought to shower first, she'd taken him deep into her mouth, sucking him off with a hungry enthusiasm that had him groaning her name and coming hard down her throat.

He'd barely stopped shuddering in release before he stripped her naked and spread her out on the priceless entryway rug, his head disappearing between her thighs. She had been so aroused, so in need, that it had taken the merest flick of his tongue against her clit to catapult her into orgasm.

Ian dropped a kiss on her forehead. "And I haven't been able to *stop* thinking about it. You know, I honestly believed that finally having you live with me, sleeping by my side every night, that it would somehow lessen my obsession with you. But it's just the opposite. I want you all the time, think about you constantly, hate being apart from you for only a few hours. You are the only thing in my life that really matters to me, Tessa, the one thing I cherish above everything else."

"It's the same for me," she whispered. "Sometimes I wonder if it's too much, if we love each other too much. I worry that the way we feel – our mutual obsession – that it's not – well, healthy."

"Never that, my love, never," he uttered fiercely, taking her mouth in a deep, searing kiss. "What we feel for each other – it's a rare and precious thing, something that very few people are ever lucky enough to find. So don't ever feel that it's too much because in my opinion it can never be enough."

They held each other quietly for a long time, simply content to embrace and enjoy the unspoken bond they always felt with the other. It was Tessa who finally, reluctantly, broke away.

"I'd better go upstairs and start getting ready for dinner," she told him. "I want to look my absolute best for you tonight, after all."

He shook his head. "You already look stunning to me, Tessa. I have no idea how you can improve on perfection."

She rolled her eyes, knowing full well she looked anything but stunning with no makeup, her hair half-escaping its untidy braid, her feet bare, and wearing one of Ian's old sweatshirts and a loose fitting pair of yoga pants.

"That's sweet, but you don't have to say things like that, you know." She reached up on her toes to whisper in his ear, "You're already going to get lucky tonight. Maybe several times."

Ian grinned. "In that case, perhaps I ought to nap for an hour or so while you're getting ready. I understand that men of my advanced age need to do that sort of thing."

"Yes, but do other men your age have this sort of incredible body?" she murmured, running her hands up and down his chest. "Or are they able to physically dominate a man ten years younger than they are?"

He captured her hand just before it slid beneath the hem of his loose fitting knit shirt. "Actually, Jesse is only twenty-seven, so he's a full thirteen years my junior. But I do confess to having had a secret advantage over him, which just might have helped me best the boy."

"Oh? And what exactly was this so-called secret advantage?"

Ian trailed a series of kisses along the inside of her arm, stopping just shy of her wrist. His eyes twinkled with merriment. "Young Jesse had a great deal of trouble keeping his eyes off of my girl. I admit to having a very sneaky motive when I suggested you wear that particular workout top this morning."

Tessa gasped, picturing the snug-fitting light blue tank top, the one she'd fretted about wearing because it had displayed a bit too much side-boob. But Ian, who normally preferred that she not expose too much bare skin in public, had surprised her by insisting the top was just fine.

"Ooh, you mean you did that on purpose?" she squeaked. "Knowing full well that I was, um, showing a little too much of the goods?"

He laughed in delight, wrapping his arms around her waist and lifting her easily off the floor. "I happened to remember that Jesse is – well, something of a breast man, based on comments he's made in the past. And since you have the most fabulous rack in the entire world, I figured you'd provide a bit of a distraction. Just enough to give me a little advantage."

Tessa pretended to give him a stern look. "That's cheating, Ian. I thought you liked to win fair and square."

He gave her a loud, smacking kiss on the lips. "Darling, winning was never my worry. Jesse may be thirteen years younger but trust me – I could kick his arse with one hand tied behind my back. He's usually just – well, very focused on his workouts, a bit too intense for his own good sometimes. It was rather amusing to see him get distracted so easily."

"Oh." His explanation mollified her somewhat, and a wicked smile spread across her face. "Well, if you really want to distract him next time, remind me to wear the teeny tiny shorts that go with the top."

Ian burst into laughter, murmuring in her ear, "Darling, you'd have the entire gym in an uproar if you wore those shorts. And while I can easily take that young whelp Jesse on, I'm not certain I could say the same for a whole roomful of horny men."

***

Tessa still wasn't sure if she should be offended, flattered, amused, or all three at Ian's mischievous confession. But she couldn't help the smile that played about her lips as she began to apply her makeup. Truth be told, she hadn't paid the slightest attention to Jesse, the young, buff trainer Ian had been sparring with, and therefore couldn't say for certain if he'd actually been sneaking glances at her or not. All of her attention had been focused solely on Ian, as it always was no matter how many other attractive men might be nearby.

He had very quickly become the main focus in her life, the one thing everything else revolved around, especially in the last few weeks when she'd stopped working at her old job.

Predictably, her co-workers had been startled to learn she was resigning, especially so soon after the fire at her apartment building. Equally as expected, they'd been extremely curious about her reasons for leaving and what her future plans were. Tessa had been obliged to be as evasive as possible, merely telling anyone who asked that she just needed a little break and would be going back to school after a time. She knew Kevin in particular was dying to ask her a million more questions, and that everyone must be puzzled about how she could afford to take some time off of work. But she became quite adept at avoiding any detailed questions, and then swiftly changing the subject.

Andrew, the only person besides herself and Ian who knew the real truth, had remained stoically closed-mouthed on the matter, not that any of the team would have dared to actually probe him for gossip. On her last day of work, the whole team – including Andrew – had taken her out to lunch, and she'd had to fight off tears as she bid them all farewell.

Ian hadn't attended the lunch – though Kevin had rather cheekily invited him – for it would have looked highly suspicious if he had joined them. He had never in the past gone out to lunch with the support staff, whether it was for a birthday or when someone left the firm, and Tessa had agreed this would have been an ill-advised time to start. They had, however, celebrated her last day at the office after hours, in a way that still made her blush when she thought of it.

Tessa had initially feared that she'd be bored without having a daily job to go to, but quickly found that to be very far from the truth. She loved living with Ian and taking care of him in dozens of different ways. Even though he urged her to sleep in, she always rose when he did each morning, making him tea and fixing him breakfast. If he had errands that needed doing, like dropping his suits at the dry cleaners, or picking up more shaving cream at the pharmacy, or buying his favorite scones at the bakery, she did all these things happily. It wasn't just a matter of feeling useful, that she was earning her keep, so to speak. She simply liked looking after her man, maybe even spoiling him a little as he loved to indulge her.

She cooked dinner for him most nights, even though her culinary skills were still very basic, but she knew he loved the efforts she made to please him. He worked so hard at the office, had so much responsibility, that she could tell he was deeply grateful for the opportunity to just relax at home after a long, stressful day. She would have a cocktail waiting for him when he arrived home, and they would sit out on the terrace or in the library, depending on the weather, and talk about their respective days before they sat down to eat dinner.

She'd had a full two weeks in between quitting her job and then accompanying him on this past week's trip. To prepare for the trip, there had been countless phone calls and emails from Andrew, with endless lists of the tasks she would be expected to do, names and numbers of contacts she would need, plus half a dozen items he would "appreciate" her assistance with if she could spare the time.

Julia had been a great help when it came time to pack for the trip, helping her select appropriate outfits for each city, for day and night, and the right accessories. And Ian had insisted she spend a day right before they left on the trip at the Neiman Marcus salon – getting her hair cut, having a facial, a mani-pedi, a massage.

He'd smiled at her, tucking a strand of hair behind her ear.

"Have whatever girly treatments you'd like, my love. With two exceptions."

She'd looked at him quizzically as he'd explained. "Don't let them cut too much of this beautiful hair. I told you before that I like it long. As for the other." He'd nuzzled her neck as his hand had slipped down past her belly to cup her sex. "No Brazilian waxes. I want this left natural."

Since the very thought of someone applying hot wax to her private parts was just about the scariest idea she'd ever heard, Tessa had readily agreed.

The trip itself had been amazing, even though they both put in long hours at each of the hotels they visited, their days filled with meetings and reviews. Tessa was thrilled to actually be doing real work – taking notes during meetings, sending faxes and printing reports, making sure the arrangements for lunch and dinner were confirmed. Ian had insisted that she accompany him to each meeting, lunch and dinner, and had made it very clear – albeit in a discreet, professional manner – that she was not only his PA but his companion as well. They stayed in the owner's suite at each of the properties, each suite with its own private butler and each one more lavishly appointed than the one before.

And on the five and a half hour flight home from Florida, Ian had locked them inside the master bedroom and initiated her into what he laughingly termed "the mile high club."

"It's my initiation as well," he'd whispered while unbuttoning her silk blouse, letting it fall from her shoulders. His lips had caressed the high, upper curves of her breasts. "I've never even brought a woman on board this plane with me before now, much less considered making love to one. So this is another first for me, too."

And of course, the very best part of living with and being with him nearly all the time, was his phenomenal sexual prowess. He was the sort of lover every woman could only dream of – the sort she in her naïve inexperience had never imagined truly existed. One night he might set out to seduce her slowly, taking his time with her, drawing out the anticipation until they were both mindless with need. And then, the very next night, he would take her roughly, demandingly, the sex wild and more than a little dirty. Tessa wasn't sure what side of him she loved better – the erotic seducer or the dominant lover.

And of course there were many and varied versions of both of his personas. But it never mattered to Tessa what Ian's particular mood called for from one day to the next – she loved them all, loved being his lover, loved making love with him. He had most definitely awakened her body to the point where she craved him like a physical need akin to breathing. She responded to not just his kisses and caresses, but to the sound of his voice, his scent, his very presence in the same room. During their business meetings or dinners, where they would strive to act like complete professionals and not the passionate lovers they were, their eyes would still meet and it would be impossible for either of them to disguise the flare of awareness that passed between them every single time.

When they were alone, she would reach for him nearly as often as he did her – snuggling against him as they slept, sliding onto his lap as he sipped his tea or drank his brandy, running her hands over his bare torso as he shaved or brushed his teeth. Sometimes he teased her about having turned her into a sex maniac, but most of the time he would groan and sweep her into his arms, kissing her into oblivion or carrying her to his bed.

Tonight, for his birthday, she had an extra special sexual experience planned for him, one she was fairly sure he would love. There was a chance, however slight, that he would balk at her idea, but she honestly didn't think so. She was going to seduce him – plain and simple – and hopefully rock his well-ordered world into another galaxy.

With that goal in mind, she applied a heavier than normal makeup – her eyes darkly shadowed and lined, her skin glowing with the application of sparkly bronzer, her lips full and glistening beneath the shiny scarlet gloss. She'd taken a long, hot bath earlier, the sunken tub filled with fragrant, vanilla scented bath salts, and then exfoliated nearly every inch of her skin. She'd spent considerable time rubbing scented lotion on her arms, legs, belly, breasts, before lightly spritzing herself with the delicate floral perfume Ian had bought her, knowing it was the scent he preferred.

But it was when she put on the new, ultra sexy bits of black lace she'd bought specifically for tonight that her confidence level zoomed up several degrees. As she gazed at her reflection in the full length mirror, she ran her fingers lightly over the plunging demi-bra, miniscule thong, ruffly garter skirt, and sheer stockings. Tessa gave herself a naughty, satisfied wink in the mirror.

'There is zero chance – Z-E-R-O – that he'll say no to anything you suggest when he sees you in this, girl,' she told herself with a chuckle. 'In fact, he's going to get on his hands and knees and beg you to do him any way you want. Too bad that's not the position I have in mind for tonight.'

***

"Let's drink a toast to Ian's birthday, shall we?" suggested Nathan. "Here's wishing you a very, very happy one, and hoping that I'll be in half as good a shape as you are when I turn forty."

Julia snickered. "Well, I'll definitely drink to that!"

There was laughter all around the table as the four occupants drank from their champagne flutes. They were enjoying pre-dinner cocktails in the lavishly appointed lounge area on the top floor of the Gregson Hotel. The cocktail lounge was adjacent to the four-star gourmet restaurant where they would be having dinner shortly.

Ian had chosen the venue for his birthday celebration quite intentionally, knowing that not only would the food and the service be superb, but that he could depend on the full discretion of the staff. Even though Tessa no longer officially worked for the company, they had agreed to keep something of a low profile for a while, at least here in San Francisco. Neither of them wanted speculation to start about exactly when their relationship had begun.

But for now he refused to worry about any of that, or anything else for that matter. Tonight was a night to relax and enjoy a fine meal with friends, and of course with the gorgeous love of his life seated to his left.

His jaw had dropped when he'd seen her for the first time tonight, walking with slow deliberation down the long, winding staircase of the house. And while Tessa always looked utterly beautiful and irresistibly tempting, tonight she was beyond dazzling. In the black V-neck Herve Leger bandage dress with its sequin embellished panels, she was a bombshell – really no other word came close to describing how sizzlingly sexy she looked. Her golden hair fell in thick, bouncy waves past her shoulders, her lush mouth looking positively sinful glossed over in a deep red. The only jewelry she wore were the diamond solitaire earrings he'd bought her recently, and a diamond cuff bracelet, with nothing around her neck to distract from the tantalizing display of her cleavage.

Ian hadn't missed all the admiring, covetous male glances directed her way, and he intended to keep her very close to his side the entire evening. In fact, probably the only male in the lounge who hadn't stared lustfully at his girl was Nathan- and that was because he had his own ultra-sexy woman sitting next to him. Julia had caused more than a few jaws to drop herself, garbed in a strapless ivory chiffon cocktail dress with a jeweled waist, and very high heeled ivory satin shoes with a rhinestone strap. Every time Ian happened to glance across the table, the engaged couple were touching each other in some way, or kissing. Even now Nathan was dipping his head to whisper something in her ear, and Julia giggled in response.

"Care to share the joke, or is it a private one?" drawled Ian in amusement. His arm circled Tessa's shoulder, his fingers splayed over the bare, warm flesh of her arm. He felt the little shimmer of awareness that traveled through her body and he smiled, pressing a kiss to her temple.

Nathan and Julia were holding hands, clearly as enamored with each other as he and Tessa were. Nathan indicated his head toward the bottle of champagne Ian had ordered – a particularly fine vintage of Perrier Jouet.

"I was just reminding my lovely fiancée here that we happened to be drinking the exact same champagne on the night of our first – uh, I guess you could call it a date," shrugged

Nathan.

Ian smiled and offered up his flute in a silent toast. "Well, I'm very glad I chose something that brought back happy memories for you."

Nathan grinned, his fingers brushing against the nape of Julia's neck. "Julia loves champagne, don't you, baby? Especially when she's in the mood to be sed- "

Julia clamped a hand over Nathan's mouth. "Don't you dare. Behave yourself, Nathan Atwood. You're going to embarrass me in front of Ian and Tessa."

Nathan winked knowingly at Ian. "Nothing either of them hasn't heard before, baby. Besides, it's pretty obvious they're as crazy about each other as you and I are."

Ian caught and held Tessa's gaze, smiling as he noticed the becoming blush on her cheeks, and the way she shyly returned his smile. "I am crazy about her," he murmured huskily. "I waited a very long time for this woman, but it was well worth it."

A hint of tears shimmered in Tessa's eyes as she touched his cheek. "And I'm crazy about you, too," she whispered. "Happy birthday, my love."

He gave her a sweet, soft kiss, then glanced up to find Julia's smiling gaze upon them. He was somewhat surprised to realize Julia's green eyes were also shiny with unshed tears.

"Oh, you two are so perfect together," she murmured. "And it's so romantic how Ian waited for you, Tessa, how he didn't want anyone else if he couldn't have you." She reached up and pressed a kiss to Nathan's cheek. "I know the feeling."

"Jesus, you're going to make me cry in a minute with all this sappy stuff," grumbled Nathan. "I've got a much better idea – more champagne all around."

Everyone laughed as Nathan refilled their flutes, and the subject was changed. They headed to dinner shortly thereafter, being shown to the best table in the place. There were, after all, a great many perks to being the owner of this hotel – and therefore the restaurant – and this was definitely one time Ian was more than content to avail himself.

It was a wonderful evening all around, and Ian was hard

pressed to remember a night when he'd enjoyed himself so much. Nathan and Julia were delightful company, and it was obvious that Tessa felt very comfortable in their presence. She was far more outgoing and talkative tonight than he'd ever seen her, and it made his heart sing to see her so happy and relaxed. Of course, he'd been plying her with a tad more wine than she normally drank while still taking care to make sure she didn't overindulge. Getting her tipsy was one thing – there was no way he'd permit her to get drunk. Not on his bloody fortieth birthday, when he was extremely optimistic that she would feel like celebrating in private once they finished dinner.

But there was no denying the obvious benefits of loosening up his shy little love just a bit. Not only did she appear to be greatly enjoying herself – laughing and giggling like a young woman of her age ought to be doing – but she was also extremely affectionate, even more so than usual. He absolutely adored all of the little ways she kept touching him – a soft caress on his cheek, the way she would rest her golden head on his shoulder, how she would slip her arm through his and hug it against her breast. In his life, Ian had always been extremely reserved, even standoffish, and he couldn't recall ever showing real affection towards a woman in public before Tessa. He knew he gave off the impression of being a rather cold, unfeeling bastard – an image he'd admittedly worked very hard to cultivate. But anyone seeing him here tonight with his beloved girl would never believe he was that same formal, proper man, the one who would never dream of kissing a young, gorgeous blonde in front of dozens of other diners.

His own father, in fact, had been in utter disbelief when he'd heard about Ian's very new and very beautiful traveling companion slash assistant. After visiting the hotel in Naples, Florida, Ian knew it would only be a matter of time before he heard from Edward. The manager of the Naples property was a very ambitious younger man by the name of Rodney Horton. He was also a former protégé of Edward's, having worked at the home office in London for several years, and was especially loyal to the elder Gregson. Ian had been well aware from the moment he'd walked into the hotel with Tessa at his side that Rodney would waste precious little time in updating Edward about this extremely interesting development.

His mother had called him at the office yesterday to wish him a slightly early happy birthday before passing the phone to Edward. His father had barely been able to conceal his rather obvious amusement.

"Well, I'd wish you a happy birthday, son, but it sounds like you've already begun the celebration. And given yourself quite a present to boot," Edward had joked.

Ian had sighed. "Good old Rodney. I'm just surprised it took him this long to broadcast the news. He must be losing his touch."

Edward had chuckled. "Oh, never fear. He called me within an hour from the time you checked in. I've just been biding my time here, waiting to see if I'd ever hear the news directly from you."

"Nosy bastard," Ian had grumbled. "Never did understand what you saw in that weasel. What exactly did the gossipy little shit say to you?"

His father's mirth had been almost impossible to contain. "That my very reserved, very stuffy old bachelor son seemed to have finally landed himself a – er – hot one, as Rodney referred to her. As you know, his language can be a bit coarse at times. I'll clean it up as we go along."

"Yes, be sure to do that, Father," Ian had retorted. "Otherwise, I might be tempted to pay old Rodney a return visit very soon. This time I guarantee he won't be tattling on me to my daddy."

"Oh, lighten up a bit, son," Edward had chided. "Rodney wasn't insulting or crude, for God's sake. However, he did say that your very charming companion was – let's see if I got this in the right order – ah, yes, blonde, beautiful, and busty."

Ian's jaw had tightened in displeasure. "There's no denying that Tessa is blonde and very, very beautiful. And, ah, rather spectacularly endowed. But she's also kind, warm, affectionate, unselfish, and I'm absolutely mad about her."

There had been silence on the other end of the line for long moments, until Edward had replied in a rather awestruck voice. "My God, it's finally happened, hasn't it? You've fallen in love. Your mother and I feared we might not live to see that happy day. I'll have to tell Joanna that sometimes prayer does work."

Ian had had the good graces to laugh. "Has she been praying for me, then? I hadn't realized she'd nearly given up hope. Well, you can assure Mother that yes, I am obsessively, completely in love with this girl and that both of you are going to love her, too."

Edward's tone had grown more serious at that point. "Rodney was also bubbling over with the revelation that your companion – er, Tessa, was it? – is quite a bit younger than you are. Is this true, Ian?"

Ian had sworn beneath his breath, cursing the weasily hotel manager for his loose lips. "It is, yes. And before you ask, Tessa is twenty-four, Father."

There had been another lengthy pause before Edward had burst out laughing. "Christ, boy, you've been robbing the bloody cradle, haven't you? Well, fortunately you've kept yourself in prime shape. You'll need to be to keep up with your hot young blonde. Good for you, son. Might as well enjoy her for a while."

Ian hadn't been in the least amused. "You don't get it, Father," he'd replied sternly. "I'm entirely, one hundred percent serious about this girl. She's the love of my life and I plan on keeping her with me for a very, very long time – as in forever."

"Jesus." Edward's disbelief had been evident. "You're really serious, aren't you? This isn't some wild, middle aged fling for you. You actually mean to marry the girl?"

"Not yet," Ian had corrected. "It's too soon for all that. She needs to get to know me better, and time to adjust living in our world. The last thing I want to do is overwhelm her. But in due time – yes, I mean to make her my wife. Tessa is most assuredly not a fling, as you so charmingly phrased it. I've never been more serious about anything in my life."

There had been more silence on the other end, and this time when Edward spoke it was with an almost reverent tone. "Well, then. When do your mother and I get to meet our future daughter-in-law?"

His good humor restored, Ian had chuckled. "You're planning a visit towards the end of May, aren't you? You'll meet my Tessa then. She's, ah, moved in with me."

Edward had made something resembling a strangling sound. "Ian, have a care, son. The men in our family have traditionally had very strong hearts, but there's always a first time. Now, this question will no doubt get your knickers in a twist but it has to be asked. Are you quite certain this girl isn't just after your money?"

The question hadn't angered Ian, and he'd only marveled that his father had not already asked it. "Very certain. I have to buy her things behind her back, make sure every damned price tag is removed, otherwise I get a very stern lecture along with threats to return everything. If you knew of Tessa's background – which she'll likely share with you at some point – you'd understand, Father. She's not some ambitious young fortune seeker. That's why she's also acting as my traveling PA, so that she feels as though she's earning her keep."

"Wait a moment there, son.' Edward's tone had changed abruptly from that of concerned father to stern CEO. "Do you mean to tell me this girl – who not only lives in your home but shares your bed when you travel on company business – is an employee? Ian - for Christ's sake – you of all people ought to know better than that."

"She's no longer an official employee, Father," he'd retorted. "And, yes, I most certainly know the rules. You might as well hear all of it, though I'm shocked that weasel Rodney hasn't already ratted me out."

Ian had explained to his father in painstaking detail about how Tessa had worked on his team for more than two years; how he'd fallen for her from the very first day but had been forced to keep his distance because she'd been a married woman; how he'd learned she was getting a divorce and how they had eventually begun seeing each other. He'd hedged over the dates as to when Tessa had actually left the company, but Edward had been mollified enough to realize she wasn't technically an employee any longer.

"So you've been carrying a torch for the girl for some time, eh? Interesting," his father had murmured. "Now that I think of it, I seem to recall that you kept staring over at the other side of the room during that last Christmas party we attended. And – ah, I see now. She was the sweet young thing that arsehole Jason was sniffing around, wasn't she? The one you sent young Andrew over to rescue?"

Ian had been dumbfounded. "How did you – I mean, I was extremely - "

"Discreet? Of course you were, you're my son after all. Discretion could be our middle name. Well, except for your brother Colin, of course, though that situation finally seems to have settled down nicely. But don't forget, son, who taught you how to observe people when they had no idea they were being watched. You learned that skill from a higher master, my boy."

Ian had chuckled, reminded never to underestimate his wily father, even though Edward was very close to turning seventy. "I concede to your mastery, Father. Now, come, let's have it."

"My opinion of the girl? Does it matter to you that much, Ian?"

"Not enough to change my feelings," Ian had replied truthfully. "I haven't been a boy of fourteen for a great many years, Father, and I'm more than capable of making my own decisions. And," he'd added firmly, "before you ask, I'm also not a man who lets his dick make these types of decisions for him."

"Never doubted it for a moment. And as for your Tessa, I do seem to recall that she was quite stunning. But I'll give you a more definitive opinion when I meet her face to face next month."

Ian had changed the subject at that point, not willing to discuss his relationship with Tessa in any greater detail. But he'd felt reasonably certain that his parents would at least keep an open mind when they met her next month. The tricky part would be breaking the news to Tessa about their impending visit. As shy and insecure as she still was, she would most likely work herself into a frenzy in anticipation, fretting unnecessarily about whether his parents would like her or not. He was going to have his work cut out for him to calm her down.

But for now, he refused to dwell on his parents and whether or not they would like Tessa. *He* liked her a great deal, especially tonight when she was laughing and having fun and when she couldn't keep her hands off of him. Grinning, he slid his hand to the nape of her neck, giving her the sort of little massage he knew she loved.

Tessa purred like a kitten beneath his touch and slipped her hand inside his jacket to latch onto his waist. "You're wearing my favorite suit," she whispered in his ear. "And you look super hot in it."

He touched his lips to her rosy cheek. "Glad you like it, love," he whispered back. "Dare I hope you've got my favorite undies on beneath that very sexy dress?"

She pressed a soft kiss to his lips. "Perhaps. Then again, maybe I'm not wearing any undies at all."

Ian bit his lip to stifle a groan, and was belatedly aware that they weren't alone at the table. He glanced up to find both Nathan and Julia grinning at him knowingly.

"If you two need a room, Ian, I'm guessing that won't be a problem given that you own this hotel," joked Nathan.

Tessa blushed profusely, and stared down into her wine glass as she took a sip. There was an awkward silence for a few moments until Julia stood, picking up her clutch bag.

"I think you gentlemen should order us some coffee and dessert while we visit the ladies room," she announced. "Tessa, let's go, shall we?"

Nathan and Ian were very well aware that theirs were far from the only pairs of admiring male eyes that followed the two gorgeous women as they left the restaurant.

Nathan lifted his wine glass in a salute. "We're lucky bastards, you and I, aren't we? As much of a jerk as I was to Julia for so long she still kept on loving me. I know I damned well don't deserve her, but I'll spend my life worshipping the ground she walks on."

"I think she would disagree with the first part of that statement, mate," replied Ian. "But you're right about the other. You and I are bloody lucky to have two such beautiful women.

And I cherish Tessa every bit as much as you do Julia."

Nathan sipped his wine slowly. "You going to marry her?"

Ian laughed. "You're the second person in as many days to ask me that question. And the answer is yes, but not just yet. Tessa – she's been through a lot in her young life. I'm trying to give her some time to get used to all this – " he waved a hand around to indicate the splendor of their surroundings, "to make sure it's what she really wants."

"She loves you, Ian," Nathan told him quietly. "That's not going to change anytime soon."

Ian sighed. "Sometimes I wonder about that. She's so young, so damned young, and she's seen absolutely nothing of the world. We've talked about her going back to college in the fall, getting her degree. One of my greatest fears is that she meets someone closer to her age, decides I'm too old for her."

"Hmm. So that's really why you're giving her time. To make sure her feelings for you are real." Nathan shook his head. "The way she looks at you – it's the same way Julia looks at me. It's the real deal, my friend, never doubt that."

Ian was about to reply, to thank Nathan for his reassurances, when he noticed the number of male heads that turned and he knew the women had returned. They made quite a contrast to the other – Julia petite and curvy, looking like a very alluring angel in her ivory dress and towering heels, and Tessa tall and shapely with those endlessly long legs, sexy black dress and the stilettos that made her look like every forbidden fantasy ever conjured up.

Tessa was beaming when he pulled her chair out for her. "Julia just had the most wonderful ideas for me, Ian. I was telling her how I didn't want to just sit around and feel useless until our next business trip, especially since the college classes I'd need to take don't start until late August. And she's thought of some ways I can keep busy and still learn something useful."

Nathan smirked as he pushed Julia's chair in. "Baby, tell Tessa that shopping is not exactly cultural enrichment."

Julia rolled her eyes at him. "Seriously, Nathan? What I actually suggested to Tessa is that she ought to take some cooking courses. There's a place over on Francisco Street that offers a whole series of one day to one week classes. The other idea I had for her was to take a course at the Berlitz Language School."

Tessa nodded and smiled a bit shyly at Ian. "Since you offered to take me to Tuscany one day, I thought it might be nice to learn some Italian."

Ian smiled back and gave her hand an encouraging squeeze. "I think both of those ideas are absolutely wonderful. I want you to sign up for both classes."

"I think I will," she agreed. "In fact, Julia said there's even a cake decorating class available. That way, I can bake you a cake next year instead of having to rely on your chef to do it for me."

He couldn't hide his surprise at the sight of half a dozen waiters and busboys who suddenly surrounded their table, and at the elaborately decorated cake ablaze with at least a dozen candles.

But the real thrill came after a rousing rendition of *Happy Birthday* when Tessa whispered to him naughtily, "The real celebration begins when we get home."

***

Simon had the weekend off so they took a cab home. Not that Ian was anywhere near being inebriated – he was as disciplined and in control about the amount of alcohol he consumed as he was with everything else in his life. But he preferred not to drive himself when he'd been drinking more than a glass or two, just in case. Besides, not having to concentrate on driving meant that he could focus all of his attention on the luscious blonde cuddled up against him.

"Did you enjoy yourself tonight, darling?" he asked.

Tessa nodded, her blue eyes glowing. "It was wonderful. Julia and Nathan are good company." She ran a finger over his mouth before whispering, "But the night is really just beginning, you know. I hope you aren't sleepy."

Ian chuckled, giving her waist a squeeze where his arm held her against his side. "Not in the least, my love. And it sounds as though you have special plans for the rest of the evening, hmm?"

Tessa gave him an impish grin and nodded. "I'm going to seduce you," she announced a bit tipsily. "I hope that meets with your approval."

He glanced up at the cab driver, who was thankfully immersed in a cell phone conversation, yakking loudly in what sounded like Tagalog. Relieved that they hadn't been overheard, he looked back at Tessa.

"Considering that all you really need to do to seduce me is be in the same room, I can say with complete honesty that I wholeheartedly approve of your plans, love." He captured her wrist as her hand began to slide up his thigh. "And you can seduce me all the way until dawn, so long as you wait until we're at home to begin."

Tessa pretended to pout, but seemed content to sit beside him rather primly and merely hold hands for the remainder of the ride.

Once inside the house, she took him by the hand and led him up the long, winding staircase. His gaze was fixated the entire time on the tantalizing curve of her ass in the form fitting dress before traveling down the long, shapely length of her legs. Her sheer black stockings had a seam up the back, and were quite possibly the most erotic thing he'd ever seen. Unless, of course, one considered the sexy black and silver stilettos on her feet, with their seductive ankle strap. He really, really hoped she planned to keep both the stockings and the shoes on while she had her wicked way with him.

At the doorway to the master bedroom, she released his hand but shook her head as he would have followed her inside. "Wait. Just give me a minute or two."

Ian hovered in the doorway with barely controlled patience. He was primed and ready for whatever "festivities" she had planned for tonight, his body already hard and throbbing just from being near his gorgeous girl. And that wasn't even taking into consideration the many times this evening they had touched and kissed and cuddled. It seemed, in fact, that the entire evening had been one long, slow seduction.

Tessa appeared back in the doorway, a sultry, mysterious smile on her face. She grabbed hold of his tie – a brand new, dark red Hermes that she'd given him as a birthday gift – and pulled him inside the room.

She'd lit a dozen or more candles, and they filled the room with their golden glow and subtle jasmine scent. The duvet had been turned down, and some soft jazz music was playing from the new iPod he'd given her recently where it rested in its docking station.

"What, no rose petals strewn over the sheets?" he asked in a teasing voice.

Tessa laughed softly. "I knew there was something I forgot. Maybe next time. Now, you have too many clothes on for what I plan to do to you. Let's start with this."

He smiled indulgently as she slid the suit jacket off his arms and draped it carefully over a chair back. "Can't have anything happen to my favorite suit," she chided. "In fact, maybe you should buy two or three more just like it – you know, as back-up."

Ian grinned, loving this playful side of her. "I'll make a note of it, love."

Tessa deftly undid his tie, before starting on the buttons of his shirt. He gasped as she nuzzled her face against his bare chest, her hands splaying over his abs.

"What a beautiful man you are," she murmured huskily. "And you always smell delicious. I'll never, ever get enough of your scent."

He groaned, his hands sliding into her hair as he attempted to kiss her, but she playfully swatted him away as she took a step back. "Tsk, tsk, Mr. Gregson. No touching until I say so. Otherwise, I might have to punish you."

He laughed in delight and acquiesced, letting his hands fall to the side. "Very well, my little Dominatrix. After all, the last time anyone spanked me was when I was a boy of five, and I made the very unwise mistake of sassing my nanny. Though I expect I'd enjoy your brand of punishment far more than I did Nanny Warner's."

Tessa laid a finger over his mouth. "Shh. No more talking. And definitely no sassing."

Ian's barely controlled mirth swiftly faded away as Tessa's

hands unbuckled his belt and unzipped his suit pants. Her fingers fluttered teasingly against his hugely swollen cock before she shoved his pants down his legs. She helped him remove pants, shoes and socks, kneeling before him as he was now clothed only in his snug fitting black briefs.

She slid her hands up the sides of his legs, squeezing the hard muscles of his thighs before her hands inserted themselves into the waistband of his briefs. Ian grit his teeth, struggling mightily for control as she slowly peeled the cotton underwear from his body, freeing his throbbing cock.

"Mmm, look at you," purred Tessa, her hand closing over his penis. "You have got to be the most magnificent man in the entire world. I want this big, beautiful cock to fuck every part of my body. My mouth – " she sucked just the tip of him, licking off the thick beads of pre-cum. "My breasts." She traced the tip of his cock between her lush tits, rubbing it up and down her cleavage. Ian was already breathing hard, his body so primed and ready he could come at a moment's notice.

"My pussy." Tessa stood and ground her fully clothed crotch against his straining dick. She took a couple of steps back so that their bodies were no longer touching, but continued to pump his cock with the long, slow strokes she knew he liked best.

"Tessa." His breath hissed out her name like an invocation, as though she were a goddess he was praying to.

"Hush, my love. Come with me now. And don't forget – you're all mine to do with as I wish tonight."

Ian let her lead him to the bed, where he laid down in the middle of the huge, king-sized mattress. He dared to run a hand along her hip.

"You have too many clothes on," he rasped.

But Tessa only laughed and removed his hand from her body, only to stretch his arm out towards the slatted headboard. "Hmm, I warned you about talking, remember? You're a very disobedient boy, Mr. Gregson. Guess I'll have to punish you after all."

And then, as she opened the nightstand drawer and drew out the long strips of satin, he knew what her little game was and struggled not to laugh. He permitted her to tie his wrists and ankles to the bed in the exact same manner that he had done to her on Valentine's Day. Except that her flimsy knots couldn't have held a kitten in place, much less a man with two hundred pounds of hard, solid muscle on his body.

But as turned on as he was at this particular moment, there was no way in hell – correction, no *bloody* way in hell – he would ever dream of letting her know that. Instead, he gazed up at her expectantly, his heart thudding wildly, his cock hard and straining and practically begging for her touch.

Tessa stood by the side of the bed, gazing down at him carnally. With one fingertip, she lightly traced along the thick length of his penis. "I think he likes me," she teased in that breathy little voice he loved.

Sweat broke out on his brow as he struggled not to come right there on the spot. "He fucking worships you," he hissed. "And he would be very, very grateful if you would put him inside one of the aforementioned orifices of your very tempting body."

She removed her finger as her hands went to the back of her dress. "So impatient, Mr. Gregson. I always thought you to be the most controlled, disciplined man I ever met. Lately, though, you seem very - um, impetuous?"

Ian gave a low growl. "I'd like to discipline you, you wicked, tempting girl."

Tessa very deliberately ran her tongue over her red, glossy lips. "And you've developed this rather alarming tendency towards violence, too. You're really going to have to watch that, my love."

As he watched her in stunned, slack-jawed disbelief, she unzipped her dress and peeled it off her lush, alluring body. Ian feared his heart would burst right out of his chest cavity, it was pounding that hard, as his eyes devoured the provocative picture she made.

Her big, round tits were almost spilling out of the lacy black bra, the cups so shallow there was barely enough fabric to conceal her nipples. The flirty, ruffly little garter belt held up those cock-teasing stockings, and the matching thong was so insubstantial she might as well have left it off entirely. As she crawled up on the bed next to him, her slow, deliberate movements like those of a hungry lioness, his cock felt like it might shatter into a thousand pieces it was that hard.

"Untie me," he croaked. "Christ, Tessa, I need to touch you. You look - "

"Later." She was crouching near the headboard, her face mere inches from his. "We have all the time in the world, all night long. This first time – let me worship you, Ian. Just – surrender."

He groaned as her lips took his in a long, searching kiss, her tongue tangling greedily with his. She was quite deliberately imitating exactly how he'd seduced her up in Lake Tahoe, taking her time with him, lingering over him. Only he was quite certain he wouldn't be able to last even half as long as she'd managed to do.

Her lips moved to his throat, tracing a path down to his chest, her hands following along. His body bowed off the bed, and he pulled on the flimsy excuses for restraints as her tongue flicked over his nipples. Tessa continued to kiss her way down his body, her hands touching him everywhere.

"Tessa. Jesus," he cursed as her hands squeezed his ass. "Darling, you've got to – I'm going to come if you keep touching me like this, that's how much I need you. Please."

"Shh. Poor baby. I've made you wait too long, haven't I?" she crooned, using the exact same words he'd said to her once. "Let me take care of my baby now. Mmm, yes."

Ian gave a shout as her lips closed over the head of his cock, sucking just the tip into her warm, willing mouth. Her hand stroked him at the same time, taking him a little deeper inside her mouth with each slow, deliberate movement. His hips bucked up in sync with the eager pulls of her mouth, and he felt his release inching closer with each thrust. And then, when he was very nearly there, ready to come long and hard down her throat, she shocked him to the very core by pressing her finger down on his prostate gland.

He cried out in a guttural, raw voice. "Jesus. Fuck, ah, God, fuck!" alternately cursing and crying out her name as his back bowed off the bed. He came instantly and violently, spilling himself into her waiting mouth with uncontrolled gluttony. And when he thought himself drained, sucked dry, he kept coming, her hands and mouth coaxing him to continue spurting his hot, sticky cum down her throat as fast as she could swallow it. With a loud bellow, he wrenched his wrists free of the flimsy bonds and shoved his hands into her hair, holding her head still as his body kept shuddering with the brutal force of the climax.

And when he was finally, completely sated, he fell back limply on the pillow, his heart racing madly. He was utterly helpless to do anything but watch as Tessa crawled up his body until she was straddling his hips. Her ripe tits were within one deep breath of falling out of that fragile bra, the silk of her stockings rubbing sensually against his bare legs. Her blue eyes were smoky, half-shut, her cheeks flushed, but the single most erotic sight had to be the thick bead of cum that still clung to her chin.

She was beyond a mere goddess, more like a succubus, a sex demon here to steal the very soul from his body. And astonishingly, even though he'd just had the most intense orgasm of his life, he was getting hard again just looking at her.

Ian knew then, in that very moment, that he would never, ever give this woman up. College boys be damned, he would fight any other man to the death for her, beat them to a bloody pulp if they dared to try and take her from him. Tessa was everything he'd ever dared to hope for, and far more than he had ever permitted himself to even dream about. She was his, and he planned to keep her with him for eternity.

Ian reached up and brushed away the spot of semen from her chin. She clasped his wrist, pressing a kiss to the inside before gazing down at him sultrily.

"Naughty man, breaking free of your bonds. We might just have to tie you back up."

"Not a chance in hell," he retorted, as he easily held both of her hands still. "And speaking of naughty, you really did almost kill me this time, love. I think we ought to start keeping a tank of oxygen by the bed. And make certain we have 911 on speed dial."

Tessa dissolved into a fit of giggles, lowering her head to his chest as his arms wrapped around her. "Does this mean you didn't like your birthday present?"

He tipped her chin up and gave her a resounding kiss. "Ah, but I haven't even finished unwrapping it yet, have I? And by the way – I like the gift wrap. Very, very much."

She laughed. "I thought you might."

With almost no effort, he scissored his ankles free of the satin straps before rolling her underneath him. "And where, my very naughty little miss, did you learn that particular trick? Don't give me that innocent look – you know exactly what I mean."

She blushed, then fidgeted beneath his intense regard before admitting in a whispered tone, "Um, Julia sort of – well, suggested it. She told me in the ladies room it would drive you wild. Did it – um, work?"

Ian laughed so hard he had tears in his eyes, rolling onto his side and wrapping her in his arms. "Good God, wait until I tell Nathan that his very wicked fiancée was giving my girl tips on blow jobs while they were visiting the loo. And, yes, my little wanton, it worked very, very well." He nuzzled the side of her neck. "Remind me to send Julia a dozen roses tomorrow as a thank you for sharing her little – ah, tip." He slid one of her bra straps down, baring her breast. As his fingers plucked the hardened peak of her nipple, he whispered in her ear, "And if your very naughty friend has any more advice she'd like to share with you, it might even be worth a new pair of those very expensive shoes she loves so much."

Chapter Twenty

Mid-May

"Now, don't be thinking that just because you've brought Tessa along with you that I'll be willing to forgive the fact it's been a very long time since your last visit."

Ian and Tessa exchanged a knowing look as Francine Carrington regarded both of them sternly. Mrs. C. hadn't changed one bit since the last time either of them had seen her. She was a small woman, almost delicate looking, but far too many people over the years had assumed from her appearance that she was also fragile in nature. It usually took less than a minute in her presence to realize that nothing could be farther from the truth.

Even in the heat of a late Arizona spring, Francine insisted on wearing one of her proper, severely tailored tweed suits and a high-necked blouse. Ian wondered if this particular beige suit had been one she'd worn while still working in London. He couldn't help but think it seemed oddly familiar to him. Her hairstyle hadn't changed in twenty years either – her obviously dyed auburn hair scraped back into a tight bun from which even one errant strand didn't dare escape. And even through the thick lenses of her glasses, her gaze was as sharp as ever, never missing a trick or the tiniest detail. Ian wasn't certain he would ever truly get over being terrified by one of her scathing glances.

But it seemed that after all these years he had finally discerned Mrs. C's one soft spot – which by some fortunate coincidence was also his own weakness – Tessa. He could have sworn he'd seen Mrs. C's eyes looking a bit moist when he and Tessa had entered her office just a few minutes ago, and the older woman had actually given Tessa a brief hug. Not so himself, of course. She would never dream of being so familiar with a superior, and had instead given him one of her surprisingly firm hand shakes.

Francine looked Tessa over critically, her razor sharp gaze not missing a thing. "You look exceptionally well, dear. I see Ian has done something about replacing that appalling Walmart wardrobe of yours, thank God." She flicked her fingers over the collar of Tessa's ivory silk blouse. "But the blouse is cut a bit too low for the office. And the skirt needs to be lowered an inch or two."

Ian shook his head in amusement. "Leave her alone, Mrs. C. Tessa is dressed exactly as I prefer her to be. I'm afraid you don't get to boss her around any longer."

Francine shot him an evil look. "But then she doesn't officially work for you any longer either, does she, Ian?" She scowled at Tessa. "I do hope you're not letting him take complete control of everything in your life. He might be the boss at work, but I trust you remember to stick up for yourself at other times?"

Tessa gave her a reassuring smile. "It's not like that at all. He's wonderful to me, treats me like a princess. And I've never been so happy."

Francine harrumphed. "Well, you deserve to be, my girl. You, too, young Ian. Don't think I didn't know exactly what I was doing when I sent Tessa your way."

Tessa frowned. "How could you have known we'd end up together? I was married, after all."

The older woman shot her a look of disbelief. "To a boy you treated like he was your brother, or your best friend. I saw the two of you together on enough occasions to realize there was nothing in the least romantic between you, not even a tiny spark. Nothing at all," she added smugly, "like what you and young Ian here have."

Ian smiled, sliding his hand to Tessa's nape and pressing his chest against her back. "And what exactly might that be, Mrs. Eagle Eye?"

Francine's mouth tightened in disapproval. "Obviously you're madly in love with the girl. A half-blind simpleton could see that from a mile away. And I'll remind you, Mr. Gregson, that I don't condone any hanky-panky in my office. I don't care if you're the Managing Director or the King of England, there'll be none of that funny business here."

He laughed heartily, stepping a short distance away from Tessa. "I'm surprised you haven't hired a chaperone for us. Though I hate to be the one to break the news – I've already taken advantage of her. Numerous times."

"Well, of course you have. I'm quite certain that the moment you learned she was getting a divorce – which, by the way, ought to have happened long before it did, in my opinion – you were making plans to stake your claim. Am I right?"

Ian was astounded to feel his cheeks flush with embarrassment at the very forthright question posed by the petite woman who was even now staring him down. "Uh, well, perhaps just a bit."

"Oh, bollocks." Francine gave an irritated little huff. "Ian, my boy, you were always a handsome young man – much more so than either of your brothers, though young Colin always thought a bit too highly of himself. I watched many, many women over the years try to catch your eye – secretaries, executives, socialites. You never seemed to notice any of them, at least not for very long. But somehow I just knew that the moment you laid eyes on my Tessa here that you'd fall hard. And, as always, I was exactly right."

Ian and Tessa exchanged one of those deep, searing looks that so frequently passed between them before he regarded Francine with a half-smile. "And just how did you know this? Is clairvoyance one of the few hidden talents you've never bothered to brag about?"

She frowned at him. "Sarcasm isn't a trait that suits you, my boy. And I knew you'd be completely taken with young Tessa here because the two of you are kindred spirits. Both impossibly beautiful on the outside, of course, but in each of your cases your true beauty is deep inside. I just knew you would see that in each other, as clearly as the light of day."

Ian took Francine's small, wiry hand and brought it to his lips. "Then I owe you a tremendous debt of gratitude," he told her in a reverent tone. "Tessa is absolutely the best thing that has ever happened to me, and I will cherish her for the rest of my days.

Now, I'll leave you two ladies alone for a bit while I meet with Vincent. I trust you've whipped him into shape by now?" he asked Francine teasingly of the newish hotel manager.

Francine waved a hand in the air. "The boy is afraid to take a piss without clearing it with me first, so I suppose he'll do. Go, I'll send Tessa to you in just a bit. If you can bear to be separated for that long."

"Just barely." Quite deliberately he gave Tessa a lingering kiss on the lips, knowing full well that Francine would be glaring at them in disapproval. "See you in a bit, darling," he whispered to Tessa.

Tessa watched him walk the short distance down the hall until he entered the hotel manager's office, already feeling bereft without him beside her.

"Good Lord, girl, he's just down the hall, not halfway around the world. No need to get teary eyed about it," scoffed Francine.

Tessa couldn't help but smile as she turned to face her former mentor. But for all of Francine's tough talk, there was no denying the softer, more indulgent expression on her face.

"I know. And I'll be seeing him soon at the staff meeting. I just – well - " Tessa demurred.

"You're just head over heels in love with the man," finished Francine. "As he is with you, dear. So tell me – when is the boy going to make an honest woman out of you?"

Tessa was startled by the question, but in all honesty not the least surprised that Francine would come right out and ask something so personal. "I, um, well – we haven't really discussed that yet. I mean, we haven't really been together all that long, and I'm not sure - "

"Oh, rubbish." Francine gave her a stern glare. "I'll tell you now, young miss, that your man there isn't going to stand for anything less than making you his wife one of these days. As controlling as that boy is, he won't be satisfied you're truly his until it's all legal and binding. The real question is – what do *you* want?"

Tessa stared at the older woman in disbelief. "Well, of course I'd love to marry him - If that's what he wants, of course. I mean, living together is one thing, but marriage is something else entirely. He might decide I'm not suitable to be his wife. Ian might as well be royalty while I'm just so – well, ordinary."

"Nothing ordinary about you, my girl," declared Francine. "And your man knows that as well. That's why he won't let you go anytime soon – if ever. Trust me, before this year is out you'll be calling me with news of your engagement. And it goes without saying I'll expect an invitation to the wedding."

Tessa was so flustered she didn't even know how to respond. "Um, well, of course. I mean, assuming it actually happens, which I can't say for certain - "

"I can. I'm never wrong," stated Francine. "I was right about you and Ian falling for each other, wasn't I? Too bad my mother instilled in me from such a young age about what a terrible vice gambling was. I could have made myself a tidy fortune by now."

Tessa laughed. "Whether or not he marries me one day, it doesn't matter. I'd follow him to the ends of the earth, Mrs. C."

"I know you would, dear. But can you honestly tell me that he hasn't swept you off your feet a bit too quickly? I mean, it's perfectly natural for a young woman like yourself to be dazzled by a man like him – his looks, his money, his position. Are you truly attracted to the man himself or simply to what he can give you?"

Tessa's smile faded abruptly and she shook her head in emphatic denial. "I don't give a damn about his money. And I'm sorry if this offends you but I really don't appreciate your suggesting otherwise. I love Ian with all my heart, more than I ever believed it was possible to love someone. That's the only reason I'm with him – the *only* one."

Francine shrugged. "It's a logical assumption to make. Come, look at it from a different perspective. He flies you down here on the corporate jet. You're staying in the owner's suite at the very hotel where you used to be a file clerk and make coffee for the meetings. He dresses you in silk blouses and five hundred dollar shoes. I know those are real pearls around your neck and that watch – it's a Bulgari which means it cost five thousand dollars – minimum. You can't lie to me, young lady, and tell me none of that matters."

"But it doesn't!" Tessa burst out, tears pooling in her eyes. "None of these – these *things* matter! You know I've lost absolutely everything I own – twice now. But those were just things, nothing that couldn't be replaced eventually. Ian is irreplaceable. If I ever lost him, if he ever left me – life wouldn't be worth living for even one more day."

Francine patted Tessa on the back as she handed her a tissue. "That's my girl. I knew deep down his money didn't matter a whit to you – I just had to hear it from your lips. And now I also know for absolute certainty what a treasure he has in you. You let me know if he doesn't treat you right, my dear. I may be the only person in the entire world that boy is still terrified of."

Tessa realized somewhat belatedly that the older woman had been provoking her deliberately, testing her, it seemed, with the sole purpose of making sure her feelings for Ian were genuine and unselfish. Then Mrs. C. startled her anew by actually brewing tea for both of them – a task that had always fallen to Tessa in the old days. Or it had once she'd proven herself capable of making a cup that would meet with Mrs. C's approval.

"Have you met Ian's parents yet?"

Tessa shook her head. "But they are visiting at the end of the month, and staying at the house. I'm a nervous wreck just thinking about it."

"Well, that's to be expected, dear. But you have nothing to worry about," assured Francine. "Edward Gregson is a charming man, it's very easy to see where young Ian gets his charisma from. You won't have any problem at all winning his approval. As for Mrs. Gregson – well, all you really need to do is give her the same scolding you just gave me, and she'll never doubt your feelings for Ian."

Tessa gasped. "I did not scold you! At least, I didn't mean to. And I would never dare talk that way to his mother. She'd think –"

"That you were more than a worthy partner for her son," retorted Francine. "And don't you dare apologize to me, young miss. It's about time you started voicing your opinions and sticking up for yourself. I'm proud of you, Tessa. You've far exceeded all the expectations I once had for you."

The rare compliment coming from the woman most people called "the dragon lady" made Tessa beam.

"I wouldn't have made anything of myself without your help. I was scared to death of you, but you did get results." Tessa took a sip of her tea before telling her former mentor, "Ian thinks I ought to go back to school, get my college degree."

"I think that's an excellent idea, Tessa. But is that what you want?"

Tessa shrugged. "Yes and no. I mean, I think it would be good for me, definitely something to be proud of. But, well, I like being able to travel with Ian like this and if I go to school full time that wouldn't always be possible."

They chatted a bit longer, Tessa telling Francine about the Italian classes she was taking at Berlitz, and the cooking courses she'd already finished and new ones she'd signed up for.

When Tessa had learned their next business trip included a stop in Tucson, she'd had mixed feelings. On the one hand, she'd welcomed the opportunity to visit with Francine and some of her other former co-workers. But, on the other hand, Tucson had held very few happy memories for her, and she hadn't especially looked forward to the visit. At least they would only be here for a day, and would be spending all of that time at the hotel.

Ian had inquired if she had any friends she cared to visit, or particular places she'd like to show him. He had very tactfully not brought the subject up again when she'd merely given him an abrupt shake of her head. He had seemed to sense after that initial inquiry that she wasn't exactly thrilled to be going back to Tucson.

Their meetings wrapped up fairly early, leaving them a couple of hours to relax and unwind before their dinner meeting. Since it was still over ninety degrees at four o'clock, a swim in one of the resort's several pools was a welcome respite. And while Tessa would have never dreamed of using the guest facilities at this time of the day when she'd been employed here, the same rules evidently didn't apply to the owner.

They swam vigorously for almost an hour, until her legs were quivering in protest and her breathing became labored. Ian kept going a while longer, and she watched him with admiring eyes as he stroked powerfully through the water. Tessa scowled as she realized several other women seated around the pool were also eyeing him hungrily. Two of them even made some very vocal comments about what a hunk he was, and how they sure wouldn't mind having a nice big helping of his brand of man candy.

Behind the cover of her oversized Chanel sunglasses, Tessa glared at the forty-something bleached blonde with the fake tan and even more obviously fake boobs who'd made that last comment. It made her wonder about all the years of traveling that Ian had done all over the world, and of the many different women who'd hit on him. The jealously she felt threatened to consume her, and it suddenly became very important to stake her claim, to make sure those – *cougars* knew that her man was strictly off limits.

Ian vaulted out of the pool, water dripping from his body, and she was there to meet him with an oversized beach towel. He smiled his thanks as he briskly toweled off his hair and chest before wrapping the towel around his hips. Tessa slid her arms around his neck, pulling his mouth down to hers for a lingering, open-mouthed kiss. He gave a little "mmm" of surprise just before his hands gripped her hips, pulling her into his body.

He was chuckling when he lifted his head. "Any particular reason for your very enthusiastic greeting?"

She pressed her breasts more fully against his chest, and ran her hands over the bulging muscles of his biceps. "Just admiring my very studly boyfriend. And making sure that all the other women around here know you're taken."

Ian smirked, sliding one large hand down to cup her ass. "What other women?"

Tessa laughed in delight. "Oooh, nicely done!"

As they walked over to their lounges, where she'd taken the liberty of having an ice cold margarita waiting for him, she kept an arm wrapped around his waist. She couldn't resist flashing a triumphant smile in the direction of the now crestfallen bleached blonde cougar. She was absurdly pleased that Ian didn't even acknowledge the presence of the other women, that the only one he had eyes for was her. It made her realize all over again how incredibly lucky she was to have this amazing man all to herself. She resolved to make very, very sure that he knew on a daily – no, make that an *hourly* – basis just how crazy she was about him, how much she cherished him. Tessa figured right now was an excellent time to start.

Ian glanced up in surprise as she plucked his margarita glass from his hand and set it down on the low glass-topped table between their lounges. She straddled him, looping her arms around his neck, and gave a satisfied little smile when his gaze automatically flicked down to the ample cleavage bared by her yellow bikini top.

She leaned down to whisper in his ear, "You know how sometimes I really, really like giving you carte blanche over me in bed?"

He ran his hands up the side of her ribcage, stopping just below the swell of her breasts. He swallowed with some difficulty before nodding. "I, ah, do know, yes."

She licked the side of his neck. "Well, I think I'm going to be in a very giving mood tonight."

***

"You look kind of – uh, tired, Ian. Late night?"

"Hmm?" Ian glanced up across the table at his dining companion. "I'm sorry, Matt, did you say something? Afraid I've been in a bit of a daze most of the morning."

Matthew Bennett gave his friend a knowing grin. "Should I assume your very hot new girlfriend is the reason for your, er, daze?"

Ian couldn't suppress the grin that spread across his features. "Jesus, mate, you wouldn't believe the half of it. But, yes, suffice it to say that Tessa is most definitely the reason I look a little out of it right now. Not to mention in dire need of a nap."

Matthew had been a good friend for several years now, the two men having met at the exclusive private health club they both belonged to. Matthew had, in fact, been one of the very first people Ian had befriended upon moving to San Francisco, and the two of them tried to meet up for lunch as often as possible, given their equally hectic schedules. Matthew was the CEO of a hugely successful software company headquartered in the city, and he was worth billions. Still, he was amazingly one of the most down to earth individuals Ian had ever met, and he considered him a very close friend.

Still, close friend or not, there was absolutely no way Ian was going to recount exactly why he was so wiped out this morning. He'd been woken out of a sound sleep at an ungodly hour of the morning, but he'd have had to be a blithering idiot to even consider complaining about it – not when he'd woken with a groan to find a gorgeous, sexy blonde bent over him, his cock in her mouth as she gave him a very enthusiastic blowjob. And then, when he'd been perilously close to coming, she'd straddled his body, positioning the thick head of his penis at the entrance to her body before impaling herself an inch at a time until he was buried to the root.

She'd looked like a pagan warrior princess as she'd ridden him, her bare, lush breasts beckoning him to touch them, her long hair waving over her shoulders. The merest flick of his thumb against her clit had sent her spiraling into climax, the tight muscles of her pussy squeezing his cock as she came, and he'd spilled himself inside of her hot, welcoming body mere seconds later.

It had been every man's dirtiest fantasy come true – the ultimate wake-up call – and Ian was really no different than most men when it came down to it. But he was definitely starting to feel the effects of missing out on some sleep this morning, especially when his voracious young lover had also kept him up rather late the night before. Tessa, he thought with a rueful smile, was quickly becoming rather insatiable.

Matthew grinned. "Has anyone told you what a lucky fucker you are? Seriously, almost every guy at the club would cut off their left nut to trade places with you right now."

Ian groaned. "I'd advise them to hold on to both of their testicles, especially if they have a wife or a girlfriend as – ah, eager as Tessa. Sometimes I wish I had a spare pair."

Matthew laughed uproariously. "Christ sakes, Ian, just how often are the two of you getting it on anyway?"

"Every single day." Ian enunciated each word slowly. "Usually multiple times. So far I've been able to keep up with her, but I'm half afraid she's going to wear me out."

"Well, if you need help keeping your woman satisfied, you can always ask Jesse," joked Matthew. "When he saw you walk by with Tessa one day last week, he made some predictably crude comment like 'Dude, I would tap that anywhere, anytime'. And then he finished up by saying it wasn't fair that you had two sweet rides – first the Jag and now Tessa."

"Is that right?" Ian's fist clenched and unclenched, and his mouth tightened in annoyance. "Well, I had already planned on pummeling that young punk into the mat the next time we sparred. Now I might consider upping the ante."

Matthew grinned, taking a sip of his iced tea. "Yeah? Whatcha got in mind for our young Casanova?"

Ian winked before reaching for his own glass of tea. "Making sure Tessa is present to watch us. And that she's wearing as little as possible."

"You're an evil bastard as well as a lucky one," conceded Matthew. "But that would serve the little shit right. He does like to flirt, not to mention brag about all the pussy he gets. Though I'm just guessing you're getting a hell of a lot more action than he is. And I *know* you're getting way more than I am. Hell, you probably got more last night than I've had in a month."

The tone of Matthew's voice clearly betrayed that things weren't as they should be in his marriage. Ian had met his wife on several occasions, and couldn't really say if he liked Lindsey Bennett or not. She'd been pleasant enough, if a bit on the flirty and empty-headed side, which hadn't bothered him nearly as much as the rather careless, off-handed manner in which she treated her husband. Matthew was just about the nicest, most decent man Ian had ever met, and had never allowed his somewhat sudden good fortune to go to his head or change the person he was. The Bennetts had two children, and Matthew was absolutely devoted to them.

Ian frowned. "Everything all right with you and Lindsey? How is your lovely wife, by the way?"

Matthew grimaced. "She's fine. A little more generously endowed these days, however. She, uh, just had her boobs done – against my wishes, I might add. Call me crazy, but I just hate all that fake shit women insist on having done to themselves."

"You're not crazy," assured Ian. "I've never been a fan myself. Fortunately for me, Tessa is – ah, a natural beauty."

A grin crossed Matthew's face, his good humor quickly restored. "Since I haven't seen a pair of twenty-four year old tits since *I* was twenty-four, tell me – do you feel like weeping every time she takes her top off?"

Ian shook his head. "More like saying a prayer, mate. Thanking Christ that she's all mine, and then begging Him that I don't wake up and find it's all been one big wet dream."

"Jesus." Matthew looked more than a little awed. "Well, all I can say is enjoy all this while it lasts, because honeymoons definitely end sooner than later. Take my word for that. Besides, all of us forty-something's at the club are rooting for you. You're sort of our role-model, you know."

Ian speared a forkful of his salmon filet but paused before bringing it to his mouth. "You don't think I'm making an ass of myself, do you? I mean, Tessa tells me all the time that she doesn't think I'm too old for her, but – well, it does weigh on my mind a lot. Especially when young bucks like Jesse are salivating over her."

Matthew waved a hand in dismissal. "Jesse salivates over most anything with a pair of tits. God, I'd better keep him away from Lindsey and her new D cups – my understanding is that he likes older women, too. And you don't have to worry about Tessa. I've seen the two of you together a few times, don't forget. The girl's got it bad for you, Ian. Even with every guy in the gym giving her the onceover, the only one she's ever paid attention to is you."

Ian nodded. "I appreciate that, mate. And I guess I must be doing something right, considering her, uh, eagerness. Now I just have to find a way to keep up with her."

Matthew chuckled and indicated his plate. "Maybe you should have ordered a cheeseburger like I did. You know, extra protein, red meat, that sort of thing."

Ian sighed. "I've already tried that. Unfortunately, all it seemed to do was raise my cholesterol by twenty points."

"There's always Viagra."

"You don't get it, Matthew. Getting an erection is never a problem with Tessa. Christ, it's like taking a triple dose of that stuff with her. The problem – if one is selfish enough to think of it that way – is having enough energy to get through the day."

"You're right – you *are* a selfish prick to even think of this as a problem. A gorgeous, sexy and horny twenty-four year old girlfriend is most men's favorite spank bank fantasy. So, as I see it my friend, you've really only got two solutions to your, er, situation."

Ian regarded him warily. "And what exactly would these solutions entail?"

Matthew gave him an evil grin. "Cutting her off to once a day, or fitting in time for an afternoon nap. And since I'm guessing there's no way in hell you'd even consider the former, maybe you should make sure there's a comfy pillow and blanket on hand in your office."

***

Late May

Tessa didn't think she'd ever get tired of the view from the deck of this house. Even though this particular morning happened to be crystal clear, and the winds were calm, she wouldn't have minded in the least if it had been cool and foggy, or even rainy and windy instead. The ocean view was breathtaking, mesmerizing, and she thought she could happily sit out here for hours with a mug of tea and a good book – much as she was doing right now.

Ian had surprised her with this getaway for Memorial Day weekend. He hadn't told her where they were going, simply to pack enough for a three night stay, and nothing that could be considered the least bit dressy. They had left San Francisco on Friday morning – he'd taken a day off from work – and driven up the Sonoma County coast in his vintage Jaguar. Tessa had never been to this part of the Bay Area before, and had been spellbound by the magnificent scenery they'd viewed en route.

They'd arrived at their destination in the early afternoon – a community of gorgeous homes built along a ten mile stretch of the coast that Ian had referred to as The Sea Ranch. The house he had rented for the long weekend was situated right on the bluff top, and was nearly as lavishly appointed as his own home in the city. Tessa, however, had more or less bypassed the gourmet kitchen, sunken living room, and huge loft space once she had glimpsed the jaw dropping view from the back deck. She had spent the majority of their stay thus far curled up on a deck chair or chaise lounge and letting the sound of crashing waves hypnotize her.

She supposed a large part of her fascination with the ocean stemmed from having lived most of her life in either desert or mountain communities. Since moving to San Francisco, she'd certainly spent some time by the Pacific Ocean, but nothing remotely like this – sitting so close to the bluffs that she could feel the spray of the water when the surf was high enough.

The fabulous home was fully furnished and equipped with everything they might need – dishes, glasses, linens. There were books to read, movies to watch, music to listen to. Ian had made arrangements with the rental agency to have a local caterer stock the refrigerator with a variety of readymade meals, snacks, and drinks. He refused to let her cook this weekend, ensuring that they would not have to do much more than relax and enjoy a blissfully quiet getaway.

Since their arrival two days ago, they hadn't really discussed the imminent arrival of his parents within the coming week. The Gregsons would be staying at the house, of course, though Ian had told her that they had offered to use the owner's suite at the hotel instead. Tessa had insisted they stick with the original plan of staying at Ian's home, knowing that he didn't get to see his family all that often. And if she was still a nervous wreck about meeting them – and hoping they didn't hate her on sight – it wasn't for lack of constant reassurances on Ian's part.

At least she felt a bit less gauche after having spent these past two and a half months living and traveling with Ian. With the help of both Julia and Marlene Brennan, she knew how to dress and accessorize, and had become fairly adept at doing her hair and makeup.

The series of one-day and weekend cooking courses she'd taken thus far had given her the confidence she needed to get more creative in the kitchen, and Ian had praised her efforts. Her Italian classes were also coming along nicely, though of course she had a long way to go before she could be considered even moderately fluent in the language.

And Ian had been teaching her a little here and there about things like art, classical music, and fine wines, mostly so that she would feel more at ease among the people she'd be meeting at several upcoming functions. Like the San Francisco Symphony benefit ball they would be attending with Ian's parents during their visit. She would have already been in a mild panic about going to the ball, but coupled with the fact that the Gregsons would be accompanying them she was almost beside herself with anxiety.

Ian had done his utmost to calm her down, assuring her that not only would his parents adore her but that she would create quite a stir when she arrived at the ball with him. But Tessa knew that she would continue to fret and worry until she'd gotten both dreaded events over with.

"Penny for your thoughts, love?"

Smiling, Tessa set her empty mug down and turned to face Ian where he stood framed in the doorway leading from the living room out to the deck. Her heart gave a little thump-thump when she saw how mouthwateringly handsome he looked this morning – unshaven, his two day stubble the sexiest thing she'd ever seen; wearing a pair of gray sweatpants and a black T-shirt that bared his chiseled biceps; like her, he was barefoot.

"Right now I'm thinking how much I love you," she told him softly. "And how much I'd really like a good morning hug."

Ian smiled and was by her side in an instant, sitting next to her on the wicker settee and scooping her into his lap. "Good morning, birthday girl. And I love you, too." He gave her a long, lingering kiss. "But I missed waking up next to you this morning. You should have woken me. "

Tessa shook her head, snuggling happily against him. "You were sleeping so soundly, I couldn't bear to disturb you. Besides, I know you've been – um, missing out on some sleep lately because of me."

He chuckled, wrapping his arms even more tightly around her. "You haven't heard me complaining, have you? I happen to like your, er, wake-up calls. Very, very much."

She pressed a kiss to his cheek, running her nose over his dark stubble. "And I love the way you make sure I sleep very, very soundly at night. Ah, but I'm not being a very good girlfriend this morning, am I? Let me go and fix you a cup of tea."

But his arms only tightened about her, not permitting her to move from his lap. "Not a chance. It's your birthday, after all, and you are not lifting one finger today. I'll make us some tea in a bit. Let's just sit here for a few minutes and enjoy the view, hmm?"

"Okay." Tessa gave a sigh of happy contentment. "I love it here, Ian. This is the absolute best birthday present ever."

He kissed the top of her head. "Perhaps I should buy the house for you. Then we could come up here whenever we like."

She laughed, convinced he was joking. "Don't be silly. You already own a home."

Ian smiled, brushing a loose strand of hair from her forehead. "Darling, many people own more than one home. My parents, for example, have a townhome in London, an estate out in Kent, an apartment in Paris, and a condo in Spain. Plus a share in the villa in Tuscany, of course."

Tessa was wide-eyed in disbelief. "You're really serious? That's just – wow. How much money do they have anyway?"

He laughed in delight at her shock. "A lot. So do I, by the way. I could very easily afford to buy a house like this if that's something you'd like, darling."

She stared out at the water again. "Better not. If I knew I

could wake up to this view every morning, I'd never want to leave here. And I think this would be just a little too over the top as a birthday gift. You've already given me way too many gifts, Ian."

Since their arrival on Friday, he had left beautifully wrapped packages in various spots around the house for her to discover. He'd spoiled her rotten, of course, gifting her with clothing, lingerie, a pair of shoes, a new purse, jewelry. With each extravagant present, she had made him promise that this would be the last one, protesting that he'd gone overboard as usual.

He kissed her hand before rubbing his cheek against her palm. "There is just one more, love. And I saved the best for last."

Tessa gave him a stern look. "You had better not have bought me that car you were talking about. I think driving your Mercedes around town will be just fine for me."

Truth be told, she wasn't very confident as yet about driving in San Francisco. The hills, narrow streets, and often nonexistent parking in the city made getting around much more difficult than it had back in Tucson. But since she couldn't rely on Simon or take taxis to get her everywhere she needed to go – and since Ian wasn't thrilled with the idea of her taking a bus – she had gradually started to drive again. He had given her the keys to his three year old Mercedes sedan, a car he claimed to rarely use since he preferred driving either the Range Rover or the Jaguar.

She'd been terrified of wrecking the expensive vehicle, a far more luxurious ride than the old compact Toyota she'd last driven in Tucson. But Ian had brushed aside her concerns carelessly, insisting she was doing him a favor by making sure the Mercedes got some use instead of sitting idle inside the garage.

"Ah, but as good as you look behind the wheel of the Benz, I think you'd be sexy as hell driving – let's say a fire engine red Ferrari," he teased.

Tessa gasped. "Oh, my, God, you are *so* not buying me a Ferrari! Or any car. Or one more thing, Ian. I mean it. Not a blouse or a pair of earrings or even a bra. Nothing. Do you understand?"

Ian grinned. "Yes, my feisty little birthday girl. But there is still one more present left. Relax – this one didn't cost very much at all. And I think you'll like it a lot."

Her curiosity was piqued as he led her back inside the house. They had breakfast first, a simple meal of granola, fruit and tea. Ian cleaned up the few dishes, still refusing to let her do any work this weekend, and then brought out a modestly sized box. This one was as beautifully wrapped as all the others had been and she eyed the box suspiciously.

"If it's more clothes, I'll tell you right now they're going back."

He smiled at her indulgently. "It's not. And you won't want to return this. Open it, darling."

She unwrapped the box slowly, lifting the lid, and then stared down at the contents in stunned disbelief. She would never in a million years have ever thought she'd receive a gift quite like this one, and her hand was shaking as she slowly withdrew one of the three items.

"My mother's books." Her voice was unsteady as she held one of the volumes with reverence, as though she were afraid it would disappear. "My God, Ian, where in the world did you find these?"

"I know several rare book dealers, both here in the States and in other parts of the world," he replied quietly. "I've had every one of them on the lookout for these for some time now. They were able to locate three of the four books your mother had published, and one of the dealers may have a lead on the fourth. Do you like them, Tessa?"

She hadn't known she was crying until she raised her gaze to his and he wiped away a tear. "This – this is the most wonderful thing you've ever done for me," she told him brokenly. "I had nothing – *nothing* – of my mother's. We moved around so much that we always had to leave things behind. And the few remaining items I had of hers burned in the fire. The first fire. All I really had left was one very old photo of her in my wallet. And, well, the second fire took that away. So, yes – I adore them. And I adore you for giving me this."

"Darling." He pulled her close against him, holding her as she wept, stroking her hair and murmuring soothing words.

When she felt in control again, she lifted her head from his chest and gave him a sweet, tender kiss. "Thank you," she whispered. "I can't even tell you what this means to me. Or how much I love you for finding these. It's just – too much for me to express right now."

He nodded in understanding. "I get it. And I'm so pleased you like your gift. Look, there's even a photograph of your mother on the back cover of this book."

Ian took out one of the other books from the box, this one a hardcover with a glossy jacket that was in excellent condition. The other two books were paperbacks and a bit on the well-used side. Tessa gasped as he flipped open the back cover, and she ran her fingers over the smiling image of her mother in stunned disbelief.

"It's really her," she murmured, starting at the image of the happy, glowing young woman who looked so much like her own self. "And this – this is how I prefer to remember her, Ian. Young and healthy and full of life. Not – not the sad, sick woman she became as I got older. This is my real mother right here."

Ian pressed a kiss to her temple. "She was beautiful, Tessa. You could be her twin, the resemblance is remarkable. And I was thinking – there's a photography studio I know of in San Francisco that specializes in restoring old photos. I'm willing to bet if we brought them this book jacket that they would be able to find a way to reproduce the image into a proper photograph. Obviously the quality wouldn't be the best, but - "

"I don't care." She flung her arms around his neck, hugging him tight. "I'll take anything, the quality doesn't matter. Thank you, thank you, thank you!" She pressed fervent kisses all along his cheeks, jaw, neck.

"You're more than welcome, my love," he whispered. "Now, come. It's your twenty-fifth birthday and no more tears, hmm? Let's vow to make this the happiest birthday of your life so far, all right?"

And it was most definitely the most wonderful birthday that Tessa could ever remember having. Not that she had very many happy memories of past birthdays. The last two years prior to this one had been spent alone, since Peter had been on a trip somewhere far away on both occasions. And she couldn't honestly remember ever having something as traditional as a birthday party as a child – that certainly hadn't been her mother's style.

But spending this day – this weekend – with Ian wiped out any memories of less happy times. They spent a quiet, blissful day together – taking a long walk on the beach; driving into the small town just north of the house to get a cappuccino; browsing through the boutiques and art galleries in town, where he bought her a beautiful copper bowl filled with multi-colored pieces of sea glass. Back at the house, they soaked in the enormous hot tub out on the deck while sipping wine and watching the wild surf below.

And they talked – for hours, it seemed. Over a beautifully prepared dinner the caterer had left – including a fabulous white chocolate birthday cake – they shared stories of their respective childhoods, though most of Tessa's memories weren't always happy ones. She told Ian more about her relationship with Peter, how they'd been almost virtual strangers when they'd married so young – still children, really. They had been awkward and uncertain around each other but had gradually grown closer and become the best of friends. Tessa confessed to having felt lonely and sad and frightened when Peter had begun to travel, and how hard she'd had to stave off falling into a deep depression at times. And it had tugged at her heart to recall Peter's almost nightly bouts of insomnia, the nightmares that had plagued him, and how it had been rare for him to actually sleep in the same bed with her.

They had moved back out to the deck by now, curled up on the wicker settee with a plush cashmere throw tucked around them, sipping a post-dinner snifter of brandy. Tessa's head was on Ian's lap as he played idly with one of her thick blonde curls.

"Is that why you love to cuddle in bed so much?" he asked her gently.

She smiled and rubbed her cheek against his heavily muscled

thigh. "Probably. Though some of that goes back to when I was a little girl. Because we moved around so much I was always a little scared getting used to a new place, especially – well, in the shelters. There were usually some creepy people living there, and my mother wasn't always in a sane enough state of mind to make me feel secure."

He rubbed her neck, and she could tell from the grip of his fingers that he was disturbed at the mental images he must be conjuring up. "I still can't bear to think of you in a place like that." His voice was rough, thick. "It makes me want to wrap you up in this blanket and cuddle you close for the rest of my life. You know I would do absolutely anything for you, Tessa, and that I will always keep you safe and protected." He bent down to place a lingering kiss on her lips. "I will slay dragons for you, my love, and whatever other monsters might try and hurt you."

She reached up to caress his cheek. "I take it back. The books and renting this house weren't the most wonderful birthday presents ever – you are."

Then, because she was fairly certain she was going to start crying again, she swiftly changed the subject and asked him about a particular matter that she'd been avoiding for months – that of his former fiancée.

Ian sighed. "It seems like such a long time ago, when it was really less than ten years. At times it almost feels like it happened to someone else, not me. But, truthfully, there isn't a whole lot to say on the matter."

He told her a bit about her – a lovely, dark-haired woman named Davina, who was three years his junior. They had traveled in the same social circles, had several friends in common, and had dated on and off for a couple of years before becoming engaged. But that had been during a time when Ian was traveling three weeks out of four, and working sixteen hour days, and they saw very little of each other.

"And Davina was an especially sociable woman – adored the whole party scene. Her family wasn't as wealthy as mine, but they could trace their roots back for centuries and had some sort of minor connection to the royal family. Davina didn't work – not really – but she was on the boards of several charitable organizations and did a lot of fundraising for them. And it didn't take very long at all for her to become extremely disillusioned with a fiancée who was rarely around to escort her places."

Tessa was sitting upright on the settee now, snuggled close against his side. "So she broke things off?"

Ian shook his head. "I did, actually. I knew it wasn't fair to her, my not being around much, but the real truth was that I simply didn't love her, couldn't envision spending the rest of my life with her. She was upset for a time, but it didn't take her very long to meet someone else. Last I heard they'd been married for several years and had a child."

"And there was never anyone else for you?"

He shrugged. "No one serious, no. I worked so hard, traveled so much, that having a relationship was a very low priority. However, I can say without a shadow of a doubt that if I had met you somewhere along the way, my priorities would have changed overnight."

"We very nearly met a couple of years before I moved to San Francisco, you know," she recalled. "I was still going to college, finishing up the certificate program. You were scheduled to pay a visit to the resort, we were all in an uproar getting ready for it, Mrs. C. insisting that everything had to be beyond perfect. Your visit was on one of the days I didn't normally work, but Mrs. C. was demanding that I be there anyway. And I would have, if the date hadn't coincided with final exams at school. There was no way to re-schedule them and I had to take them, she knew that. But she wasn't at all happy with me, and I could never figure out why."

Ian grinned. "I'd say it was rather obvious, wouldn't you? She wanted us to meet, likely knowing full well what would have happened the moment I laid eyes on you."

"And what would that have been?"

He threaded a hand into her hair, tipping her head back so that he could stare into her eyes. "What wound up happening eventually anyway – I fell instantly and hopelessly in love with you at first sight. Only it's not so hopeless any longer, is it?"

They stayed out on the deck a while longer, not saying much

more, content to simply gaze at the stars and bask in each other's company. And when the night air grew a little too brisk they moved inside to watch a movie.

And, though they had touched, kissed, caressed frequently throughout the day, they didn't have sex that night. It was odd, because there had been extremely few nights they had spent together when they hadn't made love – the night she'd told him about her past; the awful night of the fire at her apartment; and a few times when she'd had her period.

But as they fell asleep wrapped in each other's arms, both Tessa and Ian had never felt closer, or more intimate with the other, than they did on this particular night.

Chapter Twenty-One

It would have surprised most people who met her to learn that Joanna Gregson had spent the majority of her sixty-seven years largely in the company of men. After all, she was a dainty, exquisitely feminine woman, always perfectly coiffed and dressed to the nines. No one looking at her now would ever envision her as a scruffy tomboy who'd roughhoused with her three brothers, and who'd played competitive field hockey during her school years.

Fate had decreed that all three of her children would also be boys, despite her secret longing for a daughter. But Joanna doted on her sons, and they in turn were completely devoted to their mother.

Hugh, the eldest, had been a placid, easygoing boy, very much like his father. He'd never given his parents a moment's worry, always the dutiful son and in later years the quintessential company man. He had married Victoria, the girl he'd fallen in love with at university, and they had presented Joanna and Edward with four beautiful grandchildren – all boys.

Colin, her youngest, had been the complete opposite of his eldest brother – rambunctious, constantly getting into mischief, and rarely doing what he was told. He'd been the wild child who'd grown up – if one could call it that – into the notorious, womanizing playboy. Joanna had wrung her hands in near despair over him for years, shuddering to learn about his latest escapade or see the most recent photo of him in the tabloids, usually in the company of some actress or model. But Colin had finally settled down in recent years, once he'd been assigned to the Asia/Pacific regional headquarters in Hong Kong and met his future wife there. Even Joanna – who wasn't easily intimidated by anyone – was rather in awe of her regal, confident daughter-in-law, the one woman it seemed who'd had the power to rein in the previously untamable Colin. Selina had given birth just over a year ago to their first child – another grandson.

But it had always been her middle son – Ian – who had given

Joanna the most concern over the years. Oh, definitely not because of his behavior or relationships or lifestyle. Unlike easygoing, affable Hugh or mischievous, fun loving Colin, Ian had always been quiet, composed and in complete control - the perfect gentleman. Joanna couldn't recall ever seeing him really lose his temper or betray his emotions. The only times she'd ever seen him let loose a bit had been in the boxing ring at school. And even then Ian had always been in total control, besting opponent after opponent, due not just to his physical strength and conditioning but to his ability to block off his emotions at a moment's notice.

Even when Ian had become engaged to Davina, he'd maintained his air of reserve, never displaying overt affection towards her or seeming truly happy. It had hardly been a shock to Joanna when the ill-fated engagement had ended after less than six months.

Since that time, and to the best of her knowledge, Ian hadn't been serious about a woman. When she and Edward had visited him in San Francisco, he had either escorted one of three or four different women – all of whom he treated more like a business associate than a girlfriend – or gone without an escort altogether. And during his visits to London, or family gatherings at the villa in Tuscany, he had always been alone – and lonely.

Joanna had always been puzzled about Ian's reticence with women, for he was undeniably the handsomest of her three sons, and she'd very clearly seen the way women vied for his attention. But when she'd quizzed him on the matter on multiple occasions, he had always dismissed her concerns, assuring her he was more than content with his lifestyle and joking that no woman would put up with his schedule anyway. She hadn't been especially reassured, however, and continued to fret over the fact that he was now forty, unmarried, and alone. He was too good a man, too kind and generous a person, to not have someone special in his life, someone to love and care for him the way he deserved. She had hoped and, yes, prayed, for years now that Ian would finally find the right woman to share his life and bring him the sort of happiness he deserved more than anyone she knew.

But when Edward had broken the news to her last month that not only had Ian apparently fallen head over heels in love, but that the woman in question was also living with him, Joanna had been immediately concerned. The very last trait she would have ever attributed to her middle son was that of impulsiveness, and this very sudden, unexpected action on his part seemed completely out of character.

The alarm bells had really begun to ring, however, when Edward had told her the final two bits of news. The woman in question – Tessa was her name - was not only a former employee of Ian's but a very young one at that. Upon hearing that this young woman was a full fifteen years Ian's junior, Joanna had immediately pegged the girl as a fortune hunter, an opportunistic gold digger, and had fretted and worried about all the ways the girl must be taking advantage of her son.

Edward, however, had only chuckled about the whole matter and dismissed her concerns. "My dear, this is Ian we're talking about after all, and not Colin. Or your thrice-divorced brother Gavin, who was unfortunately one of Colin's role models. Ian is the most sensible, level-headed person I've ever met, and lovesick or not there is no possible way he would let anyone take advantage of him. Have some faith, Joanna. After all, it does seem that all of the praying you did for him over the years has finally shown results."

"My prayers didn't include a twenty-four year old floozy who's only interested in his money," grumbled Joanna. "Well, it's a good thing we're paying a visit next month so we can see for ourselves what's going on. Hopefully it's not too late to save Ian from this little schemer."

No amount of reasoning on Edward's part had served to change Joanna's mind. And since she wasn't about to accuse Ian over the phone of taking up with an eager little fortune hunter, she was obliged to keep her opinions to herself during their conversations. He did sound extremely happy, far more so than she could ever recall, and he assured her that she was going to fall in love with Tessa as quickly as he had. Joanna had to bite her tongue on those occasions, and rather stiffly tell her son that she was looking forward to their visit very much.

But now that they were actually here in San Francisco, their luggage being loaded into Ian's Town Car by Simon, Joanna found herself dreading what she feared was going to be an awkward and unpleasant encounter. If this young woman was in fact the greedy, opportunistic little tramp that she feared, it was going to make for a very long, uncomfortable visit.

Simon was as efficient and accommodating as he'd been during their previous visits, loading up their luggage and driving them smoothly out of the airport with a minimum of polite conversation. But Joanna was uncharacteristically chatty with Ian's chauffeur, anxious to get his opinion on this Tessa and to pry whatever information she could from the very proper Welshman.

"So, Simon. What can you tell us about Mr. Ian's new, ah companion?"

Edward frowned at her. "Joanna, let's not put Simon in an awkward spot. I'm sure he doesn't indulge in idle gossip."

"It's not a problem, sir," assured Simon from the front seat. "And to answer your question, madam, I can assure you that you'll be quite taken with Miss Tessa. She's a lovely girl, just lovely, and Mr. Ian is completely besotted with her. You'll be rather – ah, amazed at the changes in him."

Joanna was visibly taken aback at this news. "Mr. Gregson and I were worried that this girl might be taking advantage of our son. Given her youth, that is."

Edward gave her a jab in the ribs. "Speak for yourself, my dear. *I'm* not worried in the least. Ian is far from a boy, after all, and not one to let his emotions take over his common sense."

"You don't have to worry about Miss Tessa," declared Simon. "She's a good girl, quiet, well-mannered, and she takes very good care of Mr. Ian. With all due respect, madam, she's the furthest thing from a fortune hunter you can imagine. You'll see for yourself very soon."

Joanna was only mildly mollified by Simon's assurances, but she did console herself with the fact that the very straight-laced chauffeur was not a man who suffered fools gladly. Of course, it was entirely possible that the little flirt had somehow wormed her way into Simon's affections as well, twisting him around her finger the way she appeared to have done to Ian.

Joanna knew very few people who would readily admit to being wrong, and she didn't count herself in that minority. But she was well bred and gracious enough to realize when she'd made a serious error in judgment, and she knew the minute she shook Tessa Lockwood's hand that she'd been completely wrong about the girl.

Ian's new companion was exquisite, and it was easy to see why he was so taken with her. Instead of the overblown sexpot that Joanna had been expecting to meet, the girl was almost painfully shy, very sweet, and clearly extremely intimidated to meet Ian's parents. The hand she placed in Joanna's was actually trembling, and her voice breathy and high-pitched as she greeted them.

Edward smiled broadly as he took Tessa's hand in his and gave her a peck on the cheek. "It's delightful to meet you, my dear. You're practically all Ian talks about these days. And you are even more beautiful than he claimed."

Joanna was astonished to see the girl blush, unable to remember the last time she'd seen a young woman react in such a way.

Ian chuckled, placing an arm around Tessa's shoulder. "You're embarrassing her, Father. And she's already nervous about meeting the two of you."

"Well, that's ridiculous," chided Edward. "You don't need to be nervous around us, my girl. We trust Ian's judgment implicitly, and since he's admittedly head over heels in love with you – well, that's good enough for us. Isn't that right, Joanna?"

Joanna glanced at Tessa, and felt a little tug on her heart when she noticed how anxious the girl appeared. She smiled warmly, taking Tessa's hands and giving them a reassuring squeeze. "Yes, it most certainly is. And my husband is right, dear. It's a great pleasure to meet you."

At that, Tessa smiled – really smiled – and suddenly whatever tension might have still existed seemed to evaporate into thin air.

Tessa served them a perfectly prepared and beautifully arranged full tea service, and Joanna was almost speechless with surprise when Ian told them proudly that Tessa had made everything herself.

"She's been taking some cooking courses, and is becoming quite the accomplished chef," bragged Ian. "In fact, we're having dinner here at home tonight. Tessa insisted on cooking for you."

Tessa offered up a shy smile. "I thought you'd be tired from such a long flight and might not want to go out. I hope that's all right."

Joanna was astonished. Neither of her daughters-in-law actually cooked. With four young, energetic sons Victoria relied heavily on domestic help to keep her sane. And Selina, who'd gone back to her job as a high-powered corporate attorney a few months after giving birth, freely admitted she could barely boil water.

Joanna herself seldom cooked, and very few of the women in their social circles – young and old – did either. So she was doubly surprised that Ian's very young girlfriend was not only taking cooking lessons but actually putting them to some use.

As they enjoyed their tea, Joanna took the opportunity to more closely observe the girl, and more importantly, her interactions with Ian. Tessa was fresh-faced and glowing, her flawless skin practically makeup free. She was wearing a charming floral print dress – dainty pink flowers on a cream background, a pink cardigan sweater, and low-heeled cream sling-back pumps. Her nails were kept on the short side and covered with a pale pink polish, and the only jewelry she wore was a pair of pearl stud earrings.

She looked classy and polished, someone that Ian would be bursting with pride to have on his arm. Joanna knew the pearls were real, recognized the shoes as Prada, and was fairly certain the dress was from Dolce & Gabbana's spring collection. She wasn't naïve enough not to realize that Ian had paid for the entire outfit, and most likely a great deal more. But none of that mattered to Joanna at this point, not when she saw how happy her son was, how often he smiled and laughed, how he looked younger, leaner, and very much in love.

And the girl clearly adored him. It was more than obvious with every look she gave him, every smile, the way she hung on his every word. And though they were both entirely discreet and restrained, they couldn't seem to keep their hands off each other for very long. Even now as they all sat in the living room finishing their tea, Ian was clasping Tessa's hand lightly in his, and they sat close enough on the sofa for their shoulders to touch.

Joanna was almost spellbound to watch her normally austere, standoffish middle son acting like a young boy in love for the very first time in his life. And she very nearly choked on one of the admittedly delicious homemade scones Tessa had baked when Ian wrapped his arm around the girl's shoulders and pressed a kiss to her rosy cheek. Tessa blushed an even deeper shade of pink and looked down at her lap shyly while Ian merely chuckled in amusement.

"Darling, you don't have to be shy around my parents," he told her. "I'm not exactly a boy of fourteen any longer."

Edward smiled. "Ah, but you were far more interested in your studies and sports when you were that age. Your brother Colin was the ladies' man, even at that young age. And I think your mother feared he would never settle down."

"Well, God does work his miracles sometimes, doesn't he, Mother?" teased Ian. "Colin is happily married and a father, and I've met the most wonderful girl in the entire world. So all is well, wouldn't you say?"

Joanna couldn't help smiling fondly at her much loved son. "I certainly would. And you look wonderful, darling, happier than I've ever seen you. I suppose we all owe Tessa here a debt of gratitude for putting that sparkle in your eye. You look a bit thinner than you did in February, Ian."

Ian patted his rock hard torso. "Just a few pounds that I'd put on over the holidays. You know what our business is like, Mother, all the dining out with clients and staff. It catches up to you after a time, especially at my age. Since Tessa's moved in, she insists on cooking for me as often as possible so I'm naturally eating healthier."

Joanna had to stifle a little gasp of surprise when Ian smiled fondly at the girl, tucking a long strand of blonde hair behind her ear and murmuring to no one in particular, "She takes very, very good care of me, don't you, love?"

Tessa didn't reply, merely beaming at him adoringly and touching his cheek lightly. It was the most innocent of caresses, and yet Joanna couldn't help but feel that she and Edward were witnessing a very intimate moment.

Before she did something ill-mannered like fidgeting, Joanna smoothly changed the subject. "Do you have any siblings, Tessa? Ian hasn't really told us much about your family."

Instantly the girl's face sobered, and Ian frowned in displeasure at the question. He bent to whisper something in her ear but she waved him off.

"It's all right," she told him gently. "It's not a secret, after all." And then to Joanna she replied quietly, "I don't have any family at all, Mrs. Gregson. My mother was really all I had and she died when I was sixteen."

Joanna was startled at this bit of news, and she couldn't help the rush of empathy she felt for the girl. She noticed for perhaps the first time the great sadness in Tessa's enormous blue eyes, eyes that suddenly seemed too old for her otherwise youthful face.

"I'm so sorry, my dear," she told her sincerely. "I've always had such a large family that I can't even imagine what it must be like to be all alone in the world. But you're not alone any longer, are you? Now you have my Ian to look after you."

Tears shimmered in Tessa's eyes as she nodded and squeezed the hand Ian had slid into hers. "I do, yes. And I know how lucky I am to have him. He's the most wonderful man in the world."

Edward cleared his throat. "Now, then, no tears, young lady. I'm the sort who tends to get a bit weepy during sad movies so allow an old man his dignity, hmm? Only happy talk allowed, are we clear?"

Ian laughed. "You'd better say yes, darling. I'm not certain I could handle seeing my father start crying like a girl."

Tessa giggled, and then all four of them were laughing and the subject changed to something more lighthearted.

Tessa seemed startled when Joanna offered to help clear away the tea service, but the girl merely nodded and thanked her graciously. Somehow, and apparently without the guidance of a mother or other relative, the girl had learned how to conduct herself like a lady, for her manners were impeccable.

"You were an employee of Ian's, I understand?"

Tessa nodded as she wrapped up leftover food and began to load the dishwasher. "Yes, ma'am. I worked on his support team for a little over two years. Before that I worked at the resort in Tucson."

A light suddenly went on in Joanna's mind. "Ah, I see. You worked for Francine at one time."

Tessa's face lit up at the mention of her former manager. "Yes, for several years. She – well, she taught me a great deal. You know Mrs. Carrington then?"

Joanna chuckled. "Yes, indeed. She was in charge of the office in London for a number of years, as you know. And that included being in charge of Edward and his brother. Everyone knew that Francine was the real boss."

If Tessa had been under the tutelage of Francine Carrington for several years, that would explain her exquisite manners and ladylike demeanor. Joanna was finally beginning to feel like she could breathe a huge sigh of relief. Rather than the aggressive, obnoxious gold digger she'd been dreading, Ian's new companion was turning out to be a very pleasant surprise.

"I see you haven't made any changes to the house as yet," commented Joanna. And indeed the only alterations she'd noticed had been an abundance of fresh flowers in almost every room she'd seen thus far.

Tessa was clearly taken aback by this statement and looked a bit puzzled. "Well, no. I'm not sure that I would have, though. I mean, this is Ian's house, not mine. But aside from that fact, I love everything about this place and wouldn't change a thing. He has such wonderful taste, doesn't he?"

Joanna smiled indulgently when she saw the dreamy look that crossed Tessa's face. "That he does, my dear. Did he pick out that dress for you?"

A guilty look came over Tessa's features and she was clearly uncomfortable discussing the subject. "Not this one, no. My friend Julia helped me pick it out."

"Ah, well, your friend has excellent taste. Does she work in the fashion industry?"

Tessa shook her head. "No, she's an interior designer. In fact, she and her fiancée are the designer and architect working on the new hotel in the Napa Valley. But Julia does have an eye for fashion so – well, she's been helping me out."

Joanna could read between the lines very easily, and figured that Tessa wasn't at all accustomed to wearing high end fashions. "Well, the dress looks lovely on you, dear. Have you chosen a gown for the benefit ball next week?"

"Not yet, no. I have an appointment with the personal shopper Ian uses at Neiman Marcus for this Friday. I'm not at all sure what I ought to be wearing to such a formal event."

"Well, I'm sure your friend – Julia, is it? – will be happy to help you out."

"Julia's very busy at the moment, actually," demurred Tessa. "Her wedding is just over three weeks away and I wouldn't even think of asking for her opinion right now. Ian thought that – well, that maybe you'd be able - "

Joanna smiled. "I'd be delighted, dear. And I've been to so many of these events that I can advise you on exactly the right dress to buy. What of your friend's wedding? Do you have a dress for that yet?"

"Not yet, no. Things have been rather hectic with our schedules lately, what with the business trips and all."

"Well, we can kill two birds with one stone and find you a dress for that at the same time. I think – well, that it would be nice for us to get to know each other a little better, don't you? After all," added Joanna kindly, "it seems that my son is intent on keeping you around for a very long time to come. And I know it would please Ian very much if you and I became good friends, don't you agree?"

Tessa's face lit up with a gorgeous smile as she nodded enthusiastically. "I do, yes. Very much. Thank you, Mrs. Gregson. You're so kind, just like Ian."

Joanna squeezed the girl's hand. "You should call me Joanna, dear. Though I expect that one day very soon that might change to what Ian calls me – Mother."

***

Ian grinned. "She told you that, did she?"

Tessa couldn't believe she'd actually confessed what his mother had told her earlier today. "I'm sure she was just being polite."

He shrugged. "Well, my mother is always polite. Unless she happens to be chasing after one of my nephews. That's usually when the gloves come off. My mother can be quite feisty when the need arises. I suppose that's what happens when you spend your life surrounded by men." He pulled the pink cardigan sweater down her arms. "But Mother never says anything she doesn't mean, polite or not. And she definitely meant that last part she told you."

"Oh. Well, that was nice of her, I suppose. Though I don't know how I'll be able to actually call her Joanna, much less, er - "

"Mother?" finished Ian helpfully. He held onto her arm as she stepped out of her shoes.

Tessa shrugged. "I mean, it's not like that's really likely to happen."

"Isn't it?" He slipped his arms around her waist, touching his forehead to hers. "We've never talked about getting married – you're not ready for that just yet. But make no mistake, Tessa – you *will* be my wife one day, sooner than later."

She stared at him open-mouthed, completely taken aback by his very matter of fact statement. But before she could even think of a reply, he was turning her to face away from him.

"Now, unfortunately, I do have an early start to the day tomorrow, so let's get you out of this very pretty dress so that I can finally satisfy my curiosity about what you have on underneath." He nuzzled the nape of her neck as he slowly lowered the zipper. "I appreciate that you chose to wear something a bit conservative to meet my parents in, but that doesn't mean I didn't fantasize all damned day about what lacy bits you have on."

Tessa closed her eyes as he worked the dress down past her hips, kneeling at her feet, and urged her to step out of the fabric. She gasped as his arms circled her hips from behind, and she felt his lips on the small of her back. His fingers toyed with the waistband of her tiny white lace thong.

"Mmm, all ladylike and proper on the outside with your pretty dress and little heels," he murmured, his hands caressing the bared cheeks of her ass. "But underneath you've got on these very, very sexy undies that make you look like a pinup girl." He slipped his finger beneath the lacy band of her sheer thigh-high stockings. "God, I love these. They always make your legs seem even longer than they are."

Tessa was trembling as he turned her slowly in his arms, his hands splayed over her buttocks as he nuzzled his face against her crotch. "You smell delicious," he rasped. "I can already tell you're wet, just from your scent. Let me see, love."

She couldn't stifle the low moan that escaped her throat as he pushed aside the fabric of her thong and slid two fingers deep, deep inside of her slit. She clutched at his shoulders as he continued to pump his fingers in and out of her in a steady rhythm. "Ian, oh God, that's so good," she whispered. "But – please – your parents will hear us."

He laughed softly. "No surprise to my father that I've been dying to shag you all day. He's probably wondering why we didn't sneak off for a quickie in between tea and dinner."

Tessa felt like her entire body was flaming with embarrassment and not just her face. "Oh, my, God, he is not! And we can't do – *that* with them right next door to us."

Ian grimaced. "I've never been able to figure out why the second largest bedroom in this house is right next to the master suite. I suppose it would have been bad manners to move my parents to the room at the end of the hall, given that it's the smallest, wouldn't it?"

Since Ian was still intent on pleasuring her with his fingers, Tessa could only nod in agreement, not trusting herself to open her mouth for fear she would emit another, louder moan. But when she shoved a fist inside her mouth to stifle the noise, he grinned and took pity on her.

"Let's try this, shall we?" He stood and hoisted her over his shoulder, her legs dangling down the front of his body as he carried her inside the walk-in closet. He set her down before closing the door, then turned to face her.

His gaze lingered on the heavy swell of her breasts, still encased in a lavish white lace bra. "Well, now that I've gotten a good, long look at you – Jesus, you're breathtaking, Tessa – there is no possible way I'm not having you tonight."

She nodded, her eyes lowering to the huge bulge of his erection against his trousers. "Is it – will this be private enough? I would be – *mortified* if your parents heard me, you know - "

He laughed wickedly. "Moan? Pant? Make all those wild noises you love to do when you're aroused? Well, you might want to tone it down a bit, but I don't think they'll hear us in here. Of course, if you really want to make sure, I've got a solution."

Her head fell back against one of the walls as he deftly unhooked her bra, his hands cupping her bare breasts. "Ah, oh. What – what's that?"

As Ian bent his head and began to lick her right nipple, he grabbed one of her silk scarves from the rack and dangled it in front of her. "I would be very happy to gag you."

As he moved his attention to the other breast, she let out a long, low moan and panted. "Um, maybe that's not such a bad idea."

***

"You're sure I look all right? I would be so upset if I embarrassed Ian tonight."

Tessa looked at herself critically in the full length mirror for perhaps the fourth or fifth time, worrying that the gown was too over the top, or that her heels were too high, or her hair not quite right.

"You look absolutely perfect, dear. Stunning, in fact. You

and Ian will definitely be the handsomest couple there tonight by far. Turn around once more."

Tessa obeyed Joanna's instructions and did a slow, 360^0 turn. The two women had commandeered the master bedroom and bath to get ready for the symphony ball, banishing Ian to use one of the spare bedroom suites. At Joanna's prodding, they'd had lunch earlier today at Neiman Marcus followed by a mani-pedi and a blowout at the in-store beauty salon. Tessa had initially resisted the idea, insisting she could easily do her own nails and hair for this evening.

Joanna had regarded her curiously. "Why on earth would you want to do that, dear? In case you weren't already aware, my son can definitely afford to pay for a few spa services for you."

Tessa had shrugged, always uncomfortable when the subject of money came up. "I know he can. But I don't like to take advantage, especially since I don't have an official job, or bring in any income. And, well, you've seen how much he's already done for me. I don't like feeling like a useless, frivolous girlfriend."

"Well, now you're just being silly," Joanna had declared. "Trust me, dear, Ian adores taking care of you. And after what you've told me about your childhood – all the sad things that happened to you – well, you can begin to understand why he'd want to do that."

"I do, yes. But he doesn't have to keep trying to make it up to me. Especially not with *things*. If I'm being truthful, I have to say there are times I wish he was – oh, I don't know – let's say a truck driver, and that we lived on a houseboat. That way he'd know for certain that it's him I love and not these – things."

Joanna had given her a gentle hug and patted her on the shoulder. "My dear girl, don't you think he already knows that? Besides, it would have to be an awfully big houseboat – he's not a small man, is he?"

After they'd shared a little laugh, Joanna had told her earnestly, "Let the man indulge you, all right? It obviously makes him very, very happy to do so and I've never see my son like this before. And don't forget, Tessa, that it goes both ways.

I see all the little ways you take care of him, and it does my heart good to know how much you adore him. God bless you, dear, for loving my boy so well."

Tessa had given in graciously after that and allowed herself to enjoy the bit of pampering she so seldom let herself indulge in. She knew it drove Ian a little crazy whenever he noticed her doing her own nails, or when she insisted she didn't need another new dress for an event and could wear something already in her closet. Joanna had given her a bit of a lecture on that subject as well.

"Ian's quite right," she'd said bluntly. "He's a very important man, Tessa, and like all of the family he gets a lot of coverage in the media. If you're going to be seen out with him, you really must dress the part, top to bottom. You have some lovely pieces in your wardrobe but that's truly only about half the number of things you really need."

With Ian's fervent blessing, Joanna had done her damndest over the past week to start filling in what she deemed the gaps in Tessa's wardrobe. Tessa was worn out from so many days of shopping with her, but at the same time she'd been grateful for the opportunity to spend time with Ian's mother and get to know her a little. She felt infinitely more comfortable around her now than she had at their first meeting.

Even though Marlene Brennan had selected an even dozen gowns for her to try on, Tessa had known immediately which one she wanted. Another Marchesa – she admittedly loved the elegance of the designer's brand – this one a sumptuous ball gown of sapphire blue tulle, the strapless bodice lavishly embroidered with gold beads, crystals and sequins. It had fit like a glove, not requiring even the slightest alteration, and both Marlene and Joanna had oohed and aahed when she had tried it on.

Metallic gold Jimmy Choo sandals, plus the sapphire pendant and earrings Ian had given her on their first date completed the outfit. Her blonde hair had been swept into an elegant French twist, and she'd kept her makeup minimal, going for class rather than flash.

"You look like a young Grace Kelly," Joanne told her with a

satisfied smile. "Beautiful, elegant and classy. Blue is definitely your color, my dear, and that dress is fabulous. I only wish I was thirty years younger and several inches taller so that I could borrow it sometime."

Tessa smiled at the thought of trading clothes with Ian's mother, admiring Joanna's own gown of pale mocha silk, with its draped neckline and elbow length lace sleeves. "You always look lovely, and like it's effortless to do so. Have you always liked beautiful clothes?"

Joanna made a rather undignified sound. "Good heavens, no. I grew up with three very rowdy brothers, my dear, and was determined to tag along everywhere with them. My poor mother would nearly tear her hair out when it came time for us to attend an event, for I would usually refuse to even consider wearing a dress. So, the answer is a most emphatic no – I was quite a tomboy until I went to university."

Tess tried in vain to picture the elegant, refined woman standing in front of her looking anything but perfectly put together. "What changed?"

Joanna winked. "I met Edward and was instantly attracted. And I could tell right away he came from money – a great deal of it – so I knew I'd need to change my image very quickly if I wanted to keep his attention. My mother actually wept with joy when I begged her to take me shopping and have my hair done."

Tessa was still laughing at the story when she and Joanna descended the staircase to the foyer, where Ian and Edward were waiting for them. Both men were wearing tuxedos – Ian in his custom made Brioni – and her pulse rate picked up considerably when she saw how magnificent he looked. And then she saw the way he was staring at her, his eyes raking over her body, not missing one single detail, and she felt a different sort of thrill.

Ian kissed his mother's cheek as she reached the landing, mouthing a silent "thank you" before handing her off to Edward. He didn't wait for Tessa to descend the final few stairs, meeting her halfway as his arm curled about her waist, crushing her against him.

He murmured "Hello, beautiful," just before taking her mouth in the sort of deeply passionate kiss that one normally would not want one's parents to witness. Tessa made a feeble attempt to break away, but his arm was like an iron band around her, holding her firmly in place as he kissed her thoroughly.

It was only the sound of Edward rather loudly clearing his throat that made Ian finally lift his head with an impatient sigh.

"Ian, my boy, if you thought the girl looked ravishing all you had to do was tell her so," admonished Edward sternly. "Your mother and I didn't need to, er, share an intimate moment with you."

"Speak for yourself," chided Joanna teasingly. "I don't blame Ian for getting a bit carried away. Tessa looks – breathtaking, there's really no other way to describe her."

"I can think of several," Ian declared. "Gorgeous, stunning, just like Cinderella. She is simply – splendid."

Tessa's eyes got misty as he whispered the last word to her, the exact same one she'd once used to describe him. But as soon as Joanna saw the shimmer of tears, she clucked in disapproval.

"Ah, no tears, Tessa. You'll ruin your eye makeup. And thanks to my very amorous son, your lip gloss is already mussed. You'll need to fix it in the limo, dear."

But as Ian escorted her out the front door and into the waiting limo he'd hired for the night, he whispered to her in a wicked voice. "I've got a feeling you'll be reapplying that lip gloss all night long, love."

The benefit ball for the symphony was being held in the grand ballroom of the Gregson Hotel, the same venue where the office Christmas party had taken place. Tessa was both thrilled and terrified at what was really her first major appearance out in public with Ian. They had been out numerous times together, of course, to dinner and shopping, the gym, and even to a few business dinners. But Ian had very intentionally been declining a number of invitations to events like tonight's ball, wanting to give Tessa some time to get used to his lifestyle, and also somewhat selfishly desiring to keep her to himself for as long as possible.

Tonight, though, it would have been nearly impossible for him not to make an appearance. The ball was being held in the hotel he owned, he was a known patron of the symphony, and his parents were old friends of the conductor. So it had been decided that this would be Tessa's unofficial introduction into San Francisco society, and she was extremely grateful she'd had both Joanna and Marlene to give her the sort of advice she would need to successfully navigate her way through the evening.

Ian remained glued to her side from the moment they arrived, and seemed more than content to let everyone else in the room come to them, rather than seek others out directly. He kept an arm wrapped possessively around her waist, his fingers splayed over her hipbone, silently sending out the message that she was most definitely his woman. Tessa sipped expensive champagne, smiled politely until her jaw ached, and instantly forgot the name of every person she was introduced to.

"How do you do it?" she murmured to Ian in a dumbfounded voice. "I don't remember the name of the last person we just met, much less the first one."

He laughed softly, pressing a kiss to her temple, ignoring the flash of the photographer's camera that captured the image. "Practice, my love. Years and years of practice. You'll learn soon enough, especially as you tend to see the same group of people at most of these events. Speaking of which." His hand gripped her hipbone just a bit tighter. "I was hoping to avoid them, blast it, but unfortunately Alicia's parents are making a beeline for us. It had to happen sometime, darling, so it may as well be now."

Even if Ian hadn't told her who they were, Tessa would have recognized Alicia's mother instantly, for the two women bore a very strong resemblance to the other. Claire Spencer had the same pale blonde hair, slender build and fake smile that her daughter did, her voice sickeningly sweet as she greeted Ian. Claire's smile seemed to freeze in place when he introduced Tessa, especially when she spied the possessive manner in which he was holding her close to his side. Still, good manners insisted that she take Tessa's proffered hand and give it a brief, polite shake.

Alicia's father – Bradley – was considerably friendlier, and

Tessa wondered if the rather obvious scent of bourbon on his breath had anything to do with that. He took Tessa's hand in a very firm grip, even bringing it to his lips. Tessa had to suppress a shudder at the feel of his cold, clammy lips on her skin and she drew her hand away as quickly as possible.

"So you're the pretty young thing we saw Ian with at dinner that night," teased Bradley in a booming, jovial voice. He was an attractive man – or had been before age and too much booze had given him a paunch and the sort of florid complexion that came from overindulging. "I was all set to come over and introduce ourselves but Claire here thought you looked a bit – er, occupied."

Ian's fingers bit into Tessa's waist, betraying his annoyance. "Well, I appreciate your consideration, both of you. And you're quite right – Tessa and I were rather intent on having our privacy that evening."

He diplomatically excused them after a few more minutes of polite chit chat, murmuring in Tessa's ear as they walked away, "Now you can see why I prefer to avoid them at these sort of events. That fat bastard Bradley never took his eyes off your breasts the entire time. Rather revolting, considering his own daughter is several years older than you."

This time Tessa didn't even try to suppress a shudder. "Revolting is the word for it, all right. Ugh, he reminds me of one of those fish with the huge lips. What are they called?"

Ian burst out laughing, not caring a whit that he instantly drew the attention of a dozen or more couples in the area. "I believe the species you're thinking of is a grouper. And yes, I do see a vague resemblance now that you mention it. But if he dares to kiss your hand again, I'll very happily shove my fist into those fish lips of his."

She grinned, resting her head on his shoulder as he plucked two more champagne flutes off a passing waiter's try. "I wonder how long it will take Claire to spread the news about me to Alicia. She's probably texting her as we speak."

Ian's hand slid to her bare shoulder, giving it a squeeze as he murmured, "Actually, darling, I'm afraid Alicia's already figured it out for herself. Stay with me now, all right? The little witch wouldn't dare say anything nasty in my presence."

But Tessa couldn't prevent the cold fingers of dread that crept up her spine as she glanced up to meet the murderous glare of her former co-worker. Alicia's normally pretty face was scrunched up into an angry, ugly expression, and if looks could kill, Tessa would have suffered a mortal wound by now.

As he'd been doing all evening thus far, Ian didn't go to Alicia and her date, but let them come to him. Tessa noted that Alicia had paled significantly, and was still staring at her with a shell-shocked expression.

Ian quite deliberately chose to act as if there wasn't the slightest thing unusual about Tessa being here this evening, and on his arm nonetheless. "Good evening, Alicia. A pleasure to see you as always. And of course, I'm sure you're delighted to see Tessa again."

Alicia's mouth opened but she seemed to have great difficulty in speaking as she stared at Tessa in disbelief, taking in her gown, her hair, the sapphires.

Tessa, desperate to fill in the increasingly awkward silence, extended her hand to Alicia. "It's good to see you, Alicia. How have you been?"

Alicia stared at Tessa's outstretched hand like it was a coiled snake. "How – why are you here?" Her voice was a hoarse whisper, barely audible.

Ian swiftly interceded. "I would have thought that the answer to that was quite obvious, Alicia. Tessa is here with me this evening as my guest."

Alicia was almost shaking with suppressed rage. "You're *dating* her?" she hissed. Her fists clenched as though she'd love nothing better than to pull Tessa's hair out of its intricately arranged twist.

Ian smiled, but it wasn't a particularly pleasant expression. "Tessa and I are together, yes. In fact, she's moved in with me." Not waiting to see how Alicia reacted to that bombshell, Ian extended his hand to her date. "Hello, I believe we may have met at our office Christmas party. Ian Gregson – Alicia's employer. Have you met Tessa before this evening?"

While Alicia's date Ross exchanged pleasantries with Ian, Tessa dared to glance up at Alicia and almost recoiled from the icy cold rage stamped on the other woman's face. Tessa was very well aware of how long Alicia had plotted and schemed to one day attract Ian's attention and date him herself. Tessa also knew that Alicia had never liked her, had overheard the scathing comments and thinly veiled insults she'd made about her. She shuddered to imagine what horrible, nasty thoughts must be going through Alicia's mind right about now.

Fortunately, Ian was very well aware of the animosity being directed Tessa's way and suavely steered her away to greet another couple. As they walked in the opposite direction of Alicia and Ross, Tessa released a long sigh of relief.

Ian rubbed the back of her neck in his usual soothing manner. "All right there, love?"

She grimaced. "Glad to have that over with, that's for sure. But can you check my back for claw marks? And I've got a terrible chill all of a sudden – must be that case of frostbite I just caught."

He snickered and caressed the bare skin of her shoulder blades. "She was green with jealously, love. Not only are you ten times more beautiful than she is, but her own date couldn't take his eyes off of you. Maybe I should have security check her bag for any sharp objects."

Tessa shook her head. "You know, I should have expected something like this to happen. I had that bad feeling I get sometimes when I have these premonitions. And of course it just happens to be a Wednesday."

"Darling, I've told you a dozen times. That's just a coincidence. I refuse to believe that bad things haven't happened on other days of the week. Or that good things haven't happened occasionally on Wednesdays."

"Not very many," she replied somewhat grudgingly. "And I still say it's some sort of weird curse."

Tessa's good humor was restored a couple of minutes later when they met up with Ian's good friend Matthew Bennett and his wife Lindsey. Tessa had never met Lindsey before, but knew Matthew from the gym and liked him a lot. He was kind and friendly, and she found it hard to believe he was actually a billionaire, for he seemed like one of the most genuine, down to earth people she'd ever met. Not as classically handsome as Ian, Matthew was nonetheless a very attractive man – a little shorter and leaner than Ian, his light brown hair cut in a short, slightly spiky style. And though he wore his tuxedo well, he didn't seem like the sort of man who liked wearing formal attire or even a suit. He also didn't seem especially thrilled about attending this ball tonight, unlike his wife who appeared to be having a wonderful time.

Lindsey was laughing, tossing back glass after glass of champagne, and also flirting somewhat outrageously with Ian – a situation that was embarrassing Matthew, pissing off Tessa, and making Ian extremely uncomfortable. Lindsey was a pretty woman, and looked amazing for being forty, the same age as her husband. Petite with glossy dark brown hair and green eyes, she was definitely making sure every male in the room noticed her rather obvious assets showcased by the slinky, low-cut black gown she wore. Tessa was certainly no expert on the subject, but she was almost positive the older woman's gravity defying breasts couldn't possibly be real.

Fortunately, Ian had long ago mastered the art of fending off unwanted female attention, and very diplomatically extricated himself and Tessa from what could have become a very awkward situation.

"Poor Matthew," murmured Tessa in a hushed tone as Ian walked them in the opposite direction of the married couple. "He looked mortified at the way Lindsey kept flirting with you. And it's a very good thing you got us out of there when you did, because if she tried shoving those fake tits of hers into your face one more time I was going to take her down."

Ian started to laugh almost uncontrollably, until he became aware of all the curious glances directed his way. Trying to muffle his laughter but not doing a very good job of it, he pulled Tessa into his arms and turned his face against her hair.

"My little tigress," he murmured, his body still shaking with mirth. "And here I thought I was the only one of us with violent tendencies when it comes to someone poaching on my territory. I'm very glad to know I can count on you in the future to – ah, defend my virtue."

Tessa couldn't help laughing along with him. "I think those kickboxing classes I've been taking have brought out my protective side. You told me once that you always look out for what's yours. You've got to know that it's the same for me." She kissed his cheek before adding softly, "You're mine, Ian, and no other woman can ever have you."

Ian's fingers bit into her waist and she could feel the outline of his erection through the fragile fabric of her gown. "Christ, I wish like hell there weren't hundreds of people here right now. Because I have the card key for the owner's suite in my pocket, and I'd love nothing better than to quietly disappear with you and lock ourselves in for a few hours."

She smiled at him in a deliberately provocative manner. "I wouldn't say no to that idea. Maybe another time, hmm?"

He gave her a lingering kiss on the mouth, evidently not giving a damn how many people were watching. "It's a date, love."

***

Alicia was seething, her barely controlled temper ready to snap at a moment's notice. She couldn't recall a time in her twenty-nine years when she'd been this angry, or so in need to throw something. Or better yet, kick someone. Especially if that someone was a certain blonde tramp who had effectively managed to ruin Alicia's entire evening. No, make that her entire life.

"Hey, everything okay?" asked Ross, who was seated to her right.

Alicia glared at her date, who she was *this close* to dumping for good. She had never considered him good enough for her, and wasn't at all sure why she was still dating such a loser. And seeing him here tonight among all of these rich, successful men only served to emphasize his shortcomings.

"Fine, yes. Why do you keep asking?" she snapped. This was

at least the third time he'd inquired about her rather obvious agitation.

Ross shrugged. "Maybe because you've been hitting the booze pretty hard tonight. Not to mention being a little – uh, testy."

Her voice was dripping with ice as she replied, "If I need a lecture my parents are seated just across the table from us."

Ross threw his hands up in frustration. "Suit yourself, Alicia. I'm just concerned about you, okay? But as usual, you snap my head off whenever I try to do something nice. I'll keep my mouth shut for the rest of the evening."

Alicia defiantly drained her wine glass. She *had* been drinking rather heavily this evening, but who could blame her? After the shock she'd suffered earlier, it was small wonder she wasn't trying to drown herself in booze right now.

When she'd continued to hear the increasing rumors about Ian and his new blonde girlfriend, she never in a million years would have suspected that woman to be Tessa. Alicia had been stunned speechless to recognize her former co-worker clinging to Ian's arm and looking like some sort of fucking princess. It was a joke, really, that the naïve, somewhat awkward girl who'd dressed in discount store clothes and clearance rack shoes would be here tonight wearing that regal Marchesa gown, with real sapphires at her throat and ears. Alicia grudgingly conceded that Tessa had always been pretty, but now, tonight, in the right clothes and her hair done up, she was striking. Enough so that Ian Gregson hadn't allowed her to leave his side all night, or been able to tear his eyes from her for more than a minute at a time.

Alicia wondered wildly how and when they had started seeing each other, and why it had been Tessa – of all people – who'd finally managed to snag the attention of the elusive Brit. She clenched her fists as she thought of all the times she and Gina and the others had gossiped freely about their boss, speculating on who he might be dating or banging, and joking bawdily about Alicia's potential chances with him one day. And all that time Miss Goody Two-Shoes Tessa had never said one word or even blinked an eyelash, keeping her nose to the grindstone as she always did and refusing to participate in any gossip. Tessa had never once betrayed any interest in Ian, and certainly their standoffish employer had always kept his distance from the support staff.

Had they been seeing each other in secret all this time, since Tessa had begun working at the office? But no, Alicia truly didn't think Mr. Prim and Proper would fuck a married woman, so this little fling of theirs had begun more recently. And the more she stewed over the matter, the more it was that certain things started to become clear.

Like why Tessa had suddenly been appointed to fill in for Andrew when that had never happened in the past. And why Ian had rather abruptly stopped being seen in public with any of his usual escorts, and then stopped attending certain events altogether. The wheels kept spinning as she realized the "hot blonde" her parents had seen Ian dining with must have been Tessa, and that the "friend" the bitch had stayed with after the fire at her apartment was most likely Ian.

And it would certainly explain why she'd quit her job, a question the whole team had puzzled over for weeks. No one had been able to figure out where she was getting the money to travel or take an extended break, though Kevin had half-jokingly guessed she had some rich new boyfriend taking care of her. Alicia had dismissed his theory as ridiculous, but now it all made horrible, awful sense.

Tessa had left the company because she'd been fucking the boss. Now wouldn't *that* make for some really, really juicy gossip. Except, thought Alicia with a snarl, it would be humiliating beyond belief to admit to her co-workers – and especially her roommate, best friend, and staunch supporter Gina – that the man she'd salivated over for the past four and a half years had chosen a slut like Tessa over her.

And any thoughts she might have of causing trouble for Ian were swiftly abandoned. First, she couldn't prove a damned thing, especially since Tessa had already quit. Alicia was willing to bet that righteous prick Andrew knew everything, but trying to pry any information out of him was a complete waste of time. If Alicia was foolish enough to ask him anything the least bit personal about Ian, Andrew would merely give her a scathing look and tell her to get back to work.

And that was yet another problem. Admittedly, she'd been slacking off a bit on the job lately, though no more so than any of the others. Andrew, however, had chosen to make some sort of example of her, calling her under the carpet for a variety of grievances – tardiness, taking too many breaks, sending personal emails (which the bastard had actually had the balls to read), and screwing up on some travel arrangements she'd made for several of the managers. Andrew had let her off with a warning, but the dickwad had actually threatened her with formal probation next time.

No, making any accusations or spreading gossip about Ian at this time would be extremely unwise, and that realization only made Alicia angrier. The need to lash out was overwhelming, but with her parents present she was forced to keep a damper on her emotions.

It became harder and harder to control her temper, though, as the evening wore on. From her place at the dinner table, she unfortunately had a good vantage point of the table where Ian and Tessa were sitting, and it made her stomach hurt to observe how lovey-dovey the two of them were acting. Each time Ian kissed the bitch's cheek, Alicia wanted to follow it up with a hard slap. When he caressed the nape of her neck, Alicia's fingers itched to yank a long strand of Tessa's blonde hair out by the roots. And when the dancing started and she watched how closely Ian held Tessa in his arms – not to mention the tender, loving way he gazed into her eyes – she feared she might upchuck the small amount of food she'd been able to consume.

But when she spied Tessa leaving the ballroom and heading towards the ladies lounge, Alicia surged to her feet like a panther scenting its prey. She ignored Ross' voice asking where she was going, or her mother calling after her in concern. She was more than a little tipsy at this point, and had to weave her way carefully around the tables. But she was determined to corner that little bitch and get a few things off her mind.

Tessa was visibly startled when she left the toilets to find Alicia pacing back and forth in the adjoining lounge. It gave

Alicia great satisfaction to see the fear in Tessa's blue eyes, the same look a small animal had when it knew it was trapped. Alicia noted with some relief that the two of them appeared to be the only ones in the lounge, though at this point she was so worked up it wouldn't have mattered if three dozen people were present.

"It won't last you know," Alicia told her boldly. "He'll get tired of you quicker than you can blink an eye. You're nowhere near good enough for a man like him, Tessa, not even close. What the hell does he see in a stupid bitch like you anyway?"

Except for the slight tightening of her mouth, Tessa didn't betray the slightest emotion, which only infuriated Alicia more.

"He loves me," was all the bitch said in a calm, serene voice that made Alicia want to scream. "And I love him. He doesn't care about anything else."

"But he will. One day soon when he gets tired of banging you, he'll realize what a mistake he's made," raged Alicia. "You're nobody, Tessa, fucking nobody. You have no education, no family, no breeding. You used to buy your clothes from Ross Dress for Less, and wear shoes with worn out heels. And you might be all dressed up tonight but deep down you're still nobody and that's never going to change."

It pleased Alicia tremendously to see the tears pool up in Tessa's eyes, and the way her lip started to tremble. But still the bitch wouldn't break, despite the fact that her voice was a little less steady.

"None of that matters," replied Tessa quietly. "To either of us. He loves me for who I am, not what school I did or didn't go to, or where I bought my clothes. Ian's a good man, the very best, and *you're* the one, Alicia, who will never be good enough for him."

"How dare you!" screamed Alicia. "I'm exactly the sort of woman he needs. I went to fucking Wellesley, the best women's college in the country. I was a debutante, my mother's family is one of the oldest in San Francisco, and my father is the top criminal attorney in the state. You couldn't pick a more perfect woman to be worthy of Ian Gregson."

"Except for one very important fact," murmured Tessa. "He

doesn't love you, Alicia. In fact, I don't think he even likes you very much."

"Shut up!" Alicia's rage was off the charts by now and she advanced on Tessa until she was close enough to grasp her by the arm. "How would you like it if I told everyone in the office that the boss was fucking one of his employees? I don't suppose that would go over very well with the higher ups, would it?"

Tessa grimaced as Alicia dug long fingernails into the flesh of her bare arm. "First of all, I don't work there any longer as you well know. And second, considering that his father is about as high up as you can get and that he knows all about us, I'm not really sure what sort of trouble you think you can cause."

"Oooh, meek little Tessa is finally growing a spine I see," sneered Alicia. "You make me sick. You were always so prim and proper, sticking your nose up in the air when we would gossip about other people in the office. I wonder why you never said anything all the times we'd talk about the boss man. Afraid of showing your cards, I'll bet. Exactly how long have you been screwing him, Tessa?"

Tessa's mouth tightened angrily. "Our relationship is none of your business, Alicia. I have no intention of talking to you about it."

Alicia shook her head. "No wonder you always seemed to get the best assignments, why Andrew always seemed to favor you. It was because the boss wanted you for himself all along. Tell me, bitch, when he asked you to do all those spreadsheets for him, were you spreading something else at the same time? Your legs, maybe?"

Tessa gasped, and was struggling to maintain her composure when a pair of heels clicked rather loudly on the marble floor of the toilet area. Alicia glanced up, ready to tell the unwelcome intruder to mind their own business, when the words caught in her throat.

Joanna Gregson was regarding Alicia like she was something scraped off the bottom of a shoe. Both Alicia and Tessa were silent as Ian's mother glided their way with carefully measured strides, a smile on her face that somehow chilled Alicia to the bone.

"Tessa, dear, you really ought to get back. Ian will be missing you," said Joanna gently. "Tell him and my husband that I'll be along shortly." When Tessa hesitated, Joanna gave her a little push. "Go, my dear. I'll join you once I have a little chat with the young – er, lady."

Tessa gave a quick nod and then hurried out of the lounge.

Mrs. Gregson refocused that chilling smile on Alicia. "You're a very pretty young woman. Your name, dear?"

Alicia swallowed with some difficulty. "Alicia Spencer, ma'am."

Joanna fingered the fabric of Alicia's pale lilac gown. "Lovely dress. Dior, I believe?" At Alicia's nod she continued. "Pretty face, beautiful dress, but such an ugly soul. And frankly, it doesn't seem that your years at a prestigious school like Wellesley did much to teach you things like good manners."

Alicia flushed and began to stammer an apology. "I'm very sorry you had to overhear all that, Mrs. Gregson. I didn't mean – I'm just - "

"Disappointed that Ian didn't choose you?" Joanna raised a dainty brow. "My dear, there have been a great many girls like you over the years who've pursued Ian – pretty, well-bred, well-educated. The woman he was engaged to once was very much like yourself. But do you know why none of them ever held his attention – why he didn't pick you over – ah, what did you call Tessa – oh, yes, a nobody?"

Alicia could only shake her head, too cowed to utter a reply.

"It's because that girl loves him for who he truly is," replied Joanna softly. "She sees far beyond the man that everyone else sees, beyond his obvious attributes like good looks and wealth and power. And that is why there will never be anyone else for either of them. Because deep down, where it really matters, they are two of the kindest, purest souls you'll ever meet, and somehow they've managed to find each other."

Alicia stared rather sullenly at her shoes, refusing to acknowledge what Ian's mother had just said. She knew – just knew – that bitch Tessa was most likely telling Ian all the awful things she'd just said to her, and wondered wildly how she was going to talk her way out of this, especially when his mother had apparently overheard every word.

"How long have your worked for our company, dear?"

Alicia was a bit startled at the question but replied, "Almost five years, Mrs. Gregson."

Joanna nodded. "Ah, well, that will look impressive on your resume, won't it? And if you don't have it up to date, I'd strongly advise polishing it up, dear. Maybe at the same time you're typing up the letter of resignation I'll tell my son to be expecting on his desk tomorrow morning. Now, do be sure and enjoy the rest of your evening, Alicia. And lay off the alcohol, dear. Otherwise your complexion will start to look like your father's before you know it."

With a charming smile, Joanna exited the lounge, allowing Alicia the dignity of sobbing her heart out in private.

Chapter Twenty-Two

June

"Hmm. Good morning." Ian glanced up from his newspaper and smiled at the sight of the gorgeous blonde framed in the doorway. Her hair was rumpled and she was in the middle of a very wide yawn. He knew that beneath her long white cotton robe with its ruffled neckline that she would be nude, and his blood immediately started pumping a little hotter at this realization. Even with a severe case of bedhead and not a scrap of makeup, his girl never failed to arouse him, often just by being in the same room.

"Tired?" At her nod, he gave her an indulgent look. "You should have kept sleeping then, love. After all, we were up a bit late last night and will probably be so again tonight."

Tessa shrugged, causing the gaping neckline of her robe to slide over her bare shoulder. "I got lonely in there without you. Why didn't you wake me up?"

Ian chuckled. "For the same reason I ought to be tucking you back into bed right now. You obviously need your rest, darling. We have plenty of time until the wedding, you know. Why don't you go back to sleep for a bit?"

She shook her head and started walking over to where he sat on the sofa. He sat up a little straighter, watching with unabashed interest as her robe parted with each step, revealing the endlessly long length of her legs. Ian held out his arms as she sat down next to him, cuddling her close and kissing the top of her head.

"Mmm, this is so nice," she purred, burrowing her head against his shoulder. "I missed waking up with you."

He stroked her tangled curls lovingly, and couldn't prevent the way his body responded all too quickly to the feel of her unbound breasts crushed against his ribcage. "I promise to stay in bed with you tomorrow morning. We'll sleep in as late as possible, all right? After all, another perk of owning this place is that I don't have to worry about trivial details like check-out times."

They were spending the weekend at the company's luxury resort in Pebble Beach, the gated community adjacent to the quaint coastal town of Carmel. Today was Julia and Nathan's wedding, and Ian was glad to see that the couple would be enjoying warm, sunny weather on their special day.

Ian nearly always used the owner's suite when he visited one of the company's properties, unless there was some dignitary or celebrity who'd requested it. At those times he would simply stay in another, smaller suite, much like the one he and Tessa were occupying now. As part of their wedding present to the couple, Ian had arranged for them to stay in the owner's suite, though Nathan had had the plush accommodations all to himself last night. Even though he and Julia had been living together for almost a year, she'd insisted on sleeping apart the night before their wedding as tradition called for, and had stayed at her parents' home in nearby Carmel Highlands. Ian gave Nathan a great deal of credit for abiding by his bride-to-be's wishes; for himself, he honestly didn't think he could ever willingly spend a night without Tessa in his bed.

"Why don't you let me fix you some tea, love? Then we can call down for breakfast when you're ready," he offered.

Tessa gave another yawn. "I can get it. Why don't you go back to your newspaper?"

"Hush. I'll read it later. I'd much rather spend time with you. Be right back."

Their suite was equipped with a state of the art beverage bar that included a Nespresso single serve coffeemaker with a wide assortment of brews, and a sophisticated electric kettle and selection of Tazo teas. He brewed them each a cup of their favorite Darjeeling blend, then carried the two steaming mugs back into the living room area.

"Mmm, thank you," murmured Tessa after taking the first sip. "Just what I needed." She had tucked her legs up under her, and he ran his hand up and down the back of her calf.

"My pleasure, love. And the least I can do, considering how many other times you're the one brewing our morning tea."

She gave him a sweet smile, the sort that never failed to make his throat catch just a little. "You know I don't mind, know how much I love taking care of you."

Ian's fingers moved to her ankle, then her instep, giving her the sort of little foot massage he knew she adored. "The feeling is very mutual, my sweet."

Tessa gave a satisfied little groan as he continued to rub her foot, the sound she made more than enough to interest his already semi-hard cock. "Oh, and that feels so good. You're way better than a professional masseuse, you know. Magic hands."

He cocked his head at her. "Even better than Sasha?"

Tessa's yoga teacher slash massage therapist had been to the house on several occasions by now, and had worked her magic on both of them. Ian had been a bit skeptical when Tessa had raved about how good she was. He'd mostly been used to receiving massages from men, largely because he didn't consider a female quite strong enough to be able to dig deep into the thick layers of muscle that covered his body. His skepticism had only grown stronger when he'd met Sasha for the first time – a slender, graceful young woman of no more than medium height. But it had become apparent within five minutes that she was an exceptionally skilled masseuse, with the knack of finding spots he hadn't even known were sore. She also had a calm, serene nature about her that soothed the mind and the spirit as well as the body.

Tessa gave him an impish grin. "Well, she might have more experience but you're way hotter. I'd much rather have your hands on my body than anyone else's."

He gave a low growl and tightened his hand around her ankle. "Well, I would most definitely second that opinion, darling. And no other man had better even think of putting his hands on this body of yours."

She blew him a kiss. "Same here. Except for Sasha, of course. At least I know when she touches you it's to make you scream with pain and not pleasure."

He laughed as he reached for the room service menu. "Feel

like eating breakfast now?"

"In a minute." She sat up on the sofa, her feet touching the carpeted floor, and he could tell by the way she was worrying her bottom lip that something was on her mind. "I, um, wanted to talk to you about something first."

Ian lounged back against the sofa cushions, his arm draped along the back. "Go ahead, love. You know you can always talk to me about anything, don't you?"

Tessa nodded. "I know. And, well, we've discussed this subject before but I just thought of a different approach to it. It's – well, about school."

He frowned. "We have had this discussion, several times. And I already know what you're going to say, Tessa. You don't want to start college in the fall because it will keep us apart when I have to travel. Darling, nothing has changed since the last time we had this talk. As awful as it will be not to see each other as often, it's also important for you to get your degree. We'll work it out, don't worry."

She lifted her gaze to his, giving a slight shake of her head. "You don't understand. Listen to me, Ian, please?" At his assent she continued. "I was looking at the university's website the other day, mostly doing some more research on courses, when I realized they have an entire online program. All of the classes I'd need to get my degree are offered via distance learning. I'd still have to go to the campus in person for mid-terms and finals and for a couple of meetings, but that's it. So I could still travel with you while getting my degree. What – what do you think?"

A slow smile crossed his features. "I think you're a very sweet and generous girl to be willing to do something like that for me – correction, for us. But, darling, part of the whole college experience involves being on campus, sitting in lecture halls, making friends. You'd miss out on all that if you chose this other option."

"I don't care about that stuff," she declared firmly. "I mean, let's face it. It's not like I'm eighteen years old and fresh out of high school any longer. Most of the students will be anywhere from five to seven years younger than I am. Plus, it's still hard for me to talk to people and make friends most of the time."

Ian cupped her cheek in his palm. "I don't want you choosing this other option because of me. I want what's best for you, Tessa."

She turned her face into his palm and pressed a kiss there. Her blue eyes were filled with tenderness. "This *is* best for me. For us. We can still be together this way, Ian, it's the perfect solution." She rose up on her knees, slipping her arms around his neck as she gazed down at him. "You told me on the night of our very first date that there wasn't anything you wouldn't do for me. Well, I'm telling you now it's the same for me. There is nothing – absolutely *nothing* – I wouldn't do for you. And if that means taking my classes online rather than in person so that we don't have to be separated – my darling Ian, that's the easiest decision I'll ever have to make in my life."

He was speechless at her impassioned words, the way she was looking at him with so much love. He stared at her for long seconds, scarcely daring to breathe because his heart was brimming over with so much love, so much desire, and so much need. He was powerfully, immensely aroused, to know that this gorgeous, giving, loving woman was his, and that she had just sworn steadfast devotion to him.

His hands were trembling as they moved to the sash of her cotton robe, the gaping ruffled neckline giving him a generous glimpse of her cleavage. He needed her naked right now, needed to bury himself inside of her as deeply as he could get, to mark her as his in the most primitive way possible.

"Take this off."

At his hoarsely muttered words, her eyes grew big and round, her mouth parting in a lush "O". But she was quick to do his bidding, untying the robe and pushing it off her shoulders to bare her ripe, glowing body to his devouring gaze.

His hands slid up her arms and into her hair, tilting her head back as his gaze bored into hers. "I need to take you, Tessa. Just – let me, all right? I won't hurt you but I can't be gentle right now either."

She gave a quick nod and he groaned, even as he stripped off his T-shirt and pajama bottoms. She gasped at the sight of his immensely swollen erection and reached out to touch him, only to have his fingers clamp down around her wrist.

"No. Like this. I need you like this."

He flipped her onto her stomach, spreading her thighs apart. He stretched both of her arms above her head, placing her hands on the arm of the sofa.

"Hold on to that tight. Don't let go," he ordered.

"O-okay," was all she seemed capable of saying in response.

Then, with one dominant surge, he mounted her and drove deep inside her tight, clenching pussy. The cry of surrender that escaped Tessa's throat was one of the most erotic sounds he'd ever heard, and he groaned as he took her hard, his chest flush against her back. This was what he'd needed to do so desperately after she'd so sweetly declared her devotion to him – to fuck her hard, to brand her with his possession, with intense and utter domination. She was the only woman in his entire life that he'd ever felt this way about, the only one in his forty years of living that he'd ever wanted to claim.

Tessa was mewling against the sofa cushions, clutching the arm rest for dear life, as he continued to pound into her with hard, powerful strokes. He worked a hand between their co-joined bodies and found her clit, hearing her gasp as he rubbed the hard little nub.

He was too far gone, too consumed with lust and need and love to care if he was crushing her or not, his body so much heavier and muscular than hers. But if he was hurting her she gave no indication, didn't try to resist his domination of her body. She whimpered when he sucked hard on the back of her neck, marking her with his love bite, and the blood roared in his ears at the little sounds she made.

Feeling himself drawing ever closer to release, he reared back onto his knees and pulled her up with him, his chest pressed against her back. Tessa's head fell back limply onto his shoulder as she gasped for breath, and then she was panting as his fingers plucked at her engorged nipple while the other hand stimulated her clit, all while he continued to fuck her with barely controlled force.

Her orgasm shook her whole body, and she would have collapsed onto the sofa if he hadn't banded an arm around her waist to hold her in place. Ian shouted incoherent, raw words of pleasure as he followed her over the edge, continuing to pump into her body long after he was empty. When he could breathe again – though not necessarily think – he folded her into his arms, dragging her onto his lap.

Tessa spoke first, her voice whisper soft. "I assume since you own this hotel that the staff will overlook the big wet stain we're leaving on this sofa."

His shoulders shook with mirth. "Let's put it this way, love. Not a one of them would have the nerve to bring the subject up."

She smiled, and tenderly brushed damp strands of hair back off his face. "I love it when you're in boss man mode. How everyone snaps to attention and bends over backwards to please you." She nibbled on his earlobe. "And I especially love it when you're the boss in our bed."

He chuckled, pulling her astride his lap and squeezing the firm cheeks of her ass. "And I love how you, uh, just bent over backwards for me."

Tessa gasped in mock outrage, giving him a little shove. "As I recall, I wasn't exactly given a choice in the matter."

"No, you weren't." Ian sobered, tracing his thumb over her lips. "I didn't hurt you, did I?"

She shook her head. "No, you could never hurt me, Ian. Though it might be a little difficult to walk a straight line today."

"I'll hold you up, darling," he murmured, pulling her head down to his for a long, lingering kiss. "Though a hot bath might help both of us. I'm a bit shaky myself."

"Not surprising, considering how you were pretty much in barbarian mode a little while ago," she teased. "I never imagined when I told you I was going to do online classes that you'd be quite so, ah, thrilled."

"It wasn't just that and you know it." He brushed a soft kiss on her lips. "It was what you told me about doing absolutely anything for me. That just – touched something in me, made me go a little crazy with needing you. All I knew at that moment was that I had to own you completely, be just as raw and honest as you had been with me."

Tessa touched her forehead to his. "I love you, Ian. And I meant every single word."

"My sweet, darling girl. You are the love of my life. Now, let's see about that bath and then breakfast, hmm? After all, we have a wedding to attend."

***

Julia looked breathtakingly beautiful, Nathan incredibly handsome, and their wedding was rather like a fairytale. At least it seemed that way to Tessa, who had never actually attended a wedding before. She and Peter had married in a brief, rather clinical ceremony at City Hall, and the extent of their celebration had consisted of eating dinner at the Olive Garden. She had seen a lot of lavish weddings being set up when she'd worked at the Tucson resort, but had never actually attended any of them, of course.

Tessa had gotten a little misty eyed while her friends were exchanging their heartfelt vows, and she smiled gratefully at Ian when he took her hand.

"It's so romantic, isn't it?" she whispered.

In reply, he merely pressed a kiss to her temple and squeezed her hand a little tighter.

The words he had spoken to her last month during his parents' visit suddenly came back to tease her – what he'd said about her being his wife one day. He hadn't mentioned anything further about marriage since that evening, and she hadn't permitted herself to think about it too much. But now, in this exquisitely romantic garden setting, with a string quartet playing, flowers everywhere, and two starry eyed lovers pledging themselves to each other, it was easy to imagine her own potential nuptials one day. At the same time, though, the idea made her a little sad, because unlike Julia she had no doting father to give her away, no proud mother watching teary eyed from the front row of seats, and no devoted sister to stand as her maid of honor. If Ian did in fact marry her someday, it would really only be his family and friends in attendance, and it occurred to Tessa for the first time since moving in with him just how alone she would be without him.

Impatiently, she forced her maudlin thoughts aside just as the minister was pronouncing Nathan and Julia to be husband and wife. With something of a twinkle in his eye, the white haired officiate nodded at the rather impatient groom.

"Well, go ahead, Nathan, it's finally time. You may kiss the bride."

Tessa joined in the applause as a grinning Nathan wasted no time in sweeping Julia into his arms and kissing her soundly, not seeming to notice that two hundred other people – including her father and uncle – were watching them intently. Somewhere to her left Tessa heard loud whoops and cat calls, as well as several suggestive comments being shouted out.

Ian murmured in her ear, clearly amused. "The, ah, cheering section there would be Nathan's old college mates that I told you about."

"The ones from the bachelor party?" At Ian's nod, Tessa glanced over at the group of a dozen or so noisy thirty-somethings in concern. "Oh, God, I hope they don't ruin Julia's wedding! From what she's told me – and what you saw firsthand - they can get a little rowdy."

Ian arched a brow. "A little rowdy? Darling, a rugby match is a little rowdy. Nathan's chums over there take rowdy to whole new levels. Think *Animal House* on steroids."

Tessa suppressed a giggle, especially when the string quartet started to play a rousing version of the Beatles' *All You Need is Love* as the recessional. She'd heard all about the drunken bachelor party – where Ian had drolly told her he'd been not only the oldest but the most sober of the attendees. It had taken place the same night as Julia's only slightly less wild bachelorette party, to which Tessa had been invited.

Fortunately, Nathan's friends quieted down long enough for him to walk down the aisle with his beaming bride on his arm, the two of them waving and smiling to as many guests as they could. When Julia saw Tessa and Ian she blew them a kiss before continuing down the white carpet to the back of the outdoor chapel.

"She looks so beautiful," sighed Tessa. "And so happy."

Ian slid his arm around her waist, guiding her out of their row of chairs as other guests began to leave the chapel. "They deserve it, darling. Like with us, it took a little time for the stars to align properly so they could be together. Now, come, the festivities are beginning."

He steered her over to the expansive patio area where champagne and hors d'oeuvres were being passed around. All of the wait staff seemed to know exactly who Ian was, treating him with extreme deference and care. At various times during the cocktail reception, the hotel manager, catering manager and head bartender all came over to shake his hand and inquire if all was well, as though he were the groom or the father of the bride instead of merely a guest. As always, Ian was graciousness personified, greeting them by name and asking about their families. It never ceased to amaze Tessa at how much respect he commanded and how eagerly all his employees rushed to please him. He was, she though fondly, like a well-loved king among his subjects.

And the two of them seemed to be drawing almost as much attention as the bride and groom. Tessa thought with a little smile that they did make rather a striking couple, both tall and impeccably dressed. With Joanna's help, she'd chosen a gorgeous pink silk pleated dress with an off-the-shoulder neckline. With it she wore killer pale pink satin Jimmy Choo sandals that had a satin bow attached to the ankle strap, plus the triple strand pearl necklace and dainty pearl stud earrings that Ian had given her months ago. He had chosen a complementing Armani suit in a pale silver gray, paired with a pearl gray shirt and a silk tie patterned in varying shades of gray and mauve. Tessa hadn't missed all the admiring female glances directed his way, and she made sure she stuck to his side like glue.

Julia and Nathan were doing their best to circulate among all their guests, stopping to greet as many people as possible. When they eventually reached Tessa and Ian, Julia pulled her down into a fierce little hug.

"Oh, you look so pretty, Tessa! God, just look at the pair of you together. Like two movie stars or European royalty," sighed Julia.

Ian grinned and bent to kiss her cheek. "Ah, but the bride is supposed to be the center of attention on her wedding day. And as lovely as my girl here looks, I think she'd agree that you are the most beautiful woman here today. Congratulations, Mrs. Atwood."

Nathan was beaming as he shook Ian's hand and then kissed Tessa's cheek. "I told you on your birthday, Ian. We're the two luckiest bastards I know. And with the two most beautiful woman in the world."

"Hey, I heard that, Nathan. And since Jules and I are identical twins, I'll take that as a compliment."

Nathan rolled his eyes as his very outspoken sister-in-law Lauren sidled up alongside Julia, slipping an arm about her twin's waist. Tessa had only met the very formidable Lauren once – at the bachelorette party that Lauren herself had organized – and she confessed to being more than a little intimidated by her. Julia's sister was utterly fearless, extremely outspoken, and could put away an astonishing number of tequila shots. She seemed sassier than ever today, though she looked far softer and more feminine in her mint green floral print bridesmaid dress.

Nathan gave his sister-in-law a good natured jab in the ribs. "Okay, the three most beautiful women in the world. You've met Tessa, haven't you?"

"I have. Tried like hell to get her drunk but I think her man here gave her strict orders to behave. Good to see you again, sweetie." Lauren turned and winked at Ian. "Hey, handsome. I'd ask how you were doing but I can see that for myself. You two look like Ken and Barbie."

Ian grinned and gave Lauren a peck on the cheek. "Lovely to see you as always, Lauren. Break any hearts lately? Or noses, for that matter?"

Lauren glared at him darkly. "I should have never told you that story. And I didn't break the little crybaby's nose, just made it bleed a little. On accident." She gave Tessa a sheepish look. "Blind date gone bad. Really bad. Ask Ian to tell you the story sometime, he thought it was hilarious."

As the call came to sit down for dinner, Tessa gave Ian an inquiring look. "I didn't realize you'd met Lauren before."

He nodded as he ushered her to their assigned table. "Once, last fall. It was at a dinner party Julia and Nathan were giving. I was lonely, and rather miserable since I was still pining away for a woman I couldn't have – namely you. I thought meeting Julia's sister might prove something of a distraction." He shook his head. "I'm not certain there's a man alive capable of taming that girl. She was definitely too much for me to even consider handling. And as beautiful as she is, she still wasn't you."

Tessa clutched his arm a little tighter. "Sometimes I wish I'd known sooner how you felt about me. I don't know how that might have changed things but - "

He shook his head. "It wouldn't have. I know you too well, Tessa, and the fact that I was attracted to you would not have compelled you to leave your husband. The way we finally got together – it had to happen that way, love. You had to end things with Peter first, and for the right reasons. As much as I wanted you, I would never have broken up your marriage."

"I know. And you're right, of course. Still - "

"Shh. We're together now and that's all that matters. Ah, here's our table."

They had been seated with several of Julia's and Nathan's co-workers – the co-owner of the firm, Travis Headley, and his partner Anton Nguyen; Nathan's PA Robyn Reynolds and her husband Dan; and Jake Harriman, the associate architect working on the new Gregson resort in Napa, accompanied by his date Abby.

During the multi-course wedding meal, Tessa learned that Travis had been the interior designer responsible for decorating Ian's home; that Anton also worked as a personal shopper at Neiman Marcus – albeit in the men's department – and that Marlene Brennan was a mentor of his; and that Robyn had originally worked with Nathan and Travis at a different architectural design firm before – as she fondly recalled – "the boys decided to spin off on their own and practically shanghaied me into going with them."

It was, all in all, a beautiful wedding with wonderful food and wine, pleasant company, and a magnificent setting. Tessa took a sip of her wine and gazed admiringly around the trellised patio.

"This is so beautiful," she told Ian. "I think this might be my favorite of all the hotels I've seen so far. Not that I've been to all that many, of course."

He nodded in agreement. "It's one of my favorites, too, and one of our most popular. Especially for weddings. But," he added mysteriously, "I have an even grander venue in mind for the day I finally make you my wife. And before you ask, darling, that bit of information is going to remain a closely guarded secret. Let's just say it will be another first."

Once the lavish meal had been cleared away, the dancing began. Tessa and Ian watched along with all the other guests as the bride and groom shared a tender first dance before changing partners multiple times to dance with parents, siblings, and the members of the wedding party. As soon as the rest of the guests were invited to join in, Ian tugged Tessa to her feet, and smoothly drew her onto the dance floor.

She went into his arms with a little sigh, resting her cheek on his shoulder, and smiled when she recognized the song.

"This is what was playing when we danced for the first time in Lake Tahoe," she told him as he guided her around the dance floor to *If I Ain't Got You.*

"I remember. Very, very well," he replied with a warm glow in his hazel eyes. "And it's true, you know, what the lyrics say – if I can't have you, Tessa, then nothing else in this whole world means a thing."

She touched his cheek, which was already starting to show signs of a five o'clock shadow. "Same here. I told your mother that sometimes I wish you didn't have all this money, that you were a truck driver or something like that, and that we lived on a little houseboat somewhere. Just so that you'd know you were the only thing that mattered to me."

He pressed a kiss to her palm and smiled. "I do know, darling. You show me that every day in more ways than you realize. As for driving a truck – I much prefer the Jaguar, thank you very much. And the houseboat – I have to confess to an occasional bout of seasickness so I'm afraid we'll have to stay on land."

She laughed along with him as the song finished, and then Ian went to claim a dance with Julia while Tessa and Nathan paired up.

Tessa couldn't recall a time when she'd enjoyed herself more – laughing with all the other guests when Nathan "accidentally" smeared cake frosting all over Julia's mouth, and then egging him on as he slowly licked it all off; watching Lauren start up a raucous conga line that was quickly joined by most of Nathan's drunk friends; and then listening dreamily to Julia's father Robert serenade his daughter with a touching rendition of *Sunrise Sunset*.

Then it was time for Julia to toss her bouquet, and at Ian's prodding Tessa joined the other single women on the floor, giggling the whole time. Save for Angela, Tessa was taller than most of the other women present and thus had a better than even shot at catching it. She actually had a hand on the gorgeous bouquet of pink and cream roses, was convinced she could snatch it up, when it tumbled instead into the hands of Lauren McKinnon.

Julia's sister stared at the bouquet with a horrified expression, as though she were clutching an angry badger instead of some beautiful flowers. Julia was squealing in delight as she realized her twin was the lucky girl, while Lauren could only murmur in stunned disbelief, "How in the hell did that happen?"

Chapter Twenty Three

July

"Okay, maybe this is my new favorite hotel. It's at least in the top five. No, make that top three. And I do understand why they call this place paradise."

Tessa stretched luxuriously as she reclined in the padded chaise lounge. The warm Hawaiian sun beat down on her bikini-clad body, and she closed her eyes in bliss.

Ian chuckled. "It will be interesting to see how your pecking order changes as you see more of our properties. But you will be hard pressed to find too many places in the world as beautiful as these islands."

They had flown to Hawaii a week ago, traveling first to the resorts on Oahu, Kona and Kauai. Ian had performed his usual inspection of the properties, held meetings and reviews with the managers and staffs, and tended to all the other matters that required his attention during visits like these. They had arrived here in Maui two days ago, and tomorrow nearly every hotel manager in the Americas Region would be arriving for a four day meeting.

The managers meeting was an annual event, and held at a different property each year. While this was obviously the first one Tessa would be in attendance at, she'd been involved the past two years with all the preparations – compiling reports, printing up name badges, coordinating with the hotel staff to ensure all the necessary A/V equipment was ready, etc. The entire management support team had been heavily involved with the preparation for what was arguably one of the most important events of the year. Andrew always attended the meeting, needing to be on hand to ensure everything ran smoothly, and he had in the past taken one of the support team along to help out. Tessa recalled listening to both Gina and Alicia rave about the trip, how luxurious everything had been, what a fabulous time they'd had. Tessa hadn't been able to help being more than a little envious, and had wondered wistfully at the time if she would ever get a turn.

She thought idly how much could change in a year's time. Twelve months ago she'd still been married to Peter, clinging desperately to save a marriage that had really been over with for a long time. She'd been working for a boss who she admired and secretly crushed on from afar, but had never dreamed he'd even noticed her. Now, a year later, she was divorced, Peter was living halfway around the world, and her boss was now her lover, the man she idolized and longed to be with every minute of every day.

Ian's phone rang and he scowled at it before reluctantly checking the screen. His phone seemed to have been ringing off the hook these past few days, and she knew he must be growing weary of all the calls.

"Damn it, I've got to take this unfortunately," he told her. "It shouldn't be long."

She waved her fingers at him. "It's okay. I'm not planning on moving from this spot for a good long while."

He squeezed her shoulder as he answered the call, walking to the edge of their private patio as he did so. From behind the lenses of her oversized sunglasses, Tessa smiled in satisfaction at the truly awe inspiring sight of him clad in just a pair of swim trunks. His heavily muscled upper body was bared to her admiring gaze, and she noted with interest at how deeply tanned his skin had become in just a few days. She loved the raw, primitive beauty of his ripped biceps, broad chest and huge shoulders. She liked that he wasn't overly hairy, just a wide strip of hair down the middle of his chest that tapered down past his waist and disappeared beneath his dark blue swim trunks. Tessa continued her unabashed inspection of his body, lusting at the sight of his long, muscular legs and taut buttocks. He was unshaven today, giving him that dark and dangerous look she loved, and his hazel eyes were covered by a pair of aviator sunglasses.

Beneath her red bandeau bikini top, her nipples peaked and her breasts felt achy as she continued to watch him. It had been over a week since they'd had sex, due to another of her heavy, painful periods. That hadn't prevented them from enjoying each other in alternate ways, though the pleasure had been largely on Ian's side. Despite his half-hearted protests that he could wait until she was over her cycle, in the end he hadn't resisted when she'd taken him into her mouth, or stroked him with her hands, or guided his fully erect cock between her breasts. She had done the latter just last night, and could still picture the look on his face as he'd come all over her breasts, the thick streams of semen marking her in a different way as she'd rubbed his essence into her skin. He had groaned as he'd watched her, taking her mouth in a soul-stealing kiss, and then whispered to her urgently that he'd been keeping very careful tally all week of how many orgasms he owed her.

Tessa smiled as she recalled those heated words, and squirmed a bit as she realized how aroused she was. Her period had finally ended this morning, to her great relief, and she'd been this close to waking him up to give him the good news. But he'd been in a deep slumber, worn out from the demands of the last few days, and she'd let him continue sleeping while she took an early yoga class at the resort's health club. But as stimulated as she was becoming now, she was beginning to regret her earlier decision.

As Ian's phone conversation continued, she flipped onto her stomach, hoping that her arousal might ebb if she stopped watching him for a while. It didn't take long at all for her to become pleasantly drowsy, loving the feel of the warm sun heating her skin while at the same time one of Hawaii's famous tradewinds kept the temperature from feeling too unbearably hot.

Like almost all of the other owner's suites she'd stayed in with Ian, this one was opulent and spacious, though decorated in a slightly more casual island motif. The real attraction of this particular suite, though, was its expansive outdoor space – the huge, partially covered patio, sunken hot tub and large private pool. The beach was mere steps away, and each night the sound of the surf had lulled her to sleep.

She felt a little guilty lazing the afternoon away, but consoled herself with the fact that she had certainly earned her keep these past few days and would be working even harder once the managers meeting commenced. Andrew had flown in late yesterday afternoon, and had eaten dinner with her and Ian last night. But even during dinner, Andrew had been all business, discussing all the things that still had to get done for the meeting, and Tessa had longed to tell him to chill out and just relax for once. Truthfully, though, she was still more than a little intimidated by him, even if she no longer officially worked for the company, and had kept her mouth shut.

Employee or not, Andrew hadn't hesitated in bossing her around this morning, assigning her tasks just as he'd done for over two years. But Tessa hadn't minded, for she liked to keep busy and feel useful, and was relieved that Andrew hadn't gone soft on her just because she was the boss' girlfriend. He had looked a little taken aback when she'd somewhat teasingly told him just that during dinner last night.

"You're a bright girl, Tessa," he'd told her. "I would never dream of insulting your intelligence by treating you like some brainless bimbo. No offense, Mr. Gregson. I know better than anyone that you'd never be interested in a – uh - "

"Brainless bimbo?" finished Ian with an arched brow. "Yes, I appreciate your unwavering faith in me, Andrew. And you're right – Tessa is exceptionally bright and you should continue to make use of her skills in whatever way you see fit."

Andrew had grimaced. "Well, I certainly miss her at the office, especially since both hers and Alicia's replacements have proven something of a disappointment so far. I think I might be losing my touch after all this time."

Tessa hadn't been able to suppress a grin at his last statement. "Keep that up and pretty soon Shelby will be one of your top team members."

Andrew had looked a little sheepish. "Actually, she's flying over tomorrow to help out this year."

Tessa had very nearly spewed out the mouthful of water she'd just sipped, and Ian had had to pat her vigorously on the back.

With watery eyes, she'd gaped at Andrew in disbelief. "Shelby? The same Shelby you used to grouse about not having more than three functioning brain cells?"

Andrew had nodded reluctantly. "Believe it or not, she's stepped up her game these past few months. When Alicia, ahem, left, Shelby volunteered to take over doing the travel arrangements. It turns out her aunt owns a travel agency and Shelby worked there part time during high school and college – who knew? And she's actually done a decent job. I think – well, it seems that Alicia wasn't very nice to Shelby over the years – would make fun of her and outright insult her on a regular basis. Since she's left, Shelby seems happier and has more confidence."

Tessa had grinned at her former supervisor. "So she doesn't quake in her boots whenever you walk by?"

"I didn't say that," Andrew had replied dryly. "After all, I still have my reputation as a stick-up-his-ass bastard to maintain." At Tessa's expression of disbelief, he'd given her a scathing look. "You think I didn't know? I know everything that goes on in that office, eyes in the back of my head and all that."

Ian had nodded in agreement. "Can't argue with that assessment. He knows far more than I do about what goes on."

Andrew, who'd consumed a pre-dinner Mai Tai and several glasses of wine during the meal, had evidently been feeling bold as he'd smirked at his boss. "Well, I did learn from the very best, sir. Watching how you observed people without them being aware of it taught me a great deal. In fact, I was even able to turn the tables on you and use those exact same tactics."

Ian had regarded his PA warily. "And what precisely does that mean?"

Andrew, who never smiled, had – wonder of wonders – actually given Ian a cheeky grin. "I knew the moment Tessa walked into your office that first day that you fell for her like a ton of bricks. No offense, sir, but you were a real open book that day."

It had been Tessa's turn to frown. "Well, I never noticed a thing. Of course, that's probably because you'd already made me a nervous wreck about meeting him – all of your rules and instructions about what I could and couldn't say. How did you know? I mean, Ian seemed as in control and professional that day as he always does."

Andrew had shaken his head. "Oh, he didn't give anything away when he met you. It was right after – when he called me back into his office to rip me a new one that he gave himself away. I'd worked for you three years already, sir, and had never once seen you actually pacing or using any form of sarcasm and there you were doing both at the same time. But the real giveaway was when I told you Tessa was married. You looked like the floor had given way beneath you."

Ian had nodded at his PA's observations. "You're spot on, as usual. Especially about the latter issue. I'd never in my life felt helpless before, never been in a situation where I couldn't make something happen if I tried hard enough." He'd turned to Tessa at that point, taking her hand in his. "When I learned you already belonged to another man – that I'd have to keep what I felt for you under strict wraps – I swear that was the hardest thing I've ever had to do in my life."

When he and Tessa had continued to hold hands and stare dreamily into each other's eyes, Andrew had cleared his throat until they had somewhat guiltily broken apart.

Andrew had seemed more than a bit hesitant to broach the next subject, a fact that had surprised Tessa since he never seemed uncertain about anything. But once he'd uttered that name, a sudden chill had traveled up her spine, despite the tropical climate, and Ian had scowled in annoyance.

"I hate to bring up such an unpleasant topic, Mr. Gregson, but both you and Tessa need to be aware that Jason Baldwin will be attending the meeting. Along with his wife – your cousin – of course."

Tessa had glanced at Ian anxiously. "He wouldn't do – or say – anything with your cousin along, would he?"

"He'd better not, if he knows what's good for him," Ian had muttered darkly. "I haven't spoken to the bastard since I kicked him out of my office last fall. But gossip travels quickly, and between co-workers and our family I'm certain Jason has heard that Tessa and I are together."

Tessa had shuddered. "All I know is that he gives me the creeps more than anyone I've ever met. How does your cousin put up with his – er, antics?"

Ian had shrugged. "Charlotte is a sweet, lovely woman but not especially bright. My aunt and uncle also coddled her well into adulthood, and she's used to getting whatever she wants. And when she met Jason, she decided he was exactly what she wanted. I'm afraid she deliberately turns a blind eye to his antics so that she doesn't have to admit to her parents – or to herself – that they were right about him."

"So your aunt and uncle don't like Jason?"

"That's putting it mildly. Unlike Charlotte, Uncle Richard is a very wise man and he saw through Jason from the very first. But, as I mentioned, once Charlotte made up her mind she wanted something, her parents had a very difficult time ever saying no."

"What I never quite understood, sir," Andrew had interjected, "was why Jason wound up working for you. I would have assumed he and your cousin met and married in England."

A look of disgust had crossed Ian's features. "They did. But after three complaints about the bastard from female employees, Richard thought a change of scenery would do him good. So he sent him my way."

"You know there have been a couple of close calls with him down in Scotts Valley, don't you?" Andrew had asked soberly. "One was a hotel guest who called our head of HR to complain that Jason made some very suggestive comments to her. And one of the office staff confided to the night manager that Jason has been getting a bit too touchy feely for her liking."

Ian had shook his head. "Well, apparently this leopard hasn't changed his spots, has he? Looks like I'll have to pay him a visit when we return home. In the meanwhile," he added sternly, "that little shit is not to get anywhere near Tessa over the next few days. I don't want her left alone where he might be able to harass her."

She'd patted his hand and tried to smile reassuringly. "Hey, I can take care of myself. You've been showing me some moves, after all."

Ian had been working with her at the gym to learn a few basic boxing techniques, and she also continued to take some kickboxing classes. He'd also arranged for her to work out with a personal trainer – a female one, of course – and she knew she was in the best physical shape of her life right now.

Ian had smiled at her rather indulgently. "And you've been a very apt pupil. But I still don't want you having to confront Jason. The safest solution is just to keep you as far away from him as possible."

Tessa couldn't help the tiny shudder that rippled through her body as she thought of having to see Jason again. And there was no doubt she would have to at least acknowledge him. Tomorrow evening a lavish cocktail reception and buffet dinner had been planned for all the managers and their guests, and it went without saying that Ian's cousin Charlotte would seek him out to say hello. There would be no polite way to avoid her for the entire duration of the meeting.

She must have dozed off a little, drowsy from the sun, and gave a little start when she felt Ian's lips on the back of her neck.

"Mmm. Hi,' she murmured, scooting over a bit as he sat down on the chaise next to her.

He ran his hand down her back, and she shivered as he slipped his palm beneath the band of her bikini bottoms to cup her buttocks. "Hi yourself, gorgeous girl," he whispered, his warm breath tickling her ear. "You should have been a swimsuit model as good as you look in this bikini. I can just see you splashed on the cover of *Sports Illustrated* with these beautiful long legs" – he traced his fingertips down the backs of her thighs – "and this sexy ass" – he squeezed her behind – "and of course these fabulous tits." He slipped a hand beneath her and squeezed her breast.

Tessa groaned and clasped his hand, holding it in place against her breast. "Don't stop. It feels so good."

His fingers found her nipple and tweaked it. "Your wish is my command, love. Are you still on your cycle?"

She shook her head. "No, thank goodness. It's, ah, been a long time."

He chuckled, his hand slipping inside her low-cut bikini top to cup her bare, warm flesh. "Are you horny, darling?"

"God, yes," she panted, trying to roll over onto her back. But his hand on her back held her in place, unable to move freely.

"Shh. I'm going to take very good care of you very soon, love. But first, you're starting to get a little pink back here. You need some more sunscreen. Ah, there it is."

Tessa gave a little squeal as he squirted the cool lotion on her sun-warmed skin, but then quickly began to purr in contentment as he rubbed it into her back and shoulder blades. As his hand dipped beneath the waistband of her bikini briefs, she gave a little wiggle, which earned her both a deep chuckle from Ian and a playful swat on the butt.

He squirted another blob of lotion on her back before deftly unhooking the bandeau top, letting the sides fall unheeded onto the chaise. He rubbed the lotion into her skin before sliding his hands beneath her to cup her breasts.

Tessa whimpered with need. "Please."

He knew what she was pleading for as he pulled her to an upright position, her knees hanging over the side of the chaise. He knelt between her thighs, his dark head at eye level with her chest.

"I take it back," he murmured hoarsely, his hands fondling her breasts. "There's no way in hell I'd want a photo of this sexy body of yours being splayed all over a national magazine, letting every horny bastard in the country ogle you. " He bent his head and licked at her nipple. "For my eyes only, darling."

"Ohh, yes," she breathed, clutching his head to her breast as he sucked her nipple into his mouth.

He lifted his head, then moved to the other breast while his thumb and forefinger pinched the other nipple. "Is this what you wanted, love? What you needed? God, your tits are so full right now, Tessa, so swollen. Let me, darling."

She was groaning as he lavished attention on her breasts, arousing her to the point where she knew it would take very little to make her come. She grabbed one of his hands and dragged it down to the low-cut waistband of her bikini briefs. "Ian. Now, please."

He took her mouth in a blistering kiss as his fingers slipped inside her briefs to find her clit. She came instantly, her body already primed for his touch and starving for release.

Tessa hadn't even come back down to earth yet when Ian laid her back on the chaise and stripped off her briefs. His lips touched her navel as he slowly thrust two fingers deep inside of her body.

"You're so ready for me," he murmured in awe. "You are needy, aren't you, darling?"

"God." Her hips bucked up off the chaise as he continued sliding his fingers in and out of her drenched slit. "I – oh – wanted you. You looked so – ah, yes, just like that – so hot standing there. So gorgeous. I need - "

He bent his head, his tongue fluttering over her clit. "What do you need, love?"

She cried out as his tongue licked at the moist folds of her labia. "I need to be fucked. Hard. Over and over until I can't take anymore. And even then I'll keep wanting more."

"Jesus, Tessa." His hands held her hips pinned to the chaise as he continued to eat her out with exquisite care. "Soon, darling. Soon I'll slide my cock inside this hot, delicious cunt and fuck you until neither of us can think straight. But first." He sucked hard on her clit, wringing another orgasm from her highly stimulated body.

When she could speak again, she clutched his shoulders, trying in vain to budge him, to pull his body to hers. "Do it now. Please."

"Not yet." His hand slid into the damp curls between her thighs, and he gave her a smile that was deeply carnal. "By my estimates, I owe you at least five more orgasms. I think I counted a total of seven that you very unselfishly gave me when you were – ah, indisposed."

She laughed huskily, placing her hand over his and stilling its motion. "Hmm, I think your count is off. I distinctly remember it was a grand total of eight."

"Eight it is then, love. After all, you're very good with numbers, aren't you?"

Tessa gave a sigh of utter bliss as he slipped three long fingers inside of her. "And you're really, really good at this. An expert, actually. But as awesome as this feels, it's you I want. I've missed you. Missed this."

He cursed softly as her hand traced the outline of his erection where it tented his swim trunks. "Don't, Tessa. Not now. Let me take care of you first."

"No." Her reply was insistent, her hand deliberate in its movements as she continued to stroke him. "No keeping score, that's just silly. I want *you*, Ian. I want *this*."

He hissed as she gave his cock a firm squeeze. Then, in one smooth motion, he scooped her up into his arms and carried her back inside the suite until they reached the master bedroom. Always a man of purpose, he didn't disappoint as in quick succession he tore back the bedcovers, deposited her on the mattress, tossed off his swim trunks, and vaulted onto the bed. In the very next instant he was surging as deeply and fully inside of her as he could get, and her head fell back against the pillows in ecstasy.

"So good," she breathed as he began to stroke the long, thick length of his cock in and out of her body. Her legs lifted to wrap around his hips, her arms about his neck as she pulled his head down to hers for a kiss.

Ian groaned. "It's fucking heaven to be inside of you again, love. The absolute best feeling in the world."

"Yes, yes," she cried, as he began to move faster, more forcefully. He unhooked her legs from around his waist and spread them wide, bending her knees up towards her shoulders. He rose to his knees, the position allowing him to thrust even more deeply inside of her. With each hard thrust, it felt like the head of his penis was butting up against her womb, and she whimpered with that particular sensation of half pain, half pleasure that he was such a master at calling forth from her body.

Her body already primed from the two orgasms he'd given her, Tessa came long and hard this time with his cock constantly rubbing against that super sensitive spot deep inside her. She was dimly aware of the tears that dampened her cheeks, the depth of emotion he was able to wring out of her almost too much to take at times like this. And when she stopped seeing stars after a time, she realize that he hadn't come yet, that he was still moving inside of her pliant body with slow, deliberate thrusts.

"Why are you holding back?" she whispered.

He groaned, his head falling back as she trailed her fingers up his chest where his skin was drenched with sweat. "Feels so good, love. I don't want this to end. I missed this, too."

Tessa gasped as he deftly switched their positions, pulling her on top of him while he reclined against the pillows, their sweat-slicked bodies remaining co-joined the entire time. Ian's hands gripped her hips as she found the rhythm he wanted.

His thumb brushed over the swollen nub of her clit. "Want to make you come again," he rasped. "Over and over, until we both lose count."

"No." She shook her head, the last remaining strands of her hair still contained in a messy bun tumbling down her back. "Don't hold back. Please. I need you wild, want to see you lose control. Like this."

She ignored his attempts to slow her down as she began to buck frantically back and forth, riding him hard. She leaned forward until her breasts brushed his chest, her nipples raking over his hot skin. He gasped as she ran her tongue over his mouth, her teeth tugging on his lower lip.

And then, before he could stop her, she slipped a hand to where their bodies were joined and began to gently stimulate his prostate gland, in the exact way she knew would drive him over the edge.

He came instantly, cursing loudly as his back bowed off the mattress again and again, and she could feel the hot, sticky bursts of his cum flooding her pussy. Almost violently, Ian pulled her head down to his, kissing her savagely as he continued to empty himself into her warm, tight body.

Tessa collapsed on his chest when he was finally replete, his arms and legs splayed out limply. She could feel the rapid thud of his heartbeat beneath her cheek and caressed his arms soothingly.

When he was able to speak, his voice was hoarse and his

words came out slowly. "The next time you use that little trick, give me some warning, eh? One of these times I might not survive the experience."

She laughed softly, sliding off his body to curl up trustingly against his side. "Maybe instead of that oxygen tank you mentioned we ought to keep a defibrillator handy. Or," she added teasingly, dropping a series of quick, sweet kisses on his mouth, "I could just learn mouth to mouth resuscitation."

His chest rumbled with laughter. "I think all three are excellent precautions." One big hand slid down her spine to cup her ass. "But I hope you realize that this only adds to the total number of orgasms I still owe you."

"What?" She gave him a puzzled little frown.

Ian grinned wickedly. "Well, considering this last one was really like five regular orgasms combined, by my totals I now owe you at least ten."

She shook her head. "Impossible. Because according to my much more accurate calculations, it's an even dozen."

"Well, then," he murmured in amusement as his lips began to trail down between her breasts to her belly. "I'd better get busy, don't you agree?"

Tessa's laughs soon turned to moans as his head disappeared between her thighs. "I, ah, think that's an excellent idea."

**

Jason Baldwin was not a happy man these days, and hadn't been for quite some time now. He hated – positively *hated* – his current job as the manager of the hotel in Silicon Valley. In addition to the nerve-wracking, time consuming commute he had to endure in both directions of the drive, he considered the position far beneath what should have been his far more elevated status in the company. Plus, he had little patience when it came to dealing with hotel guests – smoothing over complaints or problems someone had if they didn't care for their particular room; schmoozing with high-profile guests and clients and pandering to their already oversized egos; handling the various personnel problems that cropped up far too often for his liking;

and having to answer on a regular basis to the regional office on one matter or another – and to a manager who had up until recently been a subordinate of his.

And his miserable situation at work wasn't helped even one bit by Charlotte's almost constant whining as of late. She seemed to be checking up on him far more than she ever had in the past – frequent phone calls and texts, wanting to know exactly what time he'd be home from the office; packing their weekends full of events and activities so that he rarely had a free moment to himself.

Their three children were all of school age now, and more than a handful, especially their youngest, Aidan, who was always getting into one scrape or another. He reminded Jason of himself at that age, and he had no more patience with his son than his parents had had with him.

All of the many and varied demands on his schedule meant he had very few hours in the day to indulge in what he referred to as "recreational time". Jason had always been a man of rather insatiable sexual appetites, dating back as far as his early teens, and he was also known to like more than his fair share of kink. He'd known from the day she'd happily agreed to marry him that Charlotte couldn't even begin to satisfy either need. In fact, she was a bit of a prude when it came to the bedroom, and more often than not these days she'd claim fatigue or stress from dealing with the children all day as a way to cop out of sex. And Charlotte would have been shocked to the tips of her very proper Ferragmo pumps to fully realize many of the more – er, unconventional things he enjoyed in the bedroom.

He'd had a very satisfactory arrangement set up with the shapely Swedish law student he'd met at one of the kink bars he liked to frequent. Greta had been a dynamo in bed, even enjoyed taking charge when he'd been in the mood to allow it, and she'd been game for almost anything – especially after he'd set her up in a charming flat in the Marina District where he could pop in for a convenient visit during his lunch break or right after work.

But that particular relationship was now a thing of the past, ever since his schedule – and his entire life – had been fucked over good with the transfer to Scotts Valley. Tired of his neglect, the hot-blooded Greta hadn't wasted any time in finding herself a new boyfriend – a filthy rich Middle Eastern real estate magnate who had neither a wife, children, nor a fucking long commute to make demands on his time.

It hadn't taken Jason long to find some new action, but he couldn't afford to start up another long term arrangement right now. Not only was his free time severely limited but so were his finances. His salary had fortunately remained the same after the transfer, but there were newly added expenses with commuting, plus the private school where all three children were enrolled had raised their already exorbitant tuition even higher. Charlotte had never had much concept about money – one of the many reasons she'd never been considered for a position with her family's own company – and spent it on frivolous items that they really couldn't afford.

And everything – every single one of his woes – could be blamed entirely on that arrogant, ruthless bastard Ian. All of this was his fault, no question about it. It was solely because of him – and that treacherous, scheming bitch he was currently banging – that Jason's life was such a miserable, fucked-up mess.

Out of Charlotte's three male cousins, Jason had always disliked Ian the most – not that he'd been overly fond of Hugh or Colin, either. But at least Hugh was personable enough to shake his hand and make him feel welcome, while Colin had been a real hell raiser in his day until he'd finally settled down in recent years. Ian, though, had always been a stuck-up, cold-hearted prick, looking at Jason as though he wasn't fit to be breathing the same air as the rest of the family.

And actually working for the bastard had been ten times worse. Ian had acted like a fucking king in the office, imposing rules and regulations that Jason had found unreasonable and often intolerable. Still, with Ian on the road almost half of each month, Jason had been able to shirk his duties with relatively little difficulty, largely by heaping work on his PA and the management support team, and by passing on assignments to lower level managers. He'd had a nice, comfortable arrangement going there, one that allowed him plenty of free time to indulge in his "recreational" pursuits.

But then everything had gone to hell overnight when that sanctimonious hard-ass Ian had caught him red-handed with the blonde bitch – literally speaking, given that he'd been very pleasurably groping the girl's big tit at the time. To say that Ian had completely overreacted was putting it mildly, and Jason had remained convinced that the real reason he'd been banished to Scotts Valley was because his arrogant boss had lusted after the tart himself.

Not that he blamed Ian, of course. From the first time he'd laid eyes on the luscious Tessa, Jason had been determined to have her. She wasn't his usual type – too young and innocent and shy – but with a body like hers – well, she was every man's type. He'd lusted after her ripe, sexy body, her full, pillowy lips, and all that long, blonde hair, and had turned on every bit of charm he possessed to entice her into his bed. The thought of spanking her shapely ass until it was bright red, or cuffing her to a St. Andrew's cross while he fucked her brutally had made him salivate at the thought of possessing her.

But she hadn't wanted to play his little game of flirting and seduction, had scurried away from him like a frightened mouse each time he'd approached her. Given some of the really filthy, obscene things he'd murmured in her ear, even he had been surprised when she hadn't turned him in to HR. But he'd also quite deliberately made sure to subtly remind her that he was her superior and, more importantly, a member of the Gregson family. The girl had evidently feared for her job security for she'd kept her mouth shut about his continued harassment.

And of course Ian's little shadow – that pain-in-the-arse, by-the-book Andrew – had always seemed to be in the vicinity whenever Jason had tried to approach Tessa. Jason now knew without a doubt that Andrew had been intentionally tasked to do just that – a task handed down by the fucking king himself.

He'd heard about Ian's new amour from Charlotte, and it hadn't taken him very long at all to put two and two together. Jason's reaction upon discovering that the beautiful blonde Ian was apparently quite taken with was Tessa had been a combination of amusement, anger, and an overwhelming need for vengeance. He blamed both of them equally for the unsatisfactory situation he found himself in, and grew more determined with each passing day to make them pay dearly.

Last evening had been the first time he'd seen either of them since Ian had effectively banished him from the regional office. His fists had clenched in fury to see the way Ian kept the gorgeous blonde tucked firmly against his side, refusing to release her even for a moment. He was too old for her, of course, and Jason had told Charlotte rather scathingly that Ian must need a boost to his ego after turning forty earlier in the year.

Charlotte had frowned at him disapprovingly. "Why would you say that? Ian looks marvelous for his age, a lot fitter than men ten years younger. He could have most any woman he wanted. No, according to Aunt Joanna he really loves this girl. And she's crazy about him, too."

"Probably crazy about his money," Jason had muttered darkly.

That was yet another gripe he had against Ian – how much money the bloke had. It just wasn't fair that he and Charlotte weren't even a fraction as rich as Ian or his brothers were. While there was no possible way that scatterbrained Charlotte could have ever held a position of any significance in the family business, there was no reason at all why Jason shouldn't be at an equal level with her three cousins.

Charlotte, of course, had insisted on saying hello to her cousin and had dragged a reluctant Jason over to greet Ian and his well-kept bitch. Tessa admittedly looked every inch the pampered and spoiled girlfriend of a very wealthy man, even in the more casual island style dress she'd been wearing. It had seemed that being Ian's bedmate agreed with her.

And there was very little doubt that she was earning her keep on a regular basis. She'd had that just-fucked look about her, gazing up at Ian with almost sickening sweetness, and the looks that passed between the pair of them were nothing less than smoldering. Oh, no, Ian was enjoying her thoroughly and often, definitely getting his money's worth from that hot, ripe body. The satisfied look on the prick's face as he held Tessa tightly against him made Jason long to shove a fist into his jaw.

Charlotte had been predictably oblivious to the thick tension in the air when both Ian and Tessa had barely acknowledged him. It had been left to Charlotte to do most of the talking, and Jason had almost cringed when she'd happily babbled on about the four of them getting together for dinner soon, or inquiring if Tessa would be joining the family later in the year in England for the holidays. Ian had smoothly changed the subject each time Charlotte hit on something awkward, and the ninny had naively never even sensed there was anything wrong.

Jason had drank steadily during the evening, his fury building each time he happened to glance over in the direction of Ian's table. It made him sick to his stomach to see the way that blonde whore fawned over Ian, touching his arm and gazing at him in adoration, like he was the fucking king and everyone else here in the room his doting subjects.

'Fuck the pair of them,' Jason had thought darkly. 'He was probably screwing her the whole time she worked there. That's why he shipped you off to bloody Scotts Valley – because you dared to poach on his territory.'

He'd thought often of filing a complaint against Ian, or at least blowing the whistle on his amorous activities with one of his staff. But every time he'd considered the idea, Jason knew it was virtually useless. Tessa had very conveniently resigned recently, removing any obstacle to having a relationship with Ian. And since Ian reported directly to his father and uncle – both of whom had been fully apprised of the situation – there wasn't a chance in hell he'd be disciplined for any of his past activities.

'No,' Jason had told himself firmly. 'You'll have to figure out a different way to get back at them. And they *will* pay for what they've done to you.'

***

Tessa had just pulled on a sheer green cotton cover-up over her emerald green bikini when a knock sounded on the door of the suite. She frowned, for the butler was usually off duty at this time of the afternoon, and Ian would have used his card key. As the knocking persisted, however, she heaved a little sigh and walked over to the front door.

It had been an especially hectic morning today, the last full day of the managers meeting, and Ian had insisted she take the afternoon off and go relax on the beach. Even Andrew had shooed her off, confirming that he and Shelby could easily handle the rest of the afternoon's scheduled events. Still feeling more than a little guilty, Tessa had nonetheless returned to the suite and changed into her beachwear.

"Who is it, please?" she asked, unable to see anyone through the peep hole.

The voice on the other side of the door was the familiar Australian accent of the private butler assigned to the owner's suite. "It's Geoffrey, Miss Lockwood. I have a delivery for you and Mr. Gregson."

Tessa still thought it a bit odd that Geoffrey was on duty at this time of the day, but supposed the rest of the staff was busier than usual because of the managers meeting. She unlocked the door and opened it slowly.

And then gasped as Jason rushed past her into the room before she could stop him, grabbing her by the wrist and yanking her along with him as he kicked the door shut.

"What the hell are you doing here?" she demanded. "What's happened to Geoffrey?"

Jason snickered. "Most likely enjoying his afternoon break, I assume. I happened to notice him leaving this suite the other day, chatted him up a bit. Did you know I lived in Australia for a time, picked up the accent in no time?"

Tessa tugged on her wrist but his grip was like steel. "Let go of me, Jason. You don't scare me anymore. And Ian will kick your ass if he finds you here."

"Oh, but he won't, sweet thing. When I snuck out of that god-awful boring meeting, he was about to start droning on about some budget bullshit. He'll be there for hours yet. More than enough time for you and I to have a little chat."

Tessa forced down the sense of panic that threatened to overtake her. "We have nothing to say to each other."

"Then fucking listen, you little bitch." His voice was filled with venom, and he twisted her wrist hard enough to make her yelp in pain. "You and your lover screwed up my life big time. He banished me to that stinking hotel, demoted me, all because I dared to put my hands on you. And all the time the fucking hypocrite was banging you himself."

Tessa shook her head vehemently. "No, no. You're wrong. We weren't together then. Ian didn't know I was separated from my husband at the time and he wouldn't have - "

"Fucked a married woman? Oh, yes, noble, honorable Ian, never doing the wrong thing, always the perfect gentleman," spat Jason. "Well, maybe he wasn't tapping you then, sweet thing, but he sure as hell wanted to. So he sent me away like I was a naughty child who'd tried to play with his favorite toy."

Tessa wished fervently that she wasn't barefoot, wasn't quite so scantily dressed. She gave another experimental tug on her wrist, which only made him tighten his grip and she knew her skin was already starting to bruise.

"What do you want, Jason?" she asked with a calm she certainly didn't feel. "Your insults aren't going to change anything. And your being here is only going to make things worse once Ian learns about it."

"He can't fire me, if that's what you're thinking, sweet thing," replied Jason arrogantly. "My father-in-law won't leave the father of his grandchildren without a steady income. Besides, you and your lover owe me big time. And now it's time for me to start collecting on that debt."

Jason shoved her up against the wall, pushing his leanly muscled – and very obviously aroused – body against hers. Tessa turned her head to the side in revulsion as he ground himself against her.

"Come on, you hot bitch. Don't pretend you don't want to get fucked. Look at you," purred Jason. "Mmm, I'll bet Ian likes to take you for a good, long ride every night. But it's time for that greedy bastard to start sharing a little. I mean, he's got it all, doesn't he? Money, power, prestige, and the hottest, sweetest piece of ass I've ever seen. I might not get my fair share of all the rest, but I'm damned sure going to take my share of you."

Tessa tried in vain to shove him off of her, wishing that she was wearing a pair of her stilettos so that she could drive a spiked heel through his foot. "Guess what, asshole? Ian doesn't share. And there is no way in hell you're putting your disgusting hands on me."

Jason laughed, an ugly, menacing sound. "And exactly how are you going to prevent me from doing that, sweet thing?"

***

"Sir, we have a problem."

Ian glanced up in irritation as Andrew approached him, an anxious look on his face. "Can it wait? The break is up in less than ten minutes and I'm really not looking forward to hearing all the grumbling from the troops when they listen to my budget talk."

"Jason is unaccounted for. Shelby was supposed to be keeping track of him but, well – she does tend to get distracted easily."

Ian swore beneath his breath. "How long?"

Andrew hesitated. "At least fifteen minutes, Mr. Gregson. We think he slipped out before the break started. Shall I go look for him?"

Ian shook his head and handed Andrew his stack of notes and reports. "No. I'll go take care of the matter. For good this time."

"Very good, sir. Should I delay the start of the meeting then?"

Ian clapped Andrew on the shoulder. "No. I want you to start the meeting. You know every damned fact and figure in those reports better than I do, not to mention exactly what I'm prepared to say about them. Now all you have to do is get up there and deliver."

Andrew looked shell shocked. "Mr. Gregson – I don't think -"

"I do. Don't let me down, Andrew. I'll be back as soon as I kick that bastard's arse. Which shouldn't take very long at all."

Before Andrew could protest further, Ian was striding out of the meeting room, nearly breaking into a jog as he headed towards his suite. He had no doubt whatsoever that Jason had gone in that direction. He only hoped Tessa hadn't encountered the bastard, or that Jason hadn't gone a little crazy and attempted to harass her in any way. Ian's hands clenched and unclenched as he continued on his way, almost hoping for an opportunity to put his fist solidly in Jason's mouth, to shatter his jaw as he'd vowed to do all those months ago.

But the very last thing he'd expected to find when he burst inside the suite was a trembling Tessa rubbing her right hand and grimacing in pain, while an astonished Jason was gingerly feeling his nose, blood pouring down between his fingers.

Ian slammed the door to the suite shut decisively, and held out an arm for his girl. She rushed to his side and he held her close against him. He grimaced as he noticed the dark bruise around her left wrist, but then couldn't help grinning when he saw the reddened knuckles of her other hand.

"Got him good, did you, love?" he asked in amusement. "What was it – a right hook?"

Tessa shook her head, wrapping her arms around his waist and burrowing her face against his shoulder. "Upper cut," she mumbled.

He stroked her hair tenderly. "Well, that is your best punch, after all."

"Fucking bitch broke my nose," muttered Jason. "I need to go have this looked at."

Ian's voice was like a whip crack. "You'll stay where the hell you are. I don't give a damn if you bleed to death. I'll deal with you in a minute." Turning to Tessa, his voice became warm and gentle. "Now, I'd like you to go wait for me down at the beach, all right? I'll be along in just a moment. Jason and I need to have a little talk."

She shook her head, touching his cheek in concern. "Don't. He's not worth it. Please."

"Shh." He pressed a kiss to her brow. "Let me deal with this, darling. I promise everything will be fine. Now go, please. I'll be there in a few minutes."

Slowly, reluctantly, Tessa grabbed her beach tote and exited the suite onto the patio. Once she was safely out of sight, Ian grabbed a dish towel from the wet bar and flung it at Jason.

"Here. Try not to bleed all over the furniture, will you? And quit sniveling. If she'd actually broken your nose, believe me, you'd know it."

Jason glared at him. "So are you going to finish the job for her then?"

Ian smiled, a cold, calculating smile. "Are you challenging me, Jason? Think I won't do it? I believe I made it very, very clear what I'd do to you if you ever touched Tessa again."

Jason flinched as Ian grasped his jaw between powerful, capable fingers. With his other fist, Ian tapped Jason on the jaw almost playfully.

"Such a weak, almost fragile jaw you have. Never realized it before now. Hmm." Ian pretended to study him more closely. "Really wouldn't take much more than a tap or two to shatter this. Ouch. Now *that* would hurt."

"You wouldn't dare," hissed Jason. "I'd sue your ass off, have you arrested for assault."

Ian gave a hoot of laughter. "Is that right? It's almost tempting to try. Don't forget, this is *my* hotel, *my* employees. There's not one person here who wouldn't back up my story if I were to state that you were assaulting Tessa and I was simply trying to protect her. You wouldn't have a leg to stand on, Jason."

He released his grip on Jason's jaw, satisfied to see the imprint of his fingers on the other man's skin. "But not to worry. I realize you're flying home to your children tomorrow, and it wouldn't do for them to see their father beaten to a bloody pulp. Besides, I've decided that breaking a few of your bones isn't a fitting punishment for you. After all, bones do heal after a time, don't they? And I intend for your pain to continue for a long, long time."

Jason eyed him warily. "I have no idea what the hell you're talking about. I suppose you've gone soft, hmm? Your hot piece of ass has you good and pussy whipped, does she?"

Ian growled, shoving Jason up against the wall and holding him firmly in place with an elbow to the gut. "Shut your filthy fucking mouth. You don't get to talk about Tessa – ever. How dare you speak about her like she's one of your dirty whores? Just remember, Jason. I don't actually have to break any bones to cause you pain – a great deal of it."

Jason threw up his hands in surrender. "My apologies. So tell me, mate. Where are you shipping me off to this time? Wherever it is you won't hear me complain because anything has to be better than where you've got me now."

Ian released his grip on Jason, circling him in a calm, calculating manner, as though he were his prey. "You may want to reserve judgment on that, *mate*, until you've heard all the details. You're quite right that your days at the Silicon Valley hotel are over. Apparently you've been up to your old ways again. Clearly, you don't follow orders well and require much stricter supervision."

Jason regarded him scornfully. "Orders? I should be the one giving orders, not having to take them. As Charlotte's husband I ought to have equal authority as you and your brothers."

Ian shook his head in disbelief. "My God, your stupidity is only exceeded by your arrogance. And your ego. You're not family, despite your legal ties to my poor clueless cousin. But Uncle Richard tolerates you because Charlotte is still determined to have you. And speaking of my uncle, Charlotte will be overjoyed to learn she'll be seeing a great deal more of him in the very near future. As will you."

"What do you mean?" Jason's tone was guarded.

Ian shrugged. "That's where you're being transferred, back to corporate headquarters in London. Oh, I know what you're thinking – back to the big city, the head office, finally getting what you deserve. And you're quite right on all three parts, especially the latter. You see, you'll be working alongside your father-in-law. Very closely, I might add."

Jason frowned. "How exactly do you mean?"

"I mean, you'll be Richard's fucking shadow," replied Ian harshly. "Your office will be right across from his, where he or his staff can see exactly what you're doing all day, every day. You'll be accompanying him to every meeting, every appointment, every luncheon. You won't have any free time of your own, every minute of your day accounted for. If you need to go take a piss in the loo you'll have to clear it with him first."

As realization began to dawn on Jason, his features took on a panicked expression. "You can't do that. Come on, Ian, be a sport. You know the old bastard can barely tolerate me. He's going to make my life a living hell."

Ian smiled with great satisfaction. "Exactly, Jason. That's why this solution is so much more satisfying than simply shattering your jaw. Your pain will go on for a long time. And don't be hoping Uncle Richard will be retiring any time soon. He may be sixty-five but he's fit and sharp and will probably go on working for at least another decade."

Jason visibly paled, his eyes narrowing. "He can't control me round the clock."

"Ah, but then you haven't heard all the good news, have you?" Ian leaned against the wall, crossing his arms leisurely, as though he were discussing the latest soccer scores. "Well, you know how expensive housing is in London, even more so than in San Francisco. And since Uncle Richard and Aunt Helen want only the best for Charlotte and your children, they're insisting that all of you move in with them. After all, they've got that huge old place out in Surrey and it's been a bit lonesome with just the two of them. So Aunt Helen is at present having the entire west wing readied for your arrival, and she's probably the happiest woman in all of England right now."

Jason looked as though someone had punched him in the gut – hard – and stared at Ian in horror. "You wouldn't. I won't stand for it, do you hear me?"

Ian chuckled. "Well, considering that even as we speak Richard is calling Charlotte to tell her all the good news, I'd say you have no choice in the matter at all. Done deal and all that. Oh, and Uncle Richard also said to tell you that you'll be commuting with him to and from the office every day. Plenty of room in the Bentley for one more."

Jason was seething. "This is an insult. I don't need a fucking keeper. And you know what Richard is like."

"I do, yes. Especially when it comes to making Charlotte happy. There's really nothing he won't do for his daughter or grandchildren. And that includes keeping you on a very short leash." Ian grasped Jason's face between his fingers, squeezing tight enough to cause pain. "You sure as hell will have a great deal of trouble whoring around as you've been used to doing all these years. Maybe you'll finally learn to appreciate the very posh life you've been lucky enough to have."

Jason snorted. "I think I'd prefer the broken bones to everything you've just described."

"Tough. The choice isn't yours to make. Uncle Richard has finally realized what a liability you are to this company, to this family, and he's prepared to do whatever is necessary to keep you in line." Ian released his grip on Jason's cheeks, shoving him away. "Now, I've got a meeting to get back to. Don't bother returning yourself. In fact, perhaps you and Charlotte ought to catch an earlier flight home, given that you'll have a great deal of packing to do. Now get the hell out of my sight before I change my mind about breaking your jaw."

Jason had his hand on the door handle but couldn't resist taking one final parting shot. "Aren't you going to go check on your slut? After all, she looked awfully delicious in that bikini. I never knew you favored blondes, Ian, especially ones with nice big - "

But before the rest of his obscene words could leave his mouth, Jason was gasping for breath, bent over at the waist and unable to make a sound after Ian had given him a hard, vicious kick to the groin.

Ian opened the door and shoved him out into the hallway, a look of pure loathing on his face. "See if you can make it back to your room without vomiting, hmm? I understand they just had the carpets cleaned recently."

Ian slammed the door shut, forcing himself to take several deep breaths. He glanced quickly at his watch, realizing he'd need to make this next part quick so he could return to the meeting. At the wet bar he grabbed one of the plastic ice bucket liners and filled it with ice.

He found Tessa pacing anxiously to and fro on the stretch of sand not far from their patio. She was still wearing the sheer swimsuit cover up over her bikini, her beach tote all but forgotten on the sand. When she saw him approach, she ran towards him a bit clumsily, her bare feet sinking into the loose sand.

"What happened?" she asked worriedly. "Are you all right? He didn't try - "

Ian chuckled, pulling her close against him. "Darling, I'll try very hard not to be insulted that you thought for one moment that little shit could possibly hurt me. The real question is – are you all right?"

Tessa shrugged. "Just a little shook up. I can't believe I actually opened the door for him, that I didn't realize he wasn't Geoffrey. He just sounded so much like him. I'm sorry."

"Shush. It's all right. And Jason won't be bothering you ever again."

He quickly told her about the arrangement he'd made a couple of days ago with his uncle after discovering that Jason was up to his old tricks down at the Silicon Valley hotel. Richard had somewhat reluctantly agreed to have Jason return to London, albeit under extremely tight controls.

Tessa sighed in relief. "Well, I'm glad to hear it. And especially for your cousin. She seems like such a sweet woman, not at all deserving of how that jerk treats her."

"I agree. Now, let me see your knuckles, hmm? If you don't get some ice on them, they're going to bruise. Just how hard did you wallop him, love?"

She grinned. "He has a weak nose. It didn't take much effort actually."

Ian guffawed in delight as Tessa applied the ice pack. "You're a natural. When we get home it will be time to up your training. But *not*," he added sternly, "with that randy bastard Jesse. You'll train with me, got it?"

She reached up and gave him a kiss. "Got it." She looked down at her bare feet and shuffled uncertainly. "You do realize what day this is, don't you?"

Ian sighed. "Are we on this again? Yes, I know it's a Wednesday, Tessa, but once again it's just a coincidence. You really need to stop this silly superstition you have about this particular day of the week."

She shook her head. "Bad things always happen on Wednesdays, it never fails. But at least this time it's ending well."

"Well, forget about it, all right? Now, I'd better get back to the meeting, especially since I left Andrew in charge of delivering my budget talk. I don't know whether he'll have completely bungled the whole thing, or if the entire room full of managers will be pissed off."

Tessa grinned. "I'd be willing to bet on the latter. Go, finish your meeting. I'll be waiting on the beach for you when you're done."

"Good." He gave her a quick kiss, squeezing her ass cheeks through the cover up. "I'll be counting the minutes until I can take this off of you."

"Me, too." She sighed against his kiss. "Ian, you didn't actually – with Jason – did you- "

He winked at her mysteriously. "No blood or broken bones, I assure you. But he'll definitely have trouble walking for a few days."

Chapter Twenty Four

August

"I want to go with you to the airport. Just let me throw some clothes on and I'll be ready to leave."

Ian gave Tessa a stern look as he sat down next to her on the bed, his shirt still half-unbuttoned and his tie draped over a bedside chair. "Tessa, no offense darling, but you look like hell right now. I'd feel much better if you stayed at home and rested. Please?"

She shook her head stubbornly. "It's just my stupid period, Ian, not the plague. Let me – oh." Tessa doubled over in pain as another killer cramp wrenched her lower body.

He grimaced, drawing her close and gently rubbing his hand over her belly. "You're not leaving this house today, my love, maybe not this bed. And I still can't believe the absolutely rotten timing of this trip to Vegas. You know I wouldn't be going if it wasn't so critical?"

She nodded in understanding, sliding her hand over his as he continued to rub her cramping belly soothingly. "Of course I know. And I'd say it's pretty important for you to be there."

Over the last few days had come the discovery that the casino manager at the Las Vegas resort had been involved in a complex money laundering operation. Ian was flying out this morning along with several of his highest level managers to meet with the FBI, the Nevada Gaming Commission, and the local authorities. He hoped to resolve the matter within two to three days, and was also keeping his fingers crossed that the problem had been uncovered early enough so that the damage was minimal.

He shook his head. "This is why I dislike having casinos in any of our properties – too damned many potential complications like this one. But fortunately it sounds like we discovered this one fairly early in the game so we should be able to straighten things out quickly."

Tessa cuddled up against him, seeking out his body heat. She'd been freezing most of the night, despite the warm August weather, and was wearing a pair of sweatpants and a thermal knit top. Her hands and feet still felt cold as ice.

"I'll miss you a whole lot," she murmured, looping her arms around his neck. "You realize we haven't spent a night away from each other since April?"

Ian stroked her sleep-mussed hair. "I'm very well aware of that, love," he told her. "But even if you didn't have that orientation at school tomorrow, there's no way I'd have taken you on this trip anyway. Not in this condition."

Her period had begun on Saturday – two days ago – and the timing couldn't have been worse, given Ian's impending trip to Las Vegas. There had been no question of Tessa accompanying him this time, since she had to attend a half-day orientation at the university tomorrow. Her online classes didn't officially begin for another ten days or so, but her attendance at tomorrow's event was mandatory. She was also planning to buy whatever books and other materials she needed for her classes at the campus bookstore tomorrow.

She'd had a restless night, plagued with cramps and a terrible headache, plus some of the heaviest bleeding she'd ever experienced. She was clearly exhausted this morning, and had shuddered to see her reflection in the mirror – skin so pale it looked as though it had been bleached white; dark circles under her eyes; her hair sticking up in a dozen different places. Ian had insisted on bringing her some tea but she'd refused any food, her cramps so severe she was almost nauseous from the pain.

Ian frowned as a chill went through her body, and he took her hands in his to warm them. "Tessa, this can't continue, you know that. It tears me up to see you suffer like this every month. I'm going to call Jordan during the flight and make an appointment for us to see him a week from today."

Tessa shrugged. They had had this discussion more than once, and she'd brushed Ian's concerns aside each time. Jordan Reeves was a good friend of Ian's, a fellow patron of the arts, and one of the top OB/GYN doctors in San Francisco. Ian had been pushing Tessa to consult with him for months now.

"I'm not sure what he's going to be able to tell us," she argued. "I tried three different brands of the pill – they all made me sick in one way or the other. The nurse at the clinic said it's rare to have allergic reactions but that's definitely what happened in my case."

"Darling, that was several years ago, don't forget. I'm sure new products have come on the market since then. Besides, there's a great deal of difference between an overworked public health nurse at a free clinic with limited resources, and the top man in his field at the best hospital here in the city. Jordan will have far more resources at his disposal so that he can work with us at finding a better solution. Because this," he gestured to her shivering, cramping form, "is not something that can go on any longer."

She sighed and began to button up his dress shirt. "I'm just not sure what other alternatives will work for me. Most everything I've researched has hormones of some sort, and that's apparently what I have a bad reaction to."

He kissed the top of her head. "Let's see what Jordan has to say, hmm? I'll tell you now, Tessa – as much as I hate the thought – I'd resort to using condoms before I see you suffer through one more cycle like this."

"No!" She shook her head vehemently, having feared he'd bring that subject up. "I'd hate that, Ian, absolutely hate that."

He scooped her onto his lap and tucked her head beneath his chin as he held her. "So would I, but it would still be better than watching you this way." He splayed his head over her belly. "And since I don't plan on getting you pregnant just yet, we'll have to do something."

Tessa gave a little gasp and lifted her head to stare at him. "We've never actually discussed that particular subject, have we?"

"No, we haven't." Ian looked pensive all of a sudden. "What are your feelings on the matter?"

She smiled and placed her hand over his. "I've always wanted children. And I especially want to have *your* children." She bit her lip uncertainly. "But – that's only if you do too, of course."

Ian kissed her, a sweet, soft gesture. "My darling girl, don't you know that one of my fondest dreams is to see your belly grow big with my baby one day?" His hand cupped her breast, drawing a hiss from her as his thumb rasped over the nipple. "Or to watch my child nursing at your breast? Yes, of course, I want children, Tessa, so long as *you're* their mother."

"I love you, Ian," she told him quietly, resting her head on his shoulder. "And I would love nothing better than to give you as many babies as you wish."

He chuckled. "Let's start with one and take it from there, all right? But," he added, in a more serious tone, "not just yet. I'm a selfish enough man to want you all to myself for a time. Which is why we are going to see Jordan as soon as possible and get this birth control situation taken care of."

"Okay." She gave an exhausted sigh, too worn out to argue any further.

Ian frowned in concern as he gently laid her back against the pillows and covered her with the duvet. "Tessa, I'm not convinced you shouldn't see Jordan before next week. Not to discuss birth control – I want to be present for that – but to check you out right now. You're so pale, darling, and your skin feels clammy. Why don't you let me set something up for today? If he can't fit you in I'm sure one of his associates can. Simon can drive you."

"No." she clasped his hand. "This isn't anything I haven't been through many times before. It will pass, it always does. By tomorrow it will have eased up, and by the time you return on Thursday it will hopefully be all done. So," she added teasingly, "you'd better get lots of sleep while you're away because you'll be expected to perform as soon as you get back."

Ian laughed as he bent and kissed her cheek. "Very well, my lusty maiden. I know what you're like after you've had to abstain for several days, so I will definitely try to get as much rest as possible. You're certain about Jordan?"

"Yes. I'll be fine. Just make the appointment for next week, all right?"

Tessa knew Ian had a lot on his plate right now, that this unexpected situation in Las Vegas couldn't have come at a worse time. They had been traveling almost constantly these past few weeks, trying to get as many hotel reviews done as possible in anticipation of their vacation next month. Ian was taking her to Tuscany in mid-September, and then to London, and they would be away for a total of two weeks. So the last thing she wanted to do was worry him, or give him cause for concern. She very intentionally didn't tell him, therefore, that this was the worst she'd ever felt during one of her periods. The cramps were unbearable, the regular doses of Tylenol doing nothing to ease her suffering. She'd been bleeding heavily for almost two full days now, and felt weak from the blood loss, almost dizzy at times. She had no energy, could barely even think of getting out of bed, and was grateful she didn't have a regular job she had to report to. She only hoped she could summon enough strength to attend tomorrow's orientation.

She hadn't realized she'd begun to doze off until Ian sat back down on the bed next to her. She gazed up at him drowsily, her thoughts more than a little unfocused.

"Hmm, what is it?" she murmured sleepily.

His brows knit together worriedly. "I'm afraid I need to leave now, darling. Simon will be arriving within the next five minutes. Are you certain you're all right? I don't have a very good feeling about leaving you this way."

"I'll be fine," she whispered, too tired to even lift her head from the pillow. "And don't forget. I'm the one who always gets those bad feelings, not you. Besides, today's a Monday. Bad things only happen on Wednesdays."

He shook his head in exasperation. "If it's the last thing I do, I'm going to clear your mind of that ridiculous superstition. Now, give me a kiss good-bye, love."

Tessa clung to him as he gave her a long, searching kiss, unwilling to let him go. In the end, he gently disengaged her arms and stood, smoothing her hair off her face as he did so.

"I'll expect frequent calls and texts from you, understand?" he told her in mock severity. "I may be tied up in meetings but I'll check my phone on a regular basis. Now, rest up and recover."

He winked at her. "We have a big date on Thursday night. Maybe I'll bring you a surprise back from Las Vegas. From the La Perla store, to be exact."

She squeezed his hand and forced herself to smile. "A gift for both of us, in other words."

Ian laughed, giving her one final, quick kiss before he walked out of their bedroom. Tessa was fast asleep before he reached the foyer.

***

After lazing away the better part of Monday, Tessa was relieved to wake on Tuesday and feel considerably better. Her period was still going on but seemed to have eased a little, and the cramps were still present but bearable. She was able to eat a decent breakfast, and felt a little stronger with some food in her system. Somewhat guiltily, she realized that she'd only had tea and saltine crackers the day before.

'God, if I wasn't having the period from hell I'd almost think I was pregnant from how I've been feeling the last few days,' she thought to herself wryly. 'Thank goodness I'm going to get this rotten IUD removed soon. I will *not* miss these horrid cycles!'

Still, even though she was feeling much better, she was glad Ian had arranged for Simon to drive her to and from the campus, since she continued to feel a little light-headed and wouldn't have felt comfortable behind the wheel of a car right now. The orientation for her online classes lasted several hours, after which she ventured into the campus bookstore to buy the materials she'd need for the four classes she'd be taking this fall.

She hadn't been thrilled to learn that one of the required courses towards her business degree was algebra, a subject she'd struggled with in high school. But Ian had teasingly offered to be her "after-school tutor", telling her with a snicker that his services came cheap.

"And I accept all forms of payment," he'd joked. "Missionary, cowgirl, oral. I'm quite flexible, in fact."

She'd gasped in mock outrage. "I'm not sure I should be

listening to this sort of talk. I'm just a naïve little college girl, you know."

"No so naïve any longer, love," he'd whispered in her ear. "And speaking of lessons, I have a few new ones I'd be very interested in teaching you sometime soon."

Tessa couldn't help smiling to herself as she recalled how that particular conversation had ended, and was still grinning as her phone rang. Hoping that it would be Ian, she dug the phone out of her purse while juggling an armload of heavy textbooks. When she saw it was Julia calling instead, she couldn't help but feel a bit disappointed.

"Hi, there, newlywed," she greeted, forcing herself to sound cheerful.

Julia's bright laughter on the other end immediately made Tessa feel better. "Well, happy to report that the honeymoon isn't over yet. In fact – mmm, never mind. I get annoyed with Nathan when he talks to his friends about – uh, stuff we do so I guess I shouldn't over-share, either."

"Probably not," teased Tessa. "Though I do appreciate some of the tips you've given me. Ian does, too."

Julia snickered. "And I always appreciate getting flowers, so maybe I'll think of some more naughty advice to pass along. But I really called to see if you wanted to meet for lunch tomorrow. I walked by our favorite place yesterday and get this – they now have salted caramel cheesecake on the menu. I mean, how can anyone say no to that – right?"

Tessa agreed it sounded out of this world and arranged to meet Julia there at one o'clock the next day. They chatted until it was Tessa's turn in line to pay for her books.

As she walked to the spot where Simon would be waiting to pick her up, she checked her phone yet again and couldn't help the disappointment she felt when there were no new texts or voice mails from Ian. She'd spoken to him only sparingly since he'd left yesterday morning, the situation in Las Vegas evidently much more complicated than he'd first hoped. They had talked very briefly this morning and as yet he hadn't replied to the three different texts she'd sent him. Tessa consoled herself with the fact that he was super busy, and wasn't intentionally neglecting her. And since the very last thing she wanted to do was act like a demanding girlfriend, she put her phone away and resolved to wait patiently for his call.

But the call didn't come until much later that evening, and Ian sounded so worn out and stressed that she didn't have the heart to keep him on the line for too long.

"And I'm so sorry, love, but I'm afraid this is going to take a bit longer than I'd hoped," he told her regretfully. "It's likely going to be Friday before I can make it home."

Tessa struggled to hide her disappointment and tried to sound as supportive as possible. "I understand. I just wish I could be there to help."

"I wish you were here, too, though in all honesty there wouldn't be much for you to do in this particular case. It's certainly not a situation I've ever had to deal with before. Now, tell me about the orientation today."

They talked for a bit longer, until he started to yawn and she teasingly told him to get some sleep since she was evidently boring him.

Tessa had a hard time falling asleep that night, tossing and turning, even getting out of bed a little before midnight to brew some chamomile tea. It was the first time in months that she'd been alone in this big house, and she automatically found herself being troubled by her old fears and depression. She drifted into the library with her mug of tea, and reached for one of her mother's books.

Ever since Ian had surprised her with the books for her birthday, Tessa had read all three volumes at least twice. Ian had just recently heard from one of his rare book dealers that they had a solid lead on the fourth book, and Tessa was eagerly awaiting its acquisition.

The tea and the book seemed to do the trick, and this time when her head hit the pillow she fell asleep within a few minutes.

***

She knew almost immediately upon waking on Wednesday

morning that something was very wrong. She was groggy and disoriented, despite the fact that she'd slept like the dead for hours. Groaning, she reached for her phone and saw she had three voice mails and two texts from Ian, each one sounding more anxious than the last. Without lifting her head from the pillow, she sent him a quick text, apologizing for having overslept and promising to call him in a little while.

It was when she tried to sit up that she realized several things at once – she was dizzy, oh, so dizzy, and had to brace her hand on the headboard to stay upright; the awful cramps were back except they were worse than she could ever remember, like a knife blade stabbing her in the gut; and she was burning up, her skin hot to the touch, and she realized she had a fever. Her mouth was so dry she could barely swallow, and her head was pounding unbearably.

In dire need of some Tylenol and a glass of water, she stumbled on shaky legs to the bathroom. It was then she noticed the blood trickling down the inside of her thighs, and she tried valiantly not to panic. There was way too much blood, even for the heavy periods she suffered from, and the way it was seeping out in a steady flow made her realize she needed to get to a doctor right away.

Struggling not to pass out, she managed to clean herself up as best she could, forcing back alarm when she saturated a sanitary pad within minutes. She called Ian first, even though he was in Las Vegas, because she desperately needed to hear his calm, steady voice telling her what to do next. She shouldn't have been surprised when the call went to voice mail, and chose not to leave a message. Simon had the day off today, though she knew he would have come for her anyway, but in the end she called Julia.

"Hey," trilled Julia happily. "Working up an appetite for that cheesecake?"

"Julia." Tessa's voice was whisper soft. "I – no, I can't make lunch. I'm – sick, something's wrong."

Julia was instantly on alert. "What is it, honey? The flu? God, you sound awful."

"Not the flu. Thought it was my period but – oh, God, the cramps – so painful. And too much blood." Tessa was fighting off the urge to retch with every breath she took.

"I'm coming over. Right now. Can you get downstairs to open the door for me?"

Tessa was desperately grateful to learn her friend was on the way. "Think so. I'll find a way. I'm sorry."

"Stop it. Nothing to be sorry for. Damn it, Nathan's already on his way to Napa. I know, I'll get Travis to drive me, he's a crazy man behind the wheel so we'll get there in record time. Tessa – if this gets any worse before we arrive, call 911 immediately, okay? I'm walking out of my office now to get Travis, and I'll have my phone in hand if you have to call. Just hang on, okay?"

"Okay. See you soon." Tessa slumped to the bathroom floor, just the effort of talking sapping the little energy she had left.

She half stumbled, half crawled into the walk-in closet to find a pair of slip-on shoes and then grabbed her purse from the bedroom. Somehow she managed to get herself downstairs, largely by sitting and sliding down on her butt one stair at a time. Try as she might, she couldn't summon the energy to get up off the bottom step, her head swimming nauseatingly and the pain in her abdomen so severe she was sobbing.

While she waited for Julia and Travis to arrive, her fevered brain vaguely recalled that she still needed to call Ian. Once again the call went to voice mail, but this time she left him a short, succinct message.

"Hey, it's me. Sorry to bother you and please don't worry because it's probably nothing. Julia is going to drive me to the doctor's office just to get checked out. I'll call you when I know more, okay? Love you."

Another vicious, stabbing pain ripped through her belly as she ended the call, and she cried out in agony, wrapping her arms around her midsection. She gasped as she felt a fresh gush of blood seep down her thighs, and this time she did panic when she saw the spreading stain on her sweatpants. Tessa had no idea what was happening to her, but she knew this was far more serious than just a heavy period.

The effort it took to crawl to the front door and open it when the doorbell rang depleted what was left of her strength. Tessa wasn't even aware when she slumped to the ground in a dead faint, and most certainly didn't hear the alarmed voices of Julia and her boss.

***

Doctors, nurses, and whoever else might have been walking through the hallways at University Medical Center were quick to move out of the way of the tall, dark haired man in the gray pinstriped suit. The look on his face was deadly serious, and passers-by glanced away hastily when they glimpsed the fire in his eyes and the tight set to his mouth. No one would have dared to think of approaching him as he strode purposefully down the hall.

Ian was fighting to suppress the rising panic he felt with each step that brought him ever closer to the visitor waiting room where Julia would be meeting him. The last few hours had been nothing less than nightmarish, and his brain was a jumble of thoughts and emotions, none of which made the least bit of sense right now. He was terrified at not knowing what was going on with Tessa, trying to remain positive and not assume the worst, but also about two breaths shy of a full blown anxiety attack. He was furious at himself for having waited so long to check his bloody voice mail, a full three hours after Tessa had left that last message, her voice barely audible. And he was cursing the casino manager for his treachery that had required Ian's presence in Las Vegas these past three days. If he hadn't had to fly out there to clean up the mess, he would have been here with Tessa, able to look after her properly.

Ian had alternately scolded and teased Tessa about the so-called premonitions she felt at times, particularly on Wednesdays, which she still insisted were cursed somehow. But he himself had woken very early on this particular Wednesday, before dawn in fact, and the unsettled feeling he'd had then continued to nag at him all morning. He'd done a full hour of swimming laps in the hotel pool, hoping it would both ease his stress and dispel these odd feelings he kept having. Not wanting to wake Tessa too early, he'd sent her a text before heading off to resume the grueling round of meetings about the increasingly complex money laundering operation. He'd excused himself at various intervals to call her, growing more and more concerned when she didn't answer her phone or reply to his messages. Then, finally, there had been that brief text apologizing for having overslept, and assuring him she'd call soon.

He'd felt instant relief at that point, assured that all was well, and had returned to the meeting. Things had begun to develop at a rapid pace at that point, and before it knew it the morning had all but disappeared and it was already noon.

In between bites of a hastily consumed lunch, Ian had fielded three rather urgent phone calls from the San Francisco office before he'd finally pulled out his personal phone to check for messages.

The voice mail from Tessa had put him on instant alert, for he could immediately sense the fear in her voice that she had so unsuccessfully tried to mask. But it was the next three messages – all placed from Tessa's phone but left by Julia – that sent him into a full blown panic.

The first message had been delivered around 9:30am, and Ian could hear the sounds of traffic in the background.

"Ian, it's Julia. Call me on Tessa's phone the moment you get this. She's being taken to the ER in an ambulance, Travis and I are following behind. Not sure exactly what's wrong but when she called me this morning to cancel our lunch, she was in awful pain and said she was bleeding a lot. When Travis and I got to your place – God, Ian, she just fainted dead away and all the blood – it was awful. We called 911 immediately and I'd guess right now we're less than ten minutes away from the hospital. I'll call you after we arrive."

Julia's next message had come about forty five minutes later, and this time the background noise was minimal at best. She'd been struggling to keep her voice calm.

"Ian, it's Julia again. I really hope you check your voice mail soon. Look, we're at the ER now at University Med Center and Tessa's being looked over by a team. At first they thought it

could be a miscarriage but one of the interns just popped out and said the ultrasound is indicating her IUD has most likely perforated her uterus. They've managed to stop the bleeding but she's going to need surgery. As soon as I know more I'll contact you. Call me, please."

The third and final message had been left just after eleven a.m., and there was no mistaking the annoyance in Julia's tone this time.

"Damn it, Ian, why the hell aren't you answering this phone? I've tried calling the hotel there in Vegas but no one will put me through to you. Please call me the second you get this. They're taking Tessa into surgery now to remove the IUD and repair the damage to her uterus. That's really all I know, they won't tell me anymore, and it's like an insane asylum in this place today. Travis has been here with me but he needs to get back to the office, and Nathan is up at the hotel site in Napa today. I'll stay here and keep you updated but you need to get back to San Francisco right away. And CALL ME!"

What had happened next – in very quick succession – still had his head spinning. He'd called Julia immediately, apologizing profusely for not returning her earlier calls, and demanded an update on Tessa. When he'd learned she was still in surgery, he'd put the next steps in motion with dizzying speed – giving his management team no opportunity to argue with him when he'd announced he had to leave at once; calling to have the corporate jet made ready for a speedy departure; contacting Simon as he gathered his belongings from the suite and arranging to be picked up at the airport in San Francisco; commandeering one of the local hotel staff to drive him to the private airstrip where his plane had been waiting. During the hour long flight, he'd called Julia three times for updates, as well as badgering Jordan Reeves' receptionist until she'd finally agreed to page the doctor. The affable OB/GYN had called Ian back promptly, and agreed to check on Tessa just as soon as the baby he was scheduled to deliver within the next half hour was born. Jordan had assured Ian that Tessa was going to be fine, that these sorts of things, while rare, were usually relatively easy to repair, and it was highly unlikely that there would be any complications.

But any reassurances Ian had been given were instantly forgotten the moment he entered the hospital. Like most people, he disliked such places, and fortunately had had to spend very little time visiting them. His anxiety only continued to increase with each step that brought him ever closer to the visitor waiting room.

Julia was busily tapping away on her iPad when he all but burst inside the room, and she sighed in relief when she saw him approach. She set her tablet aside and stood. "Ian. Thank God."

"Where is she?" he demanded. "I need to see her right away. She's been out of surgery how long now?"

Julia laid a hand on his arm, trying to calm him down. "About forty five minutes or so. But she's still in recovery, so no one can see her yet. One of the nurses said the surgeon will be out to talk to us any minute now."

Ian shook his head. "Not good enough. I want to talk to someone now. Where's this nurse you spoke to?"

"Ian, you've got to calm down, okay? I realize all of this has been a shock to you, but you're not going to help Tessa a bit by freaking out and going into boss mode. Sorry to break the news, but you aren't the boss here," she told him sternly.

He heaved a sigh of frustration, raking a hand through his hair. "You're right, of course. It's just frustrating as hell. I should have been here, Julia. I should have been the one taking care of her, bringing her to the hospital. And then to ignore all of your messages – Christ, I'll never, ever forgive myself if she doesn't come out of this all right."

"Hush." Julia took both of his much larger hands in hers. "And don't blame yourself. Tessa seemed fine when I spoke to her yesterday. I think this happened very suddenly, so there's no possible way you could have anticipated it."

Ian squeezed her hand gratefully. "It's more than that. This damned IUD of hers – I've been after her for months to get it removed, to consult with a doctor about alternatives. But we've been so busy with one thing or another, she just kept putting it off. When I left her on Monday morning, I could tell she was in a bad way but she kept insisting it wasn't anything out of the ordinary. God *damn* it!"

Julia gave a little start as he slammed a fist against what was fortunately a very sturdy wall. "Why don't we sit down, hmm?" she suggested calmly. "Look, let me go try and find that nurse, see if she has an update for us. And you look like you could use a cup of tea. Maybe a nice, calming blend like chamomile?"

Ian made a face. "Hate the stuff, have ever since our old nanny tried to pour it down our throats to make us sleepy."

Julia eased him into a chair and patted his shoulder. "OK, Darjeeling it is then. And I need a really large cup of coffee, plus the biggest piece of pie I can find. I'll be back in a bit, all right? And," she added with a smile, "try not to punch any holes in the wall while I'm gone, okay?"

He couldn't help but smile a little in return. "I'll try my best. And Julia – thank you. Thank God you and Travis were able to get to her so quickly. I owe both of you a long weekend at one of our hotels. Your choice. Unless," he added with a wink, "you'd rather have a new pair of shoes."

Julia's green eyes sparkled merrily. "Wow, what a decision. I did love that weekend Nathan and I spent in Santa Barbara last year. But I've also been eyeing a new pair of Jimmy Choos, too. I'll get back to you, okay?" Then she sobered before telling him, "It was no trouble at all. I'm just glad we could help. And when we found her." She shuddered. "God, it will take me a long time to forget that sight."

She disappeared down the hallway before Ian could quiz her further, and the frightening images her words called to mind only served to increase his anxiety.

But then in the next minute the tall, broad-shouldered form of Dr. Jordan Reeves sauntered into the room and Ian instantly sprang to his feet.

"Well, it's about damned time that baby was born," groused Ian. "Boy or girl?"

Jordan grinned, his black hair mostly hidden beneath the dark blue surgical cap that was the same color as his scrubs. "A girl. Seven pounds nine ounces and she's pissed as hell. A real screamer if I've ever heard one."

Ian managed a wry smile as he shook his friend's hand. "Just your type from what I'm told. And *I'm* going to be the one who starts screaming soon if that good for nothing surgeon doesn't arrive soon to tell me about Tessa."

"Relax." Jordan squeezed Ian's shoulder. "First of all, Danny Shapiro is just about the best surgeon on staff here. And second, I just had a long chat with him about your lady and offered to give you all the details. Which is fortunate, considering he's got another emergency surgery to rush into." Jordan glanced around the nearly empty waiting room. "You here alone?"

Ian shook his head. "Tessa's friend – correction, our friend – just left to get us some tea. Julia was the one who called 911 earlier today. She's been here the whole time."

Jordan's gray eyes sparkled with interest. "Please tell me Julia was the really, really hot babe that I just passed in the hallway. Long hair, tight skirt, high heels, stacked like a brick shithouse?"

Ian shook his head. "Forget it, mate. That is definitely Julia but afraid she's already spoken for. Tessa and I were at her wedding back in June."

Jordan sighed. "Damn it. She's just my type, too."

Ian rolled his eyes. "I didn't realize you had a type. Other than young, female and beautiful. Now, enough about your love life. I need to know every single detail about *my* woman, including how soon I can see her."

Jordan explained in a quick, concise manner about the laparoscopy that had been performed on Tessa to repair the damage to her uterus. It had been a minimally invasive procedure, requiring only a very small incision in her abdomen.

"And of course they removed the offensive little device that caused all this trouble. Saved me the effort in extracting it, I suppose. How long did you say she's had the IUD?" inquired Jordan.

"Going on eight years, I believe."

Jordan nodded. "They're usually good for about ten years before they have to be replaced. This – what happened to Tessa – is actually quite rare. Fortunately there won't be any lasting damage. The perforation was fairly easy to repair."

Ian sighed in relief. "Thank God. That's the next question I was going to ask. This won't affect her ability to have children, will it?"

"Nope. Not in the least." Jordan cocked his head to the side, regarding Ian curiously. "Why? Planning on knocking her up soon?"

"Jesus, you've got a helluva bedside manner," complained Ian. "I hope you don't talk to your patients that way. And no – I don't plan on knocking her up as you so charmingly put it for at least a couple more years. That's why we need an alternative form of birth control as soon as possible."

A deep laugh rumbled from Jordan's chest. "A bit touchy there, Ian? Hey, I can't blame you. Enjoy her for a while before you start procreating. But you'll have to hold off on the fun and games for a bit, I'm afraid. She'll need some time to recover from this."

"Obviously. Well, I abstained for two and a half years while I was waiting for her. I suppose a few weeks will seem like nothing in comparison."

Jordan stared at him in disbelief. "Two and a half *years*? Seriously? I don't think I've gone two and a half *days* without some action since I was about sixteen."

Ian shook his head. "Knowing you as I do, that doesn't surprise me in the least. Now, when can I see Tessa and how soon can I bring her home?"

"I'd say another half hour to the first question and maybe a couple of days to the second. We'll have to keep a very close eye on her for any sign of infection. That's a fairly common complication for this sort of thing, and I see from the reports that she already had a fever when they brought her in."

Ian's spine stiffened at this news. "What does that mean? And I assume if an infection does occur that it's easily treatable?"

Jordan nodded. "Almost always, yes. And the fact that she was running a fever on arrival isn't anything to get alarmed over. I noticed they've already started her on a pretty high dose of antibiotics, most likely as a precaution."

Ian was interrupted from asking any further questions by the return of Julia, who was balancing two large coffee cups, a paper bag, and her oversized leather satchel. Jordan, always a sucker for a pretty woman, rushed to offer assistance.

"Let me take those for you," he offered with a killer smile as he took the two cups. "We don't want to have to treat you for a third degree burn, do we?"

Julia gave him a polite smile in return, and it was very clear that she recognized Jordan for the notorious player that he was. "Thank you, the one with the tea bag is Ian's."

Jordan introduced himself, sparing Ian the trouble, and couldn't resist turning on the charm even though he knew Julia was already spoken for. "I understand from Ian that you're recently married. My very, very bad luck. I don't suppose," added Jordan teasingly, "that you've got a twin sister tucked away somewhere?"

Julia's eyes widened as she and Ian exchanged a look of mutual horror. Jordan glanced between the two of them with a puzzled expression.

"I was actually making a joke," he explained. "Why the panic stricken looks?"

"Because I actually do have an identical twin," replied Julia. "And I'll do you a huge favor and *not* set you up with her. As I understand it, the last time someone was crazy enough to do that, her date wound up with a very bloody nose."

***

Ian refused to leave Tessa's side once she was moved to a private room. He might not have been the boss here at the hospital – as Julia had sternly reminded him – but that didn't mean he wasn't fully capable of getting things done. With Jordan's help, he arranged to have a sleeping cot set up in the room; sent Simon to the house to pick up whatever clothing and toiletries he might need; and set up a mini-office space, with his laptop, cell phone and tablet within easy reach. He'd been relieved to hear that the situation in Las Vegas was nearly wrapped up, and that his absence hadn't had much impact on the proceedings. Andrew had been fully apprised of the situation with Tessa and was under strict orders about what calls to forward along.

Unfortunately, the only thing that Ian – or anyone else, for that matter – had not been able to control was the fast-moving infection that was taking over Tessa's fever-wracked body with each passing hour. And each time the doctors and nurses upped her dose of antibiotics, they seemed a little less sure of themselves when they insisted this was normal, that she'd be fine, that she was a young, healthy woman who could fight this off in no time.

But, as the hours ticked by and Tessa showed no signs of improvement, Ian began to unravel a little at a time. He paced anxiously, ran his hand through his hair until it was standing on end, refused to eat or sleep, and snapped irritably when anyone urged him to calm down. Tessa was in obvious discomfort from the fever, tossing and turning, sleeping fitfully. She whimpered in her sleep, plucked at the bedcovers, turned her head from side to side. The nurses checked her temperature every half hour and tried to keep their facial expressions passive when her fever wouldn't break, and especially when it started to surge higher. Ian made frequent trips to and from the bathroom, filling a small plastic basin with water so he could sponge her hot skin. Her cheeks were bright crimson from the fever, but her hands were ice cold despite his continued attempts to warm them.

Towards dawn he finally laid down on the cot, and fell asleep almost instantly, completely exhausted from the last eighteen hours of stress. It was only Jordan's arrival to check on his patient around nine a.m. that woke him, and he grumbled to realize he'd slept so long.

"How is she? Any changes?" he asked anxiously as he stumbled sleepily to Tessa's side.

Jordan shook his head. "Her temperature is still hovering around 104°. We'll keep pumping the antibiotics, sometimes these infections are stubborn bastards and it takes a bit longer than we'd like for them to start working."

"But they *will* start working, correct?" asked Ian in a fierce tone.

Jordan paused. "Yes, they should. We'll keep a very close watch on her as we've been doing all along. So far it doesn't appear that the infection has spread and we need to make damned sure it stays that way."

Ian didn't like his friend's tone of voice. "What the hell does that mean? And what happens if it does spread?"

The dark-haired doctor, clad in a charcoal gray suit this morning, hesitated. "Let's not go there right now, hmm? She's not even twenty four hours post op so it's very premature to start worrying about things like sepsis. I promise you, Ian, that we'll take every precaution to make sure it doesn't get that far. Now, if you don't mind my saying so, you look worse than Tessa. And you've had those clothes on since yesterday. Get yourself together, man, and be quick about it."

Jordan practically shoved him into the en suite bathroom to shave, shower, and put on clean clothes. Ian was just emerging from the bathroom when Julia and Nathan entered the hospital room carrying coffee cups and white paper bakery bags.

"Scones," announced Julia. "Tessa told me the name of your favorite bakery once so we stopped on the way. You," she told Ian, "are eating at least two of them. Plus the fruit cup. Don't argue. Nathan will tell you it's futile."

Nathan nodded in agreement. "I think Julia was a Jewish mother in a former life from the way she insists on feeding people. So give in gracefully, my friend."

Ian ate without actually tasting the food, knowing he needed the calories to get through the day. While Julia sipped her coffee and munched on a chocolate croissant, she tenderly brushed aside damp strands of Tessa's sweat soaked blonde hair.

"Her skin is so hot," she murmured in concern. "The fever hasn't broken yet?"

"No." Ian spoke in between sips of tea. "Jordan was in a little while ago, said it's too soon to start worrying about sepsis, but I'm half afraid he's bullshitting me."

"I don't think he'd do that," consoled Julia. "He doesn't seem the sort who'd keep the truth from you."

Nathan frowned. "And how would you know that, baby? Is that the guy who hit on you yesterday?"

Julia looked flustered. "Jesus, Nathan, he did not hit on me.

Though he did ask if I had a twin – jokingly, of course."

"Baby, I hate to break the news, but he was definitely hitting on you if he asked a question like that." Nathan glared at Ian. "This guy's a friend of yours?"

Ian smiled. "Best OB/GYN in the city."

"I don't care if he's the best in the whole country. I'll tell you now, Julia," Nathan vowed to his wife. "Whenever you get pregnant, he is *so* not going to be your doctor."

The Atwoods stayed for close to an hour, until they regretfully had to get back to the office. Ian assured them he'd call as soon as there was any change in Tessa's condition and thanked them again for everything they had already done.

The day dragged on with no real change in Tessa's condition. The infection continued to rage through her body but thankfully didn't appear to be spreading further. Still, it was taking a definite toll on her and Ian was grateful she remained largely out of it. Once in a while her eyelids would flutter open, but he was never really certain if her feverish brain actually recognized him or knew where she was.

He tried to get some work done, desperate for any sort of distraction to ease his worry over Tessa. He took phone calls from his parents, his brother Hugh, from Matthew Bennett, all of whom had heard the news about Tessa from Andrew, and all expressing their concern. Simon stopped by midday, bringing along lunch for the two of them, but Ian barely touched his.

As Simon stood up to leave, there was an unmistakable sheen of tears in his eyes as he squeezed Tessa's limp hand. "She'll pull through this, Mr. Gregson, I just know she will. Such a sweet, kind girl – she certainly doesn't deserve this after everything else she's been through."

Ian had to fight back his own tears. "I know, mate. Keep her in your prayers, will you?"

"Constantly, sir. Please call me if I can do anything else. Anything."

It was early evening, and Ian was half-dozing in the bedside chair when Andrew and his girlfriend Isobel poked their heads inside the room.

"We brought dinner," announced Andrew, holding up a large

paper takeout bag. "Bento boxes, I hope that's all right."

Ian grimaced. "Why is everyone who stops by today trying to feed me?"

But he managed to eat almost half of the salmon teriyaki, rice, and miso soup before pushing the takeout container away. Isobel got a phone call that she excitedly exclaimed was from a gallery owner, and dashed out into the hall to answer it.

Ian raised a weary brow to Andrew. "Pleasant enough girl but frankly doesn't seem your type."

Andrew returned his gaze steadily. "Are you referring to the tattoos, the piercings, the purple hair or the funky clothes?"

Ian smiled. "Ah, I suppose all of those. You're much more conservative than she is."

"You think so?" inquired Andrew. "Guess you've never noticed these, hmm?"

He pointed to the holes in his right earlobe and above his left eyebrow where some sort of hoop or stud would normally be inserted.

"Obviously I don't wear any jewelry to the office. And there's one more piercing in – um, let's call it a more private spot."

Ian couldn't suppress the shudder that went through him at the thought of a piercing – *there*. "Any tattoos?"

"Six of them at last count," confirmed Andrew. "All of them well hidden under my suits at the office. No purple hair, but during college I did have a ponytail. Down to here." He pointed to the middle of his back. "And the funky clothes come out on the weekends, though it's mostly just jeans and T-shirts, nothing too out of the ordinary."

Ian's grin grew a bit wider with each revelation. "Will wonders never cease. I do believe you've bested me at my own game, Andrew. I would never in a million years have guessed at any of these hidden secrets of yours. So your image as a stick in the mud was all just one big hoax, hmm?"

Andrew dared to glare at him. "With all due respect, sir, it's vital to the continued operation of the office that this stays strictly between us. If anyone else knew, I'd lose all respect and then it would be complete and total anarchy in that place."

Ian laughed, the first time in over twenty four hours he'd come close to doing so. "I agree. So for the sake of maintaining control over the troops, your secrets are safe with me."

Isobel returned then, beaming with the news that a local gallery owner was very interested in displaying some of her sculptures. She seemed anxious to get back to her latest project, so Ian shook both their hands and thanked them for dinner.

"My treat next time," he surprised himself by saying. "When Tessa's fully recovered, we'll make it a double date – you two pick the place."

Andrew glanced uncertainly at Isobel. "Sir, I'm not really certain that's a good idea. We probably shouldn't be socializing outside of the office."

"Oh, quit being such a stuffed shirt, Andrew," scolded Ian. "You're getting to be ten times worse than I ever was. Besides, I'm a little curious to see some of these tattoos of yours. But not," he added hastily, "the other piercing you mentioned."

It was quiet after they left, and still no significant change in Tessa's condition. The doctor making evening rounds assured Ian that she was holding her own, and that they should expect to see some change one way or the other within the next twelve hours or so.

Ian frowned. "What exactly does that mean?"

The youngish doctor seemed to hesitate a bit before replying. "She's more than twenty four hours post op now, so either her fever will break and the infection will start to clear up. Or, well, the fever will continue to spike and the infection could spread. But we'll continue to keep a very close eye on her as we've been doing and look for any changes. You should really try and get some sleep yourself, sir."

But Ian knew he wouldn't be able to sleep, not so long as his beloved Tessa was still so sick and unresponsive. He tried reading, doing a bit of work, but all he could think about was her. After a while, he simply sat down in the chair next to her bedside, holding her hand, and pressing occasional kisses to her forehead or cheek, still alarmed by how hot her skin felt.

"You know, darling, if you don't wake up soon, we'll have to delay our trip to Italy next month," he told her. He knew she couldn't hear him but he was desperate for any sort of distraction. "And that would be a great pity, because you'd completely ruin some very carefully laid plans I've made."

Ian brought her hand to his lips. "I've never brought a woman to the villa before, so this will be another first for me. And it will be an excellent opportunity for you to practice your Italian, so you really need to wake up now so you can start recovering in time."

He brushed a damp strand of hair off her forehead. He'd tried to comb the tangled locks earlier in the day but had given up when she'd kept turning her head to and fro in distress.

"I know you're a sleepyhead, Tessa, but this is getting ridiculous," he joked. "Besides, this mattress is a poor substitute for ours. You know how much you love the Hypnos, so please open your eyes now so I can bring you home."

He touched his forehead to hers. "God, Tessa, you have to wake up, have to get better. I'm lost without you, darling. Didn't you know I was lost for my entire life until I met you? I used to joke that I was married to my job, that work was the only thing I really needed in my life. My poor mother had given up hope that I would ever meet someone, or give her a grandchild. Speaking of which, I've been giving it a lot of thought. I think I'd like a daughter first, one with your blonde hair and blue eyes, and if you like we could name her Gillian, after your mother."

Carefully, he eased himself onto the bed beside her, being mindful of the IV tube and monitors as he took her in his arms. "You've brought so much light, so much happiness into my life, Tessa. I was alone and lonely and didn't even know it until that day you walked into my office. You were so damned young and innocent – too young, I told myself – and then I discovered too damned married as well. My heart broke into a thousand pieces that day. I knew I should have sent you away – I almost did – just so I didn't have to face the pain of seeing you every day and knowing I couldn't have you."

Tears began to trickle unheeded down his cheeks and he buried his face against her neck. "But in the end I couldn't bear the thought of not seeing you again. So I kept you nearby, where I could still see your beautiful face every time I walked past your desk. Even though I couldn't have you for myself, I still thought it preferable to not seeing you at all. So you have to wake up now, darling. Because I didn't waste two and a half years waiting for you only to have you taken away from me now."

Ian, a man who never cried, at least not since he'd been a boy of three who'd fallen down and skinned his knee, now wept as though he were that same small child. His tears fell unchecked onto Tessa's hospital gown, the cotton fabric already dampened by her feverish body, and his body shook from the force of his sobs.

The touch was so light, so imperceptible, that at first he wasn't even aware of it. He thought perhaps he was dreaming, that his exhausted body had finally succumbed to sleep, or that his weary brain was playing tricks on him.

But then, in addition to the whisper soft touch of a hand stroking his hair, he began to hear the barely discernable murmuring as well. He forced his eyes open to find Tessa gazing at him drowsily.

"Ian."

Her voice was weak, her hand against his cheek limp, but there was clarity in the half-lidded blue eyes that gazed steadily at him.

"Tessa." His hands cupped her cheeks, his lips finding hers in a soft, careful kiss. Anxiously, he felt her brow, and his tears fell anew as he realized her fever was finally beginning to break. She still felt a little warm and definitely clammy, but not burning up as she'd been for far too many hours.

"What – what happened?" she whispered wearily."

"Hush." He brushed his lips against her cheek. "Plenty of time for all that."

"No." She clutched his hand a little tighter. "Vegas. You're supposed to be in Las Vegas. Your meeting - "

"Went on very well without me there," he assured her. "The whole damned world can get on without me for as long as it takes to get you out of this place and have you well again."

She shook her head. "But your meeting was important."

"No. No, Tessa. *You* are important. You're the only important thing in my entire life," he told her urgently. "Without you, nothing else exists for me. So forget about the meeting, or work, or anything besides the two of us. You are the only thing in my life that matters."

Tessa touched her fingers to his cheek. "You've been crying. Am I – was it that bad?"

He shook his head. "I was worried, that's all. And you're going to be fine now. After all, I've got all these plans for our trip to Tuscany next month, and there is no possible way I'm going to allow you to spoil any of them."

She linked her fingers with his and nodded. "Well, we can't have that, can we? And speaking of surprises, weren't you supposed to be bringing me one back from Las Vegas? But I guess you didn't have time to go shopping."

He grinned at her. "Actually, I did. And I've got your surprise here in the room. Want to see it?"

"Hmm. Black lace, I suppose?"

"Of course. You know how much I love you in black lace." Ian didn't bother to add that he'd also bought her a number of other things from La Perla, in a wide variety of colors.

Tessa thought about it for a moment before giving a little shake of her head. "Maybe later. I'm so tired. Besides, I don't think black lace would go very well with this hospital gown."

He laughed and hugged her close. "Darling, don't you know? Black lace goes with anything. So long as you're the one wearing it, that is."

Epilogue

September

Tessa gazed out at the acres and acres of vineyards spread out in the valley below, as the sun slowly began to set. It was cooler now, something of a relief after the heat of the day, and she thought about going back inside the house for a wrap. But it felt too good to lay back on the chaise and admire the gold and purple colors of the Tuscan sky. Ever since she and Ian had arrived here at his family's villa two days ago, they'd done very little besides what he'd jokingly referred to as their "S" activities – swimming, sleeping, sipping wine and sex.

This was their last night alone here, since Ian's parents were due to arrive tomorrow, and his brother Colin and his family the day after that. They were to remain here another week at the grand estate, located about an hour's drive south of Pisa, before flying to London for a few days. There Tessa would meet the rest of Ian's family, including his brother Hugh and Uncle Richard. What was definitely *not* on their schedule was a visit with his cousin Charlotte and her husband Jason, for rather obvious reasons.

It had taken her some time to fully recover from the uterine perforation and resulting infection. Though she'd been able to leave the hospital two days after her fever had broken, she'd been on strict instructions to rest and take it easy for at least two more weeks. Ian of course had taken those directions to the extreme and hired a nurse to look after her while he was busy at the office. It hadn't been until a follow-up visit with Jordan, where the handsome OB/GYN had proclaimed her fully recovered, that Ian had reluctantly agreed the nurse's services were no longer required.

Jordan had also prescribed a new brand of birth control pills for her, these with a very low dose of hormones, and so far she hadn't experienced any type of side effects. The issuance of her new prescription had coincided nicely with the timing of her recovery, along with Jordan's blessings – given with a huge grin – to resume sexual activity.

Ian had been gentle, tentative even, afraid of hurting her, until she'd rather impatiently taken control of things and straddled him. Since then they had scarcely been able to keep their hands off each other, not only making up for lost time but being conscious of the fact that they wouldn't be alone after today for well over a week.

"And unfortunately centuries-old Italian villas are not nearly as well insulated or soundproofed as our home back in San Francisco," he'd told her. "Plus there's no walk-in closet to hide inside, either. So while my family is here I'm afraid we'll be restricted to using the shower for any amorous activities."

"Or you can just gag me again," she'd offered teasingly. "That seemed to work out just fine the last time."

He had laughingly told her he'd give the matter some thought, but he did buy her a beautiful silk scarf during their shopping excursion earlier today to the nearby medieval town of Volterra. When she'd protested that she had more scarves that she could possibly use, Ian had whispered that this one wasn't meant to be tied around her neck.

The live-in groundskeeper and his wife, who resided in a separate cottage on the property, not only tidied up the villa each day but also cooked beautiful, elaborate meals for them. Tessa, who'd lost almost ten pounds during her hospitalization and recovery, was certain she'd gained at least half that amount back just by eating two days of Luciana's cooking.

Fortunately, she'd recovered enough to have started her online classes on time. It was proving to be a bit more work that she'd imagined, but Ian was as good as his word and helped her when she had questions or didn't understand a particular theory or problem. He was exceedingly proud when she got perfect scores on the two algebra quizzes she'd completed thus far.

This morning over breakfast he'd discussed with her an idea

he'd been floating around for some time – that of delegating more responsibility to both his managerial staff and also to Andrew. Evidently the PA had done an admirable job in delivering part of Ian's budget talk during July's managers meeting, enough so that Ian was seriously considering the idea of having Andrew take over some of the hotel reviews he did.

"Frankly, I'm getting awfully tired of being on the road so much," he'd admitted. "And while having you along certainly makes it more bearable, I'd still prefer to be at home with you a lot more often. So, we'll see. With the right training and some experience, Andrew might be able to take some of that load off of my shoulders in the near future."

Tessa had thought to herself that she honestly didn't mind whatever Ian decided to do. Whether they were on the road or staying at home, so long as they were together it didn't matter. But she knew Ian must be weary after spending so many years of his career traveling, and she decided to fully support any decision he made about cutting back.

She was wearing a plum and white patterned cotton maxi dress with spaghetti straps, something she'd picked up from a street vendor during their trip to Hawaii, and she thought it was one of the most comfortable things she'd ever owned. Her feet were bare, as were her shoulders, and this time she did shiver a bit as the sun set a little further behind the horizon.

"I thought you might need this. At this time of the year the temperatures can drop quickly once the sun goes down."

Tessa turned her head slightly and smiled at the sight of her handsome lover walking towards her. Like her, he was barefoot and very casually dressed in a pair of lightweight beige trousers, and a cream colored shirt with the sleeves rolled up to his elbows. He hadn't shaved since they'd arrived, though he had joked earlier today about how his mother would be sure to nag him about it when she arrived tomorrow.

Tessa had pouted playfully, caressing the dark stubble that made him look so incredibly sexy. "Well, I don't want your mother to scold you – or be annoyed with me for encouraging you – so I guess you'd better shave tomorrow morning."

She saw now that he was carrying two wine glasses, an

opened bottle of red wine, and had her new silk crochet shawl draped over his arm. He had bought it for her this morning during their shopping trip.

Tessa accepted the shawl gratefully, draping it over her shoulders as he poured them each a glass of wine. It was a rich ruby colored Chianti that he'd bought at the winery in the adjoining town where they'd lunched earlier today. And even though the wine cellar here at the villa was already bursting at the seams with its stellar collection, Ian had wanted to buy a bottle to commemorate Tessa's first visit to Italy.

"*Salute,*" they told each other simultaneously as they clinked glasses and sipped their wine.

"Would you like some cheese and fruit?" he inquired. "Luciana left a plate for us."

"Maybe in a bit," agreed Tessa. "After all, I saw what she has prepared for our dinner and I don't want to fill up on *formaggio*."

He grinned. "*Molto bene', cara.* You see, your Italian is coming along quite nicely. You were actually able to speak to the shopkeepers and the winery owner a bit today."

She shrugged. "I've still got a long way to go until I'm as fluent as you are." She'd been enthralled to hear him converse so easily with the owner of the winery in the language she had barely begun to learn.

"I've had a lot more practice than you have, don't forget. You'll get there, darling. Plus, you have an awful lot on your schedule these days between school, work, your cooking classes, and of course," he added with a lascivious look, "your most important duty of all – taking care of your very demanding lover."

She reached out for his hand and drew it to her lips. "That's not a duty, my love. I think of it as a privilege."

Ian's eyes darkened. "Tessa – God, I'm not sure it's possible to love you more than I already do, but when you say things like that I begin to wonder."

"I love you, too. And I love being here in Tuscany with you, at this beautiful villa. As wonderful as all of the company's hotels are – well, this is actually a home, isn't it?"

He nodded, and traced a finger over her lips. "Let me guess. This is now your new favorite place in the entire world."

Tessa laughed. "You're very perceptive, aren't you? But actually, I've come to the realization lately about what my absolute favorite place in the entire world really is."

"And where is that, darling?"

She turned her cheek into his palm, pressing a soft kiss there, before gazing at him adoringly. "It's wherever you are. Whether that's San Francisco or Italy or London or anywhere else in the world. Wherever you are at that particular moment is always going to be the best place in the entire world to me."

Ian stared at her with so much heartfelt emotion stamped on his handsome features that it made her heart ache. "There you go again," he murmured. "Saying such beautiful things to me that I can't possibly tell you how much it means to me. So I suppose I'll have to try a different approach."

Tessa tilted her head towards him in bewilderment. "I don't understand."

He smiled mysteriously, brushing his thumb over her knuckles. "Do you know what day it is today, love?"

"Hmm." She wrinkled her nose and shook her head. "September twenty-something. I'm afraid I've lost track of time very quickly over here."

"Well, I know exactly what day it is. It's the twenty-third of September. And, to be more specific, it was three years ago today that you walked into my office and into my heart."

Tessa stared at him in surprise. "Really? I mean, I knew it was this week sometime but I didn't remember the exact date. But of course you'd remember. I've never seen anyone as amazing with details as you are."

Ian shook his head. "Not with employee dates of hire. For example, I couldn't even tell you what *month* of the year it was when Andrew started working for me, much less the exact date. But with you – it was still fairly early in the morning, I think just after nine a.m. I even remember what you were wearing – a little red dress with a black belt. You were easily the most beautiful girl I'd ever seen and I fell head over heels the first time I heard your voice."

She gave his hand a gentle squeeze. "And I never guessed, never ever imagined that you even noticed me from day to day. I felt like a teenage girl with this huge crush on her favorite movie start. I never imagined we would someday be together like this."

"Sometimes fate can be cruel to us, Tessa. You've certainly had more than your fair share of that, after all. But then at other times fate chooses to smile fondly on us, like it's doing right now. And I hope it will continue to do so for many, many years to come."

They each sipped at their wine and gazed out at the landscape, now bathed in the soft glow of twilight. Ian drew Tessa to her feet, wrapping an arm around her waist as they stood against the balcony of the terrace.

"There's another occasion to commemorate today," he said quietly. "At least, I'm hoping there will be."

"What's that?" she inquired teasingly. "I already know it's not the anniversary of our first kiss. *That* date I do remember very well."

Ian smiled. "As do I, my love. No, this is something new to commemorate. Hopefully to celebrate."

As she watched wide-eyed, he dropped down to one knee, keeping her hand clasped in his. Tears were pooling in her eyes before he could even open his mouth to speak.

"Tessa. My darling girl. Will you take pity on this very old man you see before you and grant him the greatest honor he could possibly imagine – that of becoming his wife?"

The tears fell freely as she nodded, too choked up with emotion to do more than whisper, "Oh, yes." And then, as he slipped a beautiful ring with a fabulous blue stone onto her engagement finger, she burst out, "And you are *not* old!"

He laughed and stood up, wrapping his arms around her waist and lifting her feet off the ground. "I think you're my very own personal fountain of youth, darling. And you have just made me the happiest man of any age in the entire world. Now, tell me, do you like your ring? I had it designed especially for you."

Tessa gazed down at the round blue stone surrounded by dozens of smaller round diamonds. The slender platinum band was also encrusted with pave diamonds. "It's gorgeous, Ian. I love it. And I'm glad you chose a sapphire since they're my favorite."

"Ah, but it's not a sapphire, love – it's a blue diamond," he corrected. "Very rare and very precious. Just like yourself." He gave her a sweet, soft kiss. "It reminded me of your eyes. And also of that dress you wore the night of the Christmas party. The night when I finally had real hope that a moment very much like this one might actually happen."

She pulled his head down to hers for a much longer, much deeper kiss. "I love you," she breathed. "And I am so honored, so proud, that you're going to be my husband. You're the most wonderful man in the whole world, and I will do everything in my power to make you happy every single day of our lives together."

Ian hugged her tightly. "And I love you, my darling bride-to-be. Speaking of which, do you recall when I told you during Julia and Nathan's wedding that I had a very special place picked out for our own special day?"

She nodded, smiling. "It's here, isn't it? That's why you were so mysterious. You wanted me to see the villa first. And yes, I love it here. I would love having our wedding here in Tuscany."

He chuckled. "We might have a bit of a problem hosting so many guests here, though. And as beautiful as this place is, how much I've always enjoyed coming here, this isn't exactly what I had in mind. Though it is very similar. Remember when we first drove up through the gates two days ago and you told me this place reminded you of somewhere?"

Tessa nodded. "Of course."

"Well, I gave a great many photographs of this villa to Nathan and told him this was the feeling I wanted to capture when he came up with the designs for our new hotel in Napa. And while there are a number of differences, the entire resort is being built to resemble a Tuscan villa. And that, my love, is where I hope to make you my bride."

She gasped in delight. "Oh, what a wonderful idea! I love it, absolutely love it! I know exactly what you mean now – why this villa looked so familiar. I was remembering all the drawings

I'd seen of the new hotel. So we would hold our wedding there on the grounds?"

"Yes, that's what I was hoping. Right now we're scheduled to hold the grand opening the second week of June. My plan," he added with a wide smile, "was to marry about a week before that time, so that ours would be the first wedding ever held in the place. And so that we would also be the very first guests to stay there as well."

"That's what you meant by another first. And I couldn't think of a more perfect time or place to get married. Yes, absolutely. As usual, you think of everything."

Tenderly, he brushed a lock of hair behind her ear. "One more thing I just thought of. Do you realize what other day this is, darling?"

Tessa arched a brow. "No, I can't honestly say that I do. What day is it today?"

Ian's eyes twinkled merrily. "It's a Wednesday."

THE END

About The Author

Janet is a lifelong resident of the San Francisco Bay Area, and currently resides on the northern California coast with her husband Steve and Golden Retriever Max. She worked for more than two decades in the financial services industry before turning her focus to producing running events. She is a former long-distance runner, current avid yoga practitioner, is addicted to Pinterest, likes to travel and read. She has been writing for more than three decades, and is the author of the Inevitable series – six interconnected but standalone books, and the Splendor trilogy. Her writing genre is steamy contemporary romance, specializing in what she likes to call "romance for romantics".

Email – janetnissenson@gmail.com

Website/Blog - http://www.janetnissenson.com

Facebook - https://www.facebook.com/janetnissensonauthor

Twitter - https://www.twitter.com/JNissenson

Goodreads - https://www.goodreads.com/author/show/7375780.Janet_Nissenson

Pinterest - http://www.pinterest.com/janetnissenson/

Instagram - https://www.instagram.com/janetlnissenson/

TITLES BY THIS AUTHOR

The Inevitable Series:

Serendipity (Book #1 – Julia and Nathan's story)

Splendor (Book #2 – Tessa and Ian's original story)

All You Need is Love (Book #1.5 – the Serendipity sequel)

Shattered (Book #3 – Angela and Nick's story)

Sensational (Book #4 – Lauren and Ben's story)

Serenity (Book #5 – Sasha and Matthew's story)

Stronger (Book #6 – Cara and Dante's story)

The Splendor Trilogy

Covet (Book #1)

Crave (Book #2)

Claim (Book #2)

Printed in Great
Britain
by Amazon